Performative Criticism

Performative Criticism
Experiments in Reader Response

Gerry Brenner

STATE UNIVERSITY OF NEW YORK PRESS

Published by
State University of New York Press, Albany

© 2004 State University of New York

For information, address State University of New York Press,
90 State Street, Suite 700, Albany, NY 12207

Production by Kelli M. Williams
Marketing by Anne M. Valentine

Library of Congress Cataloging-in-Publication Data

Brenner, Gerry, 1937–
    Performative criticism : experiments in reader response / Gerry Brenner.
        p. cm.
    Includes bibliographical references (p.) and index.
    ISBN 0-7914-5943-8 (alk. paper) — ISBN 0-7914-5944-6 (pbk. : alk. paper)
        1. English literature—History and criticism—Theory, etc.   2. American
fiction—History and criticism—Theory, etc.   3. Reader-response criticism.
I. Title.

PR21.B74   2004
820.9–dc22
                                                                                            2003059108

10   9   8   7   6   5   4   3   2   1

Table of Contents

To Terry, *sine qua non*

Acknowledgments

My debts of gratitude are numerous and varied. Naturally I am deeply indebted to critics and scholars whose research and publications I have learned from and been challenged by. In some of the essays that follow I list, in bibliographic entries or footnotes, their work—hopeful of partially acknowledging what must seem conspicuously absent in my essays—the extent and depth of the research that always went into the preparation of each of them. I am grateful as well for the opportunities to teach a wide and varied group of writers and courses during my thirty-some years at the University of Montana, for those opportunities enabled me to discover issues that scholars had overlooked or disregarded in a number of great texts. As well, I am grateful for years of good students here and abroad who, while fretful because of my reputation as a challenging and demanding teacher who gave out top grades charily, enrolled in my courses because word got out that not only did I read their work carefully (as had my great teacher at the University of Washington, Bob Heilman) but I also created an engaging classroom, provoked thought and good discussions, enjoyed teaching, and gave interesting writing assignments. Editors, colleagues, students, family, and various friends—near and far—have suffered my questions, indulged my eccentricities, read various drafts, fetched resources, and favored me with their help, criticism, suggestions, doubts, and encouragement. Whether I can number them all is daunting, but I will try. Thanks, then, Bari Burke, Joanne Charbonneau, Drew Colenbrander, Paul Dietrich, Dick Dunn, Ulysses Doss, Katharina Erhard, Judith Fetterley, John Glendening, Bernard Harrison, Udo Hebel, Tom Huff, Bob Kindrick, Bill Marling, Bob Pack, Jim Phelan, Doug Purl, Peter Rabinowitz, Rena Sanderson, David Schuldberg, Carl Schroer, Merton Sealts, Paul Smith, Mike Steig, and Jacquie Tavernier-Courbin.

I am grateful to several game editors who first published essays reprinted in this volume:

Laurence Goldstein: "A Letter to Nick Carraway: Fifty Years After." *Michigan Quarterly Review* 23 (Spring 1984): 196–206.
Ralph Norman: "Readers Responding: An Interview with Biblical Ruth." *Soundings: An Interdisciplinary Journal* 73 (Summer/Fall 1990): 233–55.

Jacqueline Tavernier-Courbin: "More Than a Reader Responding: Hammett's Re-feathered *Maltese Falcon.*" *Thalia: Studies in Literary Humor* 10 (1989): 48–56; and "Manolin on Hemingway's Santiago: A Fictive Interview." *Thalia: Studies in Literary Humor* 19 (2000): 3–13.
Susan Stanford Friedman: "More Than a Reader's Response: A Letter to 'De Ole True Huck.'" *The Journal of Narrative Technique* 20 (Spring 1990): 221–34.
Rena Sanderson: "Once a Rabbit, Always? A Feminist Interview with María." *Blowing the Bridge: Essays on Hemingway and "For Whom the Bell Tolls."* Westport: Greenwood, 1992. 131–42. © 1992 Greenwood Press. Reproduced with permission of Greenwood Publicity Group, Inc., Westport, CT.

As must be true for most scholars, I, too, am deeply indebted to various librarians. So, thanks to colleagues and staff at the Maureen and Mike Mansfield Library at The University of Montana–Missoula: Karen Hatcher, Dick Dunn, Bill Elison, Chris Mullin, Erling Oelz, Sue Samson, Linder Schlang, and Ying Xu. Special thanks first to Marianne Farr and, then, Patricia Collins, and The University of Montana Interlibrary Loan staff, without whose electronic wizardry, cheerful assistance, and herculean efforts I could never have explored the by-ways into which my essays led me: Ginny Bolten, Rosemarie Fishburn, Gary Frazer, Don Kimmet, and Shawn Lake. I also thank two University of Montana former students and now friends in our Computer Information Services who have rescued me on many occasions from the tribulations of adapting to different software programs: Vicki Pengelly and Janet Sedgley. And I gratefully acknowledge the ever-cheerful assistance given me by James Peltz, the editor in chief of State University of New York Press, as well as his acquisitions assistant, Lisa Chesnel, my copy editor, A&B Editorial, production editor Kelli Williams, and an anonymous reader for State University of New York Press whose valuable suggestions for revision helped make this a better book.

Not least, my debts to my recently deceased wife, Terry, cannot be counted: her belief in and encouragement of this project—and her love and skillful editing—sustained and inspired me.

Introduction

At their best, literary critics do many good things. Foremost they explain texts, clarifying large and small patterns of meaning. They identify thematic structures and integrate important literary scholarship and biographical, historical, and cultural information. They uncover subtexts, latent agendas, and "hidden" meanings. They situate texts within established literary conventions. And they discover esthetic designs that enrich an appreciation of the art and craft of texts. Moreover, good literary critics formulate concepts, terms, methodologies, taxonomies, and theories, all of which better enable a reader to discern and apply them to the assumptions, processes, and results of reading texts. They demonstrate skillful rhetoric and cogent argument, revealing the strengths of their ideologies and critical approaches. They equip a reader with issues and interpretations needed to participate productively in literary conversation and controversy, be it to argue a view, to test others' conclusions, or to question the grounds of the discourse. Most of all, good literary critics enrich the special pleasures, public and private, of reading literary texts and, thereby, promote a culture of literate citizens. In a word, good literary critics always answer the short, rude, implied question lurking in many a reader's mind: So what? or Why should I care about a text and what someone writes about it? and What bearing has it on my life and concerns?

At their worst, literary critics can be faulted on many grounds: for being stuffy, dogmatic, overly ingenious, esoteric, formulaic, pedantic, simplistic, erudite, jargon-ridden, wrong-headed, silly, and, of course, boring. One cause of these faults is surely the expectation that literary criticism should be written with the depersonalized objectivity of a scientific report, much as if the voice behind the language of a critical essay ought ideally to reflect only a ratiocinative mind, cleansed of personality, divested of any personal stake in the issues at hand, professorially circumspect, uninfected by suppressed presuppositions.

One virtue of reader-response criticism has been its allowance—some would say indulgence—of every reader's interaction with the text he or she reads. Diverse though reader-response theorists and practitioners are, fundamental to the theory is its seldom-expressed goal of democratizing the practice of literary criticism. In theory it emancipates readers from subservience not only to the meanings assigned to a text by figures of authority and even its author, but also to the authority of the presumably objective text itself and linguistic structures that supposedly control readers' constructions of meaning. In theory it also enfranchises readers of any age, training, agenda, or orientation, permitting, even challenging, them to become the makers of a text's meaning, validating their experience of a text, however idiosyncratic, provided it be intelligible and supportable. And in theory it empowers readers to tell what the text they are reading and interacting with makes happen to them, what temporal event or events the text occasions in themselves as they respond to it.

But the exemplary theorists and practitioners of reader-response criticism—Fish, Holland, Bleich, Mailloux, Fetterley, and Iser, to name representative figures—continue to subscribe to the performance ideology of most literary criticism.[1] They write, more or less, in the academic style of most literary critics. In other words they write from *outside a text*, as observers. Yet if reader-response critics seek to promote good literary criticism and make it even more effective—to make it something readers will be drawn to if not seek out—they might wish to consider taking the next step. That next step, I would argue, is to compose criticism *from the inside*. Doing so requires participating in the realities and experience of the text critics are writing about, becoming or impersonating a character in or close to a text so that the criticism becomes a literary event itself, a performance in which an audience can become as emotionally engaged as when it interacts with a good literary work.

I am writing, of course, about the kind of performative criticism I have collected here. A description of what it is and tries to do, followed by discussions of its arguable function of inverting or subverting conventional interpretations and of its place among schools of reader-response criticism and antecedents, leads to brief characterizations of the problems and approaches I deal with in the twelve experiments and a brief statement of my aims in writing performative criticism.

I call the essays in criticism that I have written here "performative" because they ask to be read as texts capable of being variously performed, orally, by a single but good reader. Admittedly, inasmuch as all texts are performative,[2] so too is literary criticism, for it can be read as if on a stage by an actor. But however well an actor modulates and inflects a text written by most academic literary critics, it is still an event as told from the outside. It looks in on fictive characters who and imaginary events which are spatially, temporally, and stylistically distant from the critics writing about the text. Indeed, the stylistic range among academic critics is relatively narrow and formal, which further contributes to the loss of immediacy and urgency to a reader, limiting a critical essay's ability to pulse with the vitality of an actual event.

Performative criticism, then, names an imaginative form of reader-response criticism that bends the genre by applying inventive rhetorical strategies to interpret individual literary works from the inside. As the essays that lie ahead will show, I variously impersonate characters or people strongly affected by a work's agendas, trying to envision them as a new situation confronts them. For instance, how might golfing pro Jordan Baker—Daisy Buchanan's best friend and Nick Carraway's transitory girlfriend—respond to his account of Jay

Gatsby when she learns, fifty years after the events of the novel, that his story has become the novel most read by college students? If she were to write him a letter, might her view of him bring an added perspective to that American classic as well as to her own character? By building on an already-created character like Jordan Baker—toward whom readers have previously formed and now will continue to form impressions, expectations, and evaluations—performative criticism practices what poet John Hollander calls "interfigurality"[3]; it tries to create a temporal event that enables a fictional character or person to become a responding reader who will, in turn, challenge readers' understanding of his or her character and the issues and meanings attached to his or her text.

When performative criticism succeeds, the drama, style, and nuances of its narrative or dialogue will draw readers into caring about or becoming emotionally as well as intellectually engaged with characters, just as they do when reading about fictive or real people—now being annoyed by, now puzzling over, now taking sides with, now formulating tentative conclusions about, finally "living with" them, perhaps as a friend or antagonist, a shadow acquaintance or family surrogate, an incubus or golem. For instance, an interview by a biblical scholar might allow Ruth, that icon of female obedience and docility, to reveal intelligence and independence, both usually denied her. And that, in turn, might redeem her as a woman long given short shrift, often misunderstood, perhaps appreciated for the wrong reasons. It might also redeem a great narrative from being read as a moralistic Bible tale.

Performative criticism may appear to be but a diverting or entertaining substitute for solid scholarship and criticism. But when successful, it can provoke readers to freshly consider or understand a text and, thereby, complement the values of good scholarship and criticism. Is there, for example, a case to be made for Robert Louis Stevenson's Edward Hyde, who, in a text saturated with reports, rumors, letters, testaments, and "full statements," is tellingly denied space or time to vindicate himself? If there is, would a reader find more persuasive and pleasurable Hyde's own full statement—told from the inside, in his style—than an argument manufactured by and in the voice of an academic professor of literature? I know of no law that prohibits entwining serious critical and scholarly issues in an entertaining discourse, provided the "entertainment" rises far above whimsy, impressionism, self-indulgence, or play for play's sake.

As these examples suggest, my rhetorical strategies include letters, interviews, and, in the case of Edward Hyde, a testamentary document. Two "dialogues of the dead," one training report, one combination letter and revised ending, and one set of several letters and an editor's column complete my experiments. In some cases, to give a bit of the game away, my experiments invert or subvert what many readers will consider the standard views of characters and, thereby, may seem to be simple inversions or subversions.

I mention this matter of inversions or subversions for two reasons. First, some readers may regard them as a programmatic approach that, once launched, can be systematically applied to any text. And they would be right to do so. Inasmuch as it is axiomatic that the observer alters the observed, then surely the way one views any text depends on one's post of observation, which is always contaminated by ideology and agendas. Dickens's Fagin from *Oliver Twist*, for instance, is always seen as a villain who exploits children and fosters criminal behavior against the well-to-do. But that view, as all views do, rests on an ideological foundation. In this case, a supposedly Christian and class-oriented culture has long established the standard yardstick by which to measure Fagin. But if *Oliver Twist* were to be studied and measured by prison inmates and their yardstick—by Fagin's cronies and ilk—quite another view might well emerge. (Similarly, if one were to stage Shakespeare's *The Tempest* in Australia's outback and gear the production to engage an aboriginal audience, a smart director would consider the many ways by which Caliban can be rendered its hero, however duped, and Prospero its relentlessly self-serving, vindictive villain. Indeed, if another director were to cast Miranda as an ugly young woman, which nothing in the play disallows, its romance would take on much darker colors and Prospero's parental benevolence and political motivations could be starkly questioned.)

In my experiments in performative criticism that pivot on an inversion or subversion of conventional interpretations, the task was never to put together a case for a character or text by shifting the grounds of vision from the outside to the inside and then inverting or subverting a conventional interpretation. Rather, the tasks were first to probe a text to discover whether and why it also deserves the view of some oppressed, ignored, or marginalized readership as well; and second to question whether an inverted or subverted reading matters or should matter to anyone and whether it can make anything happen. When I found that an inverted reading did matter to someone and could make something happen—sometimes serve the claims of justice or its brother, revenge— then the task was to put a case together in such a way that the development of its evidence and argument unfolds with some degree of nuance, drama, surprise, even reversal. In a word, effective performative criticism must contain the conflict, tension, ambiguities, ambivalence, and duplicity of all literary texts. More, it must show people in motion: growing, gaining insight or perspective, developing from one state of being to another.

The second reason I mention the matter of whether my performative criticism merely inverts or subverts standard interpretations is that it bears on issues raised by James Phelan in a critique published and reprinted simultaneously with my essay on *Huckleberry Finn*.[4] Four issues may be important to readers and thus warrant some discussion here.

First, complimentary though Phelan is of my inventiveness in seeing Twain's novel, his narrator, and Jim himself through Jim's eyes, he discredits his own interpretation of "my" Jim as a strongly self-interested narrator whose motive is to aggrandize himself in the eyes of his immediate audience, his wife and son. Phelan claims he cannot convince himself that such a "subversive covert text . . . is really *hidden* beneath the text that [I] constructed" (470; emphasis added). But of course such a "subversive covert text" is there, just as it is in any first-person narrative, lyric, or, for that matter, expository text. The question Phelan raises is whether, in shaping my account, I consciously "hid" that subversive covert text for him or others to find: Did I intentionally conceal a covert text for smart readers to unearth? Or did I "unwittingly" allow such a covert text to be discerned by a creative, skeptical reader? Phelan emphasizes this distinction because he wishes to differentiate among three kinds of covert texts and, though he does not say so, the legitimacy of the meanings derived from each. Phelan holds that when a critic reconfigures a text, presumably irrespective of the author's configuration of it, the result is a "critic's covert text." When an author shapes his or her material but includes "another story told by that shaping that its shaper may not be aware of" (471) but that a critic discovers, the result is an "author's covert text." When a critic both reconfigures a text and discovers a story the author was unaware of, the result is a "hybrid covert text," which is how, at some points, Phelan classifies my essay.

The shortcoming in Phelan's formalist scheme is his insistence on classifying all interpretations of meaning as covert. That implies they are all hidden and await being made overt, thereby revealing the agent of their hiding. And that agent must either be a careless and "unwitting" author, a cleverly designing and duplicitous author, an author whose unconscious gets the better of his or her conscious crafting, or, as the case may be with *Huckleberry Finn*, an author who yields to the reality and control of a character he has created. Except in the case of allegorical texts, say, for example, George Orwell's *Animal Farm*, critics do not unearth hidden meanings and covert texts. Rather they discern, I would argue, latent meanings, ones awakened by interacting with always-duplicitous, unconscious-laden, dialogical texts and influenced by conventions of reading.[5]

Second, Phelan rightly questions the "certain license" I take in "having Jim introduce signs into the story that Huck never mentions" (473). True, "my" Jim alters some details and even contradicts Huck's version of selected events, as does "my" Jordan Baker. But the license is not to establish "facts" crucial to the case I am making. Rather, it is to justly call into question the authenticity and factuality of all first-person narratives. No two witnesses to any event—a crime scene, a domestic event, or a brief adventure—report the same details. Thus to make "my" Jim's account authentic requires some discrepancies between his and Huck's version of their adventure. Furthermore, the discrepancies call into question Huck's identity as a "reliable" narrator, no small matter.

Third, Phelan cannot shake loose his allegiance to "the traditional interpretation of Huck as naive, . . . record[ing] things without knowing the full import of what he is recording" (475), this despite the seldom-addressed question of *when* Huck narrates his adventures—soon after them or years later. For Phelan, if Huck is a "self-conscious narrator" who "knows much more than his audience" and "is deliberately deceiving, then Twain must have created him that way" (475, 476) and it then must follow that I am writing "intentionalist criticism," not reader-response criticism, because I am discovering Twain's authorial intent. Far from being interested in the vexed matter of Twain's intentions, my concerns are to grant Jim the authority to hear a consistently self-conscious narrator and, thereby, to entitle him to his ethical right to report how Huck's self-interested narrative affects him. Phelan can draw up "all the recalcitrant material" that Jim's case "has to overlook or explain away" (477). But his enumeration, with all due respect, is little more than a listing of the impediments every good critic can find in an interpretation he or she chooses to contest. Recalcitrant material, I suppose we might acknowledge, is often that evidence that rubs against any interpretation, be it conventional, subversive, or alternative.

Fourth, Phelan repeatedly commends my essay as inventive. But he states that "as long as we work in the realm of the inventive rather than the subversive, our ethical ends will not include critiquing the original texts" (478). I fail to see the legitimacy of the either/or categorical distinction or the conclusion he wishes to draw, for an inventive essay can also be subversive and can strongly critique "the original text" on which it focuses its ethical attention. The more pertinent matter, however, is Phelan's equivocation over whether to call my essay inventive or subversive, which brings me back to the matter of whether a majority of my essays in performative criticism simply invert or subvert conventional readings and interpretations. Indeed they do, as long as my readers ally themselves with prevailing interpretations. But to readers who take issue with a prevailing interpretation, it is *that* interpretation which is subversive, for it assigns a meaning contrary to the meaning that opposing or resisting readers would argue ought to prevail. (In "my" Jim's eyes, Phelan's interpretation of Huck as a naive or "unself-conscious recording narrator" is a subversive reading.) As Steven Mailloux remarks, all reading, and thus every interpretation based on reading, "is historically contingent, politically situated, institutionally embedded, and materially conditioned."[6] In short, calling a text or interpretation subversive is simply name-calling by anyone who wishes to raise a skeptical eyebrow at some radical, unpopular, against-the-grain, or resisting interpretation. Rather than perpetuate the use of "subversive" as a critical category, loaded as it is with political resonance, it would be better to refer to "alternative" interpretations.

Where, some readers might well ask, does performative criticism fit among the various schools of reader-response criticism? Insofar as none of the practitioners in any of the various schools, however categorized, applies his or her theory from inside a text as a character or even as a narrator producing a revised version, it is difficult to guide such readers to performative criticism's nearest kinship. And inasmuch as all of the "responding readers" in my experiments are more than "implied" (Iser), "informed" or "intended" (Fish), "resisting" (Fetterley), "identity-themed" (Holland), "subjectivist" (Bleich), or "competent," "inscribed," or "ideal" (Culler[7]), aligning performative criticism with other schools of reader-response criticism is difficult. Nevertheless, my experiments share characteristics of these various schools. In several cases one could argue that where my reconstituted characters may seek to vindicate themselves, they act out what Holland would insist is their "identity theme." For instance, if the primary villains of Dickens's *Oliver Twist* and *Nicholas Nickleby*, Fagin and Ralph Nickleby, believe they have been mistreated and maligned by a hypocritical, patriarchal, Christian culture, as readers they may share an identity theme rooted in an Oedipal fixation. But in other cases, such as the revision of the ending of Dashiell Hammett's *The Maltese Falcon*, my reader, Brigid O'Shaughnessy, may be appropriately classified as a "resisting" reader, as may be María of Hemingway's *For Whom the Bell Tolls* in response to a feminist interviewer. Jim's response to his son's reading of Huck Finn's account of their adventure may fit the criteria David Bleich expects in the "response-analysis statement" of a subjective reader. And Fagin and Ralph Nickleby might well constitute what Stanley Fish would call an "interpretive community."

But perhaps the matter of categorizing performative criticism according to its shared characteristics with one or another school of reader-response criticism is academic. After all, performative criticism is not a new invention. One of its forms dates back at least to Plato's dialogues, which inventively reconstruct conversations between Socrates and his contemporaries. Another of its forms, dialogues of the dead, was first practiced in Greece by the Syrian rhetorician Lucian and, in the seventeenth and eighteenth centuries, became a literary genre commonly used by French authors Fontenelle and Fénelon and British authors Matthew Prior, Elizabeth Montagu, and George, Lord Lyttleton.[8] Yet another form of performative criticism occurs in the nineteenth century in Walter Savage Landor's "Imaginary Conversations," which influenced Robert Browning's dramatic monologues and suggested a lively form that literary and cultural criticism could take. And when Serenus Zeitblom reads Adrian Leverkuhn's musical testament in *Doctor Faustus*, Thomas Mann inserts a fictional act of reading into a fictional object, as if to invite other readers to read Leverkuhn's testament differently, to challenge the authenticity and worth of Zeitblom's interpretation. It is but a small, derivative step from imaginary conversations and dramatic monologues to performative criticism and its fictive interviews, letters, reports, and full statements.

Must such dialogues and conversations, because imaginative, fall outside the pale of academic critical discourse? Indeed, do they fail to advance its epistemological enterprise? I do not think so. Humanists, philosophers, and artists have long argued the truth-values of fictive creativity, the special knowledge that poetic and virtual realities can communicate, and the wondrous capacity of language to bring into existence worlds previously nonexistent. Nevertheless our institutionalized, professional commitment to the science, certainty, and stability of critical objectivity seems to have discouraged crossover experiments that bend the genre of literary criticism.

A few academics seem to have leapt the barrier. Among them is Austin M. Wright. His novelistic construction of a four-day debate over Faulkner's *As I Lay Dying* brilliantly develops a significant discussion of criticism, pedagogy, and the profession.[9] Among them may also be John Glavin. His recent *After Dickens* transmogrifies several of Dickens's most familiar novels, recasting them as inventive adaptations, even including a performative transcription of *Nobody's Fault*, Glavin's made-over, theatricalized rendering of *Little Dorrit*.[10] Among them might even be numbered a performative-writing practitioner such as Peggy Phelan. She argues the importance of self-referencing, "autobiographical" commentary as a way of insisting to readers that every commentator is a theatricalized presence, more than a flesh-and-blood scrim between reader and text.[11] The call for "creative criticism" exists, but relatively few academics have responded to it or have achieved prominence or influence in opening new pathways of academic professionalism.[12]

With so-called creative writers matters are—and have long been—otherwise. Boccaccio, Chaucer, Shakespeare, and Milton, to mention obvious instances, appropriated for their own purposes others' stories, histories, and biblical accounts, freshly investing them with characters and complications that generated new questions, revisionist perspectives, and strong interpretations. George Bernard Shaw's *Pygmalion*, Archibald MacLeish's *J.B.*, Robert Graves's *Homer's Daughter*, and, of course, James Joyce's *Ulysses* could be included. More recent examples are novelist John Gardner's *Grendel*, a sympathetic retelling of the story of Beowulf from the monster's point of view; Valerie Martin's *Mary Reilly*, a reenvisioned version of Stevenson's *Jekyll and Hyde*; John Updike's *Roger's Version*, a densely textured reworking of Hawthorne's *Scarlet Letter*, and *Gertrude and Claudius*, a prequel that reconstructs *Hamlet*'s background; German writer Christine Brückner's *If You Could Talk, Desdemona*, a collection of fourteen monologues by women (including Christiane von Goethe, Katharina Luther, Eva Braun, Mary, and Sappho); Jane Smiley's *Thousand Acres*, a reworking of *King Lear*; and, quite recently, Madison Smartt Bell's "Small Blue Thing," which reconsiders Poe's "The Raven" from the point of view of the bird, which, forgiving Poe's "poetic license," confesses to being a mere crow.[13]

These instances of "creative writing," of course, are strongly intertextual, and the list could multiply exponentially, especially were I to enlist poems, beginning, say, with Keats's "Ode on a Grecian Urn" or Auden's "Musée des Beaux Arts." Like the previously mentioned collection of poems about art works gathered by John Hollander and John Seelye's *Lines of Thought: Triangulations in American Art*, an unpublished collection of poems on American paintings and statuary, all imaginative works that build on preexisting texts depend to greater and lesser degrees on their predecessors for how their readers respond.

∽

A sketch of the essays ahead that I have not already mentioned, and the various approaches I take in them may whet my reader's interest, may help focus his or her attention, and may justify the diverse texts I have experimented on. I have sequenced the essays chronologically and included two short works, "The Book of Ruth" and Melville's "The Bell-Tower"; two well-known but controversial narrative poems, *Sir Gawain and the Green Knight* and Browning's "Childe Roland to the Dark Tower Came"; and two translated works, "The Book of Ruth" and Camus's *The Stranger*. With that range I intend to indicate that problematic texts of any period, genre, language, or gender lend themselves to performative criticism, even though all of mine are narratives. In several essays I have suppressed the bibliographic information, withheld lengthy lists of works consulted. Others, however, should make clear that performative criticism is not whipped up without careful and extensive research. For instance, the interview with Ruth required working with a text not only variously translated, but also contested, its cruxes often pivoting on lexical and linguistic distinctions, its meanings and interpretations confounded by omitted details. Biblical and literary scholars have worked through many of these difficulties, but whether they have enriched the text at the cost of impoverishing Ruth's resourcefulness, her views of her mother-in-law, and her relationship with her second husband, Boaz, is disputable. Similarly, the criticism and scholarship on *Sir Gawain* is formidable. Merely gathering it is a lengthy process. But for all the brilliance and erudition of much of it, there remain questions about the Green Knight/Bertilak's motives, authority, and final benevolence toward Gawain, questions that Gawain himself surely would have answers to, especially after the many tests the Green Knight/Bertilak has subjected him to. But rather than interview him, too, there is better drama in having him talk with Childe Roland, a failed candidate for knighthood whose own character, narrative, and poem's meanings have long perplexed scholars and critics and whose experiences and training make him a worthy friend or rival to help discover a large social pattern that affects more than themselves or knighthood.

In Fielding's *Tom Jones; The History of a Foundling* an important detail in the plot hinges on how Tom and Partridge happen to choose their London lodgings. Couple that with Tom's refusal to marry a woman who secretly offered herself to him, and empower that very minor but intelligent woman to complain to Fielding for his betrayal of her identity by publishing her letter in his "history," and soon she can put the entire novel into the context of a major philosophical debate in seventeenth- and eighteenth-century England. Likewise, if Fagin and Ralph Nickleby were given an occasion to be each other's "brother's keeper," what is to keep a conversation between them from revealing the ways by which the valorization of Good Samaritanism informs and deforms their world of nineteenth-century England, arguably contributing to a rehabilitation of their own characters and motives while undermining those of their adversaries, the "good" people of their novels?

My approach shifts with Melville's story "The Bell-Tower," customarily dismissed because of its didactic but confused conclusion. Inasmuch as the scholarship lacks information about the acceptance of this story for magazine publication, it seemed ripe for another reading to fill in the gaps. That required boning up on the House of Harper, one of Melville's publishers, on the editor of *Harper's Magazine*, George William Curtis, and on Curtis's "Easy Chair" columns in each issue. Then the problem was to fabricate documents that would read as originals and to show Curtis as a man of letters who, when faced with Melville's story, has reason to doubt his own abilities and must wrestle with the story's meaning and Melville's intentions. A similar experiment in "literary forgery" is behind my letter from Dashiell Hammett to Lillian Hellman and "Hammett's" revision of the ending of *The Maltese Falcon*, a novel whose main shortcoming is its selling short the shrewd Brigid O'Shaughnessy.

The challenge in making dramatic the two interviews with Hemingway's characters María and Manolin, from *For Whom the Bell Tolls* and *The Old Man and the Sea*, respectively, now seems like a pushover. Create interviewers antagonistic to the characters and play out the consequences when the interviewers find their subjects, now decades older and arguably wiser, more than they bargained for. And finally the task of contributing to the volumes of criticism on Camus's overly celebrated *The Stranger* seemed most possible by lifting it out of its literary domain, treating it as a transcribed account of an analysand's "free-association" monologues, and putting it in the hands of a psychoanalytic trainee as one of her qualifying tests.

The aim of my experiments in performative criticism is not to persuade resisting or uncommitted readers to accord such merit to my scholarship, inventiveness, and evidentiary arguments that they favor my interpretation over other critics' and scholars' interpretations of the same writer or work. Winning adherents and converts is the goal of politicians and evangelists. My primary aim is to create—or re-create on the page—a world whose characters and issues become a theater wherein literary criticism comes to life. But since that theater is only on the page, readers must collaborate with my texts to animate them, just as they do when they complete the dormant poem, story, or drama on the page. And they can applaud or remain silent in response to their collaboration. They can decide on the basis of their diverse tastes, values, and ideologies whether my experiments and the styles I have written them in have been sufficiently authentic, nuanced, and developed to arrest and sustain their attention. They can decide whether my experiments have taken them out of their world and into one that I have restored or reconstituted; whether my experiments have figuratively and literally given voice to characters—representative human beings—

sometimes in the cause of a just hearing, sometimes in the cause of revising received wisdom; whether, in a word, my experiments have provided a lens by which readers can view a text differently.

My secondary aim is to illustrate some of the directions reader-response and performance criticism might consider taking. Where my experiments have failed or been insufficiently nuanced and thus only partly successful, better and more inventive minds than mine can find strategies, techniques, and language to create better letters, interviews, dialogs, "forgeries," or forms of discourse. Indeed, the shortcomings of my experiments might well goad or inspire better critics to venture into composing better and quite different examples of performative criticism. There is pleasure in the task and the challenge to make literary criticism an eventful experience.

An Interview with Biblical Ruth

INTERVIEWER: . . . dispense with "preliminary pleasantries."[1] Indeed, I have an agenda, a few topics on which I hope to elicit your considered and respected response. It was merely that on occasion it has been quite dramatic to allude to—or to ask my biblical interviewee to identify—some scholar whose commentary or interpretation has seemed especially outrageous or wrongheaded. Thus, I thought my mention of May and Carmichael might have sparked some lively retort.[2] Why, you should have heard—or should read—the tirades with which Delilah, Aaron, and Daniel began their interviews when—

RUTH: Your agenda, sir?

INTERVIEWER: Indeed. You'll forgive, I am confident, my enthusiasms? Well, then, let me see. Ah! My notes remind me that I had hoped, were you amenable, for some dialogue on your relationships with your mother-in-law, your husband, and, to be sure, your God. And, if it please you, I might even cajole you into shedding some light, along the way, upon some of the riddles which have for so long vexed scholars of your book?

RUTH: Riddles? "'Out of the eater came something to eat?'"

INTERVIEWER: Ah! Well, not exactly riddles like that of Samson's. Ought I rather call them puzzling questions? One instance: How old *was* Boaz when he pledged himself to you on the threshing-floor?[3] A second: Had Boaz and Naomi never met before she sent you to the threshing-floor? Another: Did Boaz ever explain to you—perhaps in, ahem, conjugal intimacy—why he had waited so long for the *go 'el* to honor his obligations? A last: How did Boaz learn of Naomi's plan to "sell" her field, if there had been no meeting between them?[4]

RUTH: Only four questions? A gentlemanly interviewer? Do you unduly curb your curiosity, sir? Really. Have you no wish to know as well, say, whether chance, providence, or my own design led

13

me to Boaz's field to glean that first day?[5] Whether it was necessary for me to glean at all, seeing that Naomi had a field of her own? Whether Naomi was truly ignorant that a nearer kinsman stood between her and Boaz?[6]

INTERVIEWER: Well, indeed: answers to those would be splendid! Even answer to why it was that townswomen—rather than you and Boaz—named your son? And whether your son's name was actually Obed.[7] And, if this not be prying beyond discretion—what actually transpired between you and Boaz on the threshing-floor? How it must amuse you—does it not?—to read your commentators on *that* question![8]

RUTH: Amuse? Disdaining the issue as one of utter irrelevance (a response common to prudes), the stuffy may be as bad as the salacious, who ferret away at cabalistic symbols, or, as common, natter like gossipy townswomen. But seriously, sir, do you sincerely expect me to answer any of the questions we've enumerated? You'll permit me to imagine, won't you, that answers would rob my history of some of its allure? More, answers from my lips would be suspect by scholars, wouldn't they? Like lawyers, your kind surely would roll skeptical eyes upon my reconstruction of past events, would discount my answers as apologia, would certainly discredit my observations: "stained by subjectivity."

INTERVIEWER: Ah. Indeed. They might look upon your answers—we would be disingenuous to ignore the possibility—as rationalizations. We must admit that hazard. You would have me, then, return to the pathways of my agenda? Nevertheless, worthy woman, allow me to forewarn you (for well do I know my frailties) that I am not above endeavoring to tease such answers from my biblical interviewees *en route*.

RUTH: The matter of my relationship with my mother-in-law, sir, came first, I believe? Which one did you have in mind?

INTERVIEWER: Which one? Why surely you had not been wife to some husband prior to Mahlon, had you? Oh! Shortsighted of me to forget: marriage to Boaz made you daughter-in-law to *his* mother, too. Odd that her existence was ignored. Well, I see I must be on my toes with you, my good woman. But allow me to illuminate the significance of your relationship with Naomi. It has caused no little wonder at and respect for you, inasmuch as your devotion to her is quite untypical of traditional mother- and daughter-in-law relationships. More common, as you must know, is resentment and rivalry between the two, some disdain on the part of the mother-in-law toward her son's wife, a woman whom the mother usually regards as unworthy of *her* son, as an interloper whose interference erodes the mother's and son's long-wrought chain of filial affection. Perhaps you might wish to comment on either what it was in Naomi's character which inspired your loyalty, or what it was in your background, values, or perceptions which taught you to assign such worth to her? After all, one of the marvels of your story is what would now be called "the bond of sisterhood" which you forged with her.[9] How that bond developed, apparently through your initiative, would be most instructive, for it overcame obstacles of age, ethnic background, cultural differences, and religious training.

RUTH: There was no bond.

INTERVIEWER: I beg your pardon? My hearing is not what it once was.

RUTH: I said, "There was no bond."

INTERVIEWER: Come, come, worthy woman. Would you have me disregard your renowned oath to her, and your other six loyal acts: of accompanying her return to Bethlehem, of bringing home to her the remainder of the meal you took in Boaz's field as well as your bushel of gleaned barley, of continuing to lodge with her all during the harvest (when you could have lodged with Boaz's other gleaning girls[10]), of obeying her instructions to visit Boaz on the threshing-floor, of impressing upon him his need to redeem her rights, and of allowing her to take Obed to her bosom as *her* son? Surely there's some bond of sisterhood in those seven acts, agreeing as they do with numerological symbolism.

RUTH: There is certainly some merit in that construction of my behavior and statements.

INTERVIEWER: *Some* merit? Is there a better construction?

RUTH: I suppose it depends upon the purpose of such constructions? Maybe we ought to ask whether that construction is even defensible, is without major flaw?

INTERVIEWER: Now surely your radical decision to pledge yourself to Naomi, to her people, and to her God must have some basis in a bond you made to her. Indeed, your break with family, country, and faith—

and your commitment to an old woman rather than to a man— must signify your decision to link forces with her and, together, seek to shape your future.[11]

RUTH: My famous pledge. My renowned oath. It has certainly hornswoggled my scholars, hasn't it? Could we set it aside and return to it after we look at my mother-in-law? We might glean some grains my scholars have overlooked in their harvesting.

INTERVIEWER: Certainly. You will find me always obliging. Any place you wish to begin?

RUTH: It matters little, one place as good as another, for though her statements are laced with ambiguity, when assembled they expose a tendency in her that may, in turn, suggest what lies within my pledge. Perhaps the scene of my return from the first day in Boaz's fields?

INTERVIEWER: Agreed. You had taken up the bushel of barley which you had gleaned, had returned to Bethlehem, and Naomi saw how much you had.

RUTH: Yes. And she said what, upon seeing the bushel?

INTERVIEWER: She—ah, indeed—she asked where you had gleaned.

RUTH: A correction, may I? Upon seeing the bushel, she said nothing. She didn't ask where I'd gleaned until after I'd also given her the leftovers I'd saved from my meal.

INTERVIEWER: Ah. Indeed. Quite correct you are. And so?

RUTH: And so? And so? Had you stood in her place, sir, might you have made some remark—shown some gesture of surprise or appreciation—at seeing the bushel I'd gleaned?[12] Does it strike you odd that she'd ask where I'd gleaned only *after* I'd given her the leftovers? Or shall we disregard her omission—*this* silence—as sign of my historian's art, his wish to keep my story briskly paced?

INTERVIEWER: Well, you are quite right to observe—such is your implication, is it not?—that Naomi is no gushy sentimentalist, refrains from rhapsodizing over other's accomplishments.

RUTH: Are her blessings without rhapsody? She's not above conferring them, you know.

INTERVIEWER: Indeed, indeed. Twice she here blesses Boaz. Once as simply the man who kindly took notice of you. Once after you identified him as the man in whose fields you worked. Both blessing he deserved, I believe, don't you?

RUTH: Yes. I've no quarrel with that. My point seems to have evaded you: if Naomi and I had some bond of sisterhood, then might she not have bestowed a blessing upon me, the person who grubbed hard all day to gather that bushel?

INTERVIEWER: Hmm. I do see what you mean. She did appear to express no appreciation of your day's work, promptly seconded his instructions that you continue to glean with his girls, and only in his fields.

RUTH: Seconded his instructions, you say? Or countermanded them? Do you ignore the difference between Boaz's statements before and after mealtime? Before, he adjured me to keep close to his girls, to glean *behind* them. After, he allowed me to glean among the sheaves—that is, *behind* the male reapers but *in front of* the female gleaners.[13]

INTERVIEWER: So it is, so it is. But countermanding his instructions—to stay close to his men—implies that Naomi had some reason for so doing. And that reason must have been her punctilious concern lest you be viewed as forward, lest you violate some custom of propriety or decorum: "a gold ring in a pig's snout?"[14]

RUTH: A proverb-spouter might even allow—mightn't he?—that by countermanding Boaz's instructions Naomi intended for my circumspection to increase her kinsman's notice of me?

INTERVIEWER: Why, indeed. Which goes to show that her thoughts of seeing you "happily settled" began at the end of your first day of gleaning, rather than at the end of the barley and wheat harvests. Thus we see her sustained concern for you, her wish to trouble herself on your behalf, her bond of sisterhood to you.

RUTH: Trouble herself? *Did* she trouble herself on my behalf? Little wonder at the riddles you earlier spoke of. To someone slow at picking up hints, at gleaning dropped grains, there must indeed be a bushel of riddles!

INTERVIEWER: May I remonstrate that—

RUTH: No. No protests yet, please. To continue to pussyfoot on the matter of Naomi, I realize, will keep us here for hours. My scholars seem to have missed a few signals that my historians and scribes so carefully recorded. Allow me to put the matter bluntly, to call Naomi (in modern parlance) by the name which her reputation on the Moab plateau had garnered for her: a self-seeking bitch.

INTERVIEWER: Not to "mince" matters, as they say? But assuming the correctness of your term (for which I will be required to find an euphemistic substitute, when I edit our interview), how am I to account for your mother-in-law's solicitousness: she bid you and Orphah return to your mothers' homes, asked the *Lord's* blessings upon you, wished you the security of new homes and husbands, and, then, kissed you.

RUTH: Solicitousness? Or a ceremonial ritual for public consumption? Well, it takes in the simple—Orphah and my scholars. Clearly they understand the ambiguous significance neither of bidding a widow to return to her mother's home nor of wishing one the security of a new husband's home.

INTERVIEWER: Am I in error to assume that Naomi's reference to "mothers' homes" indicates the widowed status of both your and Orphah's mothers (*rather* too coincidental, I will agree)? Or if not that, then am I in error to be persuaded that Naomi's reference is to the place best able to comfort a widow?[15]

RUTH: One of my scholars notes that a "mother's house" locates the symbolic place where marriage matters were hatched.[16] But he ignores the pattern of Naomi's insults, of which this is an early example. So he fails to see that she here imputes to Orphah and me the motive of eager interest in scurrying back home to brew up new marriages, to find fresh flesh of new husbands to cleave to, and to end the fruitlessness of our wombs. Queer that my scholars haven't considered the resentfulness in Naomi's farewell. After all, the ten years' barrenness which both Orphah and I suffered was, in Naomi's eyes, an indictment of *us*, not her sons. In fact, while I can't speak for Orphah, can you imagine my being made to feel that the death of Mahlon was a consequence of his marriage to me, an "alien?" A double curse though we might have been in Naomi's eyes, she dared not privately or publicly express such a sentiment, cautious that we might have recourse in recrimination, I suppose. And so her ceremonial farewell: it allows for sincerity, if read with no awareness of the patterns of her behavior. But it allows for sarcasm, if read with full awareness of them.

INTERVIEWER: Well! Now that is, I must confess, an original—albeit quite idiosyncratic—theory.

RUTH: Theory? Your condescension implies that still you fail to discern the pattern of her self-centeredness. Consider, then. Did Naomi, after the deaths of her sons and husband, choose to return to Bethlehem *because* she felt guilt for having abandoned her homeland during its famine over a decade earlier? Or is there opportunism in her choice to return "because she had heard while still in the Moabite country that the *Lord* had cared for his people and given them food?"

INTERVIEWER: Since you ask, I—

RUTH: Did she adjure Orphah and me to return home when the three of us still dwelt in "the place where she had been living," or only when we were on "the road home to Judah"—that is, sir, after we were no longer useful to Naomi's journey?

INTERVIEWER: Surely—

RUTH: After Orphah and I wept and insisted upon returning with her to her people, did she pause to reason with us, to explain the difficulties of being aliens in Bethlehem? Or did she abruptly begin to insult us? Did she impugn us for expecting her to find or bear us new husbands? Did she insinuate that we were too lascivious to restrain our appetites until two new sons, whom she could give birth to, could, in turn, marry us? Did she mock us as creatures of little patience and less sexual restraint?

INTERVIEWER: If you will be so good as—

RUTH: Did she, in her alleged "mordant self-deprecation,"[17] show concern for our recent loss, the freshness of our grief? Or did she—heedless that her womb had yielded two sons and ours none—rub salt into the disgrace of our childless marriages by claiming that her lot was more bitter than ours?

INTERVIEWER: Uh—

RUTH: Please. Save your interruption until I've finished! Did she acknowledge my existence or plight when we reached Bethlehem and met her townswomen? Or did she harp again on God's bitter treatment of only herself? Was she stoical? Or did she bellyache about His pronouncements against herself, the disaster He had let fall upon herself? And those six measures of barley, which Boaz sent me home to Naomi with, after my night on the threshing-floor: Did they symbolize his marital pledge or his knowledge of her reputation for acquisitiveness?

INTERVIEWER: A veritable litany of rhetorical questions!

RUTH: And to end them, Naomi's *third* silence (the *second*, recall, was when I arrived with that bushel of barley): When Obed is entrusted to her care and her own future security is guaranteed, her townswomen proclaim that her daughter-in-law, me, "'has proved better to you than seven sons.'" Did Naomi admit this to be true? Did she make any gesture, say anything my history records? Was her silence to acknowledge the obvious truth of the women's proclamation? Or was it of a piece with her cold, ungrateful, proud self-centeredness?

INTERVIEWER: Quite an eruption, I might call it? But given all of this feeling— shall it be termed "exhumed acidulousness"?—toward Naomi, esteemed by some as your story's heroine,[18] your oath to her (we may now return to it, may we?) is quite, well, irrational. Were she the self-centered female canine whom you identify, then your pledge to her makes no sense at all. Surely you must see that.

RUTH: My words to her on the road to Judah: Are they to be read only as a commitment of affection, an emotion quite at odds with my "eruption?" Are my reasons for such an oath so incalculable, truly as hidden as Abraham's thoughts when he was about to sacrifice Isaac?[19] Has it never occurred to you to attempt to read my oath as a curse, to consider that it answers Naomi's insults? No. Please, no answer. Can you so quickly forget her impugning Orphah and me with her slurs, brush aside her making light of our bitter lots, ignore her insensitivity to our tears of grief over our recently dead husbands and over the harshness and abruptness of her rejection of us? In the face of such insults can't you imagine the explanation behind her *first* silence— after I spoke my "oath?" Was she silent because of its respectfulness and modesty? Or because in articulating it I revealed some unexpected resoluteness, because it bordered on being radical, and because I spoke it with an ambiguous solemnity to cause her to wonder whether it was a pledge or a curse? Might her silence have acknowledged her astonishment at my determination, behind which—do you further suppose?—might have lurked an unarticulated vow to make her eat the imputation of her words? Were someone to consider you a leech, an obstacle impeding his or her future, sir, might your injured pride be tempted to retaliate with an oath?

INTERVIEWER: Of course, of course. But now you thoroughly compound my confusion. To think you would attach yourself to a woman you deeply disliked; well, I must say that it strikes me—and may strike others—as perverse.

RUTH: Mechanistic logic? Because I disliked Naomi's egotistical bitchery, must it follow, QED, that I would shun all contact with her, that I should have found in her, therefore, no qualities deserving emulation?

INTERVIEWER: A normal conclusion, I think I can safely say. Or am I to understand that in her you recognized value?

RUTH: Her value lay in her pluck—brass, to some. After all, from the statements my historian, storyteller, or scribe assigns to Naomi, even you must see that she was no passive, submissive woman. Even before I became her daughter-in-law she had agreed to the risky venture of leaving Bethlehem during its famine, showing that she was game to wrest with, rather than meekly submit to, fate or providence—much less to some domineering, patriarchal husband. My oath, part curse that it was, also contained a pledge to what Naomi represented: her aggressively irascible independence.

INTERVIEWER: Thus, in your oath resides not one iota of a pledge of obedience, I am to understand? In it is no vestige of your very son's name, no commitment to being a servant?

RUTH: Of course there's commitment. But to a woman whose disrespect and defiance represented personal values that challenged custom, law, people, and God. Why within seven verses (more numerology, sir!) she complained that the Lord had "been against" her, had sent her a "bitter lot," had brought her back to Bethlehem "empty," had "pronounced against" her, had "brought disaster on" her. You'd be naive, sir, to think that these outpourings were the first time she'd expressed such irreverence within my earshot. Uttered with impunity, they should begin to suggest what it was in Naomi's character which won my loyalty. In my oath was a pledge of obedience—to a principle of assertive independence.

INTERVIEWER: I believe I begin to wish your mother-in-law had never left the Moab plateau. Your view of her begins to give me some intellectual heartburn, if you will. Indeed, I begin to have some reservations about you as well, begin to suspect you of no little art in your relationship with Boaz, begin to reassess my well-schooled dismissal of the scholar who first broached the silly notion of you as a wily woman,[20] begin, I confess, to find you less to my liking than I had expected.

RUTH: As if I'd clamored for this interview, sir? As if my agreement to suffer it had also stipulated that I seek your admiration? But I've entertained you with my correctives on Naomi's character, and both you and I know that "Whosoever loveth correction loveth knowledge."[21] So why not correct me with your suspicions of my artful relationship with Boaz? Proceed. Please do.

INTERVIEWER: Curious that I had pooh-poohed that off-putting translation. It now begins to make sense, especially the rendering of the first verses of chapter 2.

RUTH: You'll be so good, of course, as to recite the translation you're referring to?

INTERVIEWER: The better to see you with, my dear: "Now Naomi knew of an acquaintance of her husband, a property holder who belonged to Elimelech's clan; his name was Boaz. Ruth of Moab said to Naomi: 'Should I go to the fields and glean among the ears of grain, in the hope of pleasing him?'"[22]

RUTH: Yes. A translation which finally allows that Naomi was not se-nile, which clarifies that she knew she had some rights due her through her husband's family, and which discloses that I had some reason for immediately gleaning in Boaz's fields. But even that translation, sir, perpetuates the interrogatory, casts me as the supplicating alien, violates my careful use of the ambiguous cohortative.[23]

INTERVIEWER: I quoted the verses, worthy woman, to emphasize none of the features to which you attend. I quoted them, rather, to point to the emphasis on which they end: your design to "please" Boaz, *'aḥar 'ašer 'emṣā-ḥēn be 'ēnāyw*, (literally, "to find favor in his eyes"). For suddenly a vision of truth crests upon my conscious-ness: Indeed, although you set out on a double mission—to glean and to please Boaz—the former was merely the means to the latter end. *There* is opportunism! And to that pair of motives add another. I refer back to your *own* information! To your de-sign in asking permission not only to glean, but to "gather grain

from among the sheaves behind the reapers." That double petition, as you—ha!—have taught me to see, sought not merely to
ask for the right which was customarily granted to all aliens and
widows, to glean *behind* the gleaners and the reapers. It also
sought special permission to glean *in front of the gleaners*!

RUTH: You will, won't you, comment likewise upon Boaz's notice of my
presence in his field? For that, too, reflects upon my artfulness,
notes that in my subject position I displayed frequent—not
just sometime—autonomy.[24] I guaranteed his notice by more
duplicity—for I gather that your use of "doubles" drifts, not very
subtly, toward that term. And so I wore to the field my Moabite
dress (didn't I?), certain that it would catch his eye, even though
no commentary observes it. And I made a point of arriving at
his field at daybreak (didn't I?), confident that Boaz would have
an overseer who could remark my display of industry and report
it to him.

INTERVIEWER: And thus, most worthy woman, the scholar correctly construes
your "luck"—the "happenstance" which, by "chance," brought
you to Boaz's field; for your "luck" lay merely in your not "*wast-
ing precious time searching for it.*"[25] Which is to say that there was
no luck at all in your arrival at his field, that you had planned to
glean in no field other than his. How it must have amused you—
did it not?—when Boaz immediately began to instruct you to
glean in no other field, to stay in his! Was it easy to suppress your
mirth, tempting to throw a wink to the overseer?

RUTH: I doubt you'd entertain any suggestion that in female volition and
human luck might be some residue of divine intentionality?[26]

INTERVIEWER: It is customary for a temptress, I have long observed, worthy
woman, to solicit fraternal magnanimity when her snares have
been discovered. Oh, how transparent your schemes are now. Of
course it was contrivance which prompted you to prostrate
yourself in false gratitude to Boaz, even though he had denied
your petition to gather immediately behind the reapers. And
naturally it was calculation when you, pressing for an advantage,
altogether avoided expressing the least gratitude to Boaz (and
you, I recollect, faulted Naomi on that very score?). Moreover,
you instead asked (and with what coyness I can now imagine!)
why it was that he "favored" you, or how it happened that you
"pleased" him, and what it was that caused him to take special
"notice" of you. And giving him ample time to let the shaft of

your subtle coquetry sink deeply into—and stir!—his nether parts, you cast that last bait, that false humility, calling yourself merely a foreigner. You are too skilled in such art for your father to have been other than a fisherman.

RUTH: You will not allow, I gather, that my question, and my admission to being a foreigner, were straightforward? Their intent could not have simply been to break through his formality, to have him own up to whether he truly knew who I was?

INTERVIEWER: Perhaps. But quite unlikely when put alongside the artful loquacity of your next speech.

RUTH: Verse 13?

"May I continue to find favor in your eyes, my lord.
Because you have comforted me
And because you have spoken to the heart of your maid-servant.
Why, as for me I am not even as (worthy as) one of your maid-
        servants!"

INTERVIEWER: As I could have predicted, you prefer that rendering to one which denies you the pretense of politeness in your opening request, which refuses you the ambiguity of the optative because your ability to elicit "acts of kindness from Boaz" obviated any need for you to resort to it: "'I must have pleased you, my lord, since you have comforted me and have spoken tenderly to your maidservant. Yet I am not even considered as one of your maidservants.'"[27]

RUTH: Quite good, sir! Correctly noted: I had no need for the optative, for I sought to express not a wish but a fact. Plainly I pleased Boaz. But in expressing that, can I disclose only artfulness, never candor?

INTERVIEWER: Was it candor for you to commend Boaz for speaking "tenderly," to your "heart?" Certainly you knew that embedded in your expression was the meaning of sexual enticement.[28]

RUTH: And certainly you will have it—to anticipate your bishop's sweeping move—that I was already snaking my way up the social ladder by inveigling Boaz to consider me not as a foreigner but as a maid-servant, a term I knew I'd find a better substitute for at a later time?[29]

INTERVIEWER: If not that, good woman, then why did you not end your speech at just that point? Hmm? Hmm? Why did you repeat the word *šiphāh*, if not to call to his attention the dilemma into which you wished to put him, of whether he would continue regarding you as merely a maid-servant or would elevate your status? And oh! how you knew to call his attention, by sincerely declaring, in artful modesty to be sure, that you were not even considered one of his maid-servants.

RUTH: Wouldn't you prefer a different translator here, despite his naive commentary about my "deferential terms" for myself, my "greater expression of humility?"[30] After all, you could certainly find impudence and coy double-dealing in "'Why, as for me, I am not even as (worthy as) one of your maid-servants.'" For did that not make Boaz—like my oath to Naomi—altogether speechless, soliciting him either to say nothing or to gallantly declare that my reputation had made me worthier than a maid-servant? Maybe you'd prefer yet another translation, one that has me asking Boaz to treat me both better than—and not at all—as a maid-servant: "'May I ask you as a favour not to treat me only as one of your slave-girls?'"[31] Love that "only." Would you like it again? Spoken with more sauce or more steam?

INTERVIEWER: What I would like is to see the act you put on at mealtime. After slaking your thirst with a drink from the jars of water, which Boaz's men had filled and from which he had invited you to drink, what did you do, worthy woman, to elicit his command that you draw near and share in the communal meal? Had you deliberately brought nothing to eat, counting upon someone's charity or pity to fill that lack? Had you conspicuously removed yourself entirely from all groups of the harvest hands, isolating yourself so as to call attention to your alien status? Surely you did something which caught Boaz's eye and played upon his susceptibility.

RUTH: In your eyes even modest withdrawal for rest and contemplation is humbuggery, the artful ploy of a designing woman? "Some men, like bats or owls, have better eyes for the darkness than for the light."[32] Is Boaz to be credited with no initiative, a victim to the mesmerizing force of my actions? My soulful eyes won from his hands a heap of roasted grain? My birdlike delicacy won from his mouth the instructions to the reapers that I be permitted to glean behind them without rebuke or innuendo?

INTERVIEWER: Setting me up for the threshing-floor scene, are you, in which he discloses how fully he has thought out the moves he must make? Well, I will not go so far as to deny him all initiative. For I find merit in the view of Boaz as trickster, a view which necessitates forethought and initiative.[33] But surely now you shrewdly try to sidestep your most duplicitous act—the betrayal of your vow, "'I will do as you say,'" after Naomi instructed you to go to Boaz at the threshing-floor. Yes, you hope—do you not?—to draw me into debate over whether Boaz was tool or trickster.

RUTH: It is a worthy debate, is it not? For in debating it, we well might weigh the tendentiousness of the trickster commentary. To see each segment of my tale compartmentalized, its functions classified within the thirty-one available to every folktale! And to what end, if its pre-charted course leaves no unresolved complications and no ambiguous characters, completely satisfies every expectation—as though every folktale were a meal one chewed and swallowed, by the numbers, from hors d'oeuvre to dessert![34] As if my tale's symmetry were merely esthetic architecture, its unifying plan were devoid of any psychological disposition.[35] As if our dialogue has brought forth no unresolved complications, has burnished no ambiguous characters, has burdened us with no unsatisfied expectations! Pish! Had my tale fully satisfied *your* expectations, I doubt that you'd have sought me out for an interview, have ever broached the question of what "transpired" on the threshing-floor, no? If I must choose between a formulaic folklorist and a fairy-tale Freudian, give me the latter, every time.[36]

INTERVIEWER: Disregarding your reference to some biblical scholar whose work has escaped me, I must admit that the debate would be profitable, if only to question whether you, putative heroine, were also a trickster, and to question whether, then, morphologists of the folktale err in assigning characters static functions, in denying them psychological reality of their own. But all of this, I repeat, is a distracting ploy to sidestep your treachery, the violation of your word to Naomi that you would do what she told you to do when you reached the threshing-floor. No translation glosses your storyteller's declaration that you did everything "exactly" as Naomi told you. But clearly, instead of waiting for Boaz to "'tell you what to do,'" *you* told *him* what to do. Indeed, upon his waking to find you at his feet, you scarcely gave him time to ask who you were before you identified yourself to him as his "handmaiden" ('*āmāh*) rather than as a "maid-servant" (*šiphāh*) as you had in the fields, insinuating your eligibility to aspire to marriage with him![37] Then you immediately instructed him to spread his

skirt over you, perfunctorily explaining that he must do so because he was next of kin. Willing as you were to go along with
Naomi's stratagem—proof one of your scheming nature—you
improved upon it—proof two.

RUTH: What would you have had me do? All of your previous accusations gather here, for pure and simple they fault me for refusing
to be a passive woman, condemn me for saying and doing things
that try to exert some control over the shape my destiny took. So
now, sir, should I have disputed with Naomi and unleashed a
pack of complaints that now even I was against her? And should
I have waited for Boaz's instructions, unsure of whether he'd repulse me as some malevolent Lilith or seize me as a vessel to
pour more of his seed into?[38]

INTERVIEWER: You should have honored your word, done as you told Naomi
you would do. In a word, obeyed her.

RUTH: Can't you see that my betrayal of Naomi's instructions was necessary to my own well-being and to my respect for Boaz? Can't
you see, for that matter, that I'd disobeyed them even before Boaz
awoke? Naomi had instructed me to wait until he'd finished eat-
ing and drinking, to observe where he went to lie down, and *then*
to approach him, bare his legs, and lie down *when he lay down*.
But exactly when did I bare his legs and lie down? "Then." But
when is "then?" He awoke about midnight. But did I lie at his
feet as Naomi had instructed, *when* he lay down, *when*, sir, he
was full of drink and food and his wits were not at their sharpest?
Or did I wait until *after* he was fast asleep, hopeful that when he
awoke he'd have slept off the muzziness of drink and fatigue?

INTERVIEWER: I do not recall *that* issue ever having drawn commentary, I will
admit.

RUTH: And, sir, while it is true that I instructed Boaz, can't you see that
my instruction was artful only in telling him succinctly that
while he might wish merely to spread his skirt over me and take
me, as mistress or concubine, into his *familias*—to fulfill his
pleasure—he should weigh my request on the scales of his levirate relationship—to fulfill his obligation as kinsman? Could
such a double-barreled statement be said with sauce or steam?[39]

INTERVIEWER: I must acknowledge that before the city gate Boaz fires both of
those barrels—in reverse order—inducing the nearer kinsman to
agree to fulfill the levirate obligation but to balk at "spreading

his skirt" over you. And in that neat inversion Boaz seems to honor the segments of your careful threshing-floor speech. Ha! Even responds to the first segment by vaulting your status from handmaiden to wife! But whether your artfulness is defensible, my latter-day Tamar,[40] hinges upon whether you knew Boaz to be, in fact, your nearest kinsman. For if you knew that he was *not*, why then, worthy woman, your cunning act of using that label exposes the culpable multiplicity of your self-seeking motives: exaggerating his status so as to heighten his interest in you,[41] bribing him with the enticements of your body to find means to supplant the nearer kinsman, and soliciting his pity for yourself, who had no legal rights to claim levirate responsibility from him. To think that in that single labeling you could rouse his pride, lust, and compassion![42]

RUTH: I tolerate your tests of my patience. But I weary of your slights to my ethical integrity. Can you think me ignorant that manipulating a person, as an object to use or agent to turn, constitutes a form of impiety, injures the soul? *Suppose* I had learned of a nearer kinsman who was married, had a family, and was the kind of man who'd snap up a chance to acquire Naomi's property but hang back from honoring Elimelech's family name. And *suppose*, sir, that I learned this through no sleuthery of mine, but simply from the gossip among the harvesters, for whom I was an object both of curiosity and marriage offers. Should I have "instructed" Boaz, "Even though I know you aren't Naomi's nearest kinsman, please take pity on me and spread your skirt over me anyway?"

INTERVIEWER: Given your suppositions, that would have been the honest thing to do, I believe?

RUTH: But it also presumes that I had no self-respect, that I went to the threshing-floor out of disappointment, that I had glumly watched the harvest end without Boaz showing much more of his hand than he had on that first day. And it forgets that I was sent there to precipitate some action from Boaz on Naomi's behalf, mortified at having to stoop to such action, but resolved to escape from it with the least harm to my own dignity, with no appeal to Boaz's pity.

INTERVIEWER: Well, I see that I must grant you that much: you never ask for pity, never thank anyone for it; you thank Boaz for his kindness, his notice of you, his not treating you as a maid-servant. But to consent to a design to precipitate Boaz into action served you as well as Naomi, make no mistake about that.

RUTH: Could I have been entirely selfless under the circumstances? Should I have had no regard for my own dignity? Please look, sir: I chose to carry out her instructions in my way, a way that wouldn't insult Boaz. Don't you see? Had I been the one to declare that I knew the existence of a nearer kinsman—supposing I *did* know—then I would have been rebuking his failure to have acted earlier. But by declaring only what everyone knew, that he was Naomi's kinsman, I tried to show my respect for him: I left to him the choice of revealing what he knew. And what he revealed was that he had not been inactive in his wish to solve a complicated problem. For he proceeded to show not only that he had weighed my acts of loyalty to Naomi and had attended to my refusal to seek after any young man, but also that he had learned of Naomi's rights to a plot of land and had discovered the identity of a nearer kinsman than he, whose values and daily habits he had made himself thoroughly acquainted with.

INTERVIEWER: Daily habits? To what do you now refer?

RUTH: The nearer kinsman's habit of passing in and out the city gates. Or do you think it accidental that he just happened to show up when Boaz sat down at the gates? In a word, sir, whether I knew the existence of the nearer kinsman is beside the point. The point, instead, is that I knew enough to identify Boaz as *a* kinsman and to let him answer the insult which Naomi's strategy of sending me to him on the threshing-floor accused him of—the insult of having done nothing to redeem her situation. His answer, both in his pledge to me and his acts at the city gates, showed he'd not been idle, even during that busiest of times of the year.

INTERVIEWER: Then his industry—observing your conduct during the harvest, ascertaining the identity and values and habits of Naomi's nearer kinsman, and devising a strategy with which to flush out the nearer kinsman's self-centeredness—all of this demonstrates that Boaz resembled the Naomi whom you have portrayed and the Ruth whose artfulness I have portrayed, does it not?

RUTH: I believe it does, for the three of us were resourceful, independent, and determined to exert some control, as I have said, over the shape of our destinies.

INTERVIEWER: Not quite the terms I had in mind: self-centered and devious. Indeed the three of you—ah! indeed, flanked by Orpah and the nameless nearer kinsman, too—make quite a despicable group, plotting and planning schemes to serve your own ends, determined, as I perceive it, to defy God's designs, as much as you were able. Why now it is even clear to me why you and Boaz allowed Naomi the rights over your son. Indeed, your act did perpetuate her husband's name and line. But it immortalized you two. Your scheming selflessness guaranteed you the immortality of history, won enshrinement in religious text.

RUTH: Our acts guaranteed immortality? Had Obed been a nonentity, wouldn't all four of us have disappeared from human memory? Could we so shape our destinies as to impress God or scribes to fit us into a genealogy important to religious people?

INTERVIEWER: Which should bring me to the last item in my agenda: your relationship to God. But I believe, worthy woman, that from what you have revealed to me and what I in turn have discovered, *your* relationship to God would also differ significantly from what "religious people" have thought it. Ha! I can even imagine, now, that you had no faith in Yahweh, merely feigned belief, used it to win yourself a wealthy husband, a man of substance.

RUTH: And to what end, sir? Domestic ease? Maternal status? Material wealth? Conjugal pleasure? Matriarchal power? Alien ambition?

INTERVIEWER: Oh, I can imagine a truly outrageous end toward which all of your actions were aimed. Shall we name it a widow's love? Shall we hypothesize that your deepest loyalty was—a trumpet fanfare, please—to your first husband, Mahlon? Shall we conceive that all of your actions were to serve his memory by marrying someone whose son by you would perpetuate his family's name?

RUTH: Sir! You amaze me with your—

INTERVIEWER: I amaze myself! But my scenario of your love story requires that it was in deference to your love of Mahlon that Boaz agreed—indeed, during those nocturnal hours on the threshing-floor, I would wager!—to the masterstroke (which *you* must have planted in his head!) of obligating the next of kin to perpetuate Mahlon's patrimony. But God—ha! or the scribes—undid your love story. For the genealogy entirely omits Elimelech and Mahlon, inserts Boaz and his father Salmon instead. There's impiety, worthy woman, injury to a soul, the manipulation of you as an object to use, an agent to. . . .[43]

A Dialogue of the Dead
Sir Gawain to the Childe Roland Came

ROLAND: Pssst! Sir! You there, sir! Hold up! Present yourself. Ah, yes. That's much better. Well, now. One of our velveted varlets has recently groused and growled about seeing a hooded knight, someone matching your description, furtively lurking about these lowly habitations—these, these quarters which those of us denied the high prize of knighthood are wont to call our "institutional residence." Do enter, lest some snooping sentinel. . . . Well, we both know how unauthorized colloquy and unscheduled assembly breeds in our keepers suspicion of seditious undertaking and cabalistic plotting. Enter, without shame, please. Surely no especial disgrace or social humiliation attaches to a knight's visit to an unsuccessful candidate, even one as smudged and besmirched as I. Perhaps, cautious sir, you wish, albeit reluctantly, to solicit, like no few of your brethren, an animated recitation of my perilous adventure to my squat Dark Tower?

GAWAIN: Not so, sir, thank you. I vie for no vocal performance of your escapade. I have scanned its cadences on sufficient occasions, have conned its complaint often. And, indeed, to deliver myself to you without disingenuousness, I have approached your dwelling on several occasions. I have been intent on questioning your claim, which you so immodestly advertise, of having been the most tormented of our brotherhood. Strictly for myself I would privately query that claim to status and privilege—or obloquy, if such be the case.

ROLAND: You're come, I presume, to humble me, deny me my status, scratch my name from that roster? And on grounds, I suppose, that it more properly belongs to you? Or perhaps to some knight you're eager to hoist, some tormented champion you boost and wish to bray about?

GAWAIN: I champion no one, sir, especially not myself. (That you shutter your windows eases my worry that perfidious eavesdroppers may be about. I thank you for that gesture of considerateness.) Furthermore, I pledge to secure our conversation in confidence, having long been taught by untoward consequences to deplore dissemination of private discourse in public arenas: No braying ass will you find me, sir. Allow me, however, to acknowledge that for a protracted period I have pondered your anomalous adventure, and I question whether the torments that beset your quest warrant any greater claim than those that others of us, similarly detained here, have endured.

ROLAND: Ah! So, you would level me? You would chop me down to some normative, yes, some de-muck-ratic mean? That way I would be the equal of my "brothers," is that it? You seek to tar my amour propre because you—and perhaps someone else—scorn it as a blemished badge of undeserved pride?

GAWAIN: I bring tar neither to your story nor to you, sir. I desire to understand your story better—and so to better judge the merit of your claim.

ROLAND: By which, am I to infer, you mean you wish to subject me to some scurvy inquiry? Let's speak bluntly, man, if converse we will. You aim to interrogate me, do you not?

GAWAIN:

ROLAND: Well, why not, why not? But. You must allow me to cast suspicion on your desire "to understand" my story, me, and my claim. I cannot accept your motive to be one of personal curiosity, academic scholarship, social justice, or—what shall I designate it?—disinterested epistemology. Your fraying green baldric blazons your identity, even in our dimmed lamplight. I have, perforce, made myself acquainted with your adventures, too. For yours rank high up in that list of readings stipulated by our severe sentence to this institution of elegant incarceration. (Better to read tales than be obliged to stoop to render "community service," I say, that's for certain.) Be that as it may, my visitor— Right?—is none other than guilt-ridden Gawain, still pouting over your shame at having been caught at a slight—or should I call it, ha! a sleight?—act of self-preservation. No need for embarrassment, man! Zounds! How your blush blanches still the scar on your neck. But come. Surely your "inquiry" has selfish motives: You wish to better "understand" my story so that you can measure the torments that tried your mettle. That way you can console, no, *commend* yourself for having suffered torments greater than mine. Ha! I've hit that one on the head, haven't I? Ha! Or would you rather I not refer to heads, inasmuch as you expected yours to be lopped off . . . Thunk . . . Plop?

GAWAIN: I have no wish to commend myself, for I know only too well my shortcomings. But once conjoined with the accounts of others' tribulations, which I have privately obtained through research and interview, our dialogue may reveal or clarify to me some baleful pattern visited upon our brotherhood. Short of that, our dialogue may provide some grounds by which I may privately measure the vicissitudes and valor of your adventures against others', if only to console me for our mutual failures.

ROLAND: Failures? Faugh! Who said anything about failures? Dare you presume to count me among failures? Did you not declare you have "conned the cadences of my complaint?" Pish! If that's so, sir, you give evidence of little discernment and less understanding. I'll have you to know these several facts: I persevered in my quest. I reached the Dark Tower. I blew my slug-horn. I survived the ordeal there to tell about it. To all but the dullest or agenda-ridden of auditors, my report, labeled by hermetic aesthetes a "dramatic monologue," surely reveals that much. I committed no wrongs. I have naught to be ashamed of, much less to repent. I withstood the trials and tests that came to me.

But sit, man, sit. Less ceremonial formality will slip the leash from our tongues. Tell you what, Gawain. I'm not opposed to your inquiry, even though its lineaments threaten to be those of a moral, perhaps political, game. I am now better able to enjoy such ludic events than I once was, before I learned, at my cost, their entanglement in all human actions. But. You must agree to allowing me to examine your adventure while you subject mine to your inquiry. Comparisons, while invidious, can also be illuminating.

GAWAIN: So be it.

ROLAND: Good. And we need to see to it that we know the rules of our game. Or, in this case, the territory over which our game will traverse. Let's agree to, well, what shall we call them? How about "yardsticks?" Good. Three should do, shouldn't it? Good. To examine—or compare—fairly the "torments" I allegedly suffered should first require us to measure the motives that impelled my imperiled adventures against the motives that impelled yours and, thus, brought about those torments, wouldn't you agree? Good, good. With what refined restraint do you nod your head. Agree as well, shall we, to compare the landscapes to which our adventures subjected us—the geographies in which my Dark Tower and your Green Chapel nested? Good, good, good. And we must, of course, agree to compare our adversaries. Hmm! A tidy threesome, these comparisons. Why, were you of a distrustful mind, you might doubt their having sprung forth spontaneously, might fancy them part of a rehearsed or preprogrammed scheme. But they should permit us—and any who wish or were to overhear us or study our colloquy—to assay and compare the respective "torments" of our adventures and our conduct in the face of them.

GAWAIN: Please know: I am loath to enable others to assay my conduct or to compare us. I deplore public parades and ceremonious contests on which spectators can gorge vicariously or bandy facile judgments and popular tastes. Thus, we shall also assent, thank you, to the uncompromising condition of private conversation. But, sir, is it your sincere wish to forgo the journey over the most prominent feature of our territory?

ROLAND: By which you mean?

GAWAIN: "By which you mean?" By which I mean the tests which forged our torments, what else?

ROLAND: Ah, yes. The tests into whose bracing bogs we were indelicately and indelibly dipped. Well, that's fair, even though mine were, as we'll see, continuous. Yours, by contrast, were numbered, neatly symmetrical. Two exchanged blows, a tit for a tat. Three exchanged gifts, a quid for a quo. And each gift you bestowed upon your Host—each of those six, curiously gendered, tormented? companionable? kisses—each bloomed from the bud-like lips of your nubile visitor whose morning ministrations both early and blatantly signaled treachery. Consequently, your daily tests posed diminishing difficulties. But. If you insist, I'll let you count them as separate tests. They may flesh out, shall we say, a yardstick that may favor you.

GAWAIN: I detect in you, sir, a capaciousness for sarcasm and oversimplification . . . and coarseness of speech.

ROLAND: Childe Roland, man. Call me Childe Roland, if you please, stressing the "childe" to acknowledge my status. The court's failure to grant me knighthood—to supplant "childe" with "sir"—is of no more concern to me now than a wart on a swine's snout or black hairs on a maiden's roseate areola. I know that arrival at the designated Dark Tower was all my brutish adventure required of me. Truly, my superiors denied my achievement, rejected the veracity of my adventure, my quest. That denial argues the shallowness of their empirical predisposition. Or the impotency of their imaginations. Or, perhaps, the quirky and querulous criteria they set for advancement to knighthood. Ha! Or yes, all three! However that may be, good fellow, let's on with it. Set forth the motives that impelled you on your adventures. Then, with the motives that impelled mine, I can trump yours, as you know I'll do quite handily.

GAWAIN: I believe, good Roland, it ill behooves me to declare my motive.

ROLAND: Motive? Motive? As if to think you had but one motive? Well, whether it behooves you well or ill, name it. Then I can properly identify its siblings, which multiply, I've learned, like lusty, well-fed, and fecund rabbits. I'll fault not your pride in choosing your motive, however grandly you may wish to ennoble it.

GAWAIN: It contains naught that could be called "grand" at all. And if, as you claim, you have acquainted yourself with my adventures, then you know as well that duty, not choice, determined them. Indeed, my adventures with the Green Knight and his cunning accomplices, you might allow, chose me. But not to make argument with that point, allow me the declaration that the motive behind my participation in those adventures was to serve loyally my uncle, King Arthur, and thereby to uphold the honorable reputation of Camelot and the chivalric virtues of Arthur's Christian stewardship—in both of which, I confess, I failed.

ROLAND: Excellent answer! Yes. Excellent. And so, Gawain, we share the same noble motive. But is that all there was to it? Self-immolating altruism alone spurred your behavior? Well, well, well. Let's just turn a bright light on—Oh, why not?—the foremost of your acts. I have in mind your response to the verdant invader's rude challenge. Your response encompassed no egotistical motives, you say? Attend.

            Item the First: You intervened in the marvelous monster's interruption of the court's merriment. Does that not argue your desire to capture continued preferment in the mind of your youthful uncle and, may I suggest, in the siren eyes of your silk-canopied queen, the graceful Guenevere?

GAWAIN: Sir, you impugn—

ROLAND: Please! Don't interrupt the leverage of my litany.

Item the Second: You paraded your preeminence in the court's hierarchy. Does that not argue your wish to vault your superiority not only over your brother, Agravain of the hard hands, but over the other famed warriors and "luflych" lords assembled but unnerved by the terms of the green man's gruesome game?

Item the Third: You exhibited your capacity to match wits against the insulting challenger. Does that not argue—on pretense of sacrificing yourself and thereby removing your king from a perilous Christmas game—does it not argue your delight in seizing an opportunity to validate your reputation as a skillful word-jockey, able to parry the garnished giant's demeaning sleights?

Item the Fourth: You displayed bold decisiveness in choosing the instrument for your stroke, the visitor's awesome axe over his harmless holly branch. Does that not argue your vanity in vaunting your shrewdness to determine precisely the terms of the exchange of blows, terms to ensure—had the emerald entrant been without magic—the safety of your own skin?

Item the Fifth: You advertised your—

GAWAIN: Allow my interruption! If it please you or not. It appears that you have more than acquainted yourself with my adventure. Your enumeration of my motives, restricting yourself to merely my earliest emergence in the history of my encounter, suggests your schooling in a species of verbal anatomy, motive-mongering, if I may be permitted such a term. Were you to continue exhuming my adventures' every action and word, even my confession before the court of my shameful scar and the adornment of the Lady's green lace upon my person as a pennant of penance, would be guarantors of my egotism. Surely, sir, you would have it, would you not, that I *advertise* my august adventures by arranging the girdle of green slantwise, thereby directing arrested eyes upward to the visible crease scarring my adjacent neck, sign of my privileged singularity, not my protracted shame? You would have it, would you not, that I *advertise* over my tunic my escape from the Green Knight's most exotic Beheading Game by unfurling the

Lady's lace as if it were brave bunting on an ambulatory grand-stand? Further, you would have it, would you not, that rather than accept my frailty without blaming the Lady, I *advertise* the treachery of womankind by wearing that skein of silk, scapegoating the duplicitous Lady and warning men to beware the bewitching snares and entangling knots hidden in the contrivances of their costumes?

Your charitable assessments of my nobler motives gives me pause to question whether our conversation will be anything less than a jousting with verbal lances, inflicting further damage to us both. I have reason to wonder if it were better to leave you to the roost from which you have chosen to crow.

ROLAND: Swanking atop a dung heap, if I take your meaning?

GAWAIN: The site is yours to name, as you wish.

ROLAND: All sites have their fragrance, as the bouquet of the squat brown tower at my journey's end attested. But of that scented land-scape anon. I delight in your discovery that I'll be beggared by none of your noble motives, however you dare to rationalize or sublimate them.

GAWAIN: By the same token, may I trust that you have subjected your own adventures to the same anatomizing?

ROLAND: Indeed I have. Will you suffer a sample?

GAWAIN: What better does our private but too-often spied-on time here afford us?

ROLAND: Splendid. Would you care to cull one or more of my grand gestures for me to motive-monger, as you term it? As you will see, it assists in what I learn is called "constructing an identity," a process that continues, I am tutored to believe, verily, as we speak.

GAWAIN: You claim we shared the same noble motive: to serve loyally the king, thereby upholding the honorable reputation of Camelot and the chivalric virtues of Arthur's Christian stewardship. I gladly allow that your account is but a truncated and terminal portion of your quest. Nevertheless, from it I am hard put to discover *my* motive of service in *your* journey to a Dark Tower.

ROLAND: Why else would I, a coneyed candidate for knighthood, have undertaken any quest, be it to intercede on my king's behalf, to honor a pledge or oath (however manipulated), or to wrest a damsel, princess, or the Holy Grail from some barbarian's clutches or traitor's captivity? One and all, such quests are undertaken in loyal service to our sovereign ruler and, through him, our Sovereign Lord.

GAWAIN: True. Thus your perseverence in addressing your steps to search out the Dark Tower—despite the failure of numerous knights, even some of your closest comrades like the disgraced Cuthbert and the traitorous Giles—your perseverence, you would maintain, was undertaken in loyal service to your mirroring sovereigns? If so, then you, being found quite fit, are acquitted of sheltering any egotistical motives, and we must linger no longer, must look to our landscapes, adversaries, or tests, would you not concur?

ROLAND: Your tone, good sir, and your pointed reference to the matter of my fitness "in addressing my steps to the search for the Dark Tower," together they announce that you await my anatomy of my motives.

GAWAIN: Verily. But permit me to advance one egotistical motive and, thereby, assist you in regaining the rampant momentum you achieved when anatomizing my motives. Your affected worry over being "fit" to continue your quest, coming in the seventh of your thirty-four stanzas, trumpets your fitness, physically and morally, and thus your superiority to the comrades who collapsed by the wayside. No traitorous Giles are you. No disgraced Cuthbert are you. No "lost adventurer" among your equals are you. You prize your singularity and your status as mere "Childe Roland," alone of a host of peers and superiors to have persevered and arrived at the destination of your quest, the Dark Tower.

　　　　　　　In three words, sir, your motive in persevering was gross self-aggrandizement. Others failed. Others abandoned the quest. Others were knights, strong, bold, and fortunate, you say. Yet only you, a mere *candidate* for knighthood, achieved what others faltered and failed at. Your status among us as "Childe" is the equivalent of my green sash, a proud pennon that hallows you with individual distinction.

ROLAND: Splendid. But my distinction lies not only in my perseverence and arrival at the requisite destination. My distinction, contrary to yours, lies in footing it to a destination without foreknowledge of what plaguey scene awaited me there. Yes, you had good reason to balk at a journey to a chilling chapel. Before its holy altar you had the happy duty of kneeling and stretching your comely neck for the reciprocal blow of a marvelous axe. But you knew, Gawain, that at the fall of that fell blade you fulfilled your pledge. You evinced as much when, blood-spurts in the snow looking back at you, you sprang into a combatant's posture, surely rattling your full leg harness—sabatons, greaves, polyns, and cuisses all.

But what, you might think to ask, what was the object of my quest, once I arrived at the appointed destination? I knew not, sir. I knew not. Nor was it my place to have inquired, either of my sovereign at the outset or my fellows on our quest. To have asked and been answered would have spelled out a purpose whose worth I might have judged and might, subsequently, have rejected, should the journey have become too troublesome for that stipulated purpose. Not to have asked radiantly testifies to the purity of my obedience to my sovereign. Certainly, lest you think I'll skirt the matter, I take pride in my obedience to what I dignify—rightly or wrongly—by calling the existential quality of my quest: I honored my sovereign's wishes and orders, however absurd they may have been or foolish others may have regarded them. Few knights, I believe, can say the same.

GAWAIN: Thus, while I was tormented by the anxieties of facing the appointed day of my presumed beheading, you were tormented, am I now to conclude, by the uncertainties of the events slated to follow your arrival at your destination?

ROLAND: Precisely. And—

GAWAIN: Patience, please. Be courteous enough to permit a favorable conclusion, speculative though it be. Your motive, then, in not properly ending your account—not reporting "what happened next," after, that is you dauntlessly set your horn to your lips and blew—your motive was to impress upon your auditor neither your achievement nor failure once you reached your predetermined destination but, rather, the virtue of trusting and loyal obedience to an enterprise whose end was indefinable and whose hardships were harsh? And if so, then am I to admire your motive for its implicit eschatological nimbus and teleological resonance? And, further. Please. Please spare me your interruption. That motive, however elegant, vouches, am I to conclude, for no mean measure of elevated self-aggrandizement?

ROLAND: Indeed it does. And my self-interested motive, as you can claim as well for your cautious conduct, also ministers to other candidates for knighthood with exemplary comportment to emulate. More, it exhibits behavior beneficial to those not of our orders or persuasions, those multitudes who question the virtue of loyal and unquestioning obedience to others' desires and objectives, however high-blown, horrible, hidden, or hideous.

GAWAIN: Perhaps. But you've sidestepped your motive for blowing your slug-horn, for declaiming the slogan by which you've become renowned. Was that not a vulgar gesture, a bugled boast announcing your arrival? As a conventional challenge to expected foes, calling them to combat, might it not puncture your eschatologically existentialist self-puffery? That is to say, respected sir, is that trumpeting not testimony to your preparedness for battle, your assumption that arrival at your destination would precipitate a clash of equipment, a contentious contest for which you saw yourself fully "fit?"

ROLAND: Like others, you take it as a given that I blew language rather than broadcast sounds, blasted words rather than bugled notes. You'd have it, would you, that first I blew my horn, as if in triumph or conquest, and then I bellowed out—basso profundo, surely—news of my arrival? Well, now. Were I illiterate, like some who slovenly file along our corridors, chatter in our courtyards, and fuel themselves like fastidious swine at delegated tables in our refectory, I might well have remarked upon my arrival in the past tense. I might have declared that I "came." I, however, attained literacy early. Were I the speaker of that infamous passage, I would have declared, of course, "Childe Roland to the Dark Tower IS come."

Thus perhaps you misconstrue the agent or source for that passage? Perhaps it constitutes my impersonation of the choric conclusion to the events that transpired after my arrival and horn-blow? And if choric, and if voiced, say, by my "lost adventurers," magically present to witness my accomplishment, do you imagine them joining in joyous chorus or rueful dirge?

GAWAIN: As well might it be the unanimous vocal verdict of the court, dismissing your candidacy for knighthood, having found that the only datum to the credit side of your candidacy was the incontestable fact that to the Dark Tower you did come but that once there you accomplished naught. Much as if you'd crossed a finish line but chose not or failed to see what your crossing—a means, not an end—required of you. That resonant announcement might also be your claim before the court, speaking of yourself as if you were a public-relations spokesperson touting a candidate's accomplishments.

It is quite interesting, of course, Roland, to parse these problematics. But you seem to have dodged the enigma of why you tooted your melodious tube. Given your disconsolateness at the beginning of your account—your "gladness that some end should be" close at hand and bring an end to your years of "world-wide wandering," should I perhaps consider that the blowing of your horn signaled—like the blanched flag of surrender—your testamentary readiness to accede to the futility of your search if its destination was to be the ugliness of the "fell cirque" at which you arrived?

ROLAND: Instead of blowing my horn, you suggest that I might, as you did, have called out on approaching the Round Tower? I could have expected, thereupon, the prompt appearance of a porter?

GAWAIN: Certainly.

ROLAND: I did but the same. You halloed from across the moat. Your noise fetched the porter. Shortly thereafter, he ratcheted down the drawbridge and drew open the castle's gates. I announced my arrival with no bravura. My horn, which instrument was as much a part of my armament as my lance and sword, emitted only my signature, a two-note, two-measure blare. I think it harmonious, not bellicose nor defeatist. Your call resulted in a welcome. Mine? Well, sir, that's not at issue, is it, eager though no few have been to ferret it out. In short, Gawain, my motive in blowing was to signal both the termination of my quest and my arrival to the Tower's residents. To attribute to it either egotistical or altruistic motives stretches the frayed fabric of a single action too tautly. It threatens to trivialize our conversation about tormenting quests.

GAWAIN: I concede the point. But since the motives attributed to us—by ourselves and each other—bear upon our characters, our identities, and thus what we represent to ourselves and to one another, do you suggest that we cavalierly ignore our work in sifting each other's motives, which constitute a portion of the very torments entwined in our adventures? Surely you'd not suggest that we methodically check off the number of altruistic and egotistic

tags we've accrued and add them up, as though they were sums
to yield a total value each of us has compiled thus far. Perhaps
we might now pick away at your perplexing motive in deciding
to travel the "ominous tract," distrustful of the cripple's counsel
and directions though you declare you were?

ROLAND: My suggestion is that we bring a different skein of cloth to our
yardsticks. It's clear to both of us that egotistical nits, fleas, and
lice lurk in the motives behind, beneath, or in any action either
of us took. And we can torment each other by setting those bugs
upon each other. The landscapes of our adventures, I believe,
came next, did they not? Or do you wish to concede the manifestly greater difficulty mine presented and let us deploy directly
to our adversaries?

GAWAIN: Readily do I grant the gruesomeness of your adventure's geography. What foulness you stomached. A leering, hoary cripple; a
blind, emaciated nag; and a baleful black bird. A weed-infested
plain with leprous grass, a frothing and flake-bespattered but
fordable river, and a mud-mired, boil-blotched terrain ending in
mounds like mine-tailings dredged from ash-heaps. I traversed
nothing quite so nauseating. My rude roads, perilous paths,
treacherous crags, ice-cold quagmires, and fierce encounters
with harassing ogres, treacherous trolls, and beastly bulls, bears,
and boars—none of these assaulted my senses with the loath-
someness of your landscapes. But the detail of your descriptions
calls into question the authenticity, the actuality, the verisimili-
tudinousness of your report.

ROLAND: By which you suggest that my account festers with blood-clots
common to melodrama or scabs of cankered fantasy, that its car-
buncular particulars are closer to hallucination than to truthful
testimony, fact-based travelogue, or objective history.

GAWAIN: Quite so.

ROLAND: And you would have verification? There being no live witnesses,
you would like empirical evidence, some hygienic mementoes of
my expedition to memorialize its legitimacy?

GAWAIN: Were some available, sir, they would go a long way toward
vouching for the credibility of your noir-like representation of
your experience.

ROLAND: Representation, indeed! I commend your adroitness in accusing me of articulating a distorted deposition, of skewing it with exaggerations or falsifications to magnify the hazards, no, the toxicity of my journey's terrain. And, true, it may well approximate what might now be called a dark "tall tale." But is the speech from the decapitated head of your jolly lime giant at Camelot's court any less melodramatic, fantastic, or hallucinatory?

GAWAIN: I think it best that we keep to the landscape of *your* adventure before turning to mine. Diversions often insinuate evasions.

ROLAND: Permit me to play along, then, with your slur that my journey was hallucinatory. Let me grant—solely for the sake of interpretation, mind you—that its pungent particulars were hyperbolical. Should we then deem my torments the "mad brewage" of some chronic inebriate who projects his delirium tremens onto the landscape he describes? Better, should we, perhaps, deem my landscape's noisome features the lunatic ravings of a deranged but fastidious madman? His repugnance of such a disease-strewn terrain would be cruelly comic. Oh, look and laugh at *that* Roland, Gawain. Watch him tip-toe across that polluted little river, squeamishly dabbing his spear's point into its bed. Gaze with superior amusement upon his fretful face as he inches his way, hysterically fearful lest a current, carcass, or cavity filch his foothold and slide him into the frothy broth. Hear *that* Roland's effeminate groan upon spearing some creature whose curdled shriek resembles an impaled infant's. Ha! Such unmanliness would be, naturally enough, cause to find *him* altogether undeserving of elevation into the bold ranks of brave knights.

GAWAIN: May I picture for you a less comic but equally unheroic Roland?

ROLAND: Of course, knowing as you do that as you dish out so shall you be dished unto—to tweak slightly some testament's monitory aphorism. Proceed, even though we must be vigilant against the footfalls of perambulatory patrollers.

GAWAIN: Your account's visual preoccupations have long drawn my attention. Tally with me your cripple's "malicious eye," your bone-staring blind horse, your blind turret, your peevish Nature's instructions to "See or shut your eyes," your day's "grim red leer" (watchful of the plain's capture of you, its "estray"), or your several references to seeing, viewing, and looking. Altogether they greet another construction of your identity, I believe. They might add up to some scopophilic fixation in you, some leering lasciviousness, were your landscape remotely erotic; that can scarcely be the case, however, given its foulness. They might sum up some masochistic obsession, were there signs you derived some depraved pleasure from being imbrued in your landscape; but I find little suggestion that you enjoy wallowing in the fetor you fulsomely describe. They might even total to some sadistic swath in you, given the mordant delight you take in rubbing your auditor's nose in those fetid scenes. I think, instead, they betoken your paranoiac anxiety.

ROLAND: My account, then, is neither fantasy nor hallucination, but a neurotic nightmare? Damnation! To be fathomed so succinctly! Ah, yes! Your fox-hunt for my crafty character stumbled, did it, over my early act of "pausing to throw backward a last view to the safe road?" And that spoke reams, did it? It discovered my demented fear of being attacked from behind by foes? My visual preoccupation, then, revealed my irrational dread of being—and surely my corresponding desire to be— caught unawares and accosted?

GAWAIN: Quite so, despite your derisive dissembling. Why, look: You animate even the hills. They are "two bulls," they are "scalped" mountains, and they are "giants at a hunting," according to your fevered fancy. To you they revel in rooting on the game, urging that you be impaled "to the heft," be given some categorical goring. Little wonder that before dauntlessly setting horn to lip you insist upon the "living frame" and "picture" by which your peers and foes, you earnestly hope and fear, will satisfy your paranoia by being in position to "view the last of" you. Neither comedy nor heroism inhere in that paranoiac portrait of you.

ROLAND: Only pathos, right? Poor chump, *that* addled Roland. Been on a quest so long that the only thing he's fit for is a mental institution—or, a carnival for exhibitionists? Interesting, good sir. But might we not add, as long as we're stimulated by the vicinity, that psychoanalytic characterization of my landscape?

GAWAIN: Do you refer to Lancelot's reading, which he regales his dissolute sidekicks with? So, I guess correctly then? The details of his Freudian interpretation, however, I am in ignorance of, for my cloistered habits thankfully preserve me from hearing all but fragments of our nattering fellows' odious blather. I would guess his formulaic equations to be preposterous, repugnant, and outrageous.

ROLAND: Preposterous, yes, but his repugnant equations amuse rather than outrage me. He fixates on the boils and blotches, leprous grass, spume-bespated river, and brutish soil of my polluted panorama. In them he sees my syphilitic spectacle. He rivets his stare on the clefts and eyes and distorted mouths I particularize. In them he catches me translating a woman's genital zone into a locus of grotesqueness. He attends to my head-chopped thistle-stalks, "toads in a poisoned tank," and the rusty-toothed tool of Tophet. In them he espies my fear of castration by woman's hand or the devouring teeth cowled in her nether eye. It's quite ingenious, the transformative power of his fixated intelligence, but I fail to recognize myself in the misogynistic terrain he paints.

GAWAIN: And the blind, round, squat, brownstone, turreted Tower? Must he not find some equally misogynistic equation for it? After all, it must somehow epitomize the torments of the repulsive, gendered landscape you crossed on foot, if his appalling allegory is to deserve even a begrudging indulgence.

ROLAND: I'm told that on that question his practice is to register irritation at his interlocutor's obtuseness. Then, sneering with condescension, he minces, "Please. Give the matter just a wee bit of thought." And then, arching always his sinister eyebrow and tapping his temple, he sidles away. A most shrewd chap.

GAWAIN: Or do you describe your own practice? For a reputed fellow recluse, you seem, sir, to know the particulars of Lancelot's reading so well that you might be suspected, might you not, of having worked it up yourself and attributed it to him, defenselessly incapacitated by STDs as the gossips' grapevine reports him to be? Be that as it may, if I were to twist my imagination into alignment with his and "give the matter a wee bit of thought," I'd surmise that the blind, round, squat, brownstone, and turreted Tower to which your quest led you is none other than a gross and grotesque distillation of woman. Stripped of ornaments, garments, corsets, cosmetics, curled tresses, and elegant settings, your abstracted column reduces her to an elemental, bestial ugliness. From her body issues a contaminating river that disfigures her country into a wasteland of woe for man. And surrounding her are mountainous mounds of vindictive men, victims of her treachery.

ROLAND: That's a stretch. But it congeals, if one is willing to give it time to clot. And it does, I'll admit, account for the utter absence of womankind in my history: Her significant absence may well argue her essential presence, disguised though she be.

      But now, good Gawain, given those various constructions of my quest's landscape—and, mind, that was but a single, searing episode from my world-wide wanderings—there can be no contest between us. The torments of my landscape were of such horrific quality that they might have overwhelmed any lesser, foot-weary knight. Surely you will now not vainly try to argue any tormenting features in the landscapes through which you and Gringolet trotted.

GAWAIN: You will allow nothing disquieting in my Green Chapel?

ROLAND: Of course I will. The discrepancy between the holy structure you expected to come upon and the swollen mound you discovered to be the site of your returned stroke, well, that would be disquieting, I admit. To arrive in time to hear the grating harmonics of the Green Knight's axe-grinding, that, too, would be disquieting. And to know that your arrival on the day of the Feast of the Circumcision betokened a beheading, that, too, ha! would be disquieting, especially were Lancelot our interpreter. So, to him, would the protuberant site of that event. I'd wager crowns against pence his crude equation would find it nothing other than a mons pubis on which a castration was to be consummated. And to him your honoring of your contract constitutes a demeaning Oedipal submission. What? Kindly spare me your surprise. It takes no perspicacity to detect your abdication of a healthy, normal, erotic desire for the object you and the Green Knight were rivals for, the Lady of Hautdesert, mother, wife, mistress, and daughter that she is.

GAWAIN: Permit me to disregard any further Lancelot-inspired equations. To return to our yardstick, setting aside my winter's journey to Hautdesert, those momentous events at the Green Chapel on the Feast of the Circumcision are my only other claim to a landscape of torment?

ROLAND: Surely you'll not stretch our yardstick by claiming the comforts of the castle or the contents of your sleeping chamber—that playground of foreplay—to be such a landscape?

GAWAIN: Why not? Allow it, too a "wee bit of thought." For your adventure your eyes were wide open. You could see what lay before you. You could anticipate your weeds, your river, your hills as you walked the designated track, however much the fading light may have played tricks on your optics. Nothing occluded your visuals.

But think on it, sir. Had I foreknowledge that the Lady of the castle would visit my chambers on any of the three mornings of my Host's hunting? Had I cause to be foresightful of the beguiling tortuousness of her "luftalk?" Had I reason to suspect the artfully rhetorical strategies of her speech, all of which, I belatedly discovered, were so contrived as to require me to treat each of her conversational sorties as commands requiring action? My reputation, principles, and precepts, my vows and code of chivalric courtesy all obligated me either to comply with those commands or, as I sought to do, to parry them with some form of felicitous noncompliance that would not offend her with rude refusal.

ROLAND: I follow your track not at all. Would you have me to believe that when that young Lady offered herself to you on the first morning she was, in fact, commanding you to lie with her in adulterous embraces?

GAWAIN: To be certain, an ambiguity dwells in her declaration that I was welcome to her "cors." Nonetheless, such a greeting calls for some allotment of action on my part, just as when, on the second morning, she again invaded my chamber and directed me to instruct her in some game of love, or, on the third morning, then appareled so provocatively, she pressed me for a love-token and, forthwith, pressed upon me presumed powers of her talismanic lace.

ROLAND: The torments in those directives must have inflicted upon you unparalleled pain and anguish.

GAWAIN: Taunt me if it please you. Your worry, by way of contrast, lay merely in navigating your nasty little river or blotched plain. Mine lay in devising artful speech to politely refuse a winsome Lady's requests. There would have been no torment whatsoever, had I felt free of the constraints of courtesy, had I liberty to inform her frankly of the exchange-of-winnings agreement extracted from me by my Host. As well could I—were I not fettered by constraints of courtesy—have scolded, nay, shamed her by enumerating my commitment to religious mandates against adultery, my chivalric code to comport myself honorably in the name of Camelot, and my sense of human decency: One does not recompense a host's genial generosity with treachery.

ROLAND: Had you uttered such things, they would have boorishly repudi- ated her: Is that what I am to glean from your constraints? Your refusals of her artful commands, then, tormented you because of the delicacy with which you had to deny her seductions but not damage her self-esteem?

GAWAIN: Quite so. But the torments were augmented by each day's ex- change of winnings.

ROLAND: You refer, I trust, to the kisses you were required to situate upon your Host's hale and hearty mouth? Indeed, the morning prospect of such an evening exchange would indeed have been unwelcome and unsavory. Unless, of course, you had—have?— a preference for the favors of intimate male comradeship. Ha! Were you to have succumbed to the Lady's erotic enticements, you'd have had a pretty time of it exchanging *those* winnings with your Host. What games! Out with Beggar your Neighbor and in with Bugger your Host?

GAWAIN: Please, sir. That nightly act of affectionate intimacy with my Host did indeed offend my person. And my preferences, thank you. But the winnings that augmented my torments were those my Host each evening solicitously surrendered to me.

ROLAND: Well, of course, of course. For were they head of the boar, hide of the fox, or heaped carcasses of the hinds, those professionally butchered bodies would remind you only of the carving that awaited you on the Feast of your uncircumscribed Circumcision. But I think this matter lifts the manhole cover beneath which the third of our yardsticks, our adversaries, putrefies. The identity of your hale Host must have ranked high among your torments.

GAWAIN: I appreciate your acknowledgment of that most vexing of matters.

ROLAND: Don't mention it. But do tell me this: Why, during some mo- ment of your stay at the castle, sought you no opportunity to pluck out the identities of your Host and Lady? Upon your ar- rival, after your change of clothing and refreshment at table, you freely disclosed your name and provenance, all to the delight of your gay Host. Was that not a good moment to inquire politely his identity and the names of his castle and Lady?

GAWAIN: It was for him and, later, her, to reveal, sir, not for me to inquire. Such inquiry would have been impolitic, discourteous, as you well know.

ROLAND: Verily, I know the cankered customs of courtesy. But surely someone as skillful in speech as you could have maneuvered your messages so as to have learned your Hosts' names. Unless—

GAWAIN: Unless what, good sir?

ROLAND: Unless you took some pleasure in not knowing their identity.

GAWAIN: And what pleasure would it afford me to ensure my ignorance of my Hosts' identity?

ROLAND: The same pleasure I had in sailing uncharted seas in an unfamiliar vessel.

GAWAIN:

ROLAND:

GAWAIN: You will, I may hope, explain your pleasure and use of that commonest of cliches?

ROLAND:

GAWAIN: I see. It's a knot for me to untie or cut? "Solve it, you!" as you adjure your auditor.
            You can be, you know, a most exasperating fellow.
            So be it. As you would say, I'll play along with your game, games being my fortune and fate, or so it has long seemed. But be still a moment. The shuffling of sandaled feet slowly slipper the pathway.

ROLAND: I believe the sandals have slipped away. So now, yes, "Solve it you."

GAWAIN: I accept that you knew not your adversary, were in utter ignorance of whom or what you would find, should ever you be delivered to your destination, the Round Tower, common though such castellated cylinders are in that other country. So, then, the critical question for me to answer is this: What gratifications were there for you in being ignorant of your antagonist?
            I would conjecture, sir, they inhered in the intensification they contributed to your quest, especially inasmuch as you willfully withhold all information about why you had undertaken it. Your ignorance, quite simply, would dilate your alertness to

every encounter Fate, Chance, or Design presented to you—such as wondering whether your hoary cripple, for instance, were your foe in disguise, able quickly to cast off his costume and present a posture of challenge. Your ignorance would attune your every sense, make you mindful of every difference of sound, every fragrance and odor, every forward footfall, lest you step into some ambush or snare. Your ignorance would, in effect, make you, shall we say, exquisitely literate? Yes, for it would train you to become a most discerning reader of your reality, keen to every sign and its possible and diverse meanings. Indeed, your ignorance would make you resemble our alleged replicas, those self-professed knights of urban metiers, the semiotic sleuths or private investigators for whom a false step or missed signal or undetected clue or overlooked particular could spell death or injury at the hand of an artful malefactor.

ROLAND: And the torment that lies in such pleasure—for me or your sleuth?

GAWAIN: The torment, you would have me acknowledge, must lie in the relentlessly alert intensity required of you. To shoulder the constant strain of such exquisite literacy demands nerves of steel, a rigorous resolve never to drop your defenses, ungird your guard, sheathe, in a manner of speaking, your sharpened sword. That torment—common to water torture—might explain your acquiescence, despite your distrust of the cripple, to turn onto the track toward which he pointed: To tread that pathway might terminate the monstrous marathon of your ambiguous quest and, thereby, the tight-twisted intensities of your pleasurable suffering.

ROLAND: Quite good, Gawain. Your analysis acquaints you with the greater degree of torment I suffered than you. After all, you neither knew nor learned during the several feast days the names or identities of your Host, Lady, and her Ancient Dame, surely a violation of the customs of hospitality. But then their crowd of Christmas revelers departed, which left you to be the castle's remaining guest. By the time our winter's weakened orb had completed one diurnal cycle, you, my astute sir, had every reason to suspect duplicity in that castle of comfort, recovery, and security. Your day's provocative visitor, your cheerful Host's gift of a burden of brittled venison, and the comely but queered kiss you had contracted yourself to bestow upon your Host—all these variations on venery warned you to be on guard against treachery. However little introspection your storyteller credits you with, only a most uncharitable reader would believe you obtuse to the likelihood of your Host's and his Lady's identities as impersonators. The marvels of their presumed friendship surely bore some shadow of the supernatural gifts of your decapitated Green Knight.

GAWAIN: You would then allow, would you, my reluctant receipt of the Lady's girdle-cloth as a potential instrument of magical power and grant that it tempted me as a talismanic hedge against the Green Knight's supernatural advantage, that it provided me, shall we say, with an equalizer?

ROLAND: Indeed I would. After all, the terms of his Beheading Game, as we are to properly signify it with capital letters, were deceitful. He withheld from you and the court the joker up his sleeve. I refer, of course, to the fact that he won your agreement to the game's contract illegally. He withheld his identity and the power of his magic. His concealment mitigated your obligation to live up to fixed and fast principles of fair play. It authorized as well your option to attempt to optimize the power of that verdant talisman.

Nonetheless, Gawain, he forgave your forgivable error, your avaricious concealment of the sash that betrayed your covetous love of life. His well-tempered and quickly administered mercy revealed not only his awareness of the advantage he had taken of you. It also revealed his warm humanity, balanced judgment, and genuine affection for you.

GAWAIN: You judge his forgiveness a benevolent act?

ROLAND: Certainly. It acknowledged your error—and sin, if you must. On the one hand it sought to relieve you of your shame for failing to live up to your chivalric code and, on the other hand, your guilt for violating your religious precepts.

GAWAIN: You know not my adversary.

ROLAND: Know him not? To be sure, I am unacquainted with Bertilak of Hautdesert. Our paths never crossed. But I can judge him well on the basis of his benevolence in trying to acquit you of grave wrong.

GAWAIN: Wherein lay his benevolence?

ROLAND: As I said, it quartered foremost in his clemency. He charitably rejected the unrealistic standards of perfection to which your Christian and chivalric codes had idealistically and foolishly bound you. As well did his benevolence dwell in his numerous declarations surrounding his forgiveness. Let me number them:

First, he disclosed his identity to you: That enabled you at last to know the adversary you were now free to judge.

Second, he identified his Lady and owned up to the temptations he designed for her testing of you: That confessed his accountability in the disingenuous games that made of you a duped pawn, a game piece.

Third, he unveiled your aunt Morgana's motives in setting into motion the New Year's Beheading Game: That allowed you to glimpse the larger exercise of which your trials were but a small part and, moreover, gave you an agent of blame, did you need one (as your misogynistic outburst proved you did).

Fourth, he invited you to return to his castle: That privileged you with the opportunity to face and take whatever action toward the Lady and your Aunt that you might wish.

Fifth, and, finally, he insisted that you keep the green lace as a souvenir of your adventure: That allotted to you the decision of how to treat that salient symbol.

In a word, Gawain, Bertilak's disclosures all constituted a confessional disrobing of himself. They congregated to stress his sincerity in ending the masquerades and magic by which he had manipulated you. They acquainted you with information on which you had independent authority to act. Most, they acquainted you with yourself, a flawed and susceptible young man.

GAWAIN: You are certain, then, that Bertilak was not another costume into which the Green Knight dressed himself? You take the varlet's instant make-over as paternal benefactor at face value, do you? And if you were to discover that role, too, to have been but another mask, would you not again feel yourself duped by that laughing knave?

ROLAND: I discern no evidence of duplicity once the Green Knight reveals his identity and compassionates you. He behaves with impeccable humanistic regard. It's quite churlish of you to think ill of him.

GAWAIN: As Host he had behaved with impeccable humanistic regard—until he, accoutered again as the Green Knight, made known the ends and engines of his game. The matter is not whether his behavior adduced evidence of deep-dyed duplicity. The matter is whether his previous conduct had so coagulated into a corrosive pattern that it warranted suspicion of continued duplicity.

ROLAND: Harsh! I think you uncharacteristically and uncharitably judge your adversary. You allow neither his role as benevolent tester nor his conversion from challenger to confessor to comrade.

GAWAIN: Look you. You may think I judge myself harshly, too. But you know not if, upon my return to Camelot, there be a yawning gap betwixt my outward behavior and my inward feelings. I ask you, sir, might you allow my spontaneous outburst against "Bertilak's" duplicitous wife and womankind to have had design in it? Might it have any shadow of a ruse, say, to determine if it would provoke from him an ardent defense of his nameless lady and my good aunt Morgana? I ask you this, too, sir. Might you allow my chastened behavior—until Bertilak and I set upon our divergent routes—to have also been a role adopted to speedily terminate our discourse and free me from his patronizing compassion, which was but a malicious testing of my sense of sin, tempting me to think lightly of the violation I had done my vows—as if it were but a weakness, a forgivable human frailty? Further, I ask you, sir, might you allow that upon our separation I might have filled the winter air with ice-clad invective toward the agents of my humiliation—none of which my agenda-driven storyteller acknowledges? Just how much a simpleton do you take me for, sir?

ROLAND: Might it be wise, sir, to mute your voice against the potential of stealthy sentinels prowling for symptoms of insurrection?

GAWAIN: Be he Bertilak, Green Knight, aunt's tool, paternal benefactor, vicar of Grace, righteous heathen, or forgiving sage, sir, that Host, oh, Roland, that man, that creature, that agent: He was malevolent. His jolly hospitality and laughing court and good-natured cheer and compassionating consolation—all of them were fiendish snares aimed at hoodwinking me. Well did he, the scheming scoundrel, know these things (Now hear my list, sir): That his wife or woman, like some diabolical incubus, would try my chaste resolve and contractual commitments. That her teasings—on my Bed Perilous—would test my passive heroism. That her games of sexual arousal would insincerely swell my susceptible but bridled manhood. That her ambiguous discourse would agitate my courtesy. That her importunate demands for daily proof of my identity would win courtly kisses. That I, in turn, would be obliged to bestow with measured amicability those ardent kisses upon my Host's lips.

That such nightly enactments would publicly put into jeopardy my very masculinity. That such acts of intimate regard would kindle gossips' natterings over whether my inclinations were straight and my preferences correctly oriented. Well did my happy Host also know that his daily hunting forays and each day's carved-up trophies, presented to me as his "winnings," would put me in mind of the more woeful carving that awaited me presently. And most well did he know these things, too: That by situating the blame for these events upon my aunt Morgana, he would minimize his responsibility. That such scapegoating would give suckle to our culture's unremitting predisposition to blame womankind for all mankind's troubles. And that by his accusation he could twist even further my dysfunctional genealogical bearings, causing me to continue stewing over extricating myself from the checkered integrity of my lineage.

ROLAND: Calm yourself, please. And do unfurl your genealogical reference. It quite mystifies me, I confess.

GAWAIN: Surely you know Arthur's lineage. Thus, you know also the paternity of my bastard half brother, Mordred. Yet you know no more of my alleged father than anyone else, including me. By placing the origin of my adventure in Morgana's brain, the Green Gamester disinterred the gnarled puzzle of my own paternity.

ROLAND: Well, just what do I know of your lineage? I know you to be the first son of the first of the three daughters born to Gorlois, Duke of Tintagel, and his duchess, Igerne: the sisters Morgause, Elayne, and Morgana. I know Uther Pendragon, disguised by Merlin to resemble Gorlois, impregnated Igerne and, thereby, adulterously begat Arthur. I know that of the four sons which your mother, Morgause, bore your father—identified in the annals as one King Lot, if memory serves—the deaths of your brothers Gaheris and Gareth have left you with only your full-blooded brother Agravain. I know Arthur's incestuous relations with Morgause, your mother and his half sister, begot Mordred, your ever-brooding half brother. But not knowing, I could make myself chew on the gristle of your aunt Morgana's antagonism toward Guenevere. And after chewing, I might spit it out and stretch it in my fingers to find Morgana's own unrecognized but incestuous desire for Arthur. After all, as surrogate mother, she shaped him from infancy in Igerne's stead, thanks, I have been told, to the abduction of Arthur by Merlin, Morgana's mentor, lover, and father to Ywain. A knotted and kinked matter, to be certain. But nothing in it chars you with questionable paternity. If anyone is entitled to consternation over his paternity, it would be Mordred, not you, Gawain.

GAWAIN: You would allow, nonetheless, would you not, that such a history of adulterous, incestuous, and treacherous family relationships contributes to genealogical misgivings and, thereby, distrust of the semblances which people, even family members, don and doff as easily as a mask for a ball?

ROLAND: Why not? But it's as easy for me to allow that regardless of whether you're Gawain, Mordred, Lancelot, Galahad, Gamelyn, Bertilak, or, indeed, me, we all suspect our parentage. What's-his-name's conception of The Family Romance would have us all, man and woman alike, swallow the belief that in childhood we share three certainties: That the blood-gouted chamber we issue from is royal. That our regal parents have had us "sent down" to be raised by lesser folk. And that they've taken that protective action to thwart the parricidal threat we pose to the imperial pair. A moronic theory, I'm inclined to think.

But I take your point. You imply that your own father, altogether absent from your story and all but shriveled in your known lineage to a mere name, King Lot, he and what he represents, behold, takes shape as the Green Knight. As well is he your Laughing Host, and your paternalistic Bertilak, perhaps even Hautdesert's priest and your penultimate tempter, your guide to the Green Chapel for act 2 of homicidally embellished "play." Recognizing in you a regicidal peril to his power and place, he concocts a far-fetched but clever plan to humble, even to mortify, you by teaching you the sizable span between your principles and your performance. But he'll place the blame, like tinder to a blaze, on women, the treacherous Eves behind all woe.

And his plan works, yes, yes. You return to Camelot chastened and unmanned. You swallow his ruse that he was acting under orders of your aunt. And that teaches you to give wide berth to womankind. You are, after all, still a bachelor, I am informed. And you are also, are you not, dead certain that neither the comely Lady, the ancient lady, your aunt, your mother, or any human rolled smooth and singularly gashed is trustworthy?

GAWAIN: Quite so, my discerning and compassionating sir. Indeed, why would my aunt, once her half-baked plot of frivolous vengeance to frighten Guenevere with the Green Knight's gruesome game failed, why would she not only acquiesce in the Green Knight's Beheading Game, but also instruct the happy Host of Haudesert—if that is truly the name of that significantly childless castle—to add other games and exchanges to it? What would she gain other than to ingrain in me a deep distrust of all friendships, brotherhoods, social intercourse, and, of course, holy matrimony?

ROLAND: Besides converting you into the shamed, joyless, and unsociable malcontent you've long been known to be, you would be well schooled to distrust your own capacities to discern the true from the false.

GAWAIN: Together they would, as they have done, teach me to withdraw to the farthest fringes of society, to acquire the habits of an alien or displaced person, and, thereby, to find myself unfit for regular relationships with kinsmen, community, and the conventions and customs of a civilized society, be it Camelot or wherever— as the court's laughter at my discomfiture upon my return and confession made so clear to me.

ROLAND: And your alien status would shrink your competitive pursuit of comely ladies, whom you would distrust and your discontent dismay. All of that means, good sir, that the culpability of your aunt, so important to the Green Knight's dodge, is a motive of his manufacture. Ha! He knew he was safe in inviting you to return to Hautdesert where he would now, oh yes, properly introduce you to his Lady and your aunt, disguised from you—was she not?—as the "Other one." He knew he could wager that you, a proud man so humbled, would decline an offer to revisit the scenes of mortification. He knew from his Lady's reports that even were you to return, you were too inculcated with courteousness to ask her for verification with such an outright yes-or-no question as Did your husband put you up to your teasing temptations? Or that you'd stoop to put it bluntly to your aunt, Are you in fact responsible for the Green Knight's visit to Camelot a year ago with his gruesome game? And was its purpose, as he reports, to frighten Guenevere to death, to test the reputation of Camelot's knights, and to challenge their pride in their perfection?

GAWAIN: Your perspicacity pleases me, Roland. But do you believe that
            I believed Bertilak's shoddy scapegoating? Did you slumber
            over the particulars of my summary to Arthur and the court, a
            selective synopsis in which I knitted no blame to the hem of
            Morgan or any woman? Upon reflection during my journey
            away from that treacherous Chapel which toyed with my
            greenness, I resolved not to be cozened by Bertilak's moral
            evasions. Nor would I perpetuate his sexist accusations by im-
            pugning their alleged perpetrator. And thus, Childe Roland,
            you are ready, are you not, to concede, then, the greater diffi-
            culties and torments posed by my most conniving, elastic, and
            demonic adversary?

ROLAND: You snub, then, the grim adversaries I braved?

GAWAIN: We have been over that ground, I believe: Your adversary was
            unidentified, which required "exquisite literacy," I thought we
            agreed.

ROLAND: That spoke only to the adversary who presumably lay in wait for
            me at the Round Tower or on my journey there. Are you so be-
            sotted with your own story that you are blind to the identity of
            the adversary to whom I told my story? Did you seek me out for
            your cheerleader?

GAWAIN: Mean you the present but inarticulate auditor to whom you
            address your monologue?

ROLAND: That's whom I mean.

GAWAIN: But of him, why am I to conclude him to be an adversary rather
            than a sympathetic friend? And why would an adversary patiently
            hear out your tale?

ROLAND: Why do you think I began my historical fragment with that
            malicious-eyed, glee-suppressing, hateful cripple?

GAWAIN: Why? Quite simply because he was the ominous agent whose
            directions pointed you the way to the Round Tower.

ROLAND: Your fine-tuned sleuthery sees in him no other shape or function?
            He has nothing in common with your adversary who can one
            minute be your gay Host, the next be your gruesome axe-wielder,
            the next your paternal benefactor?

GAWAIN: You would have me see, would you, condensed in your hoary
            cripple your auditor, a man who disdainfully tolerates in disbelief

your account but who is obligated by some duty to hear it out? If so, then you might as well ask me to see your auditor condensed also in the shipman's "mocking elf" and hear him in the hills' malevolent chorus asking that you be stabbed to death. Did we not earlier consider these to be arguable proof of paranoia?

ROLAND: They were candidates for such an interpretation, although I believe the jury is out on that, is it not?

GAWAIN: Ah! Of course! I am in your debt for your juridical hint. I believe I am led now to see: Your adversarial auditor is a judge or a jury of your presumed peers, any or all of whom bring at best skepticism, at worst thoroughgoing disdain to your history. And your history, then, is not a recitation of your adventure—least not a mere poem of measured pentameters and quaint rhyme-scheme. Rather it is an appeal. It is your request that your candidacy for knighthood be reconsidered.

ROLAND: Excellent fellow, excellent! My auditors' (yes, quite plural, thank you, their) prejudice against my candidacy and their silence throughout my deposition called forth my reference to a deathly ill man and his insensitive friends, my mention of disgraced peers, my allusion to brutes and mad brewage, and my rich detailing of my adventure's loathsome geography—all as a way to thrust into their smug faces an ordeal others failed at, an ordeal that few men could endure. I exaggerated nothing in my adventure. But I confess to coloring it slightly to heighten its horror. And to make my judge or jury wince. And to exhibit my courage.

GAWAIN: How hateful it is, except for exhibitionists, among whom I confess I early counted you, how hateful to have to pour out to others—however compassionate, objective, or well-meaning they may be—an accounting they will judge and assign meaning to, a judgment and meaning that may be far from what one intended or hoped to communicate. How much more hateful it is to have to pour out an accounting before an adversary, who will begrudge every detail, certain it can only be predictably defensive and self-serving.

ROLAND: Are you ready to pitch in the proverbial towel and concede the subtler torments of my adventure? Or does our contest still matter?

GAWAIN: The contest was of your conception. Is it that you wish to nullify it before we run our last lap, to compare our tests, my stipulated yardstick?

ROLAND: I believe we have compared our respective tests in the process of comparing our motives, landscapes, and adversaries—as I expected we would when I identified them as the triangulating yardsticks that would enable the examination of our separate expeditions.

GAWAIN: Then you would no longer denigrate my enumerated tests as consisting of neatly symmetrical blows and exchanged gifts?

ROLAND: Of course not, man! I knew when we began that your tests were every bit as continuous as mine. What folly to think of tests as formal, discrete events for which we must prime our pumps to pour forth the requisite oils, when summoned. As you yourself expressed it, every morning visit of that nubile lady to your sequestered chamber and its canopied bed comprised an unswerving series of tests. To each exfoliating event in her discourse you had to contend, parrying every overture, flattery, wish, directive, tease, chastisement, and double entendre with graceful reply. Indeed, the Green Knight's—or Bertilak's—invitation to return to Haudesert was every bit as much a test as his request that you remove your helm (complete with mail aventail) and bare your gleaming white neck-flesh to his strokes, which he did his best to make theatrical. And his accusation of your aunt as the malignant genius behind your ordeal was yet another test whose aim had to have been to observe your conduct upon receiving his incriminating information.

GAWAIN: Indeed, there were, in addition, the public tests: How to explain my substitution of a fluttery sash for the fixed pentangle. How to gloss the still-healing scar on my neck. How to answer to the court's laughter at my shameful chronicle. And how to comport myself once the court appropriated my symbol of dishonor and glibly transmuted it into an insignia of fraternity.

ROLAND: Quite so. To think of tests as distinct, formal events is the way schoolchildren are taught to think of them. Faugh! As if tests were a cooked set of numbered questions or cramped problems with outright answers or simple solutions for prim teachers and prissy quiz-masters to quickly grade. As if real-world tests were nothing more than a straight-up game of lawn-bowls or a carnival's pop-gun firing range for fetching up Kewpie dolls or teddy bears.

GAWAIN: Exactly my conclusion, I am surprised to say, finding myself, again, in agreement with you. But we have yet to carry our project to its destination, its Round Tower or Green Chapel.

ROLAND: By which you mean, if you'll forgive my occluded sense of your drift?

GAWAIN: I mean why do we undergo any tests? What is it in us or our culture that compels us to submit to them in the first place? What purpose do they serve? Specifically, what is their relationship to the rituals of initiation you and I underwent, you for much longer than I, if their end can be either failure to be knighted in your case or, in mine, failure to live up to the ideals I thought myself capable of chinning myself on?

ROLAND: Your questions, if you don't mind my saying so, sound like academic test questions awaiting an extended, expository essay. Let me put the matter differently. Who is the adversary who engineers the tests we and our brotherhood, nay, all humankind, undergo? Your Green Knight was shrewdly sexist to name your aunt Morgana as the perpetrator of your adventure. His scapegoating of her was cowardly. Or it was craven flattery, a backhanded compliment to women's backroom, behind-the-scenes power, a sop to simple feminists. Nevertheless, the pointing of his accusatory finger is testimony to the presence of some agency or impulse that compels us to be tested or seduces us to test ourselves. Would you not agree?

GAWAIN: Quite. But need it be an adversarial agency or impulse? Academics, athletes, and entrepreneurs all champion tests, contests, and competitions, however imaged, as hurdles whose crossing improves skills and techniques, invigorates endeavors, establishes performance marks to compete against, validates identity, promotes individualism, and projects a model of life's vicissitudes to whose varied occasions they must rise.

ROLAND: And instructs them in strategies for coping with failure when a rival strides away victoriously and they sulk empty-handed from their zero-sum games?

GAWAIN: Or, ribbon in hand, return home nicked and chastened to win the laurels of laughter?

ROLAND: It's that laughter, erupting throughout your adventures, that tempts me to conclude that the agency or impulse compelling us to be tested and to test ourselves is adversarial and baleful. But I think, Gawain, you've already arrived at that conclusion and are testing me, are you not?

GAWAIN: I have arrived at that conclusion, but I'm seeking your concurrence, not sizing you up as a test subject. Let me speak candidly, for you prove yourself a kindred spirit.

During my years of solitude here, I have studied rites of passages, the transition rituals of innumerable cultures and secret societies, of which your quest and my contest are but two examples. Based on my studies, I have become convinced that all such rites and rituals are steeped in malice or subscribe to a program of human diminution, however rationalized, sublimated, or consecrated by their sanctimonious perpetrators, self-congratulatory communities, gullible initiates, and time-honored traditions. Separation rituals like yours and mine subject initiates to experiences of estrangement, ambiguity, humiliation, and hazard, typified in blindfoldings, masquerades, deceptions, and journeys into the bush, forest, desert, or waterways to face unfamiliar and unpleasant trials. Integration rituals, which my adventure ended with, subject all those seeking communal embrace or ceremonial acknowledgment—yes, the survivors of separation rituals, minors, and outsiders—to discomfiting, mortifying, or mutilating ordeals which anoint them into adulthood, membership, or citizenship.

ROLAND: Easy does it, good Gawain. I've read my van Gennep, Eliade, Malinowski, and Lévi-Strauss. I, too, have dabbled in the lore of cultural anthropology, the quirks and ceremonial kinesics trumped up by spiritual legerdemain. So, spare me your lecture. And, please, your apologies, for I'm not offended. Rather, let me second your conclusions: The result of such rituals, I wholeheartedly agree, is neither to enable individuals to discover nor to aggrandize themselves by confirming and celebrating their achievements, much less to welcome them into a healthy community. Rather it's to impress upon them, as with me and you, their inferiority and inadequacies, surely to compel them to discover their vulnerability and dependency.

GAWAIN: You continue to amaze me, Roland. And so, when you, too, observe attractive insignias—

.

ROLAND: Like swastikas, crosses, iconographic badges, freemasonry emblems, and totemic amulets—

GAWAIN: And formulaic gestures—

ROLAND: Such as queer handshakes, salutes, the sign of the Cross, and ceremonial dances by guru, troupe, or dervish—

GAWAIN: When you, too, hear oaths and communal hymns—

ROLAND: Such as collective creeds, prayers of petition, and pledges of national allegiance; ethnic anthems, protest songs, secret-society vows, political chants, and incantatory mantras—

GAWAIN: When you, too, come upon codified diets and prescriptive purifications—

ROLAND: Such as Lenten fasts, kosher victuals, sacramental lustrations, and the cannibalistically expiatory Eucharist; baptisms, pedilavia, ritual fumigations, and sweat-lodge purgations—

GAWAIN: And when you, too, read of mortifications and adornments of the flesh—

ROLAND: Such as sacrificial scapegoats and ceremonial immolations; circumcisions, clitoridectomies, and cicatrizations; teeth-filing, tattoos, tabooed body-scratching, body-piercing, and spectacular scarifications; decreed hair-dressings and dictated vestments, cultic costumes and propitiatory paraphernalia—

GAWAIN: Yes, when you read of all such forms of initiation rituals, are you not made to feel it incumbent upon you to subscribe to their threefold virtues of stabilizing societies against unruly innovation, of attuning individuals to the numinous dimensions of the spirit world, and of psychotherapeutically reducing the manifold anxieties that accompany the changes in individuals' life processes?

ROLAND: Scarcely! You and I, ha! we know better. Rites of passage cheapen individuals. Initiations like yours and mine exist to toy with an initiate's capacity to survive, to withstand the hazing punishment and suffering, to endure the squeeze of pain and torment. All initiations strive to subordinate an individual to collective hocus-pocus. Their aim is to browbeat an initiate into sucking up to irrational and arbitrary conventions, to subject him, demeaned, to propitiatory humiliation in the eyes of his already-debased communities. Failure or refusal to submit to such rituals guarantees punishment, shame, or censure.

GAWAIN: Or the gift of the brand of Cain, the pariah, the outsider, which brand you and I wear, do we not? What especially galls me is knowledge that our initiation rituals entertain readers and viewers. As in all rites of passage, participants, priests, perpetrators, and spectators find splendid theater in our difficulties, see good sport in our endeavors, make festival out of our frailties, take delight in our ceremonies of diminished and devalued humanity—because our shrunken selves comfort spectators' need to laugh at those who would achieve superiority.

ROLAND: I wondered when you'd furl your rant and return to that galling laughter. For it is key, I would wager a pregnant purse, to your conclusion about the dehumanizing ceremonies on which cultures erect, sustain, and stagnate themselves.

GAWAIN: Indeed, my most discerning sir: The abundant laughter during my adventures, which long bothered me, I slowly discovered had less in common with the guffaw of comedy than with the sneer of malice: I became an object of laughter. I was the dupe of others' pranks. I was the butt of the joke. I was laughed at. Never was I laughed with.

ROLAND: And like all jokes, the ones played on you were sadistic, intended simultaneously to harm you while giving erotically tinged pleasure to their perpetrators and audience. And the jokes succeeded, for you were humbled. You were taught you were imperfect. You were instructed in your covetousness. You were compromised so that you could not take precaution with an alleged talisman, that infamous green sash, without violating your vows. In three words, Gawain, you emblemize flawed humanity: you are laughable because someone or something will always trip your self-ideal as you march onward, head held high, toward what you think of as your ennobling destiny. Your destiny, like mine, is nothing less than a pratfall. And pratfalls, in vaudeville or village, castle or court, play or earnest, are occasions for others' merriment.

GAWAIN: And that experience humanized me, did it?

ROLAND: I believe you were expected to laugh at yourself. That act would have humanized you.

GAWAIN: Or would it have diminished me? I find no laughter at yourself
              in your history. Have you since laughed at yourself?

ROLAND: Indeed I have. But it has been bitter laughter. That's the only
              kind I can imagine issuing from your mouth, too. For like you, I,
              too, had grand aspirations. I believed I was fit to defy the failure
              prophesied for me and "The Band," especially after my com-
              rades fell by the wayside to disgrace or dishonor, frustration or
              futility. To return to the former of your two questions, my bitter
              laughter has diminished me. And the laughter of your friends
              and foes alike diminishes them, which must be the quintessen-
              tial purpose of all comedy, to lower humankind to some com-
              mon level, winning consent to that shrunken status with
              conspiratorial laughter.

GAWAIN: To that I wholeheartedly agree, my marvelous fellow. And
              though I vowed long ago nevermore to extend the right hand of
              brotherhood to another mortal, confident that treachery would
              be its issue, I wish now to do so, if you find my offer of fellowship
              acceptable.

ROLAND: For me, my comradeship, you would quit your status as a solitaire?

GAWAIN: Indeed, my years of solitariness I hereby suspend. For in you,
              Childe Roland, I believe I have discovered a comrade in whom
              confidential conversation and a free-flowing exchange of ideas—
              genuine discourse with unchecked candor—is secure.
                  The firmness and warmth of your handshake heartens me.
              And the sincerity of your gladsome smile resurrects my faith in
              friendship and limited fraternity. A comradely embrace? This is
              most welcome, indeed.
                  But what sounds are these? Do I hear the approach of a bois-
              terous deputation of our fellow inmates? It sounds as if they are
              making their way hither through the courtyard. I gather that we
              can be assured of no prolongation of our privacy. So I bid you
              adieu.

ROLAND: One moment. You've been here long enough to know the rules
              as well as I. We have surely violated the interval permitted for
              colloquy between inmates, especially one not authorized.
                  But even if we have not, the deputation comes at my be-
              hest. Their boisterousness informs me of their success in hear-
              ing and recording our conversation. Unless they've altered

their plans, they are planning, I believe, to broadcast our colloquy tomorrow night, piping it from the auditorium over our
station to all residents.

GAWAIN:

ROLAND: The broadcast should be entertaining and informative, don't you
think?

Do you suppose my claim to being the most tormented
among us was deliberately rumored in the expectation of drawing in such knights as you to challenge my claim? Do you suppose it was a test? If it was, do you imagine you are now being
tested as well, for auditors to judge your reaction?

Dare I say that you remind me of my history's "One stiff
blind horse, his every bone a-stare," standing stupefied?

GAWAIN:

ROLAND: I confess, Gawain. I ought to have procured your consent to let
our conversation be recorded. But, good fellow, you took the
bait and sought me out, not I you. And when you stipulated my
guarantee for the confidentiality of our conversation—when
you took my silence for agreement to that condition—I saw no
reason to disabuse you of your assumption. You neglected to insist or press the point. Indeed, I thought it better to leave you in
the dark. That way you wouldn't second-guess or carefully
frame your responses, mindful of how anyone other than I
would hear you.

You'll come to hear the recording, won't you? It would give
me great pleasure were you to join me as my guest and brother
in the auditorium. At its end I have been assured of my induc-
tion into the ranks of a select society whose identity, I regret to
say, I am forbidden to divulge. I care less for that and its signet
ring, however, than for the perquisites with which my collaboration will be rewarded; the insufficiencies of my accommodation
and hospitality, of which you've kindly taken no notice, will, I'm
assured, be promptly corrected.

GAWAIN:

ROLAND: You're neglecting your share of our conversation, sir. So, let me
own up to the skullduggery required to keep track of your library investigations. And to the stimulants to keep myself alert
while reading those scholars. Your occasional marginalia, nota

benes, and exclamation points suggested the direction of your thinking. All quite interesting. And it rather whiled away many otherwise tedious hours here.

GAWAIN:

ROLAND: Do you suppose we'll be laughed at for having taken ourselves too seriously?

GAWAIN:

ROLAND: Will you say nothing?

GAWAIN:

ROLAND: So be it.

Yes, yes. Do come in my fine fellows. The door's unlocked.

The Widow's Epistle

To Tom Jones's Historian, Henry Fielding, Esq.

Friday, 14 April 1749
47 Lombard Street, London

Henry Fielding, Esq.

Sir,

Yesterday's *St. James's Evening Post* advertizes a new Edition, in four volumes, of your *History of Tom Jones, a Foundling*: For the Success of which, now in its third Printing (I am given to understand), you shall receive ample Congratulation. It is to be imagined, however, that your Rival, Mr. *Richardson*, will frown upon the Frivolities so liberally sprinkled in your Pages. Indeed, Sir, it is to be more easily imagined that your *History*, despite its Vogue, shall distress moral Philosophers because of your Heroe's flagrant Disregard of right moral Principles.

Their Distress, howsoever Sincere, is merely Abstract; mine quite Actual. To spare you the Labour of thumbing to the last Page, of an Epistle whose Weight has already threatened of its Length, permit me to discover myself at once: I am that Woman, whose secret Offer of Matrimony to Mr. *Jones*, both he and you have injured by your Betrayals: the Widow, Mrs. *Arabella Hunt*. Betrayals? Most decidedly: Mr. *Jones*'s in his Dishonouring the Request which closed my Letter to him, wherein I beseeched him, could he not shew my Offer his Favour, then 'to let it remain an eternal Secret.' His most courteous Reply gave me no Cause whatsoever to expect my Secret was other than Safe in his Breast. Yet, Mr. *Jones* hath played me False, by delivering into your Hands my Letter and a Copy of his (as your Printing of both, in Book XV, Chapter xi, will remind you—should you have forgotten the Letters to which I refer and which the Facts of your *History*, sir, record for posterity and the Publick). Howsoever else, Sir, could the Letters have come into your Possession? His Betrayal, tho' harmful, hath done far less Damage than yours: For it was the Inclusion of our most brief Correspondence in your *History* which has visited upon me unwelcome and recent Changes, of which my Life, already and amply beset with Misfortune, had little Expectation.

You will be quick to surmize, perhaps, from my Address, that I no longer reside on *Bondstreet*, nearby the House formerly occupied by Mrs. *Miller*. My
Home, you will perceive, is on the very street, which your Condescension
slights, on which 'modern wise men' reside. Please allow me to acquaint you
with the Chain of Causality, which your Betrayal has recently wrought for me,
and which has occasioned this Change of Address. Then kindly suffer my Discourse upon several topics: *viz.*, your *History's* injurious Use of me; the self-
interested Inducements which unravel the nobility of your Heroe's Behaviour
during the Interval of his lodging with Mrs. *Miller*; and the *Mandevillean* Cynicism which artfully buttresses the Palladian Pile, which is your *History*. You
will, I trust, discount neither my Faculty of Understanding nor Capacity for
Penetration on the shallow grounds of my Womanhood. You acknowledge, recall, that during the first year of my Widowhood, I divided my Time between
Devotions and Novels; yet, you neglected to learn of and so to acknowledge either my earlier Reading and Study of our English moral Philosophers, or the
excellent Instruction I received, during my otherwise barren Years of Matrimony, from my sage paternal uncle, *Bernhardt Harrison*, an octogenarian Don
at Oxford (quite falsely rumoured to be in his Dotage!).

In the Interval of the Three Years which have passed since the Events and
Facts your *History* records, I had gone about my uneventful Life, resolved to
wrest from my domestic ease what Meaning and Enjoyment soever I could.
But near the End of February last, Signs which betokened that I was an Object
of Obloquy were unmistakable. Passers by would stop to gawk and prattle outside my Home. My Cook *Phoebe* began returning from the Marketplace all in
a Dither at the Gossip and Tittering which there were directed at her. Even my
Lady-in-waiting was humiliated by Raillery, which neighbourhood companions aimed at her; so much so that she gave Notice in early March; and hath
since left my employ. It was a Hand-full of Allusions, accompanying her Notice, which prompted my purchase of the six-volume duodecimo Edition of
your *History*, which was published, if my recall is accurate, on the last day of
February. After reading it and seeing my Secret discovered, it was scarcely a
Surprize when in mid-March my late husband's Family wrote, disclosing to me
the Mortification which the Forwardness of my secret Proposal had caused
them; they even apprized me of their deep Grief at having to sever all Bonds
of Kinship with me.

Were my domestic Distress not enough, the Women of virtue on *Bondstreet*
began shewing me the Backs of their Skirts. Their Disdain I could disregard;
but the loss of my best Friend's Companionship and regard wounded me: to
the very Quick. Naturally I refer to Mrs. *Miller's* refusal to countenance further
Intercourse with me. Returned and mysteriously Unopened came three Weeks'
Letters, which had enquired about Arrangements for my now-customary mid-
Winter Visit to the *Somersetshire* Estate, which old Mr. *Nightingale* bought for

his Son and Daughter-in-law, and where Mrs. *Miller* and her Daughter *Betsy* also reside. Imagine, sir, my Anxiety, that she was Indisposed, having been stricken down by some plaguey Sickness. Whereupon arrived her formal Letter, explaining I gave her no Choice but to consider our Friendship at an End. Your Imagination, Mr. *Fielding*, can easily conjure her Letter; so you have no need for me to enclose it as Evidence of the Events I narrate. Indeed it brimmed over with maternal concern; further Intercourse with me would 'endanger' Daughter *Betsy*'s Understanding of virtuous Behaviour; the 'peccadillo' of my Offer to Mr. *Jones* shewed a 'shocking Tendency toward Concupiscence'; having misjudged so blindly daughter *Nancy*'s Infatuation with Mr. *Nightingale*, she could spare now no Endeavours to protect *Betsy* from Lapses in the highest of moral Precepts and Practices. The 'heretofore hidden Truth' of my Character, which my secret offer revealed, so gave the Spur to my erstwhile Friend, that she could not check herself from yet other startling Revelations. She rebuked my Enquiries of her and her Daughters about Mr. *Jones*'s Character, Virtue, and Goodness (Enquiries to which your Printing of my Offer refers). In retrospect, Mrs. *Miller* sagaciously concluded, my Inquiries were not as she had taken them: Signs of disinterested neighbourly Curiosity; rather they were self-interested Questions, which discovered my 'ulterior Designs' upon the noble young Man; therefore I was not a Widow of virtue, tho' I 'masqueraded' as one; indeed I was 'scarcely better than a Demirep,' like your Lady *Bellaston*. (Mrs. *Miller*, I might point out to you, Sir, appears to have forgotten the Facts of *her* scandalous Behaviour, in the third from last Chapter of your *History*: wherein she falsely tells Miss *Sophia* that I, 'a sweet pretty young lady, and a swingeing Fortune' was 'absolutely dying for Love' of Mr. *Jones*, and had gone so far as to offer a Proposal which he had refused, a Proposal which, she confesses, 'went a little beyond the truth again.' Again indeed! Inasmuch as I had never disclosed my Offer to a Soul, her Behaviour was certainly reprehensible, an Issue on which I had resolved to seek Clarification, during the mid-Winter Visit that was to have been, you can be most certain.)

By mid-March I had begun the Task of leaving *Bondstreet*. Fortune was with me in this Task, and to my new Home I also brought my maiden Name, hoping to spare myself further Grief or Shame on account of your *History*. Slowly I am establishing myself in good Society, handicapped tho' I am by my Thirty-three Years, by my lack of a Family, which always causes Suspicion, and by my Silence or subtle Evasions when asked about my Past.

Trusting to the infinite Discernment of a late-*Westminster* Magistrate, I little need to acquaint you with the Degrees of Anger, toward you and your *History*, which have swelled my bosom this past Month and a Half. As Anger abated and Reason regained her Ascendency, I repeatedly puzzled over the Question: Why it was necessary that you include at all my brief relationship with your Heroe? I have now read your *History* four Times over; and the more

Leave I gave myself to ruminate on that Question, the more Answers I found. Temperamentally inclined as I have been, to think the Best of others' Motives, I considered good Reasons for your Inclusion of my secret Proposal. At that Period during which I became acquainted with Mr. *Jones*, his engagement in a Commerce of Gallantry with a Woman of Fashion, cast no small Shadow over his Motives and Character. As tho' you perceived his benevolent Intercessions on behalf of Mrs. *Miller*'s Daughter *Nancy* insufficient to buff up his tarnished Reputation, perhaps, Sir, you saw fit to discover my Proposal, shewing thereby that, tho' again in dire Need of a Source to replenish his ebbed fortune, yet he could muster Resistance to Temptation, could refuse my Offer out of engaged Affection, devoted Loyalty, and genuine Love for *Sophia*. Perhaps, then, you deemed it best to include my Offer so as to move 'discerning Readers,' as you frequently address them, to think well of Mr. *Jones*'s agonised Refusal: For it shews—or appears to—that, with Time and Experience in the World, he hath learned to deny the twin Lures of Carnality and Currency; and that his ready Capitulations to the Comeliness of female Flesh will not trespass beyond that seductive threesome: *Molly Seagrim*, Mrs. *Waters*, and Lady *Bellaston*.

Consoled tho' I am at the Reflection, of having been spared the Role of Partner in a demeaning Marriage of Convenience, I find no Merit in having my secret Offer, and Mr. *Jones*'s Rejection, blabbed to a scandal-hungry Publick. Was it necessary for my good Name to be sacrificed upon the Altar of his Reputation? Must a Woman be Surety for the Bond of Man's good Character? Confess it I will, that upon Receipt of his Letter, my Admiration for him increased, believing that his pledge to a Woman of Virtue also shewed a genuine Concern for my Feelings; For he was unwilling to give his Hand, could not his Heart accompany it. The Pain which his Letter gave was off-set by the Pleasure I derived from learning, that there still existed noble Hearts, which would remain devoted, howsoever hopelessly, to Women of Virtue.

But, Mr. *Fielding*, the Refurbishment of Mr. *Jones*'s Character had been well on its Way, without divulging the Facts of my Offer and his Rejection. His repeated Deeds of Benevolence to the highwayman Mr. *Anderson*, his Integrity in the Resolution to return to Miss *Sophia* her Pocket-Book and its Bill, and his Endeavours on behalf of poor Miss *Nancy*: these had shewn the Goodness of his Heart, had they been more than an idle Shew design'd to perswade Others of the tender susceptibilities of that Organ.

May it not be, that your Inclusion of my secret Offer allowed the Opportunity to exhibit Mr. *Jones*'s gallant Letter and the high Point of Honour to which he was capable of climbing? May it not be, that his Letter of refusal was an Action calculated to augment in my Eyes the Virtue and Goodness of his Character? And may it not be, that he entertained some Hope that I might share the Substance of my secret offer with Mrs. *Miller*, whose Regard he appears especially intent upon winning? May it not be, even, that his ardent Wish was to win, in my Eyes as well as others', as high Regard for his Principles as he had already won for his Person? In a Word, may it not be, that Mr. *Jones* used me as an Instrument in some larger Plan, cunningly manipulated me as Vehicle for some self-interested Goal?

When first I gave Consideration to such a malignant Notion, my indignation readily led me to accuse him of deepest Deception. No Stranger to the Signs of my Infatuation with his Person, he had made a Point of it to learn of my Enquiries of Mrs. *Miller* and her Daughters about his Character. And his Questioning of them about me, as he cunningly knew, would guarantee Mrs. *Miller*'s Report to me of his Interest, thereby giving the Spur to my Fancy, that he would entertain my Offer, if not accept it out-right. He had but to await that Offer, whereupon he could dismiss it on the high Points of Honour which his Letter reveals.

Do I amuse you by permitting you to read of my high Dudgeon? Does my Suspicion display the Pique which a Man of your worldly Experience and Wisdom has come to expect from a spurned Woman? So, too, did I chasten myself, as a jealous Creature whose Doubts but testified to a Lack of Christian Charity. 'Before accusing Mr. *Jones*'s Behaviour of harbouring calculated Self-interest, *Arabella*,' I adjured myself, 'you must establish a broad and repeated Pattern of Evidence, which would convict Mr *Jones* of a regular and settled Disposition to make use of Others to serve self-interested Goals.' To scoff myself utterly out of the uncharitable Frame of Mind (which had settled upon my Soul like the worst Stench of our wintry, Coal-smoak-full, and poisonous Air), Mr. *Fielding*, I challenged myself with this Notion: 'To ascertain deep Hypocrisy in Mr. *Jones*, seize upon some outrageous Instance, such as that he used, to ultimate Advantage, Mrs. *Miller*.'

You may imagine my Surprize when, awakening in the Middle of the Night during my first Week in this House, attributing my Sleeplessness to the Newness of my Surroundings, and taking recourse to a Cup of warmed Milk in my Kitchin, the Illumination lay sudden hold of me: I had been awakened by the Knowledge, that Mr. *Jones* had indeed used Mrs. *Miller*, most calculatingly, as an Instrument to further private Goals! Why had it never before dawned on me, I reproached myself, that there had been deep Design in taking Lodgings at Mrs. *Miller*'s? I flew to my Parlour, seized the fifth Volume of your *History*, and fevearishly thumbed its pages till I located Book XIII, Chapter v, wherein you tell, that your Heroe 'had often heard Mr. *Allworthy* mention the Gentlewoman at whose House he used to lodge when he was in Town.' No Accident was it, then, that Mr. *Jones* dispatched *Partridge* expressly for Lodgings with Mrs. *Miller* in *Bondstreet*. Nor was it Accident, I began to perceive, that during that Residency he performed so many benevolent (but always Publick, never Private or Secret or Silent!) Deeds. Of his inimitably generous Offer, the *full* Amount of his recently acquired £50, to remedy her Cousin *Anderson*'s Plight,

I thought I would never hear an End; for Days she embroidered upon that Scene. In like Fashion did she marvel both at Mr. *Jones*'s Modesty upon meeting Mr. *Anderson*, and his earnest Endeavours at concealing and denying any Kinship to Mr. *Allworthy*. But her Encomiums on those Deeds were but a parlour Clock's chiming to the tolling of *St. Paul*'s Bells, when she descanted upon his Intercession on behalf of the violated *Nancy*, and his Supererogation in saving from Disgrace the Family threatened by her Fall from Virtue. The politicking and preaching he had to practice upon the *Nightingales*, Father, Son, and Uncle, to make an honest Woman of *Nancy*, and to staunch the Grief and shame of Mrs. *Miller*, provided Scripture for many a Day's Sermon. Certain you can be: Her Reports of Mr. *Jones*'s honourable Deeds (mock them now tho' I do) played to no little Effect upon the stirrings of my Interest in forming some better Alliance with him.

Mr. *Jones*'s Selflessness certainly warranted your Conclusion, after the brief Ceremony which wedded Mr. *Nightingale* to *Nancy* at Doctor's Commons (Book XV, Chapter viii, should you wish to confirm the Quotation), that his Offices to poor Mrs. *Miller* and her Daughter shewed that 'He was never an indifferent Spectator of the Misery or Happiness of any one; and he felt either the one or the other in great Proportion as he himself contributed to either. He could not therefore be the Instrument of raising a whole Family from the lowest State of Wretchedness to the highest Pitch of Joy without conveying great Felicity to himself.' To be sure, Mr. *Fielding*, your Conclusion quite explains Mr. *Jones*'s Motive for troubling himself with the Affairs of others; it wondrously accounts for his very considerable Interest in bringing to final Consummation the Affair between Mr. *Nightingale* and Miss *Nancy*: Felicity is a Goal which the Goodness of his Heart seeks. But may I presume to call to your Attention a Discrepancy? Your Conclusion sits ill with a Declaration, in Book V, Chapter x, *viz.*, 'We never chuse to assign Motives to the Actions of Men, where there is any Possibility of our being mistaken.' Will the Motive for Mr. *Jones*'s Behaviour permit of only one Conclusion? And might not that Conclusion be badly mistaken?

As but merely one of your discerning Readers, my conclusions and Explanations may count for little. You may cry 'Pish' at them. You may chide my Reason, turned rancid by personal Bitterness. Yet, required by your Commission as *Middlesex* Magistrate to give Ear to Adversary and Advocate, I must trust that, if only out of judicial Habit, you will do me the Courtesy to hear my case against your Heroe, which hinges upon Mr. *Jones*'s calculated Design in taking Lodgings with Mrs. *Miller*, and in making the Residents of that House the Recipients of so many exemplary and publick Deeds of selfless Benevolence.

Allow me to put this Problem: How might a banished Foster-son, denied audience with his Foster-father, seek to redeem himself in that Parent's Eyes? My Answer: the best High-way is to perform such Actions as will perswade Models of Virtue, who have the Foster-father's Ear and Trust, to vouch for the

Virtue and Character of the Foster-son. If this High-way made itself known to Mr. *Jones*, then it would appear to follow (would it not?), that upon arriving in London he would search out the only Person, of whom he had heard Mr. *Allworthy* speak, who met that Condition: Mrs. *Miller*. (You do remark, in Book XIII, Chapter ii, Mr. *Jones*'s having also 'heard that a Cousin of *Sophia* was married to a Gentleman of the name *Fitzpatrick*'; but that Cousin's Reputation Mr. *Jones* knew to be smirched; therefore disqualifying her as Audience for a premeditated Scheme of Self-redemption.)

Mr. *Jones*'s Excesses in (what shall I soever term it?) 'benevolence afore-thought' are Contrivances to woo Mrs. *Miller*'s Regard, thereby to guarantee, should ever she have the Opportunity (of which you avail her one in Book XVII, Chapter vii), that she will sing forth to Mr. *Allworthy* the Praises of his Nephew's Benevolence, Hymns rehearsed first in my Presence. Surely his impulsive Liberality, offering the entire Sum of £50 to forestall the Evils to descend upon the Family of Mrs. *Miller*'s poverty-stricken Cousin is tainted with Calculation. Having ample Opportunity to measure Mrs. *Miller*'s sentimental Inclinations in her lachrymose Relation of the Tale of the *Andersons*, Mr. *Jones* can be entirely confident, that her Conscience will not allow Acceptance of the full Sum. He can be moreso confident, that his imprudent Selflessness will ignite an Agony of Transport, which will fire Expressions of Incredulousness at such unheard-of charity. He can be further confident, that his Benevolence, displayed so grandly and so early in his lodging with her, will firmly fix his Reputation for virtuous Behaviour.

(Surely it is confirmation of Mr. *Jones*'s counterfeiting Nature that, upon hearing Mr. *Nightingale* recommending the *Andersons* to Mr. *Allworthy*'s Charity, Mr. *Jones* neither enquires about the Gentleman alluded to, nor divulges his Acquaintance with him. Naturally Mr. *Jones*'s advocates, among whom you number, will defend his silence here, arguing that he was desirous of imposing no prior Claims upon Mrs. *Miller*'s Estimation of his own character. His Adversary, I ask that his Silence be considered Evidence of his Apprehension that Mr. *Allworthy* had written Mrs. *Miller* of the banished Scapegrace, and put her on the Alert against him.)

(Perhaps you will permit of a second Digression, a Device with which you are not unfamiliar? If Mr. *Jones* knew well the Particulars of Mr. *Allworthy*'s having interposed in Mrs. *Miller*'s Behalf, as you have her relate them in Book XIV, Chapter v, then might not an Adversary be justified in raising the Question of still a deeper Design, *viz.*, that your Heroe is desirous that she glimpse, in the seeming Spontaneity of his Offer of £50, the shadow of Mr. *Allworthy*'s regular Annuity to her of £50 a Year? Indeed, the sinister Allure of such Thoughts leads me to entertain an equally violent Suspicion; even tho' you may cry 'La, she is but raking out that *Jakes*, her own Mind': In Mr. *Allworthy*'s Role as benefactor to Mrs. *Miller*, is it that he performs an altogether disinterested

Deed of selfless Good-Heartedness? What Felicity might he convey to himself by such a Deed? Merely the Felicity of doing Good for Others? Or the Felicity of guaranteeing, that to one Family, from whom he makes no Endeavour to hide his Identity, he will be regarded, if not revered, as a Saviour? Or the Felicity, as well, that lies in the Reward of procuring to himself the proud and certain Satisfaction of contemplating on his own Worth?)

How, then, might an Adversary soever construe Mr. *Jones*'s Motives in seeing to it that the knavish Mr. *Nightingale* make an honest Woman of *Nancy*? My Case must argue thus: your Heroe, in Imitation of Mr. *Allworthy*, seeks to save a Family from Ruin, which Action, in turn will redound to his Credit; contingent, of course, upon Mrs. *Miller*'s finding Occasion to tell Mr. *Allworthy* of that Action. Indeed, should Mr. *Allworthy* learn of his Nephew's Behaviour, he might discern in it Instructions in Ways to better administer Justice. Unlike the Uncle, the Nephew halts not solely with inveighing against Mr. *Nightingale*'s conduct, and reprobating his Treachery; he exceeds such *Allworthian* Practice, slyly dissembling before old *Nightingale*, taking Risques on Behalf of Justice to which the Squire would never stoop. Naturally, should Miss *Sophia* also become acquainted with Mr. *Jones*'s Deeds, she too would find Impressive his Gallantry, an Intention I believe him not above considering.

You begin to perceive, Sir, I am capable of discoursing at Length upon Mr. *Jones*'s Deeds, which appear actuated by the noblest of Goals, but are also, if not in Fact only, attributable to low Motives of Self-Interest. Might it suffice to take Notice of some dextrous Recoveries: the Readiness with which he dissembles when Lady *Bellaston* abruptly walks in upon his and Miss *Sophia*'s accidental Meeting at her Home; or his out-right Lie to Mrs. *Miller*, in Reply to whose Admonishment that he bring no more Ladies into his Lodgings at Night, he asseverates that Lady *Bellaston* was a 'near Relation,' falsely insinuating family Kinship with her, and shewing that which you elsewhere commend in him, his Art of Concealment? Or review your Heroe's Duplicity, in congratulating old Mr. *Nightingale* on the excellent Match he has provided his Son, in seconding the Fortune that such a Wife will bring to their Marriage. Not the least of Mr. *Jones*'s self-serving Deeds, of course, is his disingenuous Offer of Matrimony to Lady *Bellaston*, notwithstanding that you led Readers into rejoicing at the Discomfiture which that Offer gives her.

You will be quick to revile my brief List of your Heroe's Dissemblings; tho' I could summon a longer one, but refrain, lest I trespass unduly upon your Patience. May I anticipate your Request, that I view his Dissemblings in the Light of the Urgency of their surrounding Situations? I acknowledge Worth in Extenuations made on that Request; in Allowances for Temporisings; yet, in turn, I must enquire whether, then, you would have me sanctify as Moral all self-interested Actions in which Urgency has some Hand; and whether there is some Alembic through which a Magistrate, erect on his Bench (or some other

Lord High Chancellor, equally erect at her Escritoire!), can filter, and so separate, as Selfish or Selfless, all Actions which are extenuated by Urgency? Moreover, Sir, if I am to subscribe to the Idea, that beneath Mr. *Jones's* artfully dissembling Behaviour lie Motives of ultimate Selflessness, then should not you, in the Name of Equity, subscribe to the Reverse: that beneath his publickly virtuous Behaviour lie Motives of ultimate Selfishness? Naturally I expect your Condescension: Reprove me for mixing Instruments and Goals, for failing to see that your Heroe's dissembling Actions are Instruments in the Service of some higher Good, whereas his benevolent Deeds are Goals in themselves, free from Taint as Instruments in the Service of any Self-Interest.

Yet, the longer I allow myself the Contemplation of the Facts of your *History*, the more I perceive that in it you offer no ultimate Difference between the Poles of Virtue and Vice, your Dedication notwithstanding. Your Book discovers only Degrees of Vice; or, if the theological Term grates, Degrees of calculated and cunning Self-Interest. Endeavour tho' you may, to portray Mr. *Jones* otherwise, his *immediate* Sacrifices and Concerns in the Affairs of others are actuated by his twin *intermediate* Objects, possession of Miss *Sophia's* Love and Mr. *Allworthy's* Esteem: For together these Two Objects guarantee him the *ultimate* Goals he pursues, the Powers of Purse and Property which Reinstatement and Matrimony will confer. Inasmuch as those Goals direct his Behaviour, be it in Urgency or Deliberation: therefore he shews the same Self-interest which covers, with finer or coarser Cloth, every Person in your *History*: *Black George*, *Partridge*, *Thwackum*, *Square*, and the Man on the Hill; the Misses *Molly Seagrim*, *Nancy Miller*, and *Sophia Western*; the Mrs. *Waters*, *Western*, *Fitzpatrick*, and *Honour*, Lady *Bellaston* and the Squires *Western* and *Allworthy*; and the *Blifils*, Doctor, Captain, Wife, and Son. Truly in this last Cluster your Heroe shews his Lineage, issuing as he did from the Loins of that most deceitful and dishonest Woman of fallen Virtue: Mrs. *Bridget Allworthy Blifil*.

Astute Readers may perceive, albeit later than sooner, I have Cause to believe, your corruption of Mr. *Pope's* Couplet from *An Essay on Man*:

> All Nature is but Art, unknown to thee;
> All chance, Direction, which thou canst not see.

The poet, of course, alludes to the Deity, the Artist and Director of this vast regular Frame of the Universe; yet, in the vast regular frame of your *History*, the only Artists and Directors are artful and cunning Machines of self-interested Humanity. Upon first Reading of your *History* I could not but commend your Success in blazoning, in heraldic Colours, the Villainy of your prime Instance of an artful and cunning Machine: Mr. *Blifil*. His malignant Self-interest so siphons my Contempt and Hatred, that you nearly hoodwinked me into feeling Pity and Admiration for Mr. *Jones*, a misunderstood Innocent. *Nearly*. Upon successive

Readings, I learned to perceive the Likeness of the Half-brothers: indeed Mr. *Blifil* stands in the Shadow of an even more artful and cunning machine, your Heroe. That Likeness strongly directs my Conclusion: your *History*'s Portraiture of human Nature, albeit ever so extensive, shews only Degrees of Self-interest, Naught which can be unfurled at the Top of a Flag-pole as selfless Virtue.

Certainly Mrs. *Miller*, 'extremely strict and nice in her Principles,' as you re-mark in Book XIII, Chapter x, is Proof against my Conclusion, is she not? So had I thought, till a clearer Perception rushed upon me in tumultuous Manner but last Sunday. The Goal, which her high-minded Behaviour ardently pur-sued, was to disguise from the World her own past Indiscretion, one Clew to which lies in the Extremity of her Anguish upon learning of *Nancy*'s lost chastity: for her Extremity reflected a Visitation of the shameful Shadow of her own youthful Error. I know that you will not feign Disingenuousness, pretend Puzzlement, and cry 'Absurd' to my Conclusion: For you planted the irrefutable Clew for penetrating Readers to find. By Design you introduced Mrs. *Miller* in Book XIII, Chapter v, as the Mother of two Daughters, the elder Seventeen, the younger Ten. Exactly one Book later, you allow her to tell Mr. *Jones* that she 'was married to a Clergyman, who had been [her] Lover a long Time before, and who had been very ill-used by [her] Father on that Account.' To which Facts you also have her add that cruel Fortune deprived her 'of the kindest Hus-bands and [her] poor girls of the tenderest Parent' after just '*Five Years*' of Mar-riage. The Discrepancy between Five Years of Marriage and two Daughters whose Ages are Seven Years apart, of course, cannot but be construed to blotch the Widow's Character; notwithstanding your Gloss, that she was 'one of the most innocent Creatures in the World.' What better Way to conceal the Blem-ish of her youthful Folly—would you call it such, Sir?—than behind a Mask of Probity and nice Principle!

My Epistle, conceived in vexation, hath now come into its Majority, and of-fers a Challenge to your *History*'s Endeavour to portray human Nature. Little did I think, when first I considered inditing a Letter to you, that the six Vol-umes of your 'new Province of Writing' could inspire me (as Victim, Reader, Witness, Plaintiff, Barrister, and Magistrate!) into applying upon them my Skills in moral Philosophy, and in *Fleetstreet* Litigiousness, on which I believe I have reason to pride myself.

As straighforwardly as I am able, here is now the Problem which the Facts of your *History* set before me. You appear Resolute in examining Behaviour, in endeavouring to establish Truths of Human Nature. But in so doing, at least as early as Master *Blifil*'s Defense of freeing *Sophia*'s Bird, you show that Behav-iour can be Genuine or False; more precisely, that *in other Persons' Eyes* it cus-tomarily discovers either an unselfish Regard for others' Welfare or a selfish Regard for one's own Welfare; few being the Persons who are capable of view-ing it as both. You complicate the problem by shewing further, that a cunning

Person (whose number in your *History* is Legion) can so manipulate *how* and *what* other Persons perceive and understand; so as to cause them to credit as Unselfish those Behaviours which are, in Reality, Selfish. The Problem before me becomes an ill-lit Hall of Mirrors: For if a cunning Person can so beguile and deceive other Persons, then *can* we ever discern Unselfishness from Selfishness? And if so, then by what Means? Or, Sir, must we throw up our Hands, and humbly confess: That we lack the Science and the Tools whereby we can ascertain the one from the other?

Tho' you do not so answer, your *History*, I believe, does: we cannot consistently or unerringly discern the one from the other. (And can it be Possible, Sir, that you know not that which the Facts of your *History* discover to its Readers?)

An Instance: Mr. *Blifil*: his Selfishness is unmasked, you shew, by the accidental Revelation of his Mother's testamentary Letter, and its Acknowledgment of Mr. *Jones*'s Lineage; which Mr. *Blifil* has long concealed. Chance, not human Penetration, rescues your Heroe from his Half-brother's Villainy. In other episodes Mr. *Blifil*'s Selfishness is vulnerable to penetrating Observers, provided they are spurred by Scepticism to enquire, where there exists any Discrepancy between the Plausability of his Behaviour and the Goals his Behaviour serves. To wit: Mr. *Blifil* defends too warmly his Unselfishness in freeing *Sophia*'s Bird; and by insinuating that Mr. *Jones*'s Thoughtlessness, of climbing the tree and falling into the Water, Caused the Bird *Tommy* to fly into the predatory Clutches of the nasty Hawk, Mr. *Blifil* weakened the Plausabilty of his Defense; for he permitted a Reader of Penetration to glimpse his self-incriminating Spite for Mr. *Jones*. But La!, Sir: what Depths of Penetration must we command to discern Mr. *Jones*'s counterfeit Good-Heartedness and selfish Unselfishness!

I might impress you at Length with my Understanding of our Country's moral Philosophers and of the subtile Barbs which you hurl at them. I could, for instance, wax Loquacious in appreciating your Asides which, with sly Irony, so abruptly dispatch Mr. *Locke*'s laboured Endeavours to distinguish 'simple' from 'complex' Ideas. (The Notions, as you mock them in Book VI, Chapter i, that the Colour Scarlet may 'be very much like the Sound of a Trumpet,' and that Love may 'very greatly resemble a Dish of Soup, or a Sir-loin of Roast-beef,' are surely aimed at the venerated Philosopher.) As well might I appreciate your equally sharp Lance Of Disdain for our Age's spurious Notion that Reason and Sentiment, like vigilant Sentinels, prohibit all Traffick between themselves in one Person; and appreciate your Scorn for the Earl of *Shaftesbury*'s anaemic Theories that Morality consists in Knowledge of the Order of the Universe, in abstract Contemplation of the Beauty of Virtue, and in Belief in the Natural Order, which inextricably knits Self-Interest to Virtue. (Well thrust at the august Earl are your Comments, in Book IV, Chapter vi, wherein, referring wittily to Mankind's Moral Sense which 'doth certainly inhabit some inhuman Breasts'), you declare, its 'Use is not so properly to distinguish Right from Wrong, as to prompt and incite [Men] to the former, and to restrain and with-hold them from the latter'; and, it 'is an active Principle, and doth not content itself with Knowledge or Belief only.' Or, finally, I might well appreciate your running Engagement with the sermons, which Bishop *Butler* of *Durham* preached at Rolls Chapel, the Substance of which advocates Prudence of such a rarefied Kind that a Man who could chuse to Conduct himself according to the Bishop's virtuous Self-Interest would scarcely consent to taste (much less to savour!) the Pleasures afforded by gratifying either an Appetite for some sensory Delight or the Desire to be a Principal in the conflicts of an ordinary Relationship.

Your rejection of these moral Philosophers leaves you the Heir-apparent, I discover, of Mr. *Mandeville*. When I reflected upon my Accusations of Self-interest in your Mr. *Jones*, it became clear, that despite your seeming Intention for Readers to conclude that his Deeds were those of a Man blessed with a Good Heart, nevertheless, the *Mandevillean* Conclusion also existed. That Conclusion, after I weighed all of his Deeds, directed me to perceive that your *History* moves upon Wheels fashioned only in Self-interest, as Mr. *Mandeville* would maintain. Certainly your Heroe grew during the Course your *History* records: he learned Prudence: For he could refrain from impulsivley gratifying his Appetites, when such Behaviour might harm others and, indirectly or eventually, himself. And he learned, that a truly prudent Man avails himself of Opportunities, which tho' his Actions might make him look Foolish in the Eyes of the World, will shew him to Advantage in the Eyes of the Virtuous. He even learned, that a Man of Prudence is he whose masquerade as the Possessor of a Good Heart doth enable him to dissemble, in such Ways as to bewitch those Beneficiaries of his seeming Benevolence into believing that his Deeds are done expressly out of Concern for their Welfare. To sum the whole—honoured Magistrate, acclaimed Author, and scrupulous Historian—the Heroe of your *History* is thoroughly *Mandevillean*; a Man whose Experience hath acquainted himself with the Advantages of Behaviour which is actuated by intelligent Self-interest.

Certainly you will not deny, Sir, that Mr. *Jones*'s Compassion for the Highwayman shews Self-interest. His Benevolence (like Mr. *Allworthy*'s for Mrs. *Miller*, may I remind you?) warrants at least one fellow Human to praise him as a Saviour, a Praise which Mr. *Anderson* and Mrs. *Miller* clamourously proclaim. Should Mr. *Anderson* dissappoint this Expectation, Mr. *Jones* can preen in the Reflection of Self-Congratulation (even without your *History* recording it), can extract Pleasure from thinking well of his Deeds. (And should some Bubble of a Reader strive to commend your Heroe's Actions as Instances of high-minded Pity, I would refer him to Mr. *Mandeville*'s 'Enquiry into the Origin of Moral Virtue' in his *Fable of the Bees*, wherein he comments that 'whoever acts from Pity as a Principle, what Good soever he may bring to the Society, hath Nothing to boast of but that he hath indulged a Passion that has happened to be beneficial to the Public.') As for Mr. *Jones*'s repudiation of Mr. *Allworthy*'s Intention to banish Mr. *Blifil* without a Penny: yet more Self-interest. On the one hand, he shews his desire to instruct Mr. *Allworthy* in charity and Mercy, thereby establishing moral Superiority and demonstrating, at a single Thrust, that Affairs in *Somersetshire* will be better conducted by the Nephew than they have been by the Uncle. On the other hand, his Appearance of benevolence toward Mr. *Blifil* shews him actuated by three Desires: First, for a measure of Glory, which will accrue to him for his Magnanimity (a Glory which, Mr. *Mandeville* hath declared, 'consists in a superlative Felicity which a Man, who is conscious of having performed a noble Action, enjoys in Self-love, whilst he is thinking on the Applause he expects of Others'); Second, for the Dependency upon him of Mr. *Blifil*, which guarantees the Latter a perpetual Reminder, that he was out-foxed by a Man whose Penetration he quite misjudged; and Third, for the secret Self-satisfaction of contemplating how Generosity will rankle with his Half-brother! Mr. *Jones* quite literally becomes His Brother's Keeper, both to those who view his Brotherliness to Mr. *Blifil* in a Christian Light, and to those of a more sceptical Mind, who will view Mr. *Jones* as Gaoler; for Mr. *Blifil* is surely imprisoned in Resentment, Envy, and Hatred, which will gnaw away at his Ease and Contentment, like some fox chewing at its foot snared in a trap, willing to leave it behind rather than forfeit his life to baying dogs. Inasmuch, then, as your *History* never once shews Mr. *Jones* perform a noble or generous Action, in *Private* or in *Silence*, it follows, in Mr. *Mandeville*'s apposite Estimation of all ambitious Heroes, that Mr. *Jones*'s 'Greediness to engross the Esteem and Admiration of Others' hath sought nothing less than 'the great Recompense,' as Mr. *Mandeville* splendidly terms it, 'the Breath of Man, the aerial Coin of Praise.'

Like the Cynicism of Mr. *Mandeville*'s *Fable of the Bees*, yours, too, casts a dark Shadow, a pessimistic Pall, over the Facts of your *History*. Much at odds with the comic Festivity of many of your Book's Episodes, the black Ribbon of Cynicism deeply flaws the Cloath of your Book, reveals in it (as Time will surely verify) an unsuccessful Act of Authorship. Tho' vulgar Readers will delight in your Rake's Triumph; eventually, common Readers will tire of the wearisome Disquisitions which halt the Progress of your entertaining Plot; and aesthetic Readers will bridle with Impatience at your authorial Intrusions, which insistently endeavour to direct their Judgment; and discerning Readers, deeming your philosophic Views morally Frivolous, will scoff at your naïve Notion that Good-Heartedness and a heaping Ladle-full of Prudence will rectify Wrongs, alleviate Misery, and promote Happiness; and penetrating Readers, among whose Ranks I number myself, will perceive the broad Smudge of Cynicism, and resent your Duplicity, which disingenuously invites them to accord Mr. *Jones* the Applause of their Esteem.

How gratifying it is to me, you must perceive, to slake my circumspect but vindictive Thirst, by apprizing you of the defects in your *History*. To transform personal Pique into philosophic Penetration! To revenge myself for your *History*'s betrayal! To scorn a Work over which you laboured long! Now that the Eye of Reflection looks back upon the Book you wrought, it discerns the Blotch, your crucial Blunder. How easy it would have been to have plotted Otherwise than you did. You had only to make Mr. *Jones* and *Partridge* to happen upon Mrs. *Miller*'s Lodgings by Accident. Another Coincidence would have imposed no excessive Strain upon your Readers' Credulity: For Coincidence and Accident are such a Part of the Facts of your *History*, that by the Time your Heroe arrives in London, few Readers would contest one more Instance. Such a delicious Irony, that one Lapse on your Part avails a penetrating Reader the Lever with which to pry open your *History* and to extract its evidence of Mr. *Jones*'s Self-interest.

Yet, the Thought lays sudden hold of me: Can it be you designed that Lapse, fully knowing to what Conclusions it might lead?

Can it also be, that I have allowed Anger to cloud Reason's discerning Power, allowed Bitterness to misconstrue your Use of Mr. *Mandeville*'s Cynicism?

Can it be I have been Miss *Graveairs*?

Now I think on it, I must enquire, whether truly you share the satiric Scorn of Mr. *Mandeville*'s Cynicism? And whether Self-interest must necessarily be in conflict with your *History*'s celebration of Mr. *Jones*'s Good-Heartedness? Can it be, Mr. *Fielding*, you have gone beyond our moral Philosophers, Mr. *Mandeville* included, by endeavouring to deliquesce, as tho' it were some inky Mushroom, the Dichotomy between Self-interest and Good-heartedness?

Hazarding your Contempt for me as a Bubble inflated by Theories of the Shaftesburians and their ilk, whose views I earlier spurned, I find that I suddenly am smitten with the Perception of what it is which your *History* accepts and celebrates: that Self-interest, like the very Noses on our Faces, is a Fact of human Nature. We wrong it by reviling and by militantly (but spuriously) setting it in Opposition to Virtue, which Flattery gulls us into declaring another Fact of human Nature. Pish! Self-interest hath not an opposite Pole. It hath merely Gradations and Degrees, tho' the obstinate and virtue-minded (endeavouring to sneak Virtue in through the back Door), will declare Selflessness its Opposite. But Virtue is a Quality, which we or Others assign to an Action, thereby judging that Action as it serves or harms Others; its Opposite is Vice. Self-interest is the propelling Motive behind every Action; a Motive which hath the Capacity to suspend in Motion, like a Juggler, several Motives, simultaneously, some of which may warrant the Term "Virtue," some the Term "Vice."

Your Mr. *Jones* (nay, *our* Mr. *Jones*) learns, in the Course of his Experience, to mount, not without frequent Backslidings, the Rungs on the Ladder of Self-interest. He never abandons the lower Rungs of Self-interest: For he will satisfy his carnal Appetite. He learns, however, that indulging it may harm himself and others. He perceives that his own Self-interest must be linked to that of others, in such a Way, that his genuine concern for their welfare cannot be at the Cost of his own ultimate Goals. True, when Mr. *Jones* leaves Paradise Hall in Book VI, Chapter xii, he denies himself the immediate Gratification of possessing *Sophia* and taking her with him, mindful of the eventual Ruin which such an Action could inflict upon her (as it nearly does to Mrs. *Anderson*). Yet this sacrifice shews him making an Investment in ultimately self-interested Returns: *Sophia's* Regard, her Love, her Hand, and her Property.

Mr. *Jones's* ultimate Goals are not deplorable: For they shew Truth about human Nature, which the Facts of your *History* so patiently, so artfully unfolds. Mr. *Jones* doth not disabuse those Persons and Readers, who wish to regard him as Angelic (as doth Mr. *Anderson* and Mrs. *Miller*). Any protests or denials, which Mr. *Jones* might or doth make, concerning the Motives behind his Deeds, get over-ridden and incite the Recipients of his Benevolence to increase their Cries of Gratitude. Granting, then, that his Love for *Sophia* is Genuine; and that he can better govern the Estates of Squires *Allworthy* and *Western* than can the Squires; and that he is entitled to have as much Right to inheriting Power, Property, and Wealth as any man, I cannot fault his self-interested Designs, even though they risque using and hurting Others.

And was I not one of those whom he hurt? Forsooth: Inasmuch as I must confess that my own Self-interest gave the Spur to my secret Offer, I have no just Complaint against Mr. *Jones's* rejection. I sought my own Welfare as well as his, and my Hurt was the Risque I ran. As for the self-interested Reply of his Rejection: I had created a Dilemma for him: For his Decision could not but harm someone: himself, by violating the honour of his Love for *Sophia*; *Sophia*, by disappointing the Hope she nursed, that his Love was Genuine; me, by rejecting my Offer.

No, Mr. *Fielding,* you rightfully endeavour to shield from Censure your Heroe's Motives and to dissolve thereby the World's facile Opposition of Self-interest and Good-heartedness. You acknowledge and shew, in his Growth and Behaviour, that to be fully Human is to be full of Self-interest; that Self-interest requires performing Actions, whose Design is to bring into Being some definite State of Affairs, of ultimate Benefit to ourselves; and that moral Growth consists in Learning to perform Actions which, tho' benefitting Society (and therefore receiving Approbation for Proof of good-heartedness), are never injurious, in any ultimate Form, to our own Welfare. La, it would be nice to believe that unselfish Deeds are a Matter of common daily Observation. But whatsoever the Eye observes (which is a Matter of Perception) is merely an Action external to the Eye. Escaping the Eye's Observation are the Motives and the ultimate Effects of that external Action. To assign to an Action the Epithet 'Unselfish' is to perform a mental and moral Judgment, of which, were every Thing known about the Actor and the Action, both Actor and Action may be undeserving, if not richly undeserving. Indeed, I now hear in my inner Ear that other couplet of our Poet, Pope:

> Self-love linked to Social, to Divine,
> Gives thee to make thy neighbour's blessing thine.

But certainly, Sir, you have no need to read from any Widow *Graveairs* the wholesome Lesson, which your *History* discloses to patient and open-minded Readers. And most certain it is, I have too long trespassed upon your Patience.

Shall I bring to an End my Epistle, Mr. *Fielding*, with the Presumption of expressing Gratitude? Which was indeed beyond Expectation when, several Hours ago, I sat down to my Escritoire, to begin an Epistle, which has grown within me over the past several Weeks. Odd tho' it may seem, I am grateful you betrayed my secret Offer against my Consent: For you have enabled me to be an Instrument of Penetration, if I may so plume myself. You have forced me (in Anger, Spite, and Contempt) to engage so personally with your *History* as to inspire me with the Conceit, that I now possess an Understanding of human Nature, of which previously I was innocent. The Episode of my Offer (a Gimlet, with which to bore a tiny Hole in the Shell of your *History*, and to peer through it intently and long) has, perhaps, given me Glimpse of your *History*'s Meaning and Significance. Your Achievement hath more than earned my 'aerial Coin of Praise.'

Shall I display even Impertinence? I cannot forbear to thank your Decision to use my actual married Name, *Hunt*: For it hath as allegorical a Meaning as doth those of *Sophia*, Mrs. *Honour*, *Square*, and *Allworthy*. Truly, Sir, with my Name you have cry'd up a hunt deserving of the best Hounds, and Horses, and Hunters. I may even claim, with your Permission, to have engaged in a Pursuit, which hath captured, alive and quivering with Pulse and Blood, one of the most cunning of foxes brought forth on British soil, your *History*.

With belated but genuine Respect, Sir, I am and will remain,

> 'Your most Obliged, and
> 'Grateful Humble Servant,
> 'Arabella Hunt Harrison'

A Dialogue of the Dead

Fagin and Ralph Nickleby

RALPH: Brother's Keeper! You? Christian notions in the mouth of an old devil Jew? Ha! Permit me license, as well, to regard you a Good Samaritan?

FAGIN: And why not, my dear? Must every old, matted-haired, fang-toothed, red-bearded, and shabbily dressed Jew be labeled 'Cain'? Must I be denied the role of Abel, the wronged brother; because of narrow-minded expectations, that I acquit myself only as some satanic agent; because of naive readers of Master Twist's history?

RALPH: Naturally not. But the presumption—indeed! the preposterous notion—that a thieving, miserly, filthy leader of a gang of snatch-purses; a conniving accomplice of a brutal murderer; a crony of a hate-filled, seizure-prone villain: that such a man dare claim place as a Brother's Keeper: it quite beggars imagination. A barrister in league with the devil himself *might* presume to make such a case; but only before credulous jurors and senile magistrates.

FAGIN: True, my dear. Not in that country, for certain, could I have hoped for a barrister who'd dare smudge himself and his profession with my case, as you call it. No more, of course, could you.

RALPH: Granted. Most speedily. But leave my case—at least for the nonce. The thought, ha! that you even dare conceive you *have* one, offers rich entertainment (that being, understandably, the last thing I expected, cabined here with you). Why look, daft old Jew, think of the scenes in Master Twist's history which exude your vileness and villainy. Here, yes, slathering over your little hoard of stolen trinkets, and then rising up, knife in hand, upon detecting the parish boy watching you. Or here, drubbing the young snatchpurses for returning to your den empty-handed. Or here, with mock graciousness welcoming Twist to the dank, earthy-smelling room after Sikes and that Nancy catch him; and then laying into him with that jagged and knotted club, after his futile attempt to flee. Or here, you 'avaricious old skeleton,' as Sikes calls you to your face, incarcerating the lad in a ramshackle building, and leaving him to the mockery and corrupting example of that pair of pickpockets. A Samaritan? Oh, doubtless!

FAGIN: Quite familiar with the history, it appears, my dear. But there must be more to the case against me. Continue your recitation of my wrongdoings, please do. An old Jew may find one excuse for his behaviour, might pluck a single instance from your list to question whether there's been, as my Artful Dodger claimed for himself, 'a case of deformation of character.'

RALPH: Seems there's little else for us to occupy our time here. Why not? Mind my thumbing my way along? Well, then; here you are, putting defenseless Twist in the hands of that abusive Sikes for the Chertsey housebreaking, knowing as you did, that Sikes would show little nicety for Twist's person, should he offer the least resistance to Sikes's orders.

FAGIN: Please to forget my cautioning Twist, that Sikes was 'a rough man, and thinks nothing of blood when his own is up.'

RALPH: Or leaving young Twist with naught to read but a history of dreadful crimes, and great criminals, and secret murders, and hidden bodies: a history terrifying to the child's inmost being.

FAGIN: Please to forget, that such a history may have much in common with a certain Holy Book.

RALPH: Or entering into conspiracy with that Cain-branded Monks— hideously birth-marked—to implicate Twist in crimes which could lead to conviction and transportation—if not get him scragged, to employ your slang.

FAGIN: Please to forget that a blue-bagged barrister may assist a wealthy client for a greater exchange of money; and under protection of law.

RALPH: I'll please to forget civility, should you continue to mutter interruptions. Hold your tongue until I enumerate the charges in Twist's history. Now, then; even setting aside your malignant plots against Twist, there's your exploitation of English youth and your role as accessory to the murder of Nancy. In the matter of the former, you've no rejoinder against the fact you trained youth in the ways of crime, took advantage of their defenselessness, plied them with drink to addiction, and so incriminated them as to wield power over them, should they, miraculously, like Nancy, grow a conscience and perceive the moral enormity of their association with you. And heartless: when five of your guttersnipes were reported to dangle from the gibbet, you were gleeful that not one peached on you, mindful of your safety, not their lives.

No, old Jew: not a word, mind; I'll finish first, please you. My thumbing for an episode tenders no invitation for interruption. Ah, here it is: yes, Nancy's imprecation after she and Sikes returned Twist to you:

'I thieved for you when I was a child not half as old as this!' pointing to Oliver. 'I have been in the same trade, and in the same service for twelve years since. Don't you know it? Speak out! Don't you know it?'

'Well, well,' replied the Jew, with an attempt at pacification; 'and if you have, it's your living!'

'Aye, it is!' returned the girl; not speaking, but pouring out the words in one continuous and vehement scream. 'It is my living; and the cold, wet, dirty streets are my home; and you're the wretch that drove me to them long ago, and that'll keep me there, day and night, day and night, till I die!'

A Samaritan, Fagin? Is this some 'out-dacious' attempt to 'demogalize' me? Even a phrenological observer (yes, your profile: thank you) would find against you. Candidate for diabolical tyrant, perhaps? Mind, not a word yet!

And there's your goading Sikes into bludgeoning Nancy. Oho! Little need to call up the particulars of that episode, I perceive: mere mention sets in motion the rhythm of your bony fingers, combing your beard, telling that the episode freshly plays its particulars in your mind's eye. Small wonder Claypole received free pardon from the Crown in consequence of being admitted approver against you. That scene recorded your manipulation of Sikes, gave witness that his murder of Nancy was predictable; the moment he dashed out the door he was little more than a puppet, perpetrating on that hysterical woman the violence in your own breast. Another proof of an old Jew acting as his Brother's Keeper, I am to reckon?

FAGIN: With submission, sir: I may now speak? Gratitude, my dear, grat-
           itude. On goading Sikes: Twist's historian, of course, recorded it;
           but what evidence of my goading saw light in court? Claypole's
           testimony, to be sure: but was he awake when I primed Sikes for
           discovering Nancy's treachery? Did he witness even half of the
           particulars of my black rage? Could he have illustrated me, like
           your 'Phiz' or my Cruikshank: the violence of my quivering lips,
           the cunning of my malicious art, as I tantalized Sikes with the no-
           tion of someone's betrayal? So heavy with sleep was Claypole that
           I, kindly note, hauled him to a sitting posture, and called his
           name, several times, before he came to his senses. By all means,
           my dear: thumb up that scene again. And did he steal down the
           stairs to overhear me at the bolted door, cautioning Sikes to be
           crafty, not 'too violent for safety?' Or had he slumped back asleep?

RALPH: Implying, eh, that the court took perjured testimony from Clay-
           pole? As if maybe the court sentenced you for shepherding a
           flock of fogle filchers—on which Claypole could truthfully
           peach—not for being Sikes's accessory? But allowing that, you've
           no dodge to the charge of nefarious ringleader.

FAGIN: Ringleader, yes; and in the eyes of the law a criminal. But are the
           eyes of the law the only eyes through which conduct is to be ac-
           quitted? May I remind you, my dear, of who first took in frail
           Master Twist, when he was on death's threshold? Did I threaten
           harm with my toasting-fork, deny him a share of the sausages in
           the frying-pan? Or did I offer comfort, a place in which to recu-
           perate, society to provide him mirth—perhaps the first his life
           had experienced?

RALPH: Making yourself out the Samaritan, I see. Well, look at this. No:
           withdraw your suety finger from the page. Squint at this illus-
           tration. Yes: young Twist, propped up with pillows in an easy-
           chair by the fireside in the housekeeper's room; 'recovering from
           Fever,' says the plate. Your growl signifies recognition of Brown-
           low; but the painting above the mantle: look: more closely. Ap-
           prehend the subject? A person, bending over a supine figure;
           donkey in the roadway. Painting of *The Good Samaritan*, would
           you agree? adorning the wall of the gentleman who became one
           of Twist's benefactors, we might further agree? No painting for
           any wall in your dismal hideouts, is it?

FAGIN: Why not, my dear? I might disabuse you of its appropriateness
           on a wall in Brownlow's Pentonville home; but that's not at issue

just now. Surely you tease, comparing Brownlow and me as Samaritans. For of all people, Mr Nickleby, given the history of your nephew, you scorn that Christian parable, understand its hypocrisy. Or do I mistake you? Can you have swallowed the humbuggery that a Samaritan aids troubled people with no thought for himself?

RALPH: Ha! Only soft-hearted psalm-singers get hocussed into believing the Samaritan is without self-interest. He knows the world: knows he must travel back through the land of your Jews: knows them an unfriendly people, to Samaritans and other strangers: knows the best insurance against incivilities upon his return: to exhibit his beneficence to an innkeeper, overpay him, and promise reimbursement for costs accruing before his return. The innkeeper doesn't live who'd check his tongue, not blather about such benevolence. Ha! Do you suppose, old Jew, the Samaritan had long prayed for such an opportunity as that which the robbed and beaten and ignored man afforded him?

FAGIN: Splendid, my dear! A man of penetration!

RALPH: Admitted: but don't seek to propitiate my favour by presents of flattery, cunning one. Dispelling the sanctimoniousness of the parable is one thing; esteeming you a benevolent Samaritan, quite another. Acknowledge: you assisted Twist's recovery because in the innocence and honesty of his physiognomy, a rare countenance, you perceived a treasure which you knew best how to turn to advantage. What was it you admitted to Sikes and Nancy, before he agreed to take Twist on the Chertsey job? Yes, here it is:

'And wot,' said Sikes, scowling fiercely on his agreeable friend, 'wot makes you take so much pains about one chalk-faced kid, when you know there are fifty boys snoozing about Common Garden every night, as you might pick and choose from?'

'Because they're of no use to me, my dear,' replied the Jew, with some confusion, 'not worth the taking. Their looks convict 'em when they get into trouble, and I lose 'em all. With this boy, properly managed, my dears, I could do what I couldn't with twenty of them.'

And when that lad Barney identified Twist as 'Wud of Bister Fagid's lads,' what did Toby Crackit exclaim? Ah: 'Wot an

inwalable boy that'll make, for the old ladies' pockets in
chapels! His mug is a fortun' to him.' So, old manipulator, expect no charity from me, no acknowledgment that your aiding
of Twist instances Christian brotherhood.

FAGIN: You have other candidates, my dear? Mrs Mann, who brought
him up 'by hand' in her branch-workhouse until he was nine?
(Whose routine dose of gin-laced Daffy, when her 'blessed infants ain't well,' resembled the beverage on which Nancy grew
up and of which she complained?) Or the beadle Bumble, who
'inwented' Twist's name and embellished his coat with large
brass buttons bearing the same image as the 'porochial seal—
The Good Samaritan healing the sick and bruised man?' Or the
fat gentlemen of the workhouse board or the red-faced gentleman in the white waistcoat who assigned Twist to learn the
trade of picking oakum? Perhaps Mr Gamfield, who wished to
apprentice him as a chimney sweep, adding one more boy to his
roster of three or four whom he'd already bruised to death? Or
the magistrate who refused the apprenticeship on the grounds
of Twist's fear of Mr Gamfield? He's a better candidate, don't
you think, Mr Nickleby? For having made that decision, he
commended Twist again to the care of the workhouse, washed
his hands of further supervision, basked in self-congratulation—
mindless of the cruel sentence he'd rendered.

RALPH: Enough, enough. The sarcasm of your list wears thin. No candidates, either among the Sowerberrys or the decent folk who
showed Twist their back-sides on his journey to London. And
there is, truth to tell, a smattering of Samaritanism in that first
picture of you, maternally tending those sausages with your
toasting-fork, bringing some gaiety into Twist's young life with
your game of handkerchief-snatching. But his benefactors were
that Rose and Nancy, Dr Losberne and Brownlow. Luckily for
Twist—although some would credit providence—the Chertsey
housebreaking landed him in the lap of a young woman who
asked no questions and directly showered care upon his injured
person. Hardly my way, of course; but *that's* behaviour which
the world expects of Samaritans who seek classification as
Brother's Keeper. And when it was discovered to Twist that
Rose was his very aunt, he refused to address her as 'aunt,' directly resolved upon addressing her as 'sister.' There! our historian all but declared his intention: to figure Rose literally as her
Brother's Keeper.

FAGIN: Yes, yes, my dear; but consider: what are the duties of a Brother's
              Keeper? To nurse an injured person back to health? To bestow
              concern and affection on the friendless? To shelter the deprived
              in a community of collective succour?

RALPH: I suppose those'll do, suffocating as you make them sound—like
              raising flowers in a hothouse, from which you dare not remove
              them, lest they wilt in weather.

FAGIN: Exactly, my dear. And now consider whether I fulfilled those
              duties. And more. When boys and girls arrived at my den, or
              when I happened on them, languishing in the cold wet shelter-
              less midnight streets of Whitechapel or Saffron Hill or Field
              Lane or St Giles or Bethnel Green: Did I not feed and shelter
              them, restore them to health, show them affection, offer them a
              community? Be they Charley Bates, Jack Dawkins, Nancy,
              Betsy, Toby Crackit, Tom Chitling, or Master Twist—did I not
              rescue them from death's door? Yes; cock the brow of cynicism;
              for you don't know their histories as I do. And so you must, if
              you will, take my word that, one and all, they faced death from
              starvation or disease when first I made their acquaintance.

RALPH: And you exploited them: one and all: for your own benefit. You
              sent them out to do the thieving that you couldn't do; for so re-
              pellent is your person, that proximity to a stranger begets his
              shudder. Samaritanism on behalf of your band of snatchpurses?
              All gammon, Fagin: Christian cant behind which to hide greedy
              self-interest.

FAGIN: Remind me of the great wealth I gathered. Remind me of the
              splendid appointments in the houses I inhabited: the polished
              furnishings which showed to such advantage on my many Kid-
              derminster carpets. Item my wardrobe: speckled silk stockings,
              smart pumps, corduroy breeches, surtouts, and swallow-tail
              coats; Wellington boots and bottle-green spencers; white waist-
              coats, small-plaited shirt frills, and white cravats. Or the luxury
              of my table: pigeon pies, and blood puddings, and hams, and
              veal, and lobsters, and barrels of oysters. Or the elegant public
              rooms which I frequented and showered with my largesse.
                  Damn, my dear! How do you think I survived to reach the
              ripeness I did? Early I learned the price of excessive ambition,
              from fellow Jews who failed to resign themselves to meager sub-
              sistence. Better *that* than their early deaths; or the life of other
              Jews: ragpickers, or hawkers of fifty-bladed penknives. Blessed

with stately form and exquisitely turned limbs and comely countenance (shall I preen?), I early resigned myself as well to a life without conjugal pleasures, mocked by every woman toward whom I endeavoured to display affection. Not to be denied all substitutes of parental pleasure, the band of snatchpurses became my family.

RALPH: Ha! Even now confessing your use of those boys, making them your children, fashioning them in your own image, ugly as it is.

FAGIN: A broad band of perverseness, haven't you, Mr Nickleby? Taunt a man, draw him out, get up his gorge, and goad him into saying or doing something impetuous. You don't need me to point out the boys' virtues.

RALPH: Scarcely. Provided one overlooks their criminal deeds, it's clear you taught them a livelihood, made them resourceful, gave them confidence. Not one among them met Monks's description: of a 'sneaking, snivelling pickpocket.' Why, that young wiper, Tommy Chitling, even considered challenging your Artful Dodger; not the behaviour of a lad raised under the heavy thumb of a despotic father or workhouse warden. The system whereby you schooled those boys seemed to have given him nerve. And that Dodger. Now there's a son to take pride in: defiant to the last, full of good British pluck. To sour your grin, however, your schooling was all in the service of crime, the which, you know, cannot be overlooked.

FAGIN: You'll not entertain schooling in the service of justice? Or give consideration to the more criminal deed: committing infants to workhouses or teaching them a livelihood, albeit in petty thievery? Please to lower your brows, my dear. Surprise, affected or genuine, doesn't become a forehead the amplitude of yours.

RALPH: I'll allow you gave those boys an opportunity for becoming something more than parish- or charity-boys; boys whose self-contempt, in all likelihood, would result in either the self-pitying helplessness of Mrs Mann's little Dick, or the bullying of others: Claypole, for instance. You may even be allowed to have set your flock free to thieve where they would—provided they return with booty. But Justice, old Jew?

FAGIN: Yes; justice: at least the best justice one could hope for in such an unjust system as existed there. For, my dear, from whom did my boys rob? Coves like Brownlow, mind; monied men who did nothing for those without it, mind; gentry with time lying so idly on their hands, mind, that they could afford to stand at a book-stall and leisurely browse on a musty old book; gentlemen, mind, with neither eyes nor nose for the miserable conditions all about themselves—much less the stomach or heart or head to set about trying to rectify the social evils lying everywhere at hand. What's a handkerchief, even a pocket-watch, to such as they? Mightn't the theft of their handkerchiefs flag their debt of compassion to unfortunates with tears in their eyes? As well mightn't the lifting of their pocket-watches exhort them: 'Heed less the time, more the times?'

RALPH: Oho! A moral philosopher, no less. But such folly, to expect any reader of Twist's history to regard those thefts as parables, read them as more covert signals and signs, which you made such a habit of sending—be it with finger to lip, knuckle on nose, nod of head, or shift of eyes. Expect next that I'll behold in your troop of prigs a, a—yes!—a juvenile version of Robin Hood's merry men: transported from the Forests of Sherwood to the Streets of London: robbing from the rich and giving to the poor? Won't do, old Jew. Not in these times. Brownlow owed nothing to your thieves; had no duty to befriend anyone, except whom he pleased. Justice means leaving each man alone, permitting him to do what he wishes to do, to be what he chooses to be. Brownlow chose to be Twist's benefactor and nobody else's; *that* was his right.

FAGIN: Couldn't be that in him you find some shadow of yourself, could it? Do you warmly defend him in order that you may defend your own behaviour, having ignored the claims upon your purse by the wife and children of your brother?

RALPH: You may run your bony fingers through my history; but all in due time. Trying to skirt the question that unravels your claim of justice, perhaps? Some file, Fagin, to pretend that your group of wipers represents a tribe of justice-seekers. Beneath that crepe lies the truth, that you needed them to fetch goods for you to fence. How stands the proof of your exploitation? In your method of gaining power over all your little prigs. You implicated them in some criminal deed so that, having corrupted each one, you could exercise coercive power over them all, harbor evidence to blow upon them, should they have endeavoured to bolt your toils. Ask me not to find any concern for justice in Master Twist's instance.

FAGIN: Come, come, Mr Nickleby: we fled our Field Lane crib, you re-
              call, as soon as Master Twist fell to the police; terrified, indeed.
              Surely, then, you recognize the necessity of implicating young
              Twist in crime. What choice had we, after his weeks of recuper-
              ation with the boys and me? Were we to permit his disappear-
              ance and await his return with the London constabulary? Were
              we to bide time and let him betray our practices and residence
              when he chose? Had we any assurance that he'd not peach on
              us, play booty on our livelihood? What other protection—never
              absolute, as Nancy's treachery proved—have thieves than mu-
              tual culpability? How else live, save in mortal anxiety of being
              hounded to death, should our activities become known? I tell
              you nothing new: every society—prigs to parsons, gamesters to
              gentry—rests upon laws whose violation starts up the engines of
              punishment. Among thieves it's taboo to blow upon one an-
              other. To give that law teeth requires first the certainty, that no
              one privy to secrets be stainless, and second the threat, that
              treachery will fire the engines of retaliation. Betrayal authorises
              recrimination and maximum penalty. That principle, of course,
              required Nancy's death.

RALPH: So you exonerate Sikes's bludgeoning her to death, even as she
              holds Rose's handkerchief toward him, poignantly beseeching
              his mercy?

FAGIN: Had he not been told she'd drugged him with laudanum, stolen
              off for her secret interview, peached on our plots and dens? Her
              treachery it was, that triggered his rage; for he knew not—no
              more did I—her pleadings with Rose and Brownlow to let both
              him and me go scot-free. Seems she had some perverse appetite
              for being abused and beaten, you might agree, courted violence
              by returning to Sikes's rooms?

RALPH: Yes, a 'precious strange gal,' as Sikes remarks; something un-
              usual from the very start about her relationship with him.
              Even declined your offer to help free her from the 'brute-
              beast.' Nevertheless, Fagin, there's no pardon for his murder,
              and your connection with him has little in it that vouches for
              Samaritanism.

FAGIN: You know, then, his history: place of origin, lineage, and the
              benevolence with which fate had blessed his infant years? No
              more, I'm certain, than you know my history. The historian of
              Master Twist, curiously, declined to document our histories,
              ones that might lighten the dark shadows cast over us.

RALPH: I anticipate a narrative; but ask me not to hear that Sikes's father was a child-molester who raised Sikes 'by cudgel' rather than merely 'by hand.' Plead not that your familiarity with similar histories of unruly brutes compelled you to mull plots of using Nancy to poison him, 'the man you hate,' before his bestiality brought you all down. Spare me such histories: I have no guarantee for their credibility, no patience for extenuations, not even an handkerchief for *lacrimae vitae*.

FAGIN: The only history I need is that which the historian has given us. Not Master Twist's, but Monks's, a history which, but for the differences in wealth and station, will do to represent the histories of Sikes and me. Admittedly, when Monks, having heard of the accomplishments of my boys, offered to pay for my assistance in staining young Twist's character with crime, I had no reason to turn him away; for his request coincided with the need to protect our own livelihood by so baptising Twist. But as our plot hatched, Monks ladled out larger and larger gobbets of his history, ones that compassionated me to him, finding in it elements of Sikes's and mine.

RALPH: Compassion, indeed, for a wicked being who harbored such venom for a frail half-brother, a bastard at that. The scar, which a neckerchief and high collar failed to hide, and the seizures, which reduced him to a writhing serpent: additional marks of his malignancy.

FAGIN: That unenlightened, my dear? It was acceptable among medieval peoples to equate birthmarks with witchcraft, seizures with sorcery, deformities with the devil. But don't you find that such equations have too much in common with other emblems—employed to sanctify the persecution of scapegoats—to grace them as other than obsolete and self-serving superstitions?

          Ah! So you were, again, my dear, taunting? Then we may skip over my sympathy for a man whose physical defects were mirror to my own? Turn instead to factors responsible for the venom of his hatred for Master Twist? Well, then; may we acknowledge that it was most regrettable that Monks's and Twist's father had been forced into wedlock with a woman ten years older than he?

RALPH: Heed me not; I attend: just thumbing for Brownlow's harangue. Yes, browbeating Monks with his description of 'the wretched marriage into which family pride, and the most sordid and narrowest of all ambition, forced your unhappy father when a mere boy,' calling Monks its 'sole and most unnatural issue.' Quite free with those superlatives, the good Christian.

FAGIN: Might the 'most unnatural issue' have been the hatred of Monks's father for him? Can there be doubt that Monks bore the brunt of all that man's loathing, both for his wife and the father who'd driven him into the (how's it called?) 'protracted anguish of that ill-assorted union?' And his brooding morbidity, once the two had separated: allowing the sores of that bond to rust and canker at his heart for years could not but have further corroded Monks's childhood.

RALPH: Little wonder that from an infant Monks had, yes, 'repulsed his father with coldness and aversion.' But do spare the heart-rending particulars. Do stint your dismissals of the hearsay allegations: that Monks was a 'fierce ungovernable boy,' one who, as Brownlow execrated him, 'from your cradle were gall and bitterness to your own father's heart, and in whom all evil passions, vice, and profligacy, festered, till they found a vent in a hideous disease which has made your face an index even to your mind.' And do skip over the years of poor Monks, growing up without a father's love. Quickly: let's directly to the will; that delicious document! For there's the loathesomest insult to Monks, agree? To be left an annuity of a mere eight hundred pounds, while to his half-brother or -sister would go the bulk of his property: 'If it were a girl, it was to inherit the money unconditionally; but if a boy, only on the stipulation that in his minority he should never have stained his name with any public act of dishonour, meanness, cowardice, or wrong.' (Ha! Suppose he'd allow *private acts* of same? Know you *any* child who grows up free from *all* stain of some meanness or cowardice or wrong?) And to this most generous stipulation add his kindest justification: that he'd resolved upon it 'to mark his confidence in the mother, and his conviction—only strengthened by approaching death—that the child would share her gentle heart, and noble nature.' Confidence and conviction, indeed! Such magnanimity!

FAGIN: And such penetration, my credulous juror. I may trust, as well, to your apprehending a reason for Monks's obsession in seeing to Master Twist's corruption? Surely you remarked Twist's likeness not only to mother, but to father, too? Yes: that question: did Monks hound Twist? or did he hound the image of the cruel father, whom he saw in Twist? Even had Monks's mother destroyed the will on which you've expatiated, nothing could have blotted his loathing for the likeness of the man who openly discredited him for his (Ah, thank you for the passage: I can read it:) 'rebellious disposition, vice, malice, and premature bad passions.' It was, of course, pathetic that Monks could not overcome the stigma of his father's pernicious characterisation. But that weakness made him deserving of my modest assistance. You perceive, I trust, that he'd been robbed of his character, beaten out of his rights, abandoned to the ditches of self-contempt, and shunned as a branded devil?

RALPH: So, Good Samaritan, to weakness, too, we must attribute Monks's ready and unexplainable capitulation to Brownlow's browbeating? As pathetic was he as was Sikes, driven to virtual self-destruction by the hallucination of Nancy's incriminating eyes. But notwithstanding the dubious case for your role as Samaritan to destitute waifs and pathetic, warped men like Sikes and Monks—men ill served by family, society, fate, and their historian—nevertheless, your Samaritanism was but a feeble candle next the radiant glow of that of Nancy, Rose, Dr Losberne, and Brownlow.

FAGIN: To many that must seem correct; but so much have that foursome in common with a foursome in your history, my dear, that I can scarce credit your sincerity. Arrival at the crossroads of our two histories was inevitable, given our mutual historian; and our sequence in his youthful career. But before we turn to your history's charitable corporation—Cheeryble, Nicholas, and Noggs, Ltd.—first allow me to extract from you one concession: That I have been wronged by readers of Twist's history; and one admission: That I am your moral superior. For the history of your niggardliness toward your sister-in-law, niece, and nephew allows you no claim as Brother's Keeper or Good Samaritan. Those Christian concepts nest poorly with usury.

RALPH: I claim no place as Brother's Keeper; but to relegate me your inferior warrants either contempt, for the dullness you share with our historian, or compliment, for the taunt of your wry reference: to his conclusion that my hatred of Nephew Nick was in consequence of his manfully standing up to me, upon our initial meeting.

FAGIN: Exquisite, my dear. Our lodging here has dimmed your wits not one whit! Yes; I was, I confess it, thinking of that first encounter, during which our historian drew such contrasts between your

old face—ah, yes, here—'stern, hard-featured and forbidding,'
and 'that of the young one, open, handsome, and ingenuous.'
Your eye, he remarked, was 'keen with the twinklings of avarice
and cunning; the young man's bright with the light of intelligence and spirit.' And then this sagacious conclusion, that none
ever feel such a 'striking contrast' 'with half the keenness or
acuteness of perfection with which it strikes to the very soul of
him whose inferiority it marks. It galled Ralph' (that's you, my
dear) 'to the heart's core, and he' (still you, sir) 'hated Nicholas
from that hour.'

RALPH: Pshaw! Quite a moral stripling, our historian: so certain of the
reason I hated my nephew; as though envy inevitably bred only
hatred. Fortunately I was, unlike you, allowed a history; it awaits
an astute reader who'll undertake the task of unravelling the
knots in which my 'hatred' is wound. Might I beseech you to accept such an appointment?

FAGIN: With humble pleasure; for your history availed me a wondrous
discovery: that in you, dear brother, dwell the qualities of Cain.
Ah! Not the discovery you anticipated? But peace: permit me to
begin, may I? Oh, where? So many knots at hand, of course.
Shall it be your avarice as a youth, ever undertaking to turn your
schoolmates' needs to your own account with gouging lending
rates, learning at a tender age your usurious life's trade?

RALPH: Must every usurer, and every Jew, be slid, perforce, like a greased
key into the patent Brahmin of received expectations?

FAGIN: Or shall it be the deep design behind your money-hunting marriage, impatient for your unsuspecting brother-in-law's early
demise, which would leave to your use the money your bride was
to inherit?

RALPH: Came by the facts of that segment of my history from our historian's mouth, did you? From my mouth, perhaps? Or from
that of a man who hated me and who chose to divulge such
'facts' in surroundings which disfavoured remonstrance—had I
deigned to dignify his slanderous tongue with answer?

FAGIN: Peace, please! Perhaps it shall be your abuse of the man to whom
you allude, that very Brooker? Or your abuse of your clerk,
Noggs; or of other misfortunate, downtrodden brethren whose
desperateness you seized advantage of? Or, more to the point,
your refusals to be, literally, your brother's keeper? Shameful, my

dear, offering so little assistance to your sister-in-law, niece, and nephew. Indeed, rather than assist them, you altogether denied them the advantage of your wealth; worse, exposed Niece Kate to the degrading conditions of a dressmaker's shop and to the 'demdest' effrontery of that bewhiskered Mantalini; worst, to the perils of consorting with such raffish libertines as Hawk and Verisopht. I'll allow, now, my dear, that sound with which our historian so frequently characterises your utterances; a growl is long overdue. No? As you wish, then.

Your resemblance to Cain is most repugnantly visible in your fratricidal venom for Nephew Nick. Found him employment with a brutal and ignorant schoolmaster, employment which could only have a violent termination. And then, unregenerate one, bribed Snawley to mask as Smike's father, merely to strip Nephew Nick of Smike. Even stooped to slander, endeavoured to persuade the Brothers Cheeryble of your nephew's black-guardly proclivities, expecting they'd dismiss him. Admitted: you killed no one; in which you differ from your Biblical predecessor; but your behaviour was lethal in its intentions and wishes, swearing as you did, to Sir Mulberry Hawk, yes, 'if we were only citizens of a country where it could be safely done, I'd give good money to have him stabbed to the heart and rolled into the kennel for the dogs to tear.' Thoroughly 'wicious,' you were, my dear, despite lacking the visible scar by which your kindred are more readily known.

RALPH: Finished so soon? I'd expected at least a parade of personages, all uniformed as Brothers' Keepers, which my Cain-like villainy could better illuminate. In the front rank of which would march in splendor the Cheerybles, Noggs, and, of course, the patron saint of children himself, our Saint Nicholas, rescuing as he did, my Smike, little Lillyvick Kenwigs, Sister Kate, and Spouse Madeline.

FAGIN: Flank them, should we, with that platoon of parliamentary did-dlers, those collective swindlers who sought to launch, in the holy name of national charity, the United Metropolitan Improved Hot Muffin and Crumpet Baking and Punctual Delivery Company?

RALPH: And at the rear that benefactor to the Kenwigs's expectations of inheritance for their proliferating progeny? yes, that pompous porpoise, so debasedly deaf to the jingle of coin in the Kenwigs's fawning, obsequious servility: Lillyvick?

FAGIN: Agreed: but only if, at the head, will march our grand marshall, your very own Uncle Ralph; whose charitable act, of willing his five thousand pounds sterling to your father, made manifest his character as Brother's Keeper—albeit by default. Wonderful, his contempt for the Royal Humane Society, to which he'd intended to will his money, for meddling in, and thereby saving, the life of a poor relation, whom he'd been slowly frying, like one of my sausages, on the low heat of a meager allowance.

RALPH: Ah, yes: dear Uncle Ralph, whose flinty habits accompanied his legacy to me; and whose seeming charity set the pattern for my nephew's history; for it was his unexpected gift which suckled the wish, common to softer hearts than yours or mine, for a benevolent figure to intercede in times of dire need. That very wish catapulted to London my nattering ninny of a sister-in-law, fully expecting me to empty my purse for her and hers, to hurl coin at her feet as though I, like her cucumber-chucking lunatic lover, would uncontrollably lavish sterling upon her sovereign senselessness.

FAGIN: But, my dear, where there exist such men as the cherubic Cheerybles, who can be proof against that fairy-tale wish? Unlike my splendidly selective Samaritans—bestowing protection and favour upon two obedient orphans, but washing their hands of any obligation to all, all the rest—yours answered to divers needs, merely awaited Trimmers's notice. Or where there exist such men as your Noggs, inebriate and indigent though he was, who abetted those in distress? Or lads like your nephew, who—

RALPH: In *whom* dwells a broad band of perversity, old Jew? Ha! But I know you have seen through Nephew Knuckleboy's game, good creature of craftiness. I grant I erred in my assumption: that his befriending of Smike sought to curry favor and fortune from Smike's father. But I erred not in my implication; for by playing Samaritan to a dim-witted, illness-ridden lad, Nephew Nick—perhaps inspired by his satanic namesake, Old Nick?—happened upon an excellent ruse. Coupled with his mourner's sleeve, it was a superb gambit in securing others' pity and goodwill. Oh, I'll not deny his sympathy for Smike; but it was a mere spoonful to his cask of self-pity, his desire that others take pity on him as he did Smike. Notice, did you, that in telling the Brothers Cheeryble his story, he hid beneath no basket the light of his charity toward one more desperate than he? For never once did either twin express surprise at Smike's existence or relationship to the Nickleby household. And did it give you pause to wonder that my nephew—under the fictitious name, yes, of Johnson—was so readily accepted into Crummles's theatrical troupe? Do you suppose it signified some off-stage histrionic ability; some appetite for melodrama; some resemblance to other actors—*not* of Crummles's troupe—who figure so hugely in the melodrama he concocts?

FAGIN: Questions rhetorical, of course; but worthy of our consideration withal. Fortunately, our historian lifted a corner of the crepe beneath which your nephew endeavoured to hide his self-interested actions; allowed us to lift, in turn, an eyebrow. Upon Miss Bray he bestowed benevolence, risked himself time and again, because he desired her love and—may I say?—person. But from whom did he withhold the same? Why from the maiden mistaken for Miss Bray, a damsel equally in need of rescue from another paternal ogre, Cecilia Bobster. Not curious at all, his utter neglect of her distress, once Noggs's error saw light.

RALPH: No more curious than his about-face on the matter of social inequities. What brave thoughts does our historian attribute to him—here!—concern that so few people 'tenanted the stately houses' while so many 'lay in noisome pens': distress that 'ignorance was punished and never taught': despondency that 'jail-door gaped and gallows loomed for thousands urged towards them by circumstances darkly curtaining their very cradles' heads': indignation at 'how much injustice, and misery, and wrong there was, and yet how the world rolled on from year to year, alike careless and indifferent, and no man seeking to remedy or redress it.' Yet upon Nephew Nick's inheriting wealth, which my having died intestate left him: wealth with which he might have found means to remedy or redress some injustice, some misery, and some wrong: why, what, then, did he? Ha! recoiled: morally squeamish at the prospect of becoming tainted by 'money so acquired' by his usurious uncle; allowed my riches to be, yes, 'swept at last into the coffers of the state,' so that 'no man was the better or the happier for them.'

Oh! that there can be sybaritic pleasure in the company of an astute sceptic, like you, old Jew; that sneering detractors, who weave such miserable figments from their malicious brains, can delight in such doings. A proposal: that we celebrate the other villains in the his-story of my nevvy?

FAGIN: Accepted, with zest; for the night's still young. (Or do you sup-
            pose it's day? Always hard to tell, here, eh?) Allow me to com-
            mence with my favourite scoundrel: Noggs. The genuine item,
            an authentic Iscariot, though lacking in the compunction of
            both my biblical kinsman and my Nancy. Befriend your
            brother's family though he did, his aims were spite and the
            wish, common company to lonely old fools, to win some slight
            measure of others' regard. Certainly: your usurious rates had
            tumbled him. But he'd perched atop a gentleman's ladder of
            rotted rungs long before he sought you out; and if not you, then
            some other usurer would've become scapegoat for his own
            reckless habits. Out of charity—an attribute which our histo-
            rian ever-so-hastily qualified, by remarking omissions in your
            account of Noggs's background to Mr Bonney (omissions he
            deemed unworthy of his attention in others' accounts)—out of
            charity you gave him employment. And your insulting treat-
            ment of him? Proof of perception, that kind treatment of
            wrongdoers customarily exacerbates their guilt, shame, and
            feelings of unworthiness; customarily turns once-plucky men
            into grovelling, snivelling worms: a perniciously double-edged
            principle, is Samaritanism. And the meager wages you paid
            him? Both to deny him wherewithal for more beverage than
            that with which he already intoxicated himself; and to do him
            sufficient injustice to keep him cheeky.

RALPH: Bravo! Then you properly admired Noggs's manfulness, too?
            Watched him, under the auspices of Nephew Cheeryble and an
            officer of the law—curiously absent from the event, eh?—sneak
            up on Squeers and crash down upon his head an old bellows? Not
            for the likes of us, is it, to question why Squeers was allowed no
            legal recourse for that invasion and assault? But what's that, now,
            you're thumbing to? Not Noggs's manly denunciation of me?

FAGIN: Precisely where my bony finger points! Denying that the
            Cheeryble brothers had tampered with him, he fronted you with
            the admission that he sought them out, told them that 'I wanted
            to help to find you out, to trace you down, to go through with
            what I had begun, to help the right; and that when I had done
            it, I'd burst into your room and tell you all, face to face, man to
            man, and like a man.' Admirable courage in such a denunciation;
            and buttressed by the security of only three glowering and grave
            witnesses; I always wondered at the meaning of that expression,
            'man to man.'

RALPH: And they all fronted me, mind, only after they'd made sure of themselves by besetting Snawley, (allow me?) here, 'to lead him, if possible, into contradictory and conflicting statements, to harass him by all available means, and so to practise on his fears and regard for his own safety.' And only *then*, mind, after they'd visited my relic Gride and 'appealed to' him, our historian terms it; another historian might have found they'd tampered, harassed, intimidated him, do you suppose?

FAGIN: But we can ill afford to overlook the greater scoundrel in your mob's actions, the truly fraternal Cain of your nephew's history. Yes; your pursing lips all but sound his name: Brooker. So arrogant was he, early forgetting his place and his debt to you, presuming to claim a share in the profits of some business he brought to you. Quickly taking his measurements, you met his challenge—as many in your business would: turned evidence on him, and saw to his arrest. But after exhibiting your power, you relented. Unlike most men, you had him freed and took him back into your employ. But even then his injured self-esteem festered; the pus from his pricked pride oozed forth; in it he hatched his atrocity: his lie about the death of your seven-year-old infant son. Add to which he committed that son to Dotheboys Hall; and no longer able to meet the terms of required payment, he ignored his duty of discovering to you his heinous deed; thereby allowing Squeers to treat your son as chattel, inflicting even more degrading consequences upon him. To all of this, Christian readers will mutter, 'Poetic justice,' for certain.

RALPH: For certain. But more: bless Brooker's charitable soul; he arrogated to himself the role of God's scourge, as—where is it? yes—'the instrument of working out this dreadful retribution upon the head of a man who, in the hot pursuit of his bad ends, has persecuted and hunted down his own child to death.' Did I read that with appropriate moral zealousness?

FAGIN: I believe you did, my dear; none save your nephew could have bettered you. But neglect not, in your benedictions, my dear, Brooker's accomplices. For they, too, murmured not the least sound of outrage at Brooker's benevolence. Much less did they favour consideration of your behaviour in the light of your loss of a son, or of the thawing influence which that child might have had upon your existence. Rather, they eagerly preferred to 'brownlow'—pardon, browbeat—you with your role in Smike's death. Preferred to ignore facts—Smike's illness-ridden frame and feeble-minded head, for which Brooker's act was ultimately culpable. Preferred to grub for fictions which fed their ill will: for it was knowingly—was it not?—that you vented 'malice and hatred' on Smike; knowingly that you made him an 'instrument for wreaking your bad passions'; knowingly that you sank him 'under your persecution?' The accomplices deserve Master Bates's praise of Sikes's dog; its hatred of 'other dogs as ain't of his breed,' proved it an 'out-and-out Christian.'

RALPH: Deserve Sikes's own praise: watching his dog lick its lips and eye 'Oliver as if it were anxious to attach itself to his windpipe without delay, Sikes laughed, "He's as willin' as a Christian, strike me blind if he isn't!"'

FAGIN: Their turn, then, is it?

RALPH: I do believe it is.

FAGIN: Shrewd scoundrels, weren't they? All Saint Simon Without, and Saint Walker Within?

RALPH: Tip-top sawyers, they were. Superior to any of yours.

FAGIN: Oh, far! Admired their ostentatious charity, I did. So handy to their purposes, a man like that Trimmers. Who'd bring to their attention news of every calamity, for which their coin could proffer partial redress.

RALPH: Who'd hawk to all who had ears the exact amount of their generosity.

FAGIN: Who'd undertake to secure their reputations as men whose twinkling merry eyes, whose dimpled double-chins, whose portliness and affability could conjure the image of some Christmastide nocturnal visitor.

RALPH: Who'd see to it that the right hands knew—and told!—what the left hands were a-doing.

FAGIN: Admired also their disinterested assistance to distressed young women, didn't you?

RALPH: Ah! Showed to such splendid disadvantage the villainous principle upon which I sought to complete Niece Kate's education: allowing for no prolongation of mollycoddling dependency, I set store by thrusting a maiden of her years into the unsheltered world, whereby she must (and Kate handsomely did!) learn to rely upon her own resources. True, true: the jealousy—hem!—of a spinster forewoman, the attentions—demnition!—of a mustachioed fop, the affectations—sigh!—of conjugal neurasthenics, the designs—ba-a-d devyles!—of unscrupulous rakes, and, yes, the indifference of a flinty uncle: circumstances which tried her character. But she survived the tests, proved herself. Only to relapse, like Miss Bray, under the Cheerybles' benefactions, Nephew Nick's protections, and spouse's suffocations.

FAGIN: Sad that neither young woman was the wiser for the contrast between your and the Cheerybles' principles. Truly sad, for Maid Madeline had promise, having inherited her father's pride: refused charity; insisted the charitable twins shroud her appeals in secrecy; and stipulated they honour the compromise she insisted upon: that the money she received remunerate her handiwork, rather than be gratuitous charity.

RALPH: To all of which they agreed; but not without disclosing their condescending contempt for that handiwork—setting Nephew Nick, here, 'to make a feint of purchasing her little drawings and ornamental work at a high price'; and here, to 'dispose' of the 'little productions' of her needle, pencil, and pen.

FAGIN: All of which discovers—albeit not to themselves—their slumbering wish: for her ineradicable indebtedness to them. Ah! Poor Charles Cheeryble: self-esteem pierced by Madeline's mother's choice of Walter Bray over himself. Then lanced by learning—according to whose version of Bray's history?—of Bray's abusive treatment of her, of his plunge into indebtedness, and, worst, of her fond love of him, even on her deathbed. How to avenge himself upon her and her unworthy spouse—although he'd never acknowledge vengeance as a motive? How to impress upon others her costly error? A problem on which Mr Charles may have pondered often and long? One solved by Miss Bray's distress.

RALPH: Solved to his advantage, rather? Dare we imagine, as an invisible memorial to Mrs Bray and her sister—whose precipitate demise deprived Brother Ned of his bride—that the twins might have solved the problem otherwise? Might they have secretly learned to whom Bray was indebted, honoured his debts, and set him free to live out the remainder of what all knew to be a life of short duration?

FAGIN: *That* would have been charity: it would have offered no affront
                  to Bray's virulent pride; for he'd have scorned the anonymous
                  simpletons who'd shown him such favour. And the brothers'
                  silent goodness would have freed them of our accusation of self-
                  interest, eh? But, vain coves that they were, they earnestly
                  sought Miss Bray's indebtedness, Mr Charles especially hunger-
                  ing for her to consider what her life could have been, had her
                  mother married wisely, chosen his sublime self.

                  Well, well, my dear. We could continue to pry open the lid
                  on the slops of the Cheeryble's designs. Could remark the insid-
                  ious methods of accomplishing *their* 'darling wishes,' of extort-
                  ing gratitude and compliancy from those beholden to their
                  despotic benevolence.

RALPH: Could even look at, say, their clerk, Linkinwater? Could study
                  the effects of their civility (yes, 'Damn your obstinacy,' 'Devil take
                  you,' 'submit peaceably,' 'have recourse to violence') on his behav-
                  iour? Could ponder his sea-changes, from violent antagonist—
                  a lion, they averred—to persnickety bookkeeper, to fearful
                  schoolboy, who had to secure permission from stern fathers be-
                  fore venturing to ask for Miss La Creevy's hand in matrimony?

FAGIN: Why, yes; yes, my dear, of course; of course! Could even, my dear,
                  cluck our tongues at his moral obtuseness. Enjoyed telling your
                  nephew the sentimental tale of the sickly bed-ridden humped-
                  back boy who grew flowers in old blacking-bottles on his back-
                  attic window-sill, didn't he? Odd that he found no example in
                  the practices of his employers—after forty-four years!—to which
                  he could apply himself with similarly intense relish. Found no
                  necessity in endeavouring to lighten the lad's misery. Asked the
                  poor sickly cripple if he might do something for him—called 'lip
                  service,' I believe? But considered no course of action which
                  might have avoided affronting the deformed child's pride.

RALPH: We could even return to Master Twist's history and study the
                  thorns in Rose Fleming's—well, why not?—her emasculation of
                  Harry Maylie? Could argue a curious connection between his
                  docility before her demands, that he abandon worldly ambi-
                  tions, and his hostility toward a man who bludgeons to death an
                  equally demanding woman, a woman who also shares Rose's
                  concern for Master Twist?

FAGIN: Why, yes, my dear; we could. We could, if you wish, even look at
                  the sibling pairs which populate your nephew's history: the

Pykes and Plucks, Scaleys and Tixes, Folairs and Lenvilles, Cur-
dles and Borums, Snevelliccies and Ledrooks, Fannys and
'Tildas, Kenwigs and Crummles *kinder*. We could annotate our
historian's endeavours to employ them for embroidery upon his
theme of brotherly keepers.

RALPH: We could even give consideration to my nephew's search for
some kind of royal father? We could sift through the teeming
assemblage of our historian's cast to observe Nephew Nick
brandishing his wrath upon all those who fail to gratify that
search? We could remark the irony of Mrs Nickleby's crackpot
suitor, the vastness of whose estates, the assortment of whose
connections, the poetry of whose romantic language, and the
thrust of whose inquiries—'Are you a princess?'—identify him
as that would-be royal parent?

FAGIN: Why, yes; most certainly we could. But why, my dear, this sudden
irascibility?

RALPH: We could look at the undersides of many things, crafty Jew. But
these coulds; what do they signal? Ha! Prolegomena to accusations. So please proceed apace, and spare me your delicacy.

FAGIN: Yes, my dear. Well, then; you are aware that however much you
and I (malignant creatures as we are), however much we calum-
niate the stealthy scoundrels of your nephew's history, we must
needs acquit you of villainy, if possible. Permit me, then, to put
you to the task of exculpating one unsavory role: accomplice to
old Gride's designs upon Miss Bray. To nourish the loathsome
scene of putting that beauty to bed with that beast condemns
you as cohort to an unnatural marriage.

RALPH: Hear ye! Hear ye! The aged are hereby denied all rights to seek
conjugal pleasures. Matrimony twixt January and May is hereby
proscribed. That it? True, part of Gride's design hinged on his
expectation of an inheritance directly upon marriage to the
'pretty chick.' But the ecstasy in his description of her charms;
the epochal wonder of a man who'd caressed only coin, giving
thought to caressing a woman; such a turn-about, a truly hu-
manising possibility, provided an unexpected surprise, for which
I had no heart to deny him my assistance. Puts me to mind of
you, caught fondling your trinkets the morning after Master
Twist's arrival. A compassionating scene for me, watching you
find gratification for your deprived sense of touch.

FAGIN: Waste no compassion on me, my dear. It might cause me to
            gloss over your villainy; and we cannot allow that, now can we?
            Humbuggery, if I may. Your *feeling* for Gride? Nothing other
            than the pleasurable glow from knowing you had another vehi-
            cle for the conveyance of your avarice.

RALPH: Nor, of course, had I any feeling for Bray. No replica was he, of
            what my own life could have been, a stern and proud man re-
            duced to penurious conditions and pathetically enfeebled by ill
            health: he stirred no sympathy in me? Nor gave I thought to the
            possibility that Gride's offer, at no cost to myself, eradicated
            Bray's debts, and, at no cost to Bray's haughty pride, enabled
            him to resume his spendthrift's ways? Nor did I find pleasure in
            his discourtesies to my nephew?

FAGIN: Next you'll ask me to credit your ruthless treatment of Nephew
            Nick with a similar design. How should it go? Allow the case:
            you knew to refuse him charity; for experience had long taught
            you its softening effects: in times of crisis made men vulnerable,
            resourceless, unable to fend for themselves, dependent upon
            others' good-heartedness; *viz.*, the stripling's feckless father.
            Allow the case: you knew the price of receiving, and relying on,
            others' charity: prostituted one's integrity; *viz.*, the Kenwigs.
            Allow the case: you knew, beforehand, the result of Nephew
            Nick's employment with Squeers: tested his mettle, tried his
            feisty pride and arrogance. But allow, too, this case: from your
            nephew's eye-opening and fist-dispensing initiation at Squeers's
            establishment you little expected his deduction: the categorical
            revelation of some deep-dyed villainy in you.

RALPH: Allow *this* case: Noggs's discovering to him a copy of Fanny
            Squeers's libelous letter authorised his right to saddle a high horse
            of righteous indignation; notwithstanding Noggs's having advised
            him of my capacity to guess the truth behind the maid's scurrility?

FAGIN: And allow the case: fancying that high dudgeon became his
            countenance and compelled a posture difficult for striplings to
            resist; he felt obliged to render a defiant performance during his
            interview with Miss La Creevy, upon his return from Squeers's
            school: 'I desire to confront him,' (you, sir) 'to justify myself and
            to cast his duplicity and malice in this throat.'

RALPH: Indeed; so allow but yet another case: the roots of such lunatic
            conclusions drew water from his suppressed outrage at Gregsbury,

who'd proposed making a toad-eater of him, and from his demeaning role as inglorious tutor to the Kenwigs's children, answerable to the pompous Lillyvick.

FAGIN: And allow, finally, this case: dander up, he cast you as scapegoat, rashly heedless of any virtuous motives in your employing him with Squeers. Much less could he begin to appreciate your gruff exposure of his alleged atrocities to his mother and sister; endeavouring, as a charitable reading of your behaviour might express it, to steel them to the prospect of a modern, urban existence, family togetherness an exception, not the rule.

RALPH: To be the object of a charitable reading, however qualified by allowances, suddenly stirs a most bizarre sensation, an unaccountable feeling of (what was it Miss Squeers called it? yes!) 'unliquidated pity' for my nephew, benighted creature that he was. After all, should I have expected different behaviour from such a chivalrous young donkey? I knew the kind of woman (horrors!) to whom my brother had chained himself (truly, in wedlock!); and I should have guessed that disdain, disregard, and disparagement of me would have been the only attitudes my nephew would have heard expressed during his youth.

FAGIN: Disregard, it was, which first threw me the hint that your history explained why you were, as Miss La Creevy called you, a 'cross-grained old savage.' To which your niece responded, here, with the timid supposition, 'It's only his manner, I believe; he was disappointed in early life I think I have heard, or has had his temper soured by some calamity.' Her uncertainty about your history— she *thinks* she has heard!—speaks folios on your brother's lack of regard for you. Until, of course, lying on his deathbed, he thought it prudent to address his impecunious family to you. Doubtful whether he ever reflected upon what growing up in your shoes was like, raised as the two of you were by an old Adam, whose favouritism could not but breed the very perniciousness which explains Cain's biblical wrath. Ah! found it; your recollection: 'comparisons were drawn between us—always in my disfavour. *He* was open, liberal, gallant, gay; *I* a crafty hunks of cold and stagnant blood, with no passion but love of saving, and no spirit beyond a thirst for gain. I recollected it well when I first saw this whipster; but I remember it better now.'

RALPH: But Nephew Nick could scarce be expected to know of this. Still less could he have guessed the source of some of my early hatred of him: here, his being 'young and gallant, and perhaps like the stripling who had brought dishonor and loss of fortune' on my head, my Leicestershire brother-in-law. Yet, were he to have known of that resemblance, it's unlikely that he'd have shown tolerance for my situation; not even did our historian choose to correct Brooker's version of my marriage, call into question my brother-in-law's cruel seizure of his legal rights over my bride, the which prevented us from normalising our wedlock and legitimising our son's infant years.

FAGIN: Nor did our historian call into question another blotting: Brooker's insinuation that the cause of your wife's elopement with another man, after seven years' marriage to you, was *your* refusal to acknowledge the marriage at the cost of losing her inheritance. Well might we wonder for whom to feel 'unliquidated pity': your nephew, or our historian! But for you—may I confess it?—I have admiration. Especially for the dignity with which you chose to conduct yourself before your accusers: neither stopping them to extenuate your past behaviour, nor to challenge Brooker's distortions; nor succumbing (like my Monks) to their hectoring. Even the dignity of your suicide I admire, cliche though it has been for stage usurers to so end their lives. In your instance exists—may I believe?—a silent dramatic declaration: your apprehending the futility of seeking understanding or compassion from any in that country.

RALPH: I bow to your applause. But on condition: that you bow, in turn, to my compliment. For may I commend your consummate performance in that dismal prison cell on the eve of your hanging, commend your final endeavour to impress upon your antagonists their thoroughly un-Christian conduct? Ah, come, come! Now is no time, crafty old Jew, to feign perplexity. Yes. I refer to your behaviour upon the arrival of Brownlow and Oliver. Not that you hadn't already won some compassion: from our historian with your courtroom conduct and from me with your action of driving away with curses those charitable and venerable men of your own persuasion, who'd come to pray beside you. Pathetic were you: desperate and fearful of dying upon the scaffold; deprived of the means to end your life with the quiet dignity of a suicide; forced to slake a mob's rapacious thirst. Oh! in the name of Justice, to be certain. But what self-command you were still capable of marshalling!

FAGIN: If any, my dear, it was generated by my outrage at Brownlow bringing Master Twist to my cell. Falsely pretending to need Monks's papers, in truth he was maliciously gloating over his triumph, impressing upon Twist the fate he'd been saved from, grinding into Twist's consciousness the eternal gratitude which he had better be sure to tender to his adopting parent.

RALPH: But the irony of your acerbic wit! Answering Twist's request to join him in a prayer, you commend his ability to gull others' belief in his sincerity, mocking the silly reliance upon prayer as corrective to the abundant social evils of that city. Encouraging his cry, 'God forgive this wretched man,' you tell him, in the savage sarcasm of disguised lunacy, 'That's right, that's right. That'll help us on.' And then, being restrained by attendants, you send him off with cry upon cry, searing his consciousness—it is to be hoped—for his callow betrayal of the first man who befriended him.

FAGIN: But best of all, my crafty hunks, did you detect the scene whose shadow I sought to mirror? Leaning upon Master Twist, pretending he was assisting a beaten man, staggering towards the cell-door in a state of distraction, pressing the scabbed knuckles of my right hand upon the bandage of linen cloth about my head: my riddle: what did I endeavour to conjure?

RALPH: Ah! What else! You crafty genius: the Jew being led off for succour by the Good Samaritan. How excellent. And lost on all the Christians, to be certain.

FAGIN: But what's this interruption? What is this dripping, ugly, small lord of creation, kicking along the floor a volume much like ours?

RALPH: Stay, my ungainly dwarf or infant phenomenon! By whose authority do you bring into these chambers a doglike smile, a malodorous cigar, a distorted face, and (what's this he's strewn upon the floor?) bloody stake, gigantic prawns, wilted watercress, and hard eggs, shells and all?

FAGIN: Dare we presume yet another, a small Cain, my dear?

QUILP: Quilp's the name. Daniel Quilp, if you please.

A Rejection Letter—And More—
for Melville's "The Bell-Tower"

For forty years George William Curtis was principal editor of *Harper's Monthly*, wrote most of its monthly "Editor's Easy Chair" columns, and had considerable say over the writing published in the successful, middle-class magazine. *Nile Notes of a Howadji* (1851) and *The Howadji in Syria* (1852) established his literary credentials and the calling cards whereby, in 1853, he gained admittance to his duties in the "countingroom" of the House of Harper. Lyceum lecturing increased his fame, involvement in various reform movements gave him political prominence, and good judgment made him indispensable to the Harper brothers.[1] Yet today his name is recognized, if at all, only by students of minor nineteenth-century men of letters, by scholars of the heyday in American magazines, and by, perhaps, a few handfuls of Melville critics.

It is this last group that may find the following five items of interest, for they document a brief sequence in the fate of "The Bell-Tower," one of the stories Melville had submitted for publication to *Harper's*. The story, on occasion denigrated as "most inept," has received its due share of critical commentary.[2]

But Curtis's heretofore unpublished responses show a surprising measure of discernment—and, it must be owned, feverishness—often denied earlier magazine editors, for he pries away at "authorial intention," an issue central to much of Melville's fiction.

The five items may engage two other kinds of readers as well. First, fellow writers who, disappointed by the return of their submissions in the mail, customarily assume that rejection letters formally terminate an editor's responses. These items, perhaps exceptional, suggest otherwise. Second, fellow readers who take interest in reading about how yet another reader confronts a text. It may be instructive to observe one who peels away his onion-layered public selves, stripping to his private, unsheathed self. It may even be consolatory to witness, perhaps, a mirror-image grappling with a stubborn text, trying to wrest from it some significance.

Rather than relegate the matter to a minimizing endnote, I wish here to acknowledge two debts. One to Judith O'Keefe Earney, now-retired curator of

110

the George William Curtis Collection in the Staten Island Institute of Arts and Sciences; without her professional assistance and encouragement and success in securing publication permission, these documents would remain all but entombed. The other to the Louise A. Froude Foundation; a generous travel grant enabled me to ascertain the authenticity of these Curtis documents by visiting the other repositories of his materials: the Abernathy, Boston Public, Fruitlands, Houghton, Longfellow, Massachusetts Historical, and New York Public libraries.

Item 134—Memorandum: Fletcher Harper to George William Curtis

[This memorandum, from the youngest of the four famous founders of the House of Harper, alludes, variously, to several stories published either in *Harper's* or its rival *Putnam's*, for which Curtis was an advisory editor[3]; to Donald G. Mitchell, a fellow editor who began "The Editor's Easy Chair" column and who had authored, under the pen name Ik Marvel, *Reveries of a Bachelor, or a Book of the Heart*; to Curtis's satirical essays, collected as *Potiphar Papers*; to the December 1853 fire that burned to the ground the publishers' Pearl and Cliff Streets establishment; to the charitable Cheeryble brothers of Dickens's *Nicholas Nickleby*; and to sobriquets identified in Item 135. The volumes itemizing Melville's correspondence contain no record of the letter that prompts Mr. Harper's memorandum.[4]]

The Counting-room, May 27, 1854

Confound it, Howadji. Rec'd another letter from Melvil—on white paper, not the customary blue.[5] This one hard on the heels of yesterday's acknowledgement of rec'pt of $100 from us for his 2-part story "Paradise of Bachelors & Tartarus of Maids" [Davis and Gilman, 168—69]. Today's letter was accompanied with two *more* stories. Yesterday I proofed galley for our June issue. I found in it another story of his: "Poor Man's Pudding & Rich Man's Crumbs." Checked the accounts on Melvil. Shows we've also paid him for 2 more stories, "Happy Failure" & "Fiddler." Plan to publish them in summer issues, do you?

No, it's not presumptuous of me to ask. After all, you know better than I the decline of Melvil's literary reputation. His novels get harder & and harder to understand, I'm told. & we know they're harder & harder to sell, as our records show. But here we are, printing his stories, one after the next, just as fast, it seems, as he writes them.

With his "Pudding & Crumbs" fresh in mind, I pulled this "Bachelors and Maids" story from the files. Read it. Confound it if I can make anything out of it. A gathering of bachelors for a convivial supper & camaraderie? A made-up story? Or true account of such a men's gathering? Melvil satirizing, like your Potiphar Papers, society? Can't help but feel that Mitchell'll see oblique barbs aimed at his Reveries. & that "Maids." A travel document? A mercantilist's journey to a manufactory? Any places you know of with all-female labour? Some humbuggery that Melvil's up to? Merry-andrewing, I'd guess.

Head of steam up, I pulled & read the stories in today's mail. "Two Temples" would get us in deep Dutch with city readers who'd instantly recognize its attack on Grace Church & its "opulent auditory." & to compare a temple of worship & a temple of entertainment as institutions of charity—to latter's favor: close to blasphemy. We could watch the Mayor's ears go beet-red over *that*, we could!

& now this "Bell-Tower." First half good. But after the artist dies the story drags. All speculation and guesswork. & ends with trite moral: pride goes before a fall!

In 3 words: viz, return both stories to Melvil.

Yes, Howadji, I lack your literary taste. & yes, I'm interfering with responsibilities I gave you. & yes, I hold a grudge against Melvil for that $300 advance we gave him (on the eve of our fire!) for his tortoise adventures—only to see them in print in Putnam's [Davis and Gilman, 164–65]. Then the gall to write us (in February, was it?) & and promise to call on us in March so's to inform us when his proverbially slow tortoise would be ready to crawl into market [Davis and Gilman, 167–68].

Yesterday's letter *continues* to ask for word about the tortoise extract. He implies that he's sent us the story. But no such item in the files. The man's a nuisance! Does he take us to be the Cheeryble Brothers?

My recommendation, Howadji: withdraw support of Melvil's literary endeavours. Of course publish "Failure" & "Fiddler." We paid for 'em. Paid for "Bachelors & Maids" too. But hold that pair until next year.

Have left Melvil's letter and stories on your desk. Odd that he mentions our reconsidering "Two Temples." Has it been here before? Or has he misdirected his letter—as he did with that oddity of a story on that scrivener. Note that he asks for "early attention," solicits us to apprise him equally early of the result.

Indeed, *Do So!* & remind him who Harper's readers are. Ha! Why not write an Easy Chair on his story? Typical of the swarms of stories that the daily mail-bag dumps on the counting-room floor, stories you have to read and return. (Or have you too much sympathy for a fellow author of exotic lands?)

Confound the bother, Howadji, to have to write all of this out. Your double duties here & at Putnam's causes no end of inconvenience. So what, if I surround myself with minute-men, as you like to say. What avails that to me, if the ablest of them is absent?

[Signed] The Major

Item 135—Letter: G. W. Curtis to Herman Melville

[Enclosed in square brackets are words and phrases which Curtis, on the holograph, crossed out. In its upper left margin—capitalized, parenthesized, and doubly underscored—is the instruction, COPY, suggesting that the letter was copied and sent to Melville. The volumes itemizing Melville's correspondence, however, show no record of his having received it.]

Franklin Square
N.Y. May 29, 1854

Herman Melville, Esq.
Dear Sir,

I have the honor to acknowledge the receipt both of your letter of the 27th inst. and of your two stories. The honor, however, is accompanied with the regrettable task of returning your stories, primarily at the [strong] urging of Mr. Fletcher Harper, who finds them unsuitable for our pages at this time.

Speaking for his elder brothers, he advises that I [apprise] remind you of the [policy] traditions of the Monthly since it first voyaged forth. Above all, the brothers have been [most] anxious that it be popular in a high and generous sense. Mr. Fletcher Harper has asseverated many a time—among ourselves and visiting literati in the countingroom—"The test of an article's excellence is if it tells its own story clearly and requires no explanation."

To this [standard] test his older brother John would often add, "A story must be proper for family reading and inspection. The House of Harper is the flagship—correct, Major? (asking concurrence from eldest brother James)—the flagship of the family." Upon which statement and interrogatory James Fletcher would utter, "Must maintain the tradition of our most famous series, The Family Library."

Early in my employment [with the estimable Methodist brethren] in this renowned House, Mr. Melville, Mr. Fletcher Harper (better known in the countingroom by the appellation "The Major") soberly commanded, "Questions of morals, doubtful words or allusions, and double meanings have no place, no place at all, in our pages." He was seconded by The Colonel, Brother John: "Our commodity is merchandise, not metaphysics." Often, during my first year, holding aloft some manuscript, The Major would declaim—to the air or to anyone within earshot—"Who is supposed to read *this*? *Our* subscribers? The *people*? The *plain* people? Or somebody else's subscribers? Philosophers and poets? Confound it! Why can't authors show readers good family courtesy?"

It is with such statements in mind that I, acting on behalf of the House, regretfully return your stories. Should you wish to [send us] write further stories for our pages, I would recommend you to the above statements in advance of [your beginning] embarking upon your authorial enterprises.

With highest respect, I remain,
G. W. Curtis

Item 136—Letter: G. W. Curtis to Herman Melville

[The headnote to this item, "Do Not Mail," repeated on the following two items as well, should explain their absence—although not the reasons for their absence—from the records of Melville's correspondence.]

Franklin Square
N. Y. June 1, 1854

Herman Melville, Esq.
Dear Sir,

It is with several misgivings that I follow my formal letter of the 29th inst. with this letter and its enclosure. Well might you wonder at my reasons. Indeed, sir, I can assure you that I wonder at them as well.

It may be that I wish to soften the blows—artistic and economic—of having your stories returned, knowing as I do that one of them, Two Temples, had earlier been returned to you with letters from Messrs. Briggs and Putnam, both editors fearful lest their church readers find its *point* disturbing [Leyda 1:487–88]. (Had I not been away, lecturing in upstate New York, I might have intervened and prevailed over their timidity.) It may be that I intend for my discourse (the enclosure) upon your Bell-Tower, however supercilious it may strike you, to give some guidance, should you care to continue sending your stories here. It may be that I wish merely to commune with a fellow author, someone whose friendship with a mutual friend (I refer of course to Miles Coverdale)[6] charges me with fraternal obligations from which I can not, nor choose not to, shrink. It may even be—as I venture to own, in confidence, to you—that I grow restive at the commercialism of my employers. (Would that you could witness the slight shudder of my frame upon hearing Mr. Fletcher Harper's predictable rejoinders; when, for instance, suddenly flanked in a colloquy on the score of moral issues, he invariably fires off, with self-satisfied jocosity, "If you come to metaphysics, I can't follow you.")

Whatever my reasons for this letter and its enclosure of my "Easy Chair" column, I must apprise you that in writing the column, I had been emboldened by Fletcher Harper's certitude that the story was poor and inappropriate for our pages. Upon completion of the column I was pleased with the ease of my handiwork. Yet, upon being awakened in the middle of the night, by harbor foghorns, I found myself reflecting further upon my handiwork. I considered its probable consequence for you, even though I had prudently guarded your identity in it. With a rush of feeling I remembered my indignation at Fitz-James O'Brien's condescending review of your work in the second issue of *Putnam's*, now over a year ago. The impertinence of his "wholesome advice," offered to prevent you from "a hundred future follies!"[7]

(You might appreciate knowing that Messrs. Briggs and Putnam chose to discontinue that projected series by O'Brien, persuaded by the warmth—if not the cogency—of my arguments.)

But who should now find himself offering advice? (How seductive is an editor's power, tempting even well-intentioned men into wielding it cavalierly.) With no little embarrassment I also remembered my initial pleasure when, scarcely a month after the "O'Brien incident," arrived a letter from my old acquaintance of Brook Farm and Concord years, Henry Thoreau. My pleasure curdled into chagrin upon discovering that the honorable member for Blackberry Pastures was requesting the return of "A Yankee in Canada." Irritated at my editing of his manuscript (especially my excisions of what to me constituted defiant pantheism), he withdrew the rest of it; Putnam's could not but discontinue the series after just three installments.[8]

Mindful, then, of the injuries which my editorial power is susceptible of inflicting, I resolved thereupon to withdraw the column which from my pen so easily flowed. Written yesterday, only the compositor and I had read it—if a compositor can be said to read any of the words which he sets in a composing stick, transfers to galley, and wedges into a chase.

I returned to the city early this morning, saw to the dismantling of the galley, and gathered up and destroyed all but one of the fugitive prints. I enclose that print, apologizing for its smudges of printer's ink.

The article may discover to you some acumen. It will be sure to discover to you more obtuseness. Whether my remarks are near or far from the mark of what you intended by the tale, however, only you can determine. (That they may be one or the other—or both?—should reflect upon what you have wrought and I have read.)

In closing, may I recommend that you mail Bell-Tower to "Harry Franco" (Mr. Charles F. Briggs) at Putnam's? As literary advisor to him and Mr. Putnam (as well as to the Cheerybles!), I am confident that I can be as influential on behalf of this story as on your scrivener story and, Mr. Salvator R. Tarnmoor, your Galapagos sketches.[9] Besides, the astute deliberations of the editorial conclave at Putnam's is constitutionally more receptive than Harper's to American writers, honoring its full title, Monthly Magazine of American Authors.

Other duties await my attention. To them I must turn before seeking the leisure of Newport society for summer respite and rustication.

> Wishing you the best,
> I am and remain,
> Truly, your friend,
> Geo. Wm. Curtis

Item 137—"The Editor's Easy Chair"

Even as we adjust our seat, turn away from rhapsodizing on the city in the summer and exclaiming the magic of the engraved heads by Samuel Laurence[10]; even as we clear a spot on our table, whereupon we may place a quire of Bath paper, and our office ink-horn; we glance reluctantly at the frowning pile of manuscripts awaiting our eyes. Our discourses upon the swarming numbers of correspondents, and lecturers, and popular song-writers, you have read; yet, we have not stretched, on the canvas of our page, discourse upon the tribe of tale-tellers, a discourse long hanging in our pen's nib.

Could our readers imagine the hosts of tales that swell our daily bags of incoming mail, tales which the Easy Chair must find time to read and pass judgment upon, then our readers might neither envy our chair's presumed power nor accept the appellation of its seat as "easy." Indeed, difficult is the time-consuming task of reading these many tales. More difficult is the responsibility of judging them.

Sometimes our judgment is swift. A tale by young Nathan Golightly, or Triptolemus, may immediately discover its shortcomings to our well-read eyes: insensitive language, vapid characters, hackneyed plot, operatic dialogue, or utter lack of poetry and feeling. Or a tale by Tabithy Toadstool may artlessly ask us to shed a "melodious tear" for her sentimental twaddle.[11] Or, again, a tale may violate our standards of family reading and inspection; may diverge from probity by addressing questions of morality; may venture to ignore the expectations of our readers. Yet, another tale may be so contrived as to prompt our swift acceptance; neither city flippant nor country dull: such as those which adorn the double columns of this very issue.

Sometimes our judgment is slow; when we recognize a respected author's name, we rekindle our alertness with his reputation; and read his tale with expectancy. Yet, on occasion, we finish it in perplexity. Such we find to be the case with a tale we have had the regrettable duty to return just yesterday to a well-known author, the mention of whose name would instantly arouse our readers. Without unveiling his name, his tale avails us of an opportunity with which to point our periods and stuff our chair. Verily, our comments, estimating his tale, may prove instructive, if not to him, then perhaps to brethren of the quill and to our readers. The tale runs thus:

A renaissance artist, renowned for his genius as architect, sculptor, and mechanician, is commissioned to create a tower, in which he chooses to install a mechanized clock. No ordinary clock, mind; his is a beautiful bell on which he has engraved twelve houri, each representing one of the diurnal dozen. The bell-ringer, neither acolyte nor octogenarian, is an automaton, sculpted and wrought to move along an iron track and strike, by dint of steel muscle, the several hours. The erection of tower and clock stirs considerable interest, both among public officials and the populace. From miles around the latter gather to observe the rise of the majestic pile and, thereby, to pay homage to its creator. At last the appointed day arrives on which the clock in the tower is to commence its mechanized destiny. At the very stroke of the afternoon's first hour, however, instead of numinous knell or musical peal, the onlookers hear but a dull sound. Officials rush up the tower's stairway and report what they find: the artist dead, felled by the automaton's hammer. One year later, to the very day, an earthquake topples the entire edifice.

Our summary strips the ornamentation from the tale, leaving it to stand before you like some half-dressed rustic, to sound like some antiquarian's anecdote. Like the sun's ray's upon mystery-filled mists, our summary evaporates the evocative and provocative hints hoarded in the tale. Evocative is the tale's power to recall to the Easy Chair the famous tower clocks of Berne, Massina, and that in the Cathedral at Strasbourg. Yet, it is the artist's automaton and its mechanical prowess, that evokes the clearer recall, Maillardet's writing doll. Wrought so ingeniously, with unbelievably intricate combinations of levers, rods, pulleys, cams, and spring motors, this gloriously Gallic invention writes one English and two French poems, draws three graceful pictures, one a veritable schooner. First seen by the Easy Chair in London, when it was fitted out as a little boy in court dress, its most recent costume was that of a French soldier. (What dress it will appear in next can only be conjectured, if not dreaded, now that it has been purchased, we are informed, by P. T. Barnum for his American Museum.) The toppling of the tower can not but evoke, as well, the destruction of so many of our metropolis's fine buildings, most recently Tripler Hall, about which we have scarcely finished writing.[12]

If our observation is penetrant, of far greater import is the tale's provocative preoccupation with questions of art. It questions, whether we should regard as artists only those whose genius demonstrates itself in the *beaux arts*: poetry and literature, music, painting, sculpture, and architecture. Should we widen our categories to include the useful arts: inventions and domestic arts, be they clocks and culinary exhibits, a retractable cane and a beautifully arranged bouquet of flowers? When our author refers to his artist as artisan, architect and *mechanician*, he asks us to consider, what differentiates an artist from an artisan? Do we draw a line at utility? If a wrought object is useful, did its maker aspire to be a mere artisan; if useless, to be an artist? Does an object's utility deprive it of regard as an object of art?

One scene in our author's tale especially probes this question, of whether an object's utility deprives it of regard as a work of art. In a scene with two town magistrates, the artist refers to an earlier commission he had fulfilled. To commemorate the republic's founder, the chief magistrate's very ancestor, the artist had wrought one hundred seals of that noble's head, seals to be used by customs officials for, we must presume, taxation purposes. The public at large, and all those who had used the five-score seals, believed them to be identical graven images. The artist corrects the magistrates; he instructs them that the image on each seal differed from its brothers in some unique respect, that no two were the same. Our author here asks whether an object's individuality as well as its lack of utility must be the other trademark of an objet d'art. Is it the task of the artisan to make a set of objects as identical to one another as possible? Is it, on the other hand, the task of the artist to make each item unique, deserving of attention to itself?

Our comments have surely whetted your appetite. "Give us the tale, Easy Chair," I hear you call. "Let us ponder the prolific themes it has furnished. Allow us to crack for ourselves its shell, pry out its nut without assistance."

Could we print only the summarized tale, we would promptly do so. Unfortunately, the tale, with matter to enchain and enchant us, does not terminate with the surprising death of the artist, stricken by his automaton's heavy hammer. Regrettably, it unravels itself for several more pages, devotes two-fifths as much space, after the events of the tale are told, as on those we have summarized for you. There is, in this last two-fifths, matter which slowed our judgment and prompted our decision to return the tale to its author.

"What," you ask, "what was in those two-fifths which made the tale unacceptable? Questions of morality? Matter violating the sacred seclusion of the family circle?"

Would that such were the case, dear readers. Were it so, there would be little call for the Easy Chair's discourse. Regrettably those two-fifths were filled with conjecture and cliche. The former trumpeted engaging mystery; the latter trampled well-worn morality. Full to the brim with such words as "suppose," "supposition," "opine," "conjecture," and "surmise," these last two-fifths of the tale dwell upon the mysteries of how the artist had become ensnared in his own engine, and why he had wrought his engine at all. The artist's secretive behavior, while alive, spurred speculation after his death as to his designs and motives. Interpreting his motive humanistically, some believed he wished to improve man's lot by creating an automaton which would spare man the dreary task of ringing the bell on each of the day's four and twenty hours. Others believed that in his actions lurked an irreligious motive: by creating a creature who could rival, outstay, and rule nature, the artist sought, Frankenstein-fashion, to rival God's creations.

The answers, to these and other conjectures, our author chooses not to provide. Shrouding in factitious mystery the very questions raised, he thwarts the very appetite to which his tale has appealed.

Such conjectures would answer, were our author to resolve them, common as they are in our ponderings of our fellow man's behaviors, eccentric or normal. Yet, our author, leaving them unresolved, suspends, in mid-air, the mystery of the artist's motive. Titillated with the expectancy of an answer, which our author seems intent on not providing, we are justified in terming him, with due respect, a coquette.

Beguiling in a tale as in a woman, coquetry can tease us into pleasurable by-paths of uncertainty and mystery. Yet, coquetry has naught to do with cliche, which walks us down a broad boulevard and onto the common of certainty and predictability. It is, however, with cliche that our author ends his tale. Declaring that his artist has stooped to conquer nature; calling his an utilitarian ambition; equating his death with some formula whereby blind slaves, in obeying blinder masters, slay them; he reduces the entire tale to a tired moral: Pride goeth before a fall. This cliche discovers our author, unhealthily, desperately, grasping for an easy harbor to which he can moor his foundering tale and its shifting cargo of meaning.

As our readers might now agree, the tale which we have—with due deliberation—found unfit for publication, deserves our decision. May the tale's author, and many less-gifted prosers, who seek the guerdon of being printed in our pages, take heed from the guidance of our somewhat sharp criticism, offered as it is, in neither malice nor mockery.

Item 138—Early-Morning Missive: Hafiz to Salvator R. Tarnmoor

[Italicized in angle brackets I have identified figures, numbers, strikeovers, and statements that virtually clutter the margins and text of this document, a foolscap holograph. "Hafiz" was a nom de plume above which Curtis wrote music criticism; Salvatore R. Tarnmoor, as previously noted, the one beneath which Melville published *The Encantadas*.]

Harbor foghorns, again! Once awakened by them, what find I in their wake, Herr Herman, but your tale. Why does it bewitch me? Berobed and touseled, I tug my muttonchops, pace my parlor. Did I not dismiss your flawed tale with my discourse? Have I not made amends for effrontery by dismantling that Easy Chair? How is it that I brought your tale to my lodgings, mingled among other papers? Earlier I laughed at such happenstance. By now I have rued such laughter. To put your tale to rest, thereby to be accorded my well-earned rest: more discourse, perhaps a palliative, or purgative? <*Left margin: a blotch of ink, fashioned into a heavily hubbed, many-spoked wheel.*> Two questions nag & gnaw. <*Superscript text, running up right margin: How soothing to shrink problems to numbers! A feint to exhibit control, mastery, certitude?*> Question One: How to view your artist's intentions? Question Two: How to view your tale's teller? *<Right Margin: Is teller INEPT? EPT?>*

<Left margin: a heavily serifed, Roman numeral I, framed in an embattled border.> To answer Question One, Good Sir, let me count the ways, as my acquaintance, E. B. Browning, enumerating on another theme, expresses it. Am I to view your Bannadonna within a frame of SCIENCE? If so, then I am to regard him, as the Easy Chair remarked, an *humanistic inventor*, am I not? Freeing mankind from enslavement to mechanical duties *<Stricken text: & routine drudgery>*, his intention is to prophesy automata of far superior skills in far distant times? Does he betoken technological artists, whose will is to serve mankind not God? *<Arrow to left margin and vertical text up the page: N.B.: No mention of either Church or Cathedral in connection with bell-tower. No Priests. Only Magistrates.>*

OR

Or is such an intention *<Stricken text: amenable to an alternative>* susceptible of subversion, perhaps brought on by the midnight hour? Is his intention that of some *satanical caricaturist*, bent on mocking man as a creature of mechanical forces? Does your now-malignant scientist *<Right margin: Cf. Coverdale's Rappaccini and Aylmer?>* seek to reduce man to an automaton? Does he scornfully insinuate the notion blasphemous, that men, will-lessly, perform only those duties *<Superscript text: & those pleasures?>* set into motion by honored agencies: Family, Society, Nature, Convention, & God? Be so kind, my nocturnal friend: *<Left margin: My Incubus!>* Choose One?

<Left margin: a heavily serifed, Roman numeral II, framed carefully in fretted trim or molding.> Am I to view your Bannadonna within a frame of RELIGION? If so, then was the Easy Chair again correct to regard him a *theological rebel*? Is his intention to rival God's creation, man, by elevating his own creation, the automaton, to such heights as will deserve the wonder & awe & worship accorded to God? Does his manufactory, in arrogant arrogation, intend the creation of an object deserving idolatry? *<Right margin, text running down the page: N.B.: Observers must look up, as in [unclear word: deference? reverence?], to artist's work?>*

OR

Or is it your artist's intention to be *biblical servant*? Is his creation "to the greater glory of God?" [Curious: no defiant gesture accompanies the artist's posture, as he stands atop the mounting pile at each day's end.] Does your artist exercise his genius in silent honor of the gifts God has bestowed upon him. (Let not the left hand, &tc. Parable of the talents?) Your choice, sir?

<Left margin: an arabic numeral 3, unadorned.> Am I to view your Bannadonna within a literal frame of ART? If so, am I to regard him a *vain-*

glorious artist? He feeds his self-esteem on others' homage, elevates himself by keeping his activities & designs shrouded in mystery, *<Superscript text: condescendingly>* conceals his contempt for his public & his masters beneath feigned concern, & supercilious modesty, & arch deference?

OR

Or, Master Melville, is it his intention to acquit himself as is becoming of a *sincere artist?* Is his behavior with the magistrates genuine, deferring to his superiors without irony or sarcasm? [N.B.: I read in their colloquy his sincere concern for their well-being; true, your "milder magistrate" terms your artist's replies "supercilious": yet, your chief magistrate tush-tushes him.] Does your artist's silence acknowledge that his motives are *<Stricken word: irreverent>* irrelevant to the work he creates? Does he maintain a curtain of secrecy as warrant for aesthetic integrity, to displace attention from himself to his creation? A choice, again, sirrah? *<Left margin: a drawing of the scales of Libra.>*
  <Left margin: the arabic numeral 4, bracketed with successively larger trims of cable, running scroll, and meander, respectively.> Can I stretch your artist one more way? Am I to view him within a frame of SOCIETY? Does he mean for himself to be seen a *republican benefactor?* Exceeding the restrictions of his commission, creating a tower which excels all other republics' monuments, is it his intention to show the artist as plebian servant of the state, undemeaned by his tasks, be they to engrave seals used by customs officials or to erect public monuments?

OR

Or is your artist but a *commercial entrepreneur? <Right margin: My ledger: a Debit for every Credit!>* He applies his talents, his gifts, only as means to an end—a commission for currency—not as an end in itself? Debasing art by making its objects commodities, he makes his skills serve the marketplace, creates objects as self-advertisements? (Will he publish notices of his "schemes of other and still loftier piles," sketches FOR SALE?)

OR

<Right margin What? Another Debit?> Or is it his intention to be viewed a *social revolutionary?* Does your artist's automaton figure forth the destruction of masters by their alleged slaves? Does your artist take especial pleasure in exercising his genius in ways which will instruct his social superiors to recognize their inferiority? Indeed, is it this which explains your orphan, your "unblest foundling," who, some may claim, jests with noble offspring of the republic's founder? At the risk of your tale foundering in its own foundry, dare you allude,

<Stricken text: and dare I pun so abominably!> as in your tale of those Tartarean Maids, to our southern institution of slavery?

<First words of the next two clauses, "whereas," are oversized, Old English text letters.> WHEREAS, your artist permits me to assign him such conflicting intentions, Mr. Tarnmoor-Melville; and WHEREAS, your artist allows me to choose among intentions; therefore, be it resolved: Either you have wrought a tale excellent or execrable. If your artist is so *<Stricken text: manipulable by>* malleable to my maunderings, then for what purpose have you, an artist, created such another artist? Or is that (OHO!) the rub? Is it *your* intention to contrive a tale which defies ascertaining *your* motive—as you represent yourself in your artist Bannadonna? If your purpose is such, then do you not challenge the assumption, *There are limits to authorial license?*

Some answers to Question One, M. Melville?

Darkness gives way to somber gray in the east, I perceive. But my eyes droop not, my skull a-buzz with Question Two: How to view your tale's teller?

But I question not. For have I not discovered to myself the answer???

All the suppositions, surmises, conjectures, & speculations: Do they not reveal the human craving to be fed (& to be satisfied with!) answers, to know & not be left in the dark, to solve mystery, end wonder, dispel uncertainty?

<Left margin: a vertical column of five, increasingly darker and larger daggers, extending to the end of the next paragraph.> Thus, sir, your tale pretends to revolve around a secretive artist. No. Not pretends. *Is* that. But more. Also revolves around any who would assign *A* motive or *ONE* intention to that artist. Those two-fifths of your tale, which elicited remonstrance from me, The Easy Chair: Do they not but discover an IN-tention to exhort one to pay serious ATtention to every artist's more vexing problem: will his creation be understood, either by the general public or by allegedly discerning viewers?

Yet more: will either audience accept the elusiveness, what your teller terms the "equivocal reference," of your creation? Will either accept, in one "fine personality," what your Bannadonna identifies as "ambiguous" faces? Or will both audiences seek, like some collector of insects, to pin your tale in its place, in a box, next some look-alike bug? Frustrating though your tale is in its refusal to permit me to fix it in some collector's box; yet, sir, does not that refusal celebrate the problem, honor the artist? [Curiously springs to mind your Bubblaluni's discourse on some work by Lombari, or whatever those names are. But I've no time to pull your Mardi from my lodging's bookshelves![13]]

To that celebration do you harness scorn *<Superscript text: or, better, compassion?>* for those who, like your magistrates or, indeed, the Easy Chair, clutch for that *one* answer to the problem? Yes. Compassion. Most for the teller of your tale. Indeed, it is he, not your artist, nor your speculating magistrates, who draws your tale's pathos, is it not? Is it not he who is your tale's pathetic "character?" You allow him to pretend to be an all-knowing teller, like those tellers of the novels into whom my friend Thackeray infuses himself. But if yours is all-knowing, an historian, then I allow, on one page, his being privy to your artist's motives. [N.B.: as your artist tarries atop the ever-ascending summit of the tower, your teller declares him, unequivocally, "wrapped in schemes of other and still loftier piles."] However, several pages later, I can not accept his ignorance in a crucial matter. Yet, ignorant your teller is: of whether, putting the finishing touches upon the figures on the bell, your artist was, *in fact*, too "absorbed" to notice the automaton sliding forward to execute its duty. Your teller, muzzy, permits that the artist's absorption was merely "surmised." <*Right margin: Surmised by whom? Himself? Others?*> [N.B.: your teller remarks Bannadonna's absorption: "absorption still further intensified, it may be, by his striving to abate that strange look of Una"; *it may be*, indeed!] (Do you grow weary? Does my tortuous thought require that you wend your way through it again? Consider your task slight in comparison with mine, given the hour.)

  <*Left margin: a drawing of a hand, index finger pointing to the text.*> It is your compassion, then is it, which leads your teller to end the tale with those horrendous cliches? With so much irresolution, for which you have had your teller strive, throughout the tale, do you sympathize with his task of having to resolve an unfinishable chord? [You will permit me the use of another of my sobriquets, Hafiz, to draw on a musical trope for discourse on a tale by Tarnmoor?] Is it, my cunning craftsman, is it your intention to permit your teller his cliches, expectant, thereby, of a discerning reader of finer sensibilities (our Miles Coverdale, perhaps?) to arrive at the awareness of their utter incongruity to the tale your teller has wrought?

  Or, revered sir, do I, victim of too little sleep, do I now commit <*Stricken text: flummoxed foibles*> felonious foolishness: do I become your tale's old blacksmith, venturing suspicions & foolish surmises? Do I assign to you a single motive for, one intention in, what you have wrought? Yea, verily: seek I to fix, with verbal pins, your very motive (correction: one of your motives) for those cliches? The habit, you must admit, is exceeding hard to break. Our appetite for certitude! Wed it to our prevalent taste for pertinency! Then admit neither to the temple of art? Leave both at the dining-room table? <*Superscript text: and the drawing room? and the countingroom?*> Allow them to wander in the marketplace? Hard discipline you impose, sir. Too aristocratic for the times?

  I droop, sir. Yet, it is not without some sense of satisfaction that I do so. Perhaps I have no cause for satisfaction, in your eyes. Perhaps you will wonder at the ponderous <*Unclear word: imponderable?*> pile of prose with which I have overwhelmed your small tale. Perhaps in the "chain of circumstantial inferences," which I have now drawn, there are many "absent or defective links?" Whether from you my labors deserve laurels or laughter, garlands or ashes, I can not now know. I believe, however, that I can now withdraw from my nibs,

& my ink-horn, & my quire of Bath paper, & my table, &, I shall earnestly hope, your tale.

Shall I send you these pages? Or the others I have, like some inebriated spider, spun? The sensible sunlight now beaming into my lodgings may influence that decision. Odd that I should have been so bewitched by your tale. Will it bewitch others, should it ever see print?

The world of commerce calls. Last duties before I seek the calming influence of Newport and, perhaps, some attentions from the eldest daughter of the Francis George Shaw family. <*Right margin: Are you not married to a Shaw? To the Chief Justice's daughter, have I not heard?*>[14]

My deep regard accompanies this madcap missive & its curious companions. I remain, honored author,

Most Sincerely,
Geo. Wm. Curtis

An Epilogue

Two final—and, some might say, fitting—twists. On June 18, 1855, from Providence, Rhode Island, Curtis, referring to a packet of stories submitted for his verdict, wrote to Joshua H. Dix, at that time one of the owners and editors of *Putnam's Magazine*. Among the stories was "The Bell-Tower," which Curtis informed Dix had "not passed muster." Yet on the following day Curtis wrote Dix again. Retracting his verdict, he now claimed the tale "too good to lose," calling it "picturesque & of a profound morality," declaring, it "has the touch of genius in it" [Leyda 1:502]. For the story, printed in the August 1855 issue of *Putnam's*, Melville was paid $37.50. But he returned the sum, declaring his belief that Dix and Edwards, *Putnam's* Publishers, had already "honored the draught" which he had "previously drawn upon" them for that amount [Davis and Gilman, 173].

Edward Hyde's
Full Statement of the Case

Och! The cramping and agony of these incarnations. Can they go on much longer? What's this? The debris next the glazed presses tells of yet another delivery of yet another chemist's sample, I see. And to no avail. From all appearances Harry has paced the floor since completing his crafted statement. Surely he has continued bemoaning the loss of control over his identity. Surely he has railed against me and the chemists, beseeched God's forgiveness, and decried his scientific enquiries. But just as surely he continued to write, believing himself clever enough to hide the octavo of his Full Statement from me.

During the struggle of what must be our final days, I have pondered whether I'll be capable of completing my own Full Statement, which I, too, have resolved to write. I ponder, too, whether Harry, should he discover my companion testament, will be able to restrain himself from hurling it into the fire, fearful that mine might lead sceptics to examine suspiciously his "confession." Indeed, I ponder as well which one, if either, of these Full Statements, Harry's or mine, will be discovered upon the termination of our twinned identities, when our "fleshly vestments," as he floridly designates them, are no more. Will that self-serving solicitor, Mr. Utterson, or the self-righteous servant, Mr. Poole, discover both his—the respectable Dr. Henry Jekyll's—and my—the reprehensible Mr. Edward Hyde's—Full Statements? Or will only that of my "creator," my fond parent's, be found? And should mine also be found, will it, too, be delivered up to interested parties for enquiry, as may so many of the other documents already entwined in these strange adventures? Or will it, like my voice and viewpoints, my remonstrances and rebuttals, be swept away and silenced, allowing me neither defence nor cross-examination, neither opportunity for acquittal nor occasion for vindication? Our judicial practice assures even a convicted felon of being asked whether he has anything to say why sentence should not be passed upon him. Shall I be denied that custom?

The wrenching alternations between our two bodily states has made painful these final days and exacerbated Harry's frantic endeavours, seeking desperately to replicate the potion that enabled our transformations from one form to the other. During that interval it can not be believed that I failed to discover and read his Full Statement. But I have chosen not to "tear it in pieces" as he fears, for notwithstanding his characteristic aspersions, I harbour no "ape-like spite." Indeed I find his statement a shrewd instance of what barristers have in mind when they engage in or fault their adversaries for "special pleading." It is a document decidedly worthy of preservation. Moreover, I have confidence, warranted or not, that the truly discerning will see through its self-pitying confession and, more important, its moralistic melodrama in which the reputable doctor grasps every opportunity and twists every incident to vilify me. Truly, the obfuscatory fog of his Full Statement, I must believe, will come, one day, to be seen through by careful and attentive readers for what it is, a document of racial scapegoating. Furthermore, when it shall be knit together with the other biased accounts of my behavior, the discernment of those same readers may well lead them to ponder whether I—and others as blighted or "deformed" in appearance as I—have been judged harshly and unjustly, according to predispositions of our culture that can not but guarantee condemnation. It is to arm such readers with pertinent considerations by which they may test Harry's bona fides that I pen this statement, confiding myself in the humanity of my fellow man.

Surely it ought to come as no surprise that I, whom some will belittle as but a Gothic gnome or troglodytic gargoyle, am literate enough to write out my Full Statement, a testamentary document to answer and challenge Harry's. The reports of my spoken words, whether by Mr. Utterson, his kinsman Mr. Enfield, Dr. Lanyon, or Harry himself vouchsafe my knowledge and facility in the use of the Queen's English. And the back-slant of my penmanship, which requires no great student and critic of handwriting to examine and opine on, will yield up to any attentive reader both the recognition that it is nearly identical to Harry's and that recognition's corollary, that my mental capacities mirror his as well. One other resistance to my Full Statement will nest in the rationalistic narrow-mindedness of persons who will protest that I could not be in possession of certain information I will refer to. Such resistance should melt away when readers recall that for the two months after my alleged murder of Sir Danvers Carew, Harry and Mr. Utterson saw each other almost daily; it should be hard to imagine that during that time Mr. Utterson had not repeated to Harry his kinsman's "Story of the Door" or his own encounters with me. What Harry knew, it should go without saying, I, too, knew. Moreover, his degrees in the law, DCL and LLD, are at my service as well as his: I am as well acquainted as he with such cases as the duplicitous Deacon Brodie and that penitential forger, Dr. Dodd. But unlike the latter, I have no Dr. Johnson to champion my cause with appeals, petitions, letters, and sermons on my behalf. Nor could I entertain hope to enlist the likes of Sir Charles Russell, were my case to be brought to the Bar.

Nevertheless, before I attempt to expose to sunlight the defamations made against me, allow me to remark the Soho flat in which I once resided and the information it can disclose to a disinterested observer. Admittedly Soho is a dismal quarter of the "great foul city," as Mr. Ruskin calls it. Its wayfares are muddy and passengers slatternly, its air is dirty and fogs unhealthful, its children are ragged and its women of many nationalities. This last particular reveals that it is in just such a quarter as Soho that alien peoples—immigrants, racial minorities, social rejects, and persons afflicted with deformities, diseases, and ugly infirmities—may find refuge or shelter. The quarter's dismal condition bespeaks the political indifference or hostility of Prime Minister Gladstone's government and the xenophobic antagonisms of Britons who cringe at thoughts of intermixing with strangers. But set to one side my political insinuations and aspersions; give attention to my rooms. Even such a suspicious or hostile visitor as Mr. Utterson would be obliged to concede the luxury and good taste of their appointments. A closet filled with wine, a chest of silver plate and elegant table linen, pictures envied by connoisseurs depending from the walls, and many-piled carpets of pleasing colour—all these, along with a cabinet of well-tailored clothes, surely testify to refined sensibilities. In a word, these accoutrements alone should suggest that I sought both to become and to comport myself as befit a gentleman. They should also result in enquiries which test such assertions about me as that made by Harry's denunciation: "That child of Hell had nothing human; nothing lived in him but fear and hatred."

But permit me to make the case, regardless of who sits on the Woolsack. Permit me to challenge Harry's characterization of my "leading characters": my "complete moral insensibility and insensate readiness to evil." Elsewhere he blasts me as "a being inherently malign and vicious" and, yet elsewhere, for being "pure evil" and "alone in the ranks of mankind." He finds me to be nothing short of a regicide who "dethroned," "deposed," and enslaved his king, a hapless victim. Moreover, not only were my pleasures "undignified" and "monstrous," but he claims also that I drank "pleasure with bestial avidity from any degree of torture to another." If the frequency and number of Harry's defamations were heard at a Summer Assize as the pleas of the Crown, might not impartial and just men have cause to question whether Harry's assertions amount to more than rhetorical ploys which, by libeling my character and distorting my actions into monstrous deeds, minimize his culpability?

Just how monstrous were my deeds, the *incidents* by which my name has been bruited about London? I beg you to consider them with an open mind. They number but four. And in them lies no little poetry of circumstance, as I might call it. Be fairly forewarned: the style of my statement means to engage the whole forces of the mind—the mind of both writer, me, and their reader, you.

Firstly. Late on in his Full Statement Harry reports that on the night I sought out Dr. Lanyon for access to the vital drawer, I was "skulking through the less frequented thoroughfares" until I was brought to a halt by a woman who spoke to me, "offering, *I think*," writes Harry, "a box of lights." According to him I "smote her in the face, and she fled." Is there nothing to palliate that offence? I believe there to be.

If Harry only *thinks* she offered me a box of lights, should not the imprecision or uncertainty of his memory discount the entirety of his statement? His incapacity or reluctance to remember fully or clearly what she offered me obliges him to withdraw his accusation—or my jury to discount it—rather than let its acidulous insinuation eat away at my name. For if he only *thinks* she offered me a box of lights, then what is to keep an advocate for me from asking whether Harry also only *thinks* she was "offering" me something and even *thinks* I "smote her in the face?" It is not incumbent upon me to declare precisely what it was the woman offered me—be it a box of lights or some other commodity, animate or otherwise. Nor is it for me either to describe the woman, to characterise the manner of her so-called offer, to acknowledge or correct the information that her gesture was an offer, or to report either on the duration of her pursuit before her offer or the language that preceded, accompanied, and followed it; for in every detail my inability or unwillingness to bring forward corroboration or evidence gives my reader, my bewigged judge or hoary-headed juror, full reason to doubt my word. But so, too, should that same judge doubt Harry's.

Secondly. Even a competent barrister would have taken pleasure in crossexamining Mr. Utterson's kinsman, Mr. Enfield, for his account of my first atrocity, my trampling of a young girl. Imagine how a barrister of the stature of Sir Charles Russell would have conducted his defence of me.

Item One: It is unlikely that Sir Charles Russell, were he defending me, would permit Mr. Enfield to evade questions that would establish the identity of the "place at the end of the world" from which he was coming when he happened upon my collision with the young girl. Inasmuch as the event happened at "about three o'clock of a black winter morning," it would certainly be of moment to determine whom Mr. Enfield had been visiting, whether he had partaken of any intoxicants, whether such nocturnal walks were routine for a well-known man about town, and whether his conduct throughout the episode was only motivated by benevolent goodwill for an injured girl or whether it had some source in guilt and penitence for some misdeeds of his own, perhaps in "some place at the end of the world" with a person of the same sex but of an age more mature than that of the little girl. Indeed, I besmirch Mr. Enfield's name and character by suggesting that he may have been avenging on me the punishment he himself deserved for brutalities against womanhood. But unless it can be established that he habitually walks the streets at night in search of women in need of rescue, which is not the customary reputation of well-known men about town, three additional oddities in Mr. Enfield's story beg scrutiny. I beg you to follow them carefully.

Item Two: If Mr. Enfield has become almost mesmerized by street after street of lamps, "lighted up as for a procession and all as empty as a church," and begins to long for sight of a policeman, then his apprehension of some imminent foul play has much in common with a wish that some foul play would occur. Thus when he sees the collision of a little man, "stumping along" at a good pace, and a young girl at a cross street, he's predisposed to turn an accident into foul play. If he's at some distance from the event, he'll not be an altogether reliable witness, and if he's close at hand, then it's a wonder that he neglected to "give a view halloa" to warn the two. Sir Charles Russell would certainly have established that distance; and in my recall of the episode, Mr. Enfield could not have been closer than twenty yards, for it took him several minutes before he collared me.

Item Three: Sift again Mr. Enfield's report of "horrible part of the thing," the alleged fact that I "trampled calmly over the child's body and left her screaming on the ground." Without question Sir Charles Russell would examine a little more carefully into that adverb "calmly." Can you not envision Mr. Enfield being asked first to describe how he would trample, say, some verminous creature? Perhaps Mr. Enfield could demonstrate to the judges and jury how he himself would trample upon that creature. And then he could differentiate *that* trampling from trampling "calmly" upon the same creature. At a time when there's little occasion for amusement, I can not keep from laughing at the image of a well-known man about town trampling "*calmly*" upon an imagined creature beneath him; his fancy footwork would partake of the sideshow. Surely a charitable observer would allow the adverb "calmly" to disclose that I was trying carefully to keep from stepping on the girl and was having a deucedly difficult time of dancing over her moving body beneath me. And at first I thought she was equally earnest in her efforts to dodge my descending footwear. But it was during our brief but odd nocturnal ballet that it suddenly came to me that our collision was no accident, which explains my inconsiderate departure, leaving her "screaming on the ground."

You do not take my meaning? Come, come, reader. I beg you to follow carefully for one moment.

Item Four: Given the instantaneous arrival of "quite a group" of people whom Mr. Enfield identifies exclusively as "the girl's own family," and given the apothecary's instant diagnosis that the girl was more frightened than hurt, might not her agility beneath my feet, her screams in excess of bodily harm, and her family's rapid appearance reveal to you as well as me that I had walked into a snare? What kind of parent would send a child of eight or ten out alone at such an evil time of night to fetch a doctor when other adults in the family, several of them women, could have more safely been sent? That people find my person loathsome upon first sight has long ceased to vex me; but the uniformity of this family's and doctor's homicidal antipathy quickly suggested to me that I was in the clutch of a conspiracy, one which Mr. Enfield was witlessly drawn into, gulled into thinking that he was ringleader of a posse comitatus when he was but a manipulable pawn, taken in by their well-rehearsed act. The prompt-ness, sequence, and severity of the group's hostility, the women "wild as harpies," their threats to make a scandal of the event or to blackmail me, and their resolve to extort one hundred pounds sterling from me—all these gave clear evidence of a scheme of urban piracy. Little wonder, I should think, that I adopted what Mr. Enfield objected to as my "sneering coolness" toward the group. Notwithstanding my sneers, I obediently went along with their unlaw-ful bullying, mindful that their numbers, size, and the tenacious vigor of their mischief-making mood put my person at some risk of injury.

That Mr. Enfield would leap to the conclusion that Harry's signature on the check I wrote was proof that I was blackmailing him is consistent with his char-acter as I construe it. He is a man who thinks in categories of sensationalism. He is a man who envisions the adventures of his life as though they were fresh from a shilling shocker. He is thus a man who peoples his adventures with characters direct from the stage of an Adelphi screamer. To this day I am perplexed as to why he never posed to himself the question of why that dour and dry doctor, who'd presumably been called out to attend to someone in the girl's family, never completed his emergency visitation? Moreover, why was it necessary that he ac-company Mr. Enfield, the girl's father, and me to Harry's back door, spend the night with us in Mr. Enfield's chambers, and after breakfast, march with us to the bank to verify that the cheque was genuine?

Verily I put at jeopardy my defence with my condescension, gloating deri-sively at Mr. Enfield's smug self-importance. But I do so to goad my reader into weighing my behavior against his. His complicity in extortion, even if it were not a scheme devised by a cunning family and artful doctor, surely constitutes an unlawful act, one that his juridical kinsman ought to have upbraided him for, rather than let pass without comment. Mr. Enfield's failure to allow that my collision could have been accidental, as well as his animosity toward me because of some inexplicable deformity, entitles me, I would hope, to a modicum of moral superiority to him.

Thirdly. Indulge a bit longer my fantasy of imagining Sir Charles Russell to be my counsel and to now proceed to anatomise—to "cut up into small pieces"—the story of my alleged murder of Sir Danvers Carew. Consider first the witness and then the strangeness, indeed the inflammatory peculiarities and unconscionable irregularities, of her deposition.

A maidservant of undefined age, she sits alone in a house near the Thames, inhabited by no one else. The moon is full, the sky is cloudless, the hour is late, and she has prepared herself for bed. But before settling herself for a night's sleep she sits upon her box beneath the window and looks out from the second storey onto the "brilliantly lit" lane below. It has been established that she is "romantically given"—a spinster or "odd woman" has not been ascertained—and that she has fallen into "a dream of musing." She feels uncommonly at peace with mankind and the world. Whereupon into view walk a white-haired, aged man, whom she has labeled a "beautiful gentleman with white hair," and then a "very small gentleman" whose physiognomy or other features she ignored, except for eventually recognizing him to be me and describing me to Inspector Newcomen as "particularly wicked looking." She admits to having seen me but once before, when I visited her master, and to having "conceived a dislike" for me, but if it is on any basis other than my visage, shape, or size seems unlikely, given her characterization of the scene beneath her window.

It can easily be imagined that such a maidservant, "romantically given," single, and living alone, might well be predisposed to view Sir Danvers Carew to be a man whose regard she would value, especially given her present pleasure in watching his face, which, she deposed, "seemed to breathe such an innocent and old-world kindness of disposition, yet with something high too, as of a well-founded self-content." It cannot be doubted that he was well attired and dignified, his white hair and gentlemanly manners inspiring some romantic aspirations in her. To her credit, she has made no claim to overhearing any words between him and me; consequently, she has testified only to what she saw.

But what she perceived is quite incomplete and leads observers to quite erroneous conclusions. For instance, she testifies that the "very small gentleman" was "advancing to meet" the aged beautiful gentleman. This description makes it appear that I, that same very small gentleman, either had arranged an appointment with Sir Danvers Carew or that I was deliberately walking toward him as if intending to halt him. Yet if I was "advancing to meet" him, then why is it he who "bowed and accosted the other," me, with, as the maid's testimony specifies, "a very pretty manner of politeness?" Would that not indicate that it was I who was walking along, minding my business, and that it was Sir Danvers Carew who was "advancing to meet" me, who was diverting his route so that his would converge with mine—a third encounter at "fatal crossroads" if you will. But allow me to enlarge upon a point: the maidservant's use of the word *accost*. That word unequivocally tells men of sense and propriety that Sir Danvers Carew was the aggressor in our encounter, for to accost anyone implies a challenge and, of course, an interference in another's private activities. Moreover, the word signifies an interruption whose aim is to initiate or perpetrate a sexual act. Indeed you will understandably protest the construction I put forward for your consideration. You will have it that the manner of Sir Danvers Carew's accosting of me, done "with a very pretty manner of politeness," pardons him of any aggressive or sexual intent. Just as Mr. Enfield's report of my "trampling calmly" militates against my alleged trampling, so too, you may wish to think, ought the maidservant's report of Sir Danvers Carew's "accosting politely" militate against his unwanted halting and solicitation of me. I beg to differ. The excessiveness of his "very pretty manner of politeness" hid, as smug sarcasm and gleeful malice often do, the depth of his ugliness. Let me be clear.

His pretty politeness made more repugnant the sexual overture of his imped-
ance of me, if only because its outward form belied his nefarious design. Surely
Harry Jekyll, who could put a good face on his behaviour, is not the only two-
faced hypocrite walking London's or Edinburgh's cobblestones. From Sir Danvers Carew's pointing, the maidservant guessed that he was "inquiring the
way"; but pointing fingers can be construed to contain other meanings, such as
instructing one to get hence, or to take oneself away to a place more appropriate to one's station or kind, or, if seeking to arrange a tryst, to meet one at some
designated place. But the maidservant, obtuse to such alternatives because of
her romantic predisposition, can not conceive of the encounter to be one in
which Sir Danvers Carew was a well-dressed deviant whose insulting solicitation had more in common with an unnatural Greek than with a disoriented
English gentleman inquiring the way of a stranger.

You think it outlandish and outrageous to impugn Sir Danvers Carew, MP,
by pointing him out to be a man who would stoop to a sexual arrangement with
"a creature" as deformed as I? If that be true, then his overture was even more
insulting, as if to sneer with a most polite expression on his face, at the very
thought of any human creature being able to tolerate an embrace from such as
I. His disgust for my shape and size, my racial difference, and my alien countenance were only exaggerated by his masquerade of "innocent and old-world
kindness of disposition" and "well-founded self-content," much as if I were barbaric and malodorous Caliban to his elegantly civilized Prospero. Even Harry
acknowledges that I had been the target of Sir Danvers Carew's "provocation,"
although he downplays it as "so pitiful a provocation." Inasmuch as our encounter occurred beyond earshot of any witness, his insult, both sexual and
racial, must have seemed to him a safe jest to play. But his impertinence tried
even my patience. And so I lashed out at him, as any gentleman has the right to
do when being insulted by an interfering and hateful stranger, regardless of how
well dressed or "beautiful" he is.

It is admitted that my thrashing of Sir Danvers Carew might well appear
monstrous to the maidservant. Add Harry's overgeneralised and melodrama-
tised version of my "transport of glee" in mauling "the unresisting body, tasting
delight from every blow," which I allegedly administered to Sir Danvers Carew.
Between the two a reader can not believe otherwise than to deem my bestial
rage to be horrendous. But Harry's version, as with the entirety of his Full Statement, is self-serving and can not be trusted: if I were such a creature of "complete moral insensibility and insensate readiness to evil," if I were an agent of
"pure evil," then surely I'd have never tolerated a night with Mr. Enfield and his
fellow extortionists, never have countenanced Mr. Utterson's interference at my
door, never broken my pace to hear Sir Danvers Carew's provocative enquiries,
and never have warned Dr. Lanyon of the danger he was putting himself in by
witnessing my imbibing of the chameleon liquor—of which more presently.

Similarly the maidservant's account can not be taken as dispassionate, literal truth either. According to her, until such time as the horror she witnessed caused her to lose consciousness in a three-hour-long faint, I behaved "like a madman" with "ape-like fury." She has claimed I clubbed Sir Danvers Carew to the ground, trampled him under foot and rained blows upon him with my cane, shattering his bones and causing his body to jump "upon the roadway." Has the maidservant ever witnessed the fury of an ape, I should like to know? If she has, what was the occasion? If not, has she been drawn into characterising my drubbing of a well-dressed scoundrel by resorting to the use of a hackneyed figure of speech to heighten its horror, to bestialise with brutality my behaviour? Was it ever established, for that matter, that she had ever been witness to the behavior of a "madman?" Or is she once again falling back upon some stage-drawn notion of how madmen behave and is, thus, unwittingly revealing herself to be an addict of shilling shockers? Indeed, might she even be a disturbed woman who artfully foists onto others her unhealthy wishes to commit hostile actions against beautiful men because they ignore or insult her with their indifference to her person? In any event, while she may well have been a first-hand witness to the several strokes of my cane, she was certainly unconscious by the time I left Sir Danvers Carew in the street, whimpering and regretting his provocation. Whether he died at someone else's hand or as the result of a stroke, I can not say. But surely I would not have left half of my cane behind me at the scene where I had committed a murder; I left it knowing I had only given him the thrashing he deserved. I fully expected him to get himself up and limp home, duly chastised and instructed by his arrant folly.

This episode needs one last enquiry: besides leading the police to Mr. Utterson on the morning after Sir Danvers Carew's death, why was the content of the unposted letter found on the MP's "incredibly mangled" body never looked into; *viz.,* what characterised Sir Danvers Carew's relationship to the lawyer to whom it was addressed? Could that relationship in any way have fueled my thrashing of the MP? But this matter has to do with Mr. Utterson, whose role in all of this I am beginning to glimpse. If there is time, and if I can hold off Harry's return, I will, I assure you, turn your eye on him.

Fourthly.

But the sudden torment of my bowels . . . the cramping of my legs and arms . . . warn me. I am losing myself . . . to Harry's reemergence. Into its hiding place . . . goes my statement . . . until he gives way . . . to my resurrection.

Och! I resume. Fourthly. After my disappearance following the murder of Sir Danvers Carew, the police are said to have dug up my disreputable past. Exhumed were tales of my callous and violent cruelty, my "vile life," my "strange associates," and the hatred surrounding "my career." Insofar as no specific incidents were identified, it should seem evident that my name had become an iniquitous vehicle on which to load any and all dark deeds perpetrated by criminals and desperadoes whom the police were unable to track down, convict, and bring to punishment. The unsolved, vicious murder of simple shopgirls, respectable elders, or hardened prostitutes; mysterious assaults or depraved acts; even pious frauds—all could be attributed to Edward Hyde without fear of contradiction or call for evidence. Surely I must be linked to the Phoenix Park murders in Dublin, too. How my name and disappearance simplified the tasks of the constabulary and Scotland Yard. They seized upon my name and made currency of it.

But their libelous scapegoating (no other term can begin to do justice to their smearing of my name) mirrors Harry's equally ill-defined and overgeneralised allegations of my craven misdeeds. What were my "undignified pleasures?" In what actions did my "vicarious depravity" consist? At what infamies did I connive? If the scrawled blasphemies on the pages of a pious book were in Harry's hand, why is it that I must be assigned the agent of their inscription, not he himself, in another of his foul moods? Why must I alone be the wicked author of such blasphemies? And why must the burned letters and the destroyed portrait of Harry's father not be laid at the feet of Harry? Is there any to vouch for Harry as such an exceptionally devoted son as to be altogether free of residual ill will or native antagonism toward his father?

Surely the foul fogs enshrouding my name, character, and deeds must begin to disperse if my impartial reader—whom I earnestly entreat to regard the matters put before him as if he were practising at taking silk—if he will put to the test the moral allegory in which Harry and his colluding fellow bachelor-professionals assign, like a cabal of Jesuitical monks, all villainy to me, but assign to him only the error of succumbing to the temptation of unbuttoning the morally respectable straitjacket in which he chose to encase himself. Indeed, before I ask you to look with me—patiently, scrupulously, and sceptically—at the rubicund rhetoric of Harry's Full Statement, permit me to escort you back to my brief visit with Dr. Hastie Lanyon, whose debilitating transformation and sudden demise is laid at what must be my cloven feet.

(Yes, I confess that I accorded to myself the right to open an envelope he had sent to Harry. From it I read the holograph draft of Harry's letter dated, oddly, 10 December but received by Dr. Lanyon in "registered envelope" on 9 January, the day of my visitation to him. I read as well the corrected draft of the "Narrative" which Dr. Lanyon wrote on 13 January. Both of these documents, I readily admit, I have burned in the fire, along with Dr. Lanyon's brief note in which he informs Harry that they were both but drafts of identical documents he has mailed to Mr. Utterson with instructions not to open them "till the death or disappearance of Dr. Henry Jekyll." In other words, while I chose not to "tear in pieces" the documents in an act of "ape-like spite," I knew them to be superfluous inasmuch as the originals were certain to be in the possession of the judicious, prudent, and circumspect Mr. Utterson.)

Like all the good gentlemen who have had a hand in the defamation and vilification of my character, Dr. Lanyon, too, upon my arrival at his home, found himself disturbed by my presence and attributed his discomfort to me, not to his own fastidious squeamishness. For him to remark "the odd, subjective disturbance caused by [my] neighbourhood" to him and to equate his reaction to my proximity with "incipient rigour" and "a marked sinking of the pulse" betrays nothing more than his yielding to rampant symptom-mongering, which a professional of his age and maturity ought to have been above. Worse is either his metaphysical innuendo, invoking the notion that his reaction to me had its source in "the nature of man," or his holier-than-thou exoneration, insisting that his feelings turned "on some nobler hinge than the principle of hatred." Surely his acknowledgment of his "disgustful curiosity" in me and my "ludicrous accoutrement" as well as my "misbegotten abnormality," which presumably entitled him to be alarmed by "the very essence of the creature that" faced him— "creature," indeed!—surely these bespeak the reactions of a bigot who abhors proximity to any human being of a significantly different race, origin, class, color, size, shape, and, perhaps, sex than he. His account, consequently, must be viewed as one strongly tinctured with that bigotry. (One must wonder whether all of the patients he sees or treats reflect or replicate his own white, male, patriarchal kind. Would a person of Arabic, Egyptian, Jewish, or African lineage be allowed across the threshold of his infirmary? Would he consent to administer medicine to even a swarthy Spaniard, Italian, or Turk in hospital?)

To be certain, I will be faulted for the consequences of permitting Dr. Lanyon to behold the metamorphosis I presently performed, once he had pointed me toward the drawer that held the ingredients for the elixir that only I could concoct. True, I taunted him. I teased him. I tantalized him. But I had cause. In the first place he had, after all, taken liberties not granted him in Harry's letter: he poked about in the drawer from the press marked "E." He examined the powders and salts, as well as assayed and sniffed at the half-full phial of pungent, blood-red liquor. And he fingered the date-filled record of Harry's experiments, spending no little time poring over its several hundred entries, greedily and jealously looking for useable information. In the second place he delayed me with his condescending manners. He refused me access to the drawer until I had sat down with him and engaged in pretty civilities, which is no less a torture than insisting a suffocating man be so good as to hold his breath for several minutes and comport himself politely before the person of the rescuing physician who has been called to respond to his emergency. In the third place, given the long relationship and rivalry between Harry and Dr. Lanyon, there is little wonder that I, again provoked and now needful of continued concealment from the police, that I threatened to stagger "the unbelief of Satan" with the spectacle of my transformation, the transfiguration of my "clay continent," as Mr. Utterson poetically calls the human body. That Dr. Lanyon succumbed to the temptation, to the dare I thrust before him, makes him responsible for the choice he made to witness the miracle.

Notwithstanding his repeated screams, his soul-sickened terror, his subsequent insomnia, and his death three weeks later, two oddities in Dr. Lanyon's account warrant closer notice. First, why is it that Dr. Lanyon credits Harry, who stayed on with him for an hour after the miracle, with neither treating nor easing his colleague's hysteria with medication? Although Dr. Lanyon's omission of such a detail is understandable, it is also telling because it suggests that Harry took no little pleasure in the suffering of the "ignorant," "hide-bound pedant," as Harry was accustomed to call his rival. Second, what was the "moral turpitude" that Harry "unveiled" to him during that hour, turpitude that Dr. Lanyon admits he "cannot bring my mind to set on paper." Rest assured that Harry would identify the agent of such moral turpitude to be me. And the moral turpitude would include such terrors and horrors as would conduce to boil Dr. Lanyon's brain, inasmuch as Harry had at his mercy the rival who had long "denied the virtue of transcendental medicine," denounced his "unscientific balderdash," and "derided [his] superiors," that is, himself. In three words, shouldn't those so eager to vilify me for my questionable actions, shouldn't they question whether Harry's actions are at least as villainous as those credited to my side of the ledger? Or will my self-defence have been so derided as an ingeniously compiled farrago of sophistry that my reader will have thrown it down in disgust?

Once again, my hands cramp; my bowels wrench; my chest, arms, and legs stretch and expand. They warn me of Harry's rebirth . . . and of the need . . . to secure my statement . . . from him. Ahhh. It is his turn . . . to depose me . . . out of life.

Och! Again I, the "insurgent horror" whom Harry would despise as inorganic and amorphous dust, aye, I return, perhaps for the final installment, albeit weakened and debilitated as I continue to become. But the business table has signs of dampness. And my handkerchief is damp as well. Harry has been weeping. There is much to grieve, but Harry deserves no mourners.

Perhaps no villainy Harry perpetrated can begin to compare with the spurious Full Statement with which he endeavours to blacken me and to burke enquiry into the self-serving calculations of his self-exculpatory confession. The entirety of his account is a gaudy bouquet well stocked with two oversized and meretricious kinds of flowers: florid melodrama and ruddy religiosity.

Harry's melodrama floribunda adulterates sentence after sentence of his "confession," in which, alas, as he insists in ever so many ways, he is a victim. Harry rues that one native element which rode him from birth was a "certain impatient gaiety of disposition." To that biological endowment was added the curse of being well-born, whose domestic blessings encouraged self-indulgence and, thereby, sentenced him to be the battleground, as he puts it, for "the perennial war among my members." Harry laments that society, not self-interest, early instructed him in duplicity and hypocrisy; that chance, not will, directed him into scientific studies; and that fate, not ambition, "doomed" him to discover the truth "that man is not truly one, but truly two." Harry bemoans "the curse of mankind," which has bound together, against his will or control, the "incongruous faggots" of his character. Harry mourns over the "fatal crossroads" to which fate steered him, its powerless pawn. And Harry complains of his enslavement to me, the "child of Hell" who robbed him of his dignity, willpower, respectability, and freedom. In a word, Harry, in accordance with the melodrama he so tenaciously manipulates, makes me his assailant, the agent of his downfall. I am the arch-villain against whom he, thwarted hero, valiantly struggles.

Oh, without question, he narrates a compelling confession. I give him full credit for his narrative dexterity. But fear of eternal fires frightened him. He might well have proudly maintained his identity as, what might I call him— Promethean challenger? Faustian overachiever? Wagnerian champion? Exemplary Brother's-Keeper? Intrepid Pioneer? or Valiant Explorer? Instead, he buckled. He yielded to cowardice. He patched together the exculpatory testament fit for a whimpering victim, hopeful that he'd be forgiven his trespasses against God's ordering of nature, God's creation, which Harry's experiments sought to alter or dissolve for his personal—and perhaps mankind's—benefit.

Harry's fear was that he would face Hell's fires, would "suffer smartingly in the fires of abstinence." That fear led him to conspire in and craft the portrayal of me, with neither complete nor convincing evidence, to be a mountain bandit, a Satanic Juggernaut, a child of Hell, pure evil—a creature fit for some utilitarian morality play or elementary allegorical melodrama. In the face of that fear Harry fashioned a new ambition: to be regarded as a latter-day Prodigal Son who would be forgiven and embraced by churchly fathers or their standins, his celibate peers. That ambition led him to characterise himself as a penitential apologist. It is with that self-characterisation in mind that he saturates his confession with the lexicon of moral discourse, sprinkled, naturally, with the allusions of religious devotion.

Scientist, solicitor, and sawbones though he was, Harry was also a seamstress. He embroiders his discourse with infantile contrasts of "good and ill," "just and unjust," "good and evil," "angel and fiend," "divine and diabolical," "my virtue, my evil." He knits into it a list of terms such as *shame, depravity, hatred, deformity, monstrous, disgrace, malignancy*, and *licence*. And then he sews on such terms as *prayers, petitions, remorse*, and *renunciation*. And he stitches it with references to his "immaterial tabernacle," his "fortress of identity," "dethroned powers," and the "empire of generous or pious aspirations." All of these rhetorical efforts— which are tailor-made for my mockery—exhibit the extent to which Harry pities himself as the "chief of sufferers." By claiming that "no one has ever suffered such torments" as himself, he seeks his reader's pity and forgiveness for himself. He also secures his reader's loathing for me. If he can beguile readers into believing that he perches at the peak of some pyramidal hierarchy of history's sufferers, then his architectural image also inveigles readers to regard me as a creature fit for the very trough of that pyramid's inverted image, the pit.

It is this shameful dragging of my character into "the slime of the pit," as he calls it, that constitutes his most heinous crime. Not content with the obloquy or questionable status of his own name, he must defame me and foist upon me a set of dubious crimes, all in hopes that the enormity of my sins will shrink his. Is that not a mean-spirited and malicious act, whether perpetrated upon an animal or fellow human being?

But Harry is not alone in his program to denigrate me. He has an accomplice, the man who, I now fully realize, will first put his pallid hands upon my Full Statement.

Indeed, I refer to Gabriel John Utterson, whose fussy, interfering, and persistent efforts at visiting Harry these past weeks I now hear—yes, hear—have reaped their reward. Again he is in the house, asking admittance to Harry. Well, well. This is a late hour for his visitation on such a wild, cold March night, well past his dinner hour and hearthside glass or two of wine. Mr. Poole's emboldened behaviour, which has become more vexing since he caught a glimpse of me a few days ago in the surgical theatre below, suggests trouble, perhaps an assault upon the red baize door and an unwelcome intrusion. Ah, well, let it be. My powers dwindle. And I weary of the wrenching agonies—which commence again—that signal the transformations Harry and I must endure. Let me be found. Or let Harry be found. Either way our life is forfeit.

But there may just be sufficient time to reveal the soil that spots those hairless hands of my—of *our*—secret foe, Mr. Utterson.

His dislike of me dates of course from that holograph Will, in which Harry designated me his friend, benefactor, and beneficiary. Mr. Utterson understandably prides himself on full knowledge of his clients, especially when his client is also a long-time friend from college days. Lacking so much as a minuscule clue to my identity surely rankled a man as vain as he. It goaded him into seeking me out, as he so unceremoniously did a year ago, stepping out of our dark courtyard entry one October night and halting my entrance with his meddlesomeness and his duplicity, falsely claiming that Harry had described me to him. Without question he suspected me of being a blackmailer, capable of twisting Harry with threat of exposing some felony, crime, sin, or indiscretion committed in his wild years. But what most galled him had to have been the prospect that in the event of Harry's death or disappearance, I, aye, Edward Hyde, would inherit Harry's assets of half a million sterling. Upon learning that Mr. Utterson's legal expertise was as a conveyancer, one of that clever and venal brotherhood of monopolistic solicitors whose business lies in drawing up deeds, leases, and other documents required for transferring titles of property, I realized that until my appearance Mr. Utterson had leverage on the disposition of Harry's—a confirmed bachelor's—

assets. Little wonder, consequently, that Mr. Utterson, spurred by base pecuniary motives, has dogged my steps. Surely it was a matter of glee when, after the murder of Sir Danvers Carew, I vanished, for that signified that Harry would have to alter his Will and designate some other inheritor. Little wonder as well at Mr. Utterson's reputation, as Harry has expressed it more than once: "it was frequently his fortune to be the last reputable acquaintance and the last good influence in the lives of downgoing men." Truly it would advantage his "fortune," as in wealth, not chance, to be the last person to influence, by fair means or foul, the disposition of the property of those "downgoing men." And who better than a conveyancer to know the circuitous ways of testamentary documents, to be adept in the legal legerdemain of which solicitors are masters?

Oh, but Mr. Utterson is of the club. He belongs to the narrow fraternity that I now discover myself to be entangled with and whose collective wrath—and, I dare say, envy—I have incited. Mr. Enfield, Mr. Utterson, Dr. Lanyon, Inspector Newcomen, Sir Danvers Carew, and Harry—all are patriarchal professionals sworn to guard and maintain their sterile brotherhoods and protectionist exclusivity. Wide and deep are the falsifications and distortions they resort to in order that their proprietary realms be protected against the likes of me and my brethren, who are Legion, we aliens, immigrants, throwbacks, and ill-formed outsiders whom they huddle together against, conspiring and collaborating in their collective witch-hunts. Fearful are they that the morality of the garlic-scented stranger, the rights of social lepers, will topple their class castle. Beware the alien who threatens to shake severely the master–servant hierarchy they strive to rigidly uphold. Guard against the immigrant whose different perspective threatens to fracture the fragile male bonding of the archaic fraternities whose glue requires constant replacement. Rally to malign the deformed outsider whose nonconformity to oppressive cultural conventions impedes their perpetuation and, thereby, engenders hatred reserved for villains but heaped upon their substitutes, who serve as scapegoats.

Ha! A wicked impulse dictates. Yes. Let me perplex Mr. Utterson by gratifying his hidden wish. In place of my name as the beneficiary of Harry's estate, I will insert his.

There. A redrafting of the simple will has been a matter of moments; and insertion of it in the large envelope—along with Harry's note to me, Dr. Lanyon's "Narrative," and Harry's "confession"—is done. Truly, now Mr. Utterson is companion to three "downgoing men." Will he decipher my accusation?

But noises outside my by-street door have interrupted me momentarily. Pacing to and fro, I have caught a glimpse of the footman, Bradshaw, and a boy, both brandishing sticks. It appears I can expect an assault upon the cabinet door and, should I have strength and seek escape, am to be felled by them. But the wrenching agonies that have knotted my body the past hour exceed those that have previously visited my frame. My time—our time—is come.

So I bring to a close my statement, fold over my octavo, and leave it in a conspicuous pocket of my jacket to compel some fellow human to touch me, reprehensible though I am said to be to so many. What will become of my statement? It is certain that Harry's busybody lawyer, "the true embodiment / Of everything that's excellent," will find it and will most probably tuck it, along with the envelopes containing Dr. Lanyon's "Narrative" and Harry's "Full Statement," beneath his greatcoat and retire to his Gaunt Street rooms to read all three. Will he then return to Harry's residence and notify Inspector Newcomen of the incident he will presently involve himself in? Most, will he turn over to the inspector all of the evidence he has handled, including my Full Statement?

Mr. Utterson calls out now for Harry, manfully demands to see him, and brusquely declares his suspicions are aroused. He boldly threatens brute force upon the red baize of the cabinet door.

"Utterson," I cry out in mock alarm, "for God's sake have mercy!"

Brute force—my body—makes me . . . writhe . . . and . . . twitch. . . .

Legibility . . . going. . . . Cramps. . . . Overwhelming pain.

Splinters. . . . The door. . . .

My life. . . . For . . . feit. . . .

Fingers! Spell. . . . out . . . my name.

Ed . . . ward . . . Hyde. Och!

A Letter to 'De Ole True Huck'

Dear Mister Finn,

It was my ability to read, you'll believe, that led to a conversation one April evening a decade ago, a conversation I wrote down soon after. But it's been my inability to stop grieving over pappy's recent death that has goaded me to locate you—no easy matter—and send you what I had written. I won't bother you with the details of how pappy, after returning with Mister Sawyer and Missus Polly from Louisiana, worked and saved his money, in time buying mammy's, 'Lizabeth's, and my freedom. Or the details of our move north into a run-down shanty on Chicago's south side, the jobs we found there, or 'Lizabeth's—and now pappy's—death. (Nor will you want me to tell you, I imagine, how, after several months, I found your most recent address.) I'll skip directly to our customary walks every Sunday, to the enjoyment we took in our little bit of finery, to our pleasure in the break from our weekday routines, to our great relief in being far from St. Petersburg. For it was on one of those Sunday walks that we were passing by a bookseller's on Davenport Street. I found my eye snagged by a title in the window: *Adventures of Huckleberry Finn*. I halted the family and read them what I saw. Naturally pappy found it mighty curious to see the name of his former raft-companion on the hard boards of a book cover.

We scrimped for the next three weeks, took on extra jobs, and saved up enough to buy a copy of your book. When I got home with it pappy thumbed it over, looking at all the illustrations. Then he declared that every night we would hear some of it, that I would read it aloud. For the next three-and-a-half weeks I read, to a very attentive audience, as you can well imagine, sir. After every stint of reading, mammy and I would ask pappy if things *really* happened as you said they did. But every night he'd only raise his hand, smile, and say, "We gwyneter hyear out Huck honey's 'hole tale. Dis book b'long to him."

For the first week I'd get angry with him for not answering our question, but I finally resigned myself to his refusal. I couldn't help but notice, though, that during several episodes he'd chuckle, or a serious look would cloud up his face, or he'd cock an eyebrow, push out his lips, and scratch his wool. And twice—when you wrote about the *Sir Walter Scott* riverboat and watching the sunrise on the river—he got up and paced back and forth, telling me, "Keep readin', chile. Keep readin', please." All through the episodes at the Phelps's farm he concentrated so intently that his corncob pipe would go out early and wouldn't get lit again until I ended the reading session.

When I finally finished reading your book, pappy rocked back in his chair and sucked on his pipe a few times, mammy and I waiting patiently. Then, in almost a whisper, he said, "Well, well. De ole true Huck. De ole true Huck." Then he began to chuckle. Then to laugh. And laugh. And every once in a while, like he was coming up for air, he'd say again, "De ole true Huck. Yes-indeedy, de ole true Huck."

Mammy and I, flies after honey, asked him to explain what he meant. At last his laugh wore itself out.

"Duz bof' o' you goggle-eyed puhsuns 'spect me to dump de 'hole load o' ole Huck's story t'night? I's gwyne let it sit fo' a day so's I kin unpack it right, wun carpetbag at a time. 'Sides, it's too late to go on 'bout dis story now. Good lan', I reck'n it's time we wuz all in bed er in de mawnin' we hain't gwyneter be wuth mo' dan," he cocked an eyebrow, "mo dan a hairball widout money." He chuck-led at his allusion, you can be sure, Mister Finn.

The next day was dreadful long before he returned from the docks. Mammy and I rushed him through dinner, got him seated comfortably in his rocker, fired up his corncob, and began nagging him to tell us about your book.

"Well, den. Heah's what I fines. Fo' thin's, I think. Mebbe mo', mebbe less, 'pendin' how you counts 'em en 'pendin' wedder I kin keep 'em sep'rate, like de cream f'om de milk. Fer wun thin', ole Huck honey's done sum mispropriatin'. En he's tol' sum o' dem 'stretchers,' as he calls 'em. En dey's *considable* buttuh spread on dat meanness o' his. But," and here he began to laugh again so that mammy and I could hardly make out what he was saying, "but all durin' dem adventures, 'spesh'ly durin' dat time we wuz at dem Phelps, I never knowed fo' sure if Huck knowed how much I wuz 'lettin' on,' as Misto Tom called it. Dog my cats ef'n I didn' pull de wool over Huck honey's eyes."

"Now jis' you wait wun doggone minute, James Alexander Hawkins!" said mammy. "You jis' stop all o' dat laffin', you hyear! Jis' you slo' down en 'splain to Johnny en me what you talkin' 'bout. Usin' dat big word, 'miss-propri-what?' 'Taint kind to be laffin' 'bout sumfn widout us gettin' a chance to share in de laff. En stop dat f'roshus rockin' b'fo' you tip yo'sef out onter de flo'. Commence to tell *us* de joke. Johnny chile, you fetch yo' pappy some o' dat good 'backy. Misto Finn's right 'bout one thin' fo' sure, James Hawkins: you mus' be de eas-iest nigger to laff dat ever wuz!"

Your "mispropriations," as pappy called them? By that he said he meant that you made it appear that you understood or did things with no help from him. He had me thumb back and find that place where you're telling about how the sun came up on the river. I found it easily, because I'd dogeared that page. I thought that some mighty fine writing, for it took me back to some mornings on the big river when I was still a slave. Pappy had me read it again. Then he asked me if I noticed anything curious about it. I told him that I saw nothing at all curious about it.

"Chile, you means to tell me dey's nuffn strange in dat?"

I read it to myself, looked up at him and shook my head.

"Johnny chile, is dat all fack?"

"No, pappy. Course not. Mister Finn described what he saw. Its poetry-like, not fact."

"Chile, is dey nuffn mo'? Duz Huck honey tell you sumfn dat he don't know fo' sure?"

"Like what, pappy," I asked, exasperated with his niggling.

"Chile, read dem words 'bout de log pile dat Huck honey writes 'bout."

So I read: "'. . . and you make out a log cabin in the edge of the woods, away on the bank on t'other side of the river, being a wood-yard, likely, and piled by them cheats so you can throw a dog through it anywheres; then the . . .'"

"Stop dah. *Now* what you see, chile?"

I just shook my head.

"James Hawkins! You leave dat boy 'lone. Stop yo' pickin' on him."

"Mammy, Johnny's de wun what's sposed to know how t' read. Well, it warn't no use fer to learn him how to read ef'n at sixteen he doan' unnerstan' what he's readin', wuz it? Now, den, Johnny chile, how could Huck honey know dat dat log pile wuz stacked by cheats 'stead o' jis' a sloppy stacker? Hain't dat kinder a funny noshun fo' him to draw? Well, jis' you guess who it wuz dat pointed out dat stack full o' holes? But *I* tol' him I reck'n'd it wuz stacked by a cheat *er* a sloppy stacker *er* a lazy hired hand. Kinder curious to me dat Huck would draw on'y de wust noshun. En so, Johnny chile, dat's what I means by Huck's mispropriatin'. He takes de credit fo' pretendin' as if he wuz de wun what saw dat leaky log pile."

And who, Mister Finn, came up with the idea that you should make up a story to get someone to scurry out to that wreck, the *Sir Walter Scott*? Pappy says that *you* were all for forgetting about those robbers, especially when that storm came along after you and he made off with their boat. But, chuckling all the while he told it, he remembered that once the two of you caught up with your raft, he suggested that you shove off to shore and get someone to rescue those robbers. He laughed at the recollection of the way your jaw dropped, claiming that you were amazed at his suggestion, that you didn't want to have anything to do with them, that they reminded you too much of your pap—that they could sink with the wreck, for all you cared. Pappy said he got his dander up then. He scolded you and told you it was no way to treat other folks, even if they were only no-account robbers. Of course, what you actually did, once you shoved off for shore, pappy had no way of knowing. He said, though, that he enjoyed my reading the story you told the ferryboat watchman, said that it was mighty entertaining. Whether it was true or not, he had no way of knowing.

For all he knew, you just rowed to shore, skulked for an hour or so, figured out what you'd tell him and came back. At least you were pretty mum, he said, when you and he saw the *Scott* floating down the river.

"Soun's like you 'ccusin' Misto Finn o' tellin' a stretcher, James Hawkins. I tho't you wuz jis' gwyne tell 'bout his miss-propri—drat dat word! But you jis' done clumb f'om dem thin's to stretchers, I b'lieve. Wun at a time, ef'n you please."

"But sumtimes, like de shingles on de roof, woman, dey ove'lap. Besides," he continued, "ef'n dat wuz a stretcher, den it wuz *small taters* to what Huck could do wif a full head of steam up."

He couldn't get over how you concocted—back at the beginning of your story—that tall tale of him being ridden by witches all over the world. He said he'd only been letting on that he was snoring after he stretched out beneath that tree, between you and Mister Sawyer. He figured it was you two up to pranks. After all, sitting in the kitchen door, he had heard the phoney meowing, and then you scrambling out your window. So when you stumbled over the root, he went out, then faked his snoring to see what you two would do. He was still awake when Mister Sawyer crawled back, slipped the hat off his head, and hung it on the limb above him.

But according to pappy, he explained to the other slaves that a spirit had caught him napping. By hanging his hat from a limb, the spirit had given him a sign. The sign warned him not to nap while white folks were still awake, for they were not above finding fun in dumping dirt on slaves.

"How dat ole Huck could stretch sumfn mos' all o' de time," pappy said, grinning wide and chuckling at the difference between your version and what actually happened.

"Well, pappy. How *did* you get that five-center piece that you still wear around your neck if it wasn't the money that Mister Sawyer left for the candles?"

Mammy got up and, with a wrinkly smile playing over her face, left the room, puzzling me.

Pappy chuckled at her exit. "Chile, doan' you know a luv token when you sees wun? Why yo' mammy wuz holdin' dis in de pink of her han' de fust day dat ever I saw her. She en Harbison's Minnie wuz in Misto' Harper's shackly brick sto' nex' to de Temp'rance Tavern on Meadow Lane. En dey wuz buyin' a piece o' linsey-woolsey fo' her missus wid dat five-center piece. My but she looked fine in her milk-white apr'n, calico print en red bandanner—looked like a new pin. En when she lef' de sto', I ax Misto Harper ef'n he'd swap dat five-center fo' wun in my pockit. He reck'n'd dey wuz no reason not to, en when I giv' him mine, he flipped his onto de flo'. I ignored de insult—mo' *trash* from de white folks—tuck it to de blacksmith, en had him work a hole in it so's I could wear it roun' my neck on a string. It's been heah ever since, a rememberer o' de fust gal I ever set eyes on what made my heart go flippity flop."

By this time mammy was back in the room, hands on her hips, her face a-scowling. "James Hawkins, jis' you stop carryin' on like dat. En stop flashin' yo' big brown eyes and yo' love-makin' grin on me b'fo' dat boy. Dat's not decent, en you knows it. Tell us mo' 'bout Misto Finn's stretchers."

"Yes, pappy. Why would Mister Finn want to brew up a stretcher about your so-called witch ride around the world? What good would that do him?"

"Well, mebbe it let Huck honey—when he sat hissef down t' write 'bout us—'ticipate de journey we wuz gwyne be goin' on. Kinder makes my ride a po' rag-doll version o' his own adventure, doan' it? Like thowin' a stick into bog water en sendin' a dog arter it—to see ef dey eny snakes in it b'fo' you foot acrost it yo'sef. En I spoze my cockeyed witch trip would make his tale pow'ful real-like by 'pari-son, wouldn' you say? En I spoze too dat dis wuz Huck's way, mos' o' de time. He awluz liked to show *me* to be de fool, a saphead, as he liked to call mos' folks."

"But pappy, you sure were a fool lots of times. It was downright embarrass-ing to read that part where you told Mister Finn—now where's that place? Yes, here it is—'I ben rich wunst, and gwyne to be rich agin.' Why, pappy, that whole page, about you investing in a cow, in a bank, in a wood-flat that some-one stole, and in Balum—why all of that makes you sound ridiculous, like all you had *inside* your head was the same thing you had on *top* of it—wool."

While I was rattling on, I suddenly realized that pappy's grinning meant one thing: *he* wasn't embarrassed by that page. I laughed out loud too.

"What you two chuckle-heads laughin' 'bout? Dat investin' stuff embarrass me. 'Splain to me, right dis minute, de joke!"

So I explained to her that pappy was only pretending to be a fool, that he was stringing Mister Finn along, inviting him to think poorly of pappy.

"But why you wan' do a thin' like dat to a young chile, James Hawkins?"

Pappy got out of his rocker, went over to mammy, lifted her hands from her mending, and explained. He told her he could feel that something was ruffling you when he finished telling you about his own escape. It dawned on him that you'd puffed yourself up pretty full, telling him about your own scheme of es-cape. But after he told you about his, you seemed to have lost some air. All he could figure was that you were nettled to discover that he appeared at least as smart as you. And when you made mock of his going without meat and bread or even mud-turkles, then he was sure he'd figured right. But your taunting, he owned, made him forget himself. He got sassy about catching mud-turkles and began boasting about knowing all the signs that would bring bad luck. When he noticed your lower lip stiffening, he realized he was seeing another sign. It meant he'd overstepped himself and that he'd best play dumb for a while. So that was why, he told mammy, he fell in with you and carried on in such a fool-ish way about his investments.

Returning to his rocker and refilling his corncob, pappy told us that during those first few days with you he kept forgetting that for all of your reputation as a worthless near-orphan you were still a proud white boy who wasn't about to treat him as an equal. He chuckled as he lit his bowl, asked me to find that scene where you and he are snug in the cave on Jackson's Island during that storm, asked me to read what he said after you declared that the cave was nice and that you wouldn't want to be anywhere else but there.

"'Well, you wouldn't a ben here,'" I read, "''f it hadn't a ben for Jim. You'd a ben down dah in de woods widout any dinner, en gittn' mos' drownded, too, dat you would, honey. Chickens knows when its gwyne to rain, en so do de birds, chile.'"

"Well, go on, chile," commanded mammy. "What duz dat Huck say den—arter yo' pappy's sass?"

"He says nothing, mammy—leastwise nothing back to pappy. He just goes on to tell about the river rising."

"See? Dat wuz my mistake. I didn' jedge right. I reck'n I was pooty chuckle-headed not to see dat even Huck didn' like to have folks—'speshly no slave—sassin' en makin' him feel dat he wuz beholden to 'em. His silence en dat stiff lip—dey bof warnded me dat he jis' might save up en fetch me a heapin' platter o' comeuppance when it wuz *his* servin' time."

"Pappy, that must explain why Mister Finn put that dead rattle-snake in your blanket. That and your refusal to talk about the dead man you found in that floating house—his pap."

Pappy told me I was "splittin' kindlin' fine." That snake-bite episode, he said, taught him that you were *far* from just a prank-playing boy. Shaking his head as if to wish it weren't so, he believed that you had a mean streak clear through, that you resented anyone who got an upper hand, and that you were mighty sneaky about bringing that person down, even though you did a swell job of concealing your meanness and sneakiness in the way you wrote your story.

"Arter dat rattle-snake bit me en I got better, I axed Huck honey how he fig-ured dat snake got on my bed-roll. But I jis' got sum hemmin' en hawwin' f'om him. So I made up my mine 'bout what I's gwyne to do. En dat wuz to test Huck honey a few mo' times to fine out jis' what he wuz made out o'."

"Test him? How'd you do that, pappy? I don't remember any tests."

"Well, chile, you need mo' lessons in 'terpretin' signs, it seems. 'Member you dat chapter dat Huck ends by saying '"you can't learn a nigger to argue?"' Well all o' dat arguin' 'bout Sollerman's wisdom en de ways de French folks talk—what wuz dat but testin'? I could see dat I had to fine out ef'n I could talk open to dat boy, ef'n he'd 'cept me as his ekal or ef'n he'd try to get back at me fo' doin' so. En you 'member what comes arter dat arguin'?"

"Wasn't it that episode where you and Mister Finn get separated in the fog? But that was—let me check to be sure—yes," I said, finding the place, "yes, that was two nights after that argument."

"Well, I be ding-busted ef'n it wuz! 'Cordin' to *Huck* it wuz two nights later. But 'cordin' to my rek'lekshun it wuz dat very night. He wuz still smold'rin' 'bout my 'sputin' wid him over Sollerman en my bestin' him in de 'spute 'bout de way de French talks. So he tuck it inter his haid to play dat low-down trick on me, lettin' on dat him en me hadn't ben sep'rated at all by de fog."

"How you 'splain, den, all o' dat glad talk, 'bout how happy you wuz to see him on de raf, en sich stuff? Wuz you genuwine 'bout dat?"

"Sholy I wuz, mammy. Arter all, I knowed dat fer all o' his swagger he wuz still nuffn mo' dan a lost young boy, didn' I? En I couldn't help but feel fo' him de way I'd feel ef'n he wuz our own Johnny, could I? Why you think I got inter dat Sollerman 'spute? Jis fo' de sake o' arguin'? Lan' sakes, but it wuz to try to teach Huck dat he wuz wuth sumfn to me en to hissef, dat I'd no mo' be wase-ful o' him dan if'n he wuz wun o' my own chillen. Why, I wuz rilin' dat boy up so's he'd see de *real* pint, dat 'spite o' Sollerman's lettin' on dat he'd chop a chile in two, he wuz a pappy who knowed how to value chillen—his own en yuther folks—en dat it wuz sholy wicked to treat enybody like dey wuz 'half a chile.' Er 'half a human'—fo' *dat* matter!"

"So wuz dat de las' o' yo' testin's?"

"Dey wuz wun mo'. When we wuz gettin' close to Cairo I could tell dat Huck wuz havin' trubbil wid his conshuns 'bout helpin' free a slave. His face wuz clabberin' up like milk sowerin'. So I jedged I'd best deal out sum kyards en see how he'd play 'em. I began to dance 'bout, like he writes, sayin' 'Dah's Cairo,' ever time I seed a gob o' lights on de sho'. En den I rattled on 'bout how arter I got free I'd save money en buy mammy's en my chillens' freedom. 'Deed, I dropped de bucket en let it sink clear down to de bottom o' de well: I 'clared dat ef'n I had to do it, I'd get sum o' dem Ab'lishunists to help steal my chillens out o' bondage.

"Well, it wuzn't hard to see dat *dat* kine o' talk put a slab o' ice on ole Huck, dat I couldn' trust him to act out o' goodheartedness fo' me. So b'fo' he set off fo' sho' in dat canoe to fine out ef'n dem lights wuz Cairo, I did sum mighty thick buttuh-spreadin' o' my own. I carried on like I wuz de mos' 'preciatin' puhsun in de 'hole world, 'clared dat I wuz beholden to Huck, dat he wuz de bes' fren' I ever had, dat he wuz de ole true Huck, de on'y white genlman dat ever kep' his promise to me. I said dem words what's in de book. But I said dem b'kase I knowed dat de on'y hope I had fer gettin' a pail o' merciful feelin's out o' him wuz to shower him wid an outpourin' o' sugared grat'tood."

"Buttuh-spreadin', is it? Wuz de buttuh you spread like de buttuh dat you 'ccusin' Huck o' spreadin'? B'kase ef'n it is, den you gots a wide streak o' mean-ness in you, too. Hain't dat so?"

Pappy pulled his pipe from between his teeth and looked at mammy with surprise—no, it was disappointment.

Mammy stared back at him. Then suddenly she broke into a laugh."Nem-mine, James Hawkins," she said. "I lay I kin joke you, cain't I? As ef'n I doan' know de diff'rence 'tween bein' mean to folks fo' de sake o' feelin' better dan dem, feelin' bigger dan dey is—like yo' Huck—en bein' mean kase it necess'ry fo' gettin' out o' bondage. But lemme take you back to dat sep'rashun in de fog. Ef'n dat Huck spreads buttah to make his meanness easy to swaller, den I doan' see eny on dat fog episode. He shows de kine o' lick-spittle feller he is dah, doan' he?"

Pappy told her she was right, that you wrote about that episode the way it truly happened. But he guessed that you wrote about it to use it as a decoy, figured that by owning up to the cruelty of that prank you probably hoped to put readers off the scent. If you could make them believe you felt bad about your treatment of him *there*, he told her, then they'd most likely think you'd learned your lesson and surely wouldn't treat him so shabbily again.

How he rattled on *then*, piling up a heap of telltale signs of your cruelty, like they were crackers from a full barrel. Those two men who were hunting for five runaway slaves? Why did you tell them your pap was sick with smallpox on the raft? he asked mammy and me. To save his skin? Maybe, he allowed. But he was sure he heard some low chuckling on your way back to the raft, and it made him wonder if you had suckered those men more to sharpen your skills in gulling others and to add two more sapheads to your belt, like, he said, "dem Injuns do wid dose skyalps."

And when you learned that you'd floated past Cairo and decided to canoe back upstream? Did you both sleep all day, resting up for the work of paddling upstream? he asked us. Were you both genuinely surprised when you found the canoe gone from the raft? Was that some more work of the rattle-snake skin? Indeed it was, answered pappy. It was the work of the rattler he was traveling with, anyway. He believed that to return to the Ohio and steamboat north would end the pleasure trip you were bent on having, would rob you of the lackadaisical floats you were lapping up. Always a light sleeper, he claimed that he woke to the midday rustle of those cottonwood leaves that were hiding the two of you. And when he saw you footing off in the direction of the raft, he hoped you weren't up to some treachery, were only slipping off to empty yourself.

It took a lot of pretending, he said, to act surprised when you and he later got to the raft and found the canoe gone. And he did his best to ignore the faint shadows of dampness on the raft—your footprints, he decided.

"It warn't no use fer me to do nuffn but t' go 'long wid Huck en t' hide f'om him my mistrust. It warn't easy lettin' on dat I wuz happy to see him when ole Jack led him out t' whar I wuz whilst he wuz stayin' wid de Grangerfords. En when he tole me all 'bout dat feud en de bullits dat dem Shepherdsons wuz shootin' en him perched in dat tree seein' all—well, I knowed agin (but I dassent p'int it out t' *him*) dat he wuz in de bes' place fo' to warn dat young Misto Buck o' de Shepherdsons circlin' roun' him and his kuzin. I jedged it bes' not to ax him why he didn' warn Misto Buck, why he didn' keep his eye peeled like he awluz did when we wuz on de river."

"James Hawkins! Dat's only spekyulashun! Mebbe dat young'n didn' see de sons o' dem shepherds one bit. Mebbe he wuz fixin' his eye on dem boys' dads! How 'bout dat? But here you go 'ccusin' him o' treachery. Oughtn't you be hangin' yo' haid fo' shame, awluz thinkin' de wust o' dat boy?"

"Good lan', mammy. Sho' nuff, it *is* spekyulashun. Sum. But I wuz dere, wuzn't I? En I 'members de way ole Huck's lip—awluz de lower wun—would stiffen up when he wuz strayin' f'om de truth er 'nittin' bombuls onto de facks. En whilst he wuz tellin' me 'bout dat gun-shootin' dat lip wuz gettin' a good freeze on it. En I doan' think it wuz b'kase de sight o' blood wuz puttin' a chill on it."

Then pappy held forth like one of those Chautauqua talkers, like he had a lecture all worked out, asking first a load of questions and then answering them all himself. He asked us to think over that stretch about the Duke and the King, to reckon up how long you and he had those two scoundrels along. I guessed about three weeks and mammy guessed four while he was gathering up breath for the next questions.

He told us to hush.

Did we, he asked, believe that he didn't see through those two trash-peddlers? And did we wonder why *you* believed it would have done no good to tell him that they were frauds? More, had we bothered to ask ourselves why you hadn't found a way—early on—to cast off without those rascals so that you and he could continue on your own? Most, could we read the signs of your fascination with that pair of low-down water-rats?

Mammy and I knew that pappy's questions weren't questions at all. Naturally he saw through the Duke and the King. After all, before I was five years old pappy had learned me by heart his favorite saying—one I was to recite only to him when we were alone: "De white folks is white," he'd say slowly, speaking like a schoolmaster, "b'kase dey is like glass. En glass," he'd emphasize, lowering his voice to sound sinister, "is what you *sees troo!*"

"Go on, go on, James Hawkins, en answer yo' questions—all 'cept dat wun 'bout wedder you saw troo de trash-peddlers. Dey's glass, o' course."

According to him you needed to believe in the uselessness of telling *him* that the rascals were frauds: you didn't want to be beholden to a nigger for working up a plan to free yourselves from them. He also knew he had to wait for you to signal your disapproval of the rascals, else you'd get uppity at his quicker perception and shorter fuse for moral outrage. Besides, he argued, you didn't want to be free from them. So you made out that you and he were the next thing to hostages, played up the fear that the rascals could catch you or else release the poster with the reward for Jim. Pappy scoffed at this, insisting that if you and he were smart enough by yourselves to escape from St. Petersburg and to get yourselves that far down river, then you could surely slip out of the clutches of that pair, cover your tracks to keep them from catching you, and masquerade yourselves well enough to dodge reward-hungry slave-hunters.

All of his answers, he continued, pointed to your fascination with those rascals. Neither their prisoner nor their lackey, you were, he was convinced, their shadow. You liked their adventures, the excitement of running risks and nudging up against danger. You secretly admired their ability to fleece others, the willow way they could bend down and scoop up out of the dirt some farfetched lie that they could usually get other folks to swallow. You were plumb in awe of their smarts, "the warehouse of tricks," pappy called it, that they always seemed to have at hand.

But even more, pappy claimed, you liked to watch them hurt people. After all, that was one purpose in all of their pranks: to fool gullible, believing folks who'd be hard put, in most cases, to replace the money and self-esteem that those rascals robbed them of.

"Dem two," he declared, stabbing his forefinger into his thigh to emphasize each word, "dem two give ole Huck de sugar tit he mos' longed fo', de wish to feel sco'n fo' yuther folks. On de wun han' ole Huck looked down his nose on dem sapheads fo' bein' sich simple lam's, so easy to shear de fleece f'om. En on de yuther han' he looked down his nose on dem rascals fo' pullin' sich low-down tricks, fo' fleecin' folks who jis' might have a streak of decency in dem.

"Yes, indeedy. Po' Huck honey. He didn' know hissef. He didn' know dat dem two frauds wuz parts o' hissef, dat dey wuz like his brudders unner de skin, dat dey wuz aktin' out de very t'ings dat he hissef wanted so much to do. On'y he could let on like he wuz jis' wun innercent bystander, sumbody yanked into sumfn he didn' want to 'ticipate in."

"Is you talkin' 'bout dat Huck wid de Duke en de King? Er is you talkin', James Hawkins, 'bout dat Huck wid dat Misto Sawyer at dem Phelps's farm?"

"Dat's de bes' question yet, mammy. Fer if'n I'm talkin' 'bout wun, den I'm sholy talkin' 'bout de yuther as well, hain't I?"

They were both going too fast for me, so I asked pappy to explain the connection that seemed so clear to him and mammy.

"Come, mammy. Le's go back en fetch John. 'Pears we done hopped a crick en lef' him on de yuther side. Chile, doan' you see de link 'tween dem two grow'd-up rascals en dat young 'un, dat Mars Tom? Huck tuck to all t'ree o' dem like a cat to milk 'kase dey 'llowed him to hide de meanness in hissef. Ef'n he could go 'long wid de pranks o' dem fust two, lettin' on like he wuz drug 'long agin his will, den it wuz sholy easy fo' him to go 'long wid de same kine o' pranks o' Mars Tom. Sholy you sees de link, doan' you?"

To my nodding head he continued. "Lemme put sum drippin's on dat co'n bread fo' to salt de taste. Tells me dis, bof' o' you. Duz Huck honey ever try to ruffle eny o' de feathers o' Mars Tom's plans? Even oncet? Duz he quarr'l er protest wid Mars Tom over eny o' dem gashly tricks dat dey plays? Duz Huck show *eny* sign o' bein' axasp'rated wid de blimblammin' foolishness dat wuz plumb wearin' me out en wuz—f'om what Nat tole me—makin' wracks o' de mines o' dat Misto Silas and Missus Sally? All t'roo dat 'hole long ordeal (bof' o' you be pleased to notus) Huck honey shows all de signs dat reveals—to enybody what kin *read* signs—jis' how full o' venom he wuz: *glass*, mine you.

"Now dat Mars Tom, he wuz plumb crazy, dey hain't no question 'bout dat. I knowed him by de back. He wuz bewitched by clap-trap, by de 'style' dat he wuz awluz talkin' 'bout. En so real livin' folks en real thin's didn' matter none to him. He lived in a kine o' dreamworld like Huck honey's pap arter he'd swill down dat rotgut. Er like me arter dat snake-bite en dat whiskey dat I had to slosh down my belly. Good lan' but dat Mars Tom wuz wun dang'rus boy.

"But dat Huck. He wuz even mo' dang'rus 'kase he let on dat he wuz a pooty good boy what'd got caught in a tight place en had no way to get out o' it. His telling makes it soun' like he wuz Mars Tom's chattel, like dat mean Mars Tom—ef'n Huck didn' do his biddin'—'d blow up de 'hole show, 'd up en tell dem Phelps 'bout de game dat dey wuz playin'."

Pappy pulled himself out of his rocker, came across the room, and took your book from my hands. He held it, turning it to one side and the other. Then he drew deep at his corncob. Slowly he blew the smoke all over your book. When the smoke rose away he said, "But ef'n you's sumwun's fren', den you doan' skaseley ever treats 'em like Huck en Mars Tom treated me en dem po' Phelps folks."

"James Hawkins, hain't you overlookin' sumfn? Hain't you overlookin' Misto Huck's sentimenterin' over dat Aunt Sally de night arter de 'scape? 'Members him startin' out o' dat house twyste er t'ree times on'y to come back inter de house 'kase he seed dat grievin' Aunt Sally sittin' in de rockin' chair, waitin' fo' news o' dat chile?"

"That was a nice gesture, mammy. I remember it making my voice wobbly when I was reading that scene. But I don't trust pappy's Huck. His swearing he'd never grieve her again reminds me of a couple other changes of heart. Huck's pap conned that fool judge into believing he'd reformed his ways. And at that camp meeting, the King put on that he was a pirate who'd seen the light. Besides, mammy, pappy's Huck made his vow only after Missus Sally'd been mothering him. That must've boosted all his bad feelings about the tricks he'd been helping that Mister Tom to heap on her head. Huck's vow, I reckon, is a sign pappy'd read different from most folks. Make a show of repentance or remorse, and what happens? Folks get all gushy and think well of you for making those signs, just like you're doing, now, for Mister Huck."

"Dat's right, chile. But dat hain't de ha'f o' it. Dem hain't de on'y signs to read. Read de res' o' dem. Huck put me in de pickle barr'l, he did, by sendin' dat doctor 'lone in de canoe. I 'spect'd ole Huck'd come 'long en give sum sign to 'lert me to up en hide. But de splash o' de paddle wuz mos' on me fo' I heard it. I skaseley had time to hide. Later I could see dat de doctor needed help to fix up Mars Tom. I kep' 'spectin' ole Huck to come back. But no sign o' him. I saw dat I had to help dat doctor er else when I did get foun' I wuz gwinter get mighty 'bused by de white folks. En when Huck doan' show up all de nex' day en durin' de nex' night, den I knowed dat Huck wuz probly fixin' up sum 'splanashun fer why he couldn' come back. En I knowed dat dey wuz mo' to his not showin' up dan jis' his 'splanashun. I could read dat sign, you bet! Huck wanted dat doctor en me to be in a pickle widout de stuff to fix Mars Tom b'kase he wuz wishin' fo' de wust to happen to Mars Tom."

"You mean to make me b'lieve dat dat Misto Huck o' yours wuz hopin' dat dat Misto Tom would die? Ef'n you duz, den *you* de crazy wun, a *mighty* sick Arab!"

"Well, mammy, mebbe so, mebbe so. But all de whiles dat I wuz nussin' Mars Tom wid dat doctor I couldn' get shut f'om my mine how ole Huck 'membered dat ep'sode in dat town whar dat Sherburn kernel shot down dat Boggs feller. Ole Huck wuz—what's dat new-fangle' word? yes, mezm'rized— Huck wuz mezm'rized by dat ep'sode en 'specially by dat kernel. Jis' like de way dat Johnny read it, Huck tole me 'bout dat kernel's speechifyin', tole it like it wuz writ on his mine, like dat man's words wuz sumfn dat Huck foun' wuth 'memberin, a Sunny school lesson. En dat kernel! Why dat wuz a man what shot dat yuther man in cold blood. En den he had de face to skold dem white folks like dey wuz nuffn mo' dan misbehavin' chillens. Dat wuz wun mean man, mammy. En Huck? Why Huck honey 'dmired him!

"So when Huck doan' show up fo' mo' dan twenny-fo' hours, den de meanin' o' dat sign come to me: Huck wanted to 'bandon dat doctor en me, hopin' dat Mars Tom'd die. Dat way he could get shut o' Tom. En den I'd be beholden agin on'y to him fo' helpin' me get free.

"I could see dat de on'y thin' fo' me to do wuz to help dat doctor all I could, to let on like I wuz snorin' when dem men came on dat skiff, en to give 'em no fight when dey grabbed me and tied me up. It wuz de easiest thin' I ever did to let on like I didn' know Huck when dem men led me, de doctor, en Tom—flat on dat mattress—back to de farm."

"En when dey tole you dat you wuz a free man, den how'd you feel? Tell us dat, fo' yo' Huck doan' writes much 'bout what you said er dun when he en Mars Tom got you out o' dem chains."

Pappy laughed long, then said he was sure he bested Mister Tom and the Duke and the King all rolled together for the handbill of roles he played in ten minutes. Believing their news just another mean-spirited prank, he pretended astonishment and began to chant to himself distractedly, "James Alexander Hawkins. You is a free man. You's no mo' a slave. A slave no mo', no mo', no mo'. YOU IS WUN FREE MAN!" Then he said he faked his gratitude, fell to his knees on the dirt floor of the hut, raised his arms, and thanked the Lord for sending his deliverers, his Moses and his Aaron, to lead him out of bondage. Then he began to dance about, like he was "settin' de flo' wid Jenny," capering like a fool with Missus Sally's calico dress still on and the chains clanging all about. Finally he fell to blubbering on your shoulder, he told us, thanking you for being the old true Huck, the best friend he'd ever had, blessing you and Mister Tom, vowing that he'd always do right by you both, pledging that for the rest of his life never a day would go by without him saying a prayer for the two of you.

"En all dat time I wuz a stoppered bottle o' water come to a bile. Dat low-'count Mars Tom, mo' vishus dan a wild dog wid de frothy mout'. Knowin' all de time dat I wuz already free! Puttin' me t'roo dem trashy tricks! En Huck wuz even mo' disgustin' fo' goin' 'long wid 'em. But did I haff to bite my tongue? Did I haff to hide my wish to thrash de two wid de chains dat wuz on my back? Did I haff to let on dat I wuz jis' a barr'l o' smiles en gladness en joy? Jis' like dat picture o' de t'ree o' us at de beginnin' o' dat las' chapter. Yes. Here. Wid my han's on de shoulders of my two bes' fren's."

Pappy closed the book, held it at arm's length and let it drop to the floor. "Nemmine what I did when I got all by mysef. You bof' gots 'maginashuns to draw you de pictures o' *dat*."

Mammy set her mending aside, went over to pappy's rocker, pulled his head to her, and began running her hand over his head, stroking it again and again and again. And all the while she repeated, "My Jim. My man. My Jim. My man."

After a bit, mammy tried to break away. But by this time pappy was holding her. And he wouldn't let go.

"Well, James Hawkins," she finally said, "what good's our long evenin' en what we's foun' out 'bout dat book—en dat boy—ef'n we's de on'y wuns what knows what we knows? Duz you think dey's eny chance dat yuther folks'll see dis story en dat Huck de way we sees it?"

"Like as not, mammy. De story'll get read by whites, mos' likely. En dey hain't gwineter be skwintin' at Huck—'cept fo' folks in New England, dem genteel folks. But it's like ole Nat, de slave what brought me de vittles, tole Mars Tom en Huck dat fust time dey come to see me in de hut by de ash-hopper. Chile, fine dat place, please, en read it 'loud? Fo' it wun mo' place dat show how smart us folks is, how we kin play dumb b'fo' white folks. It's dat place, chile, whar Nat's axin' Mars Tom en Huck not to tell nuffn 'bout de dad-blame witches singin' out when Huck en Mars Tom come into de hut. Fine it, chile? It's whar Nat's 'splainin' 'bout how hard it is to make Mars Silas b'lieve in witches."

"Here it is, pappy. Nat says, 'I jis' wish to goodness he was heah now—*den* what would he say! I jis' bet he couldn' fine no way to get aroun' it *dis* time.'"

"Now slowly, chile," pappy interrupted.

"'But its awluz jis' so; people dat's *sot*, stays sot; dey won't look into nothin' en fine it out f'r deyselves, en when *you* fine it out en tell um 'bout it, dey doan' b'lieve you.'"

"Hain't dat de truth, mammy," pappy asked as he pulled her into his lap, kissed her hard and buried his head in her neck.

"It sholy is, James Hawkins. It sholy is de truth. 'People dat's *sot* stays sot.'"
They laughed. And I laughed too.

But, Mister Finn, I'm not quite so sure that it is true, now that I've copied out what I wrote down a decade ago. Of course for years after that long evening we'd occasionally pull your book from the cupboard and I'd read aloud a scene or two. Mammy and I'd marvel at pappy's resourcefulness. How quickly he could size up a situation and fall in with it. Like the time you and Mister Tom pretended you didn't know him when the two of you stepped into his hut at the Phelps for the first time and he blurted out your names. And we got many a laugh from his scheming. Like at the Grangerfords, how he got you to follow Jack in hopes of seeing a stack of water-moccasins, only to come upon him instead. We laughed most at all those times he was faking sleep, pretending to snore, knowing full well what was going on and anticipating what he would do.

For many years, then, Mister Finn, I've had a pretty low opinion of you because of the way you exploited my pappy, used him for your adventures, pretending an interest in freeing him. You all but forgot about him when some better adventure came along, like with the Grangerfords, the Wilks, and all through those dupings by the Duke and the King. You treated my pappy like dirt, plain and simple. A sick Arab, outfitted like some outlandish King Lear, whoever he was! You didn't mind seeing my pappy humiliated, ever.

And of course you tried to cover up your abuse of him by pretending moral distress. Several years ago I asked pappy about that, having read again the long passage where you resolve to find and free him from the Phelps. I told him that your moral dilemma, your agonizing, made me sympathize with you. When you chose to "go to hell," to tear up the letter you had written to Miss Watson, then I felt you showed you were capable of responsible human feelings.

"Well," pappy said, "I doan' rule out sich feelin's in Huck. En mebbe it wuz a close place fer him. But, chile, you gots to 'member dat Huck wrote 'bout all o' dem adventures *arter* dey wuz over. En ef'n you think 'bout dem adventures all by demsefs, den mebbe you see dat dey make Huck look like a pooty low- 'count dog, jis' goin' 'long wid de bes' adventure dat comes to han'. Well, den, to make hissef look better mebbe he planted dat passage you mentionin', like it wuz a flower bed of moral worryin', jis' de same as he did back when we tho't we wuz near Cairo. Dat way he gets folks to think well o' him, keeps folks f'om trowin' him onter de trash pile wid dem yuther rapscallions dat hain't got so much moral feelin's as a bitch in heat. Mebbe I'm hard on ole Huck. But dat long passage soun' like it wuz writ en rewrit lots o' times, like ole Huck knowed dat he needed to put a gob o' bootshine on de scruffy parts o' his adventure to make de toes o' it shine up fo' de Sunny School folks. I guess, chile, I'd call dat long passage nuffn mo' dan a pair o' moral galluses. Dey keep his pants f'om fallin' down en showin' dat he wuz a bare-rumped boy out fer de wick'dest fun he could fine."

Since pappy's death I've pulled your book from the shelf and read it clean through, twice. For days after each reading, I've found myself repeating Nat's words and asking myself, "Am I 'sot?' Am I so set in *our* way of understanding your book that I can't see it any other way?"

To answer that question I've begun to wonder if, when writing your book, you got a glimmer of pappy's intelligence, his survival shrewdness, his skill in letting on. What makes me wonder *that* is my inability to shake from my mind those words you remember the Duke saying after you led him and the King to think that it was the Wilks's slaves—whom those two had already sold—who had stolen and taken with themselves the six thousand dollars in gold pieces: "'It does beat all, how neat the niggers played their hand. They let on to be *sorry* they was going out of this region! and I believed they *was* sorry. And so did you, and so did everybody. Don't ever tell *me* any more that a nigger ain't got any histrionic talent. Why, the way they played that thing, it would fool *anybody*. In my opinion there's a fortune in 'em. If I had capital and a theatre, I wouldn't want a better lay out than that—and here we've gone and sold 'em for a song.'" Of course the Duke's praise is unfounded, for the Wilks's slaves had nothing to do with the disappearance of that money. Still, Mister Finn, by this time— if not then—you must've learned a good deal about the shrewdness that our people are capable of, shrewdness we've been forced by the evil of slavery to learn, shrewdness our wish for survival has mandated.

As I sit here, thinking how to end this, I also wonder if maybe, when you wrote your book, you felt some deep itch, one you couldn't get a finger on to scratch. Maybe some itch of guilt and wish to make amends for the wrongs you did my pappy? Maybe some unruly feelings of love for my pappy? Maybe you realized the truly noble purpose behind all of his actions: to get himself free so that, in turn, he could free his family? If so, I wonder whether those spells of lonesomeness that find their way into your book express lonesomeness for the one man who was as close to a loving father as you would ever have—my pappy. Maybe your regard for him explains your use of *that* pronoun when, rousing him to begin the flight from Jackson's Island, you said, "'They're after *us!*'"

Maybe I'm wrong. Maybe you'll only laugh and call my notions "sentimentering." But that doesn't matter. What matters is that pappy's "alive," thanks to your book. And maybe, if your book doesn't die, other readers will learn to read signs the way pappy could, the way pappy, bless him, the smartest man I've ever known, taught me to read them, too.

Sincerely yours,
John Isaac Hawkins

Jordan Baker's Letter to Nick Carraway

A Half Century After *Gatsby*

Dear Nick,

Who, you're wondering, could have written you such a hefty letter, one postmarked from Long Island? Might it be someone you knew on that riotous island many years ago? Someone who remembers—still with some vividness—the events of that party world that swelled and swept ashore one summer, smashing that singular man, Jay Gatsby? Yes, Nick, one person who was witness to those events still survives: your once-upon-a-time sweetheart, Jordan Baker Rittenhouse.

Well of course I married, Nick. One of the Philadelphia Rittenhouses, just in case you know your Eastern society bloodlines. No, not quite a Cabot or a Lodge—and not a Kennedy. But good blood, anyway. Yes, Nick, I've had a good life since that summer. Even won a few golf tournaments, until arthritic elbows forced an early end to my glorious, golden career. And, believe it or not, I even bore my husband two daughters. One is a beautiful little fool—the best thing a girl can be in this world, according to Daisy. The other's a sensible girl who, in turn, has also had a pair of daughters. Oh yes, legitimate ones, born in wedlock.

Why, you wonder, do I wish now, so late, to tell you about my family? Well, it's partly to let you know that I was not quite the selfish, dishonest, frigid, unmaternal woman you portrayed me to be in that book you wrote. But my wish is actually prompted by seeing the feature story about your retirement on television last week. It's also been prompted by Gloria's, my granddaughter's, questions. For you see, Nick, she read your story during this past semester in a literature course at Bryn Mawr. The two events made me pull your book off the shelf and reread it—for the first time since it came out. You can be sure that the binding's been broken. And I'm amused to see some of the obscenities I'd scrawled in anger along the margins, so furious had your story made me at that time, Nick. But Gloria tells me that your book is regarded as a classic, read and loved by generations of college students, that it was—so her professor said—one of the top ten books that college students read last year.

So between your book's success and your "rise to prominence" on television, I decided it was time you got some comeuppance—from an unexpected quarter. By the bye, though, you did look good, even to a widow like me. Your silvered hair, your clean, lean face, and your Paul Newman–ice-blue eyes still make you look the man of probity, of rectitude, of moral integrity. And it seemed fitting, then, that you had taken your father's hardware business and built it into a national chain. "True Value Hardware." That's perfect, Nick: Truth and Value. Sounds like the same I'm-one-of-the-few-honest-people-I've-ever-known Nick, all right.

I hope you're seated in a comfortable chair, Nick, for there are a few pages to this. Maybe a snifter of Napoleon brandy or amaretto to sip from when my letter seems a bit harsh might be a good suggestion, too. I know you won't be disturbed by family, Nick, for unlike me, you never married, had no children, as I could have predicted at the end of that Long Island summer—and as the brief television feature on you confirmed. More of that anon.

Rereading your account of the illustrious James Gatz, I must admit that I was charmed: by the way you tell the story, by the wonderful particulars of Gatsby's bizarre parties, by the way you manipulate the materials to cajole even me into sharing your admiration for Gatsby, your censure of Tom, Daisy, and me. A cunning man you were, Nick. But too cunning, finally. And it's your cunning that has made me ask questions—not about your story, but about you. Why, I wondered, did you see fit to write the story at all? And why did you write it so artfully, skipping back and forth as you do about Gatsby's background, about his and Daisy's prewar romance? And why did you airbrush Daisy and Gatsby's adultery? More significant, Nick, why didn't you tell Tom—on that October afternoon when you ran into him on Fifth Avenue—that Daisy had been driving the car, that it was she who ran over Myrtle Wilson, tearing, as you seem determined to insist, her left breast so that it swings "loose like a flap?"

Dishonest, supercilious, and calculating though you portrayed me, Nick—the hard, evil snow-queen—I've matured, become tolerant, even charitable. And so I can find good reasons for commending your writing Gatsby's story. Maybe you just wanted to tell a story to entertain people? The rise and fall of James Gatz. A good story. But I've learned—from experience—that few storytellers ever tell a story just to entertain others. They all have reasons, personal ones. Their stories always have some private significance, some lesson, some self-aggrandizing motive, some wish or anxiety that they are compelled to express. And, Nick, you were never entertaining, anyway, so that motive for telling your story would be entirely out of character.

How about another reason? Sure.

The Twenties were riotous, rollicksome, roustabout—and morally repugnant—years. (See, Nick, even I can roll off some alliteration; it's easy, after a refresher of you.) And sure, those years needed a historian, someone to document "the way it was," to use the phrase of some American writer. And your story certainly documents for future generations that wild, postwar atmosphere in America—at least along the eastern seaboard. Were that your only motive,

Nick, to be a social historian, I'd have no cause to write you this letter. But you are no more interested in writing social history than in writing an entertainment. After all, you aren't an objective, disinterested historian. What's more, you can't even set down a straight chronology of events, as the confused sequence of the story shows. (Even if you could, I've come to learn that historians are unreliable, too, that they interpret events, mascara them to make them fit a theory, ignore or omit events that don't jibe with their notions.) So, Nick, no historian's motive prompts your story, either.

And even if you were just trying to be the didactic moralist that you are, I'd have no cause to write this letter. You're certainly good as an unfrocked priest, looking sourly down upon the events of that summer, pursing your lips as you instruct your readers about the perilous, corrupting world of the East. But contrary to what you say and, perhaps, still believe, Tom and Gatsby and Daisy and I did not possess, as you put it, "some deficiency in common which made us subtly unadaptable to Eastern life." We adapted. You didn't. And as far as that goes, Nick dear, the Midwest or the West differs little from the East in kind. In degree, maybe, but not in kind. Tom and Gatsby and Daisy and I brought with us our corruption.

You want it straight? Okay. I learned my dishonesty where you learned yours, Nick, in the Midwest. After all, even Gatsby's dishonesty about who he was, as you tell us, started out there in Little Girl Bay when James Gatz told Dan Cody that he was Jay Gatsby. While you'd like, then, Nick, to teach the moral that the East's an evil place, that moral has some rusty holes in the bottom of its bucket. (For a guy in the hardware business, you'd appreciate that old metaphor, wouldn't you?)

Or, how about the carelessness of the rich? Sure, Nick, Tom and Daisy were "careless people—they smashed up things and creatures and then retreated back into their money or their vast carelessness, or whatever it was that kept them together, and let other people clean up the mess they had made . . . ." But the rich have no corner on that market, do they? Myrtle was careless, wasn't she? And her sister, too? I think there are lots of people besides the well-to-do who are irresponsible, who make messes that other people have to clean up after them. Even you, Nick. I'm trying to clean up the mess you left—rather the mess you made but artfully concealed. So, two strikes against your role as moralist: if your attempt was to teach the have-nots that the haves are a special breed whom the have-nots should despise rather than envy, then that lesson, too, has rusty—well, let's call them rotted—holes in it.

So what prompted you, my moralist, to write your honest story? To record your moral approval of a man for whom you also felt "unaffected scorn?" To put yourself on the side of idealists who acquire money to use it for "noble" reasons? To endorse dreamers who have nonmaterial dreams, who seek an ideal world? To celebrate the naifs, the innocents who will get crushed by the calculating, the corrupt? Perhaps, Nick. But despite your attempt to glorify Gatsby by making him the Great Gatsby, despite your making sure that we hear you shout across his lawn, "'You're worth the whole damn bunch put together,'" despite your back-patting about reserving judgments, I don't believe you ever approved of Gatsby. Indeed, Nick, you don't approve of anyone—except yourself.

You know, Nick, your book is depressing because you're so down on people. I mean, look: Not only do you have it in for your fellow men, but for women, too. A chilly vision you present, Nick, of men who deserve our scorn: cruel Tom, naive Gatsby, lunatic George, bumbling Owl-Eyes, parasitic Klipspringer, my escort at that first party—"a persistent undergraduate given to violent innuendo"—molar-cuffed (and so, rapacious?) Wolfsheim, feckless Mr. Gatz, easily duped Dan Cody, and even Chester McKee, a banal photographer who can't even shave without leaving a spot of lather on his cheek for fastidious you to wipe off—with your handkerchief, of course.

While you're hell on men, Nick, you're worse on women. I get off easy. I merely lie and am "incurably dishonest," something that made no difference to you: "Dishonesty in a woman is a thing you never blame deeply—I was casually sorry, and then I forgot." Or so you say. But it sure as hell was something you made certain to get on the record, wasn't it? So, shame on me for denying that I'd left the top down on the convertible and so let it get soaked in a downpour. Shame on me for lifting my ball out of a bad lie during a tournament and then lying about it. Charity was never your strong suit, Nick. Neither was research or even a journalist's regard for accuracy. It will do no good for me to tell you that I didn't move the ball, or that when I left the convertible, the top *was* up. But it's true. You're not the only one who wanted to slander me. There were other envious people who lit rumors about me, ones they hoped would unnerve me, get me off my game. The sports world is ruthless, Nick dear. And you heard only what you wanted to hear, accepted as truth rumors that fed your scorn for me and for other women.

While I come off easily, Nick, my "sisters" don't. What a profile—I believe it's called a "hatchet job," now—you do on your beautiful cousin Daisy. (By the way, I trust you know that she died in 1931—cancer of the breast. And I suppose that you enjoy that poetic justice, don't you? After all, it so beautifully parallels Myrtle's flopping breast. Not quite tit for tat, but close, if you'll allow an old woman's crude pun.) Anyway, to you Daisy became the frivolous flirt, a mannikin mama, an adulterous wife, a disloyal lover, an unrepentant homicide, the virginal whore. And Myrtle? A vulgar slut with cheap taste whose nose, bloodied by Tom, you exult in. Her sister, Catherine, a lying lush; and Mrs. McKee, an ingratiating simp ("'I like your dress, Mrs. Wilson. I think it's adorable . . . it looks wonderful on you, if you know what I mean'"). And then there's that lachrymose soprano and the yellow-dressed strippers and that aggressive, back-home girl who tried to compromise you by insinuating your betrothal—the one who caused you to scurry East to begin with.

(And come, come, Mr. Carraway, who is really the source for some of the statements in your book? Like the one you include about Gatsby: "He knew women early, and since they spoiled him he became contemptuous of them, of young virgins because they were ignorant, of the others because they were hysterical about things which in his overwhelming self-absorption he took for granted." Perhaps some faulty attribution, as journalists term it? The Jay Gatsby we knew was contemptuous of no one. Sounds to me like a sentiment you wish he'd made though? Some "projection," if memory of my psychiatrist's jargon is sound.)

Not the least of your gallery of contemptible women, of course, is Ella Kaye, the woman who symbolizes all our gender in your eyes: the castrating bitch. It wasn't enough for you to allude to the "none too savory ramifications by which Ella Kaye, the newspaper woman, played Madame de Maintenon to [Dan Cody's] weakness and sent him to sea in a yacht." No, Nick, you also incriminate her by remarking that she boarded Cody's yacht "one night in Boston and a week later Dan Cody inhospitably died." That, Nick, is "violent innuendo," the quality you objected to in my "persistent undergraduate" escort. And female greed? Ella Kaye again: the woman who orchestrates the "legal device" that deprives Gatsby of a mere twenty-five thousand dollars and lets her inherit intact the millions left in Cody's estate.

Well, Nick, in comparison with that gallery of wicked women, Hillside stranglers and Atlanta maniacs have nothing on you.

Why, then, Nick, do I think you wrote your story? Why were you so harsh on everybody? It's quite simple, Nick. You wanted to feel morally superior to everyone else. That's why you're such a moralist, why you want the world at moral attention—so that you can stand tall in that rank of humans whom you ask us to judge. And why do you need to feel morally superior? Well, here's one answer. Because you have nothing else to recommend yourself. Yes, Nick, some people, as some writer once expressed it, have to be right; it consoles them for being nothing else.

Time for another double jigger of Napoleon, Nick? Why not? As you can feel from the heft of what's left, I'm not done. And you may as well get comfy. I am. No, I'm not all in white, buoyed up on an enormous couch, snuggling my painted toenails into a deep-piled ivory carpet. Nor am I standing jauntily like some dowager model, chin lifted, pouring this all out into a dictaphone for a chic secretary to type out. You, Nick, were the one who liked those fashion-plate scenes, not I. I sit at an old desk, cluttered, of course, with odds and ends, a couple of golfing trophies that remind me of a few moments in the sun.

And you, Nick? What mementoes surround you? Halos if you had your choice, I imagine. Oh, yes. The Good Son, Mr. Clean, The Man Who Fled the Corrupting East, Mr. Superego. That's right, Nick. Just like those spectacles you wrote of—Dr. T. J. Eckleburg's—you, too, like to peer down, morally censorious of everyone's behavior. The conscience that would punish malefactors, the voice of guilt whispering, "Shame, shame on you." And why? Well, Nick, I've come to learn this, too, about people. When they behave in extremes, then their behavior conceals contrary feelings, wishes. This means, just in case you're getting a bit dotty, that your moral priggishness, your starchy rectitude, conceals your repressed desire to behave immorally.

A bit slower, you ask? Okay.

You wrote about Gatsby's and the Buchanan's world of pleasure because you secretly envied that world, because you deeply desired to be able to let yourself go, to throw yourself with abandon into a life of sensuous pleasure. Not true? Well, why then, for example, didn't you break off early with the Buchanan's? Why didn't you refuse to attend those orgies at Gatsby's? Why didn't you reject Tom's shouldering you into New York with Myrtle that summer Sunday? Why did you tag along for the blowup when Daisy told Gatsby that she indeed had loved Tom, too? Because, Nick dear, you're a first-class voyeur—a Peeping Tom, a snoop who conceals his eavesdropping behind his moral censure. I think my old psychiatrist calls it reaction formation. You falsified what you saw that summer, you distorted it, exaggerated it. Yes, compulsively you insisted, protested too much, that the party world was reprehensible.

You're like those moral zealots, those book burners, those pornography hunters, Nick. You're a closet voyeur, someone who hides behind the front of being a companionable guy to whom anyone can tell a tale, can unload his cares on. How many wild, unknown men have made you privy to their secret griefs? I wonder. Quite a few, I imagine, because you seek them out, not they you. You need their sordid stories so that you can get a moral high on, don't you?

Just irrational insults from a hysterical woman, Nick? Well, perhaps. So let me end with *two charges*—to resort to fiercely legal language.

Charge number one? Moral hypocrisy.

Charge number two? Accessory to Gatsby's murder.

Your moral hypocrisy? You pretend moral righteousness, but you allowed yourself to be the go-between for Daisy and Gatsby. Hide their adultery though you try, it existed, as you and I both know. And why do you hide it, dear old Nick? Because it makes you into a pander, a pimp, if you will. Not a nice "job" to have on your record, is it? (How you must have rubbed your hands in leering glee at the change written into the script for that movie Paramount made from your story—was in it 1949? For who turns out to be the pimp? Me! And I didn't have a morally defensible motive, for I pimped on the condition that Gatsby pay me off with a Duesenberg—a classy auto for jaunty Jordan to wheel about in, huh? At least the 1974 film—so I'm told—corrected *that* lie.) You had a morally defensible motive for your pimping, didn't you? You were just trying to be a good guy, trying to help out a couple of frustrated lovers? If so, there's still some malice toward Tom in your act. What's more, you knew both Daisy and Gatsby. So you knew that eventually his dreamworld would crumble when he stood the real Daisy against the colossal vitality of his five-year dream of her. And you knew that she'd sooner or later see that he was just too dreamy and that she'd purposely disappoint him. And you, Nick, yes you, wanted to witness that collapse, the wreckage. For, once again, it would prove to you how contemptible we women are, prove to you your moral superiority.

Do I begin to sound like some high-toned old Christian schoolmarm? Excessively self-righteous and morally overbearing? Well, Nick, I don't pretend purity. I'll even own up to you a couple of adulterous affairs I had, just to let you know that I'm human—susceptible to the lure of the flesh and of the fresh. I even thought that I'd marry again, once I'd gotten bored with being a widow. But the suitor wanted convenience not companionship. And I got tired of my own hypocrisy, pretending love for him so as to dredge up some genuine feeling in him. So then: I confess to my hypocrisy. I even laugh at some of my stupid attempts to inflate my moral character. But that, along with menstruation, is a thing of the distant past.

But back to your moral character, Nick. Indeed, it's kindness to call your actions on the heels of Myrtle's death mere moral hypocrisy. After all, you were privy to what Tom actually believed, that Gatsby had run Myrtle down. You knew that Tom was urging revenge upon that half-crazed Wilson. And even more, Nick, you abandoned Gatsby on the day Wilson killed him.

Abandoned? Yes. You knew how crazed Wilson was. You knew that the loss of Myrtle just might tip him over the edge. You knew that he'd be the kind who'd try to trace that flashy car and avenge the manslaughter. But you, old eight-to-five Nick, you just had to go to work, didn't you? And all day long you stewed, anxious about Gatsby? Well, Nick, that anxiety also had mixed in it a wish, the wish that Wilson would find Gatsby and that Gatsby would be vulnerable to his attack.

Now, then, Nick, you could have warned Gatsby to be on the lookout for Wilson. You could even have spent the day with him. You could have done lots of things. But you, like Tom, wanted Gatsby, the foolish dreamer, dead. Sure, you did rush anxiously up the steps of Gatsby's mansion when you drove home from the train station that afternoon, largely because you wanted to be among the first to see the havoc you secretly hoped Wilson would have done.

So guilty are you, so guilty did you feel, Nick, that it's even evident in the way you write about Gatsby in the pool. Wonderful technique, Nick. Don't look at Gatsby at all; just look immediately around him. Sure, that'll make readers put on that mattress the figure they each want to see. How superbly you avoid being the sentimentalist. A lesser writer would have written about Gatsby's bewildered gaze, the perplexity on his brow, the ever-friendly but now-frozen smile on his face, his mouth halfway through its predictable

"Hello, old sport." But the technique, Nick, is a technique of concealment. You don't want to look at Gatsby, not because of artistic technique, but because you can't stand to face the man whose death you permitted, by abandoning him.

And now, Nick, I even better understand why the story you tell gets told so haltingly, so much by fits and starts, why it doesn't come across with a clear chronology of events, an easily remembered sequence. You write it in that artsy way to hide as much as possible your culpability, your guilt, your hand in Gatsby's death. Naturally, it was Daisy and Wilson who were the out-and-out homicides.

But you were the accomplice to Wilson's murder of Gatsby. You and your friend, Tom, for he, too, desired Gatsby's death.

It makes you squirm to be put into the same pigeonhole with Tom, doesn't it, Nick? And you try so hard to wriggle from it, try to separate yourself from him by making sure that your readers know that Tom never knew that Daisy was driving the car that ran over Myrtle. And why didn't you tell Tom that Daisy did it? Moral generosity? To protect Daisy? To allow Tom to stay ignorant? Perhaps, Nick. But for me the deeper reason is that once again you wanted to maintain your moral superiority, conceal your moral contempt for him and Daisy behind the impression that you were, I repeat, Mr. Good Guy.

So, I have to tell you that I've come to appreciate your confession of guilt, hidden though it is. But for you I feel pity. I used to feel contempt for your attempts to rationalize your role in that summer's events, your attempts to put the blame outside yourself—on the East, on the Rich, on the lunatic. But you don't deserve contempt. Rather you deserve and you get my pity. Anyone who so maliciously pulls other people down so that he can stand above them, anyone who so badmouths women—showing his moral contempt for their behavior—in order to conceal his deeper fear of them; anyone who sets himself up as a discerning moral arbiter only to applaud his own moral superiority, well, anyone so desperate deserves my pity. You, Nick, retreated from the East, from humanity, from the moral taint of all people. And what have you gotten out of it? Well, you've duped many people into believing that you're one heck of a good guy. Is it nice to bask in others' applause when you know that you're not the guy they believe you to be?

I'm about at the end, as you can see. I've other things to get to. Got to drive the afternoon Meals-on-Wheels van to see that the elderly get their daily nourishment. Yes, Nick, your Jordan drives. And drives well. Much better than you, I'm sure. And if my letter—or should we call it an epistle?—if it upsets your sunset years, I don't apologize. Your being upset is fifty years overdue, for you had some rejoinder coming from me that long ago. And please don't bother writing me back. I've had enough of you for one lifetime.

Scornfully yours,
Jordan Baker Rittenhouse

P.S. How utterly amused I was to reread your reconstruction of our drive in a Victoria through Central Park. Do you remember the scene? It's just after you have me "sitting up very straight on a straight chair in the tea-garden at the Plaza Hotel." Me? Me, Nick, in a straight chair? Me, sitting up straight? Why, Nick, such posture was neither fashionable nor in character for me. I always slouched—becomingly, of course—always draped my lean body upon any piece of furniture. Anyway, it's just after you report my telling you about Daisy's romance with Jay Gatsby and her marriage to Tom. And then, on our drive you report my telling you of Gatsby's request: that you invite Daisy over some afternoon and let him come too. All of that's fairly correct, Nick.

But your account of your behavior during the rest of that drive? Fantasizing there, aren't you? In the dark, as the Victoria dipped beneath a little bridge, you say that you put your arm around my "golden shoulder," drew me to you and asked me to dinner. I recall the dinner. But your romantic gestures? No, Nick. No. Not then. Not ever. Not from Nicky-Nice Guy. Nor when we passed a barrier of dark trees and "the facade of Fifty-Ninth Street, a block of pale light, beamed down into the park" did you draw up the girl beside you, tightening your arms, pulling her wan, scornful, smiling mouth to your face. All pretense, Nick. Pretense that you were capable of feeling romantic toward a woman whom you scorned. I was as right then, as I am now. And I thank you for accurately reporting at least that much: you were not the honest, straightforward person you made yourself out to be.

But you wrote so well that readers, then and now, sure fell—and fall—for your version. It'll stand, for certain, just as it's stood for the past fifty years. But now that the feminist movement has come to maturity, your version may just stand a bit shorter, may even stand at a bit of a tilt, may lean—off center. Maybe, Nick, a True Value Hardware store has something to prop up a leaning edifice?

Ciao, old sport.

Hammett's Refeathered Maltese Falcon

I sought respite for weary eyes, back, and derriere after poring several hours over early Frank Norris holographs in Berkeley's Bancroft Library. I turned away from the view of the bell tower, which the east windows so splendidly frame, and browsed on nearby bookshelves, which bracket gray manuscript boxes. The call to rescue one such box, which appeared ready to tumble from its place, I could not resist. Intending merely to nudge it back in line with its companions, and so to spare its already scuffed corners from further bruises, I stepped to it. The label on the box intrigued me: "MISCELLANY, UNIDENTIFIED: Items 638–663." A curious researcher, I eased out the thickest manilla folder, 647.

I am no booster of detective fiction, popular though that genre is among many of my students and no few of my lesser colleagues. But I was certain I could identify the author and addressee of the letter that caught my eye. "Dash" would be none other than Dashiell Hammett; "Lily" the recently deceased Lillian Hellman.

There's a tiresome story to tell about the exasperations of toiling among literary executors and pettifogging lawyers, codicils and copyrights. Suffice it that within a scant eleven months I secured the necessary permissions to publish my accidental findings. While they are of small interest to me, they may be instructive or entertaining to those who interest themselves in popular authors. (Indeed, an envious colleague, learning of my discovery, quite assured me that it would be a "super" addition to an anthology of reader-response criticism which a friend of his at Hamilton College in New York was assembling. I chose to decline, having little sympathy for new-fangled schools of literary criticism.)

I am indebted to J. Edward Struthers, curator of the Bancroft, for his most able assistance throughout these past several—and stressful—months.

Item 647A—An Unmailed Letter, Dashiell Hammett to Lillian Hellman

[This letter and its accompanying revision are undated. A modicum of research, however, (namely, Miss Hellman's Introduction to a 1967 collection of five

Hammett stories in *The Continental Op* yielded their probable date of composition: the winter months of 1932. That year saw the "completion" of the play to which Hammett refers, Hellman's *The Autumn Garden*. The quotation marks signify that Miss Hellman completed the play that year, but that it aborted in rehearsal. Many years later she recast the play, setting its events in 1949. Curtains opened to it in 1951, but it failed commercially. Other details in Hammett's letter may be confirmed by Miss Hellman's aforementioned Introduction.]

Dear Lily,

You won't get this letter. You sure as hell won't see the work I've done during this week, a week filled with your absence. So why, you'd insistently ask, do I write at all? For penance, I might have said, years ago. To make amends for my snarling criticism of your play, your first play. My censoriousness—"It's worse than bad, it's half-good"—still must burn in your ears. And my insistence that you tear up the play, throw it away, and start over is likely eroding the wall of some reservoir of self-esteem that I may have helped you build these past months. (But has anyone guaranteed that TB victims are above inflicting pain on others?)

After you left the room and shortly the house, I began imagining the labor you'd be in for, the difficulty of the task I'd insisted on, the months of revision lying ahead—provided I hadn't killed your play altogether. Could you do it, I asked myself? Have you the self-discipline and dedication that serious writing requires? Could you do it with me around, a guy who seems to have thrown in the towel, who's yanked himself from the game in the fifth inning? Could I do it?

That, Lily, is the question. Could I do it? There, sure as hell, is the damn rub. You know who poured himself a stiff one. And a stiffer second.

I turned the tables. Had Lily, I asked myself, ever cocked a Semitic eyebrow at work I'd written? Sure. Some of the early stories for *Black Mask* you found amusing. But any signal from you of a major flaw?

Walking off the blurring from the stiff ones, I recalled our first meeting in that Hollywood restaurant, your helping me get over a five-day drunk, later sitting in my car and talking until daylight. For a twenty-four-year-old you were surprisingly well-read. And I was flattered you'd read so much of my stuff. Buoyed by the tide of five days' booze and the fresh breeze of your infatuation, I dismissed your remark about my "treatment" of Brigid O'Shaughnessy in the last pages of *Maltese Falcon*. "She's bright. Too bright to stand there and swallow in silence your detective's reasons for not 'playing the sap' for her." Those were your impertinent words, if I remember correctly. I gave you little heed, had little reason to probe whether you had reason or the literary credentials to fault a work you'd probably read hurriedly—for entertainment, at that.

You'd know, if I sent this letter and showed you the pages accompanying it, that I pulled *Falcon* from its nest, and sat up until late morning rereading it.

Later that afternoon I woke, drank black coffee, paced the floors, took a walk, and stewed, all to the accompaniment of two packs of Camels. Finally I admitted the irony: my novel's ending deserved the snarling criticism I'd dished out on the draft of your play, "It's worse than bad, it's half-good."

It was after midnight before I sat down to the typewriter and began the labor I knew I had to be willing to do if I expected the same from you. Oh, sure: I'm dissatisfied with this ending. Never happy with my "finished" work, I can't imagine any good writer who ever is. This ending, you'd see, reveals too blatantly the. . . . Well, never mind about what I saw in what I'd written, what I see in what I've revised. Hell, it's got to stand on its own.

The week you've been gone has been productive, even though what I've done will never see printer's ink. I'll not even tell you what I've done to fill the time—any more than I'll tell you about the girl in San Francisco. The silly one who lived across the hall in Pine Street. I wait now for your return, confident in it, confident the pain of my criticism will have blunted itself against your toughness, confident we'll both see your work—much revised—play the boards before the year is out.

Love, Dash

Item 647B—A Revised Scene for *The Maltese Falcon*

[Across the top of the first page of the uncorrected typescript are the following handwritten instructions, which conclude with Hammett's initials: "Replace the last nine paragraphs of the final scene between Sam and Brigid with these pages. To be exact, insert this revision, in its entirety, just after Sam says, for the seventh and last time, that he 'won't play the sap' for Brigid. Keep the last scene between Effie and Spade. D.H."]

Brigid drew away from him and stepped toward the armchair.

Turning on her heel, she pointed an enameled fingernail at him.

"So, you won't play the sap," she smirked. "Well, you are one, Sam, send me over or not. 'I won't play the sap for you,'" she mimicked. "Your tedious refrain protests too much. It hoists a fluttering flag, signals that your fancy reasons for sending me over are a front. Why, Sam," she laughed, the throb gone from her voice, "you're as phoney as that bird. Sure, I'm a fraud. But so are you, shamus. So you've got seven reasons for sending me over. Maybe more? Well, any guy who drums up that many reasons to justify what he does, shows he's trying to hide his real reasons.

"Sit down, Sam. Take a load off. You've got time, before Dundy and Polhaus show up to chauffeur me off, time to hear me out. Broad I may be, but not a dumb one. You can't expect I've listened to your spiel without hope of answering back. Besides, this may be your last chance to learn something about yourself."

Spade stepped into the passageway. He leaned his erect body against the door frame and crossed his arms on his chest. "Go ahead. Lift the lid on my reasons for sending you over. Entertain me one last time, angel, with what you're best at—lies."

"From the top, Sam. First. So you're supposed to 'do something about it' when your 'partner is killed.' Like doing something to honor him, to show you know how to be your brother's keeper? To show how morally right-minded you are, is that it? Well, Sam, we both know you've been bedding Miles's wife. What's her name? Iva? Yes. So, feeling guilty, you're stung by your disloyalty to Miles and stained by the hypocrisy you had to muck around in when he was blind to her infidelity and your treachery.

"How does a guy like you rub out guilt? Simple. You find his murderer—murderess in this case—and send her over. Simple arithmetic. A plus cancels a minus. A college kid across the bay at Berkeley might find amusement in unraveling why Sam Spade, Moralist, wishes to be his partner's avenger. Why else but to balance the scales, offset with a legal right the moral wrong you did him."

The face beneath Spade's blood-streaked eyeballs tightened. He uncrossed his arms. From his pocket he pulled his tobacco and rolled a cigarette, his hands steady. He fired the end, inhaled deeply, then softly laughed, his mouth empty of smoke.

Brigid watched him, then stepped to the padded rocking chair. She wagged her head and smiled. "Still bears the impress of Gutman's bulbous body," she said. Sitting, she continued. "Second. You're a professional, and," mimicking again, "'when one of your organization gets killed it's bad business to let the killer get away with it . . . bad for every detective everywhere.' Now a defender of the faith? A priest of the profession? Verily, a knight errant? Do you expect anyone to believe you care a rat's"—she paused—"a rat's whisker for your 'brothers' in the profession? More 'brother's keeper' hooey, Sam. As you know, inside yourself. Why, you're a loner to the end. You took not one day to mourn Archer's death or to remove his name from the office door. You'd as lief—an ugly, old-fashioned word you like to favor—you'd as soon have the rest of your detective fraternity bumped off. Then you'd have the business all to yourself. Professional obligation? It sits poorly on your shoulders, Sam. Call it a bad fit."

Spade shrugged his shoulders and tapped the ash from his cigarette. His lip twitched over his eyetooth.

"Third," she snapped, crossing her shapely legs and bobbing the blue slipper that had fallen away from her heel. "'To play the sap' for me would be unnatural. To expect a detective to 'run down criminals and let them go free is like asking a dog to catch a rabbit and let it go.' Is my intonation right, Sam?"

Spade slowly mashed his cigarette into the door frame. Black and brown bits of tobacco dropped to the scuffed floor. He let the butt fall, then ground it with his heel. "Not bad," he growled. "Not bad at all. Work on getting more snarl in it, though. You may find time to practice it at San Quentin, darling." His yellow-gray eyes glinted.

Brigid lifted the arched eyebrows over her dark-lashed eyelids."It's unnatural, is it, to train a dog to capture prey but not harm it? Never heard of bird dogs, Sam? Hell, you bird-dog people, catch criminals, and, tail wagging with pride, keep the soft clamp of your bite on them until the law pats you on the head, takes your captives, and twists off their necks. Your folderol about expecting a dog to release a rabbit he's caught lets slip your natural destructiveness.

"Get it clear, Sam. You get off on violence, enjoy tracking criminals. Like that predatory bird, that raptor we've all been trying to get our hands on, you've got a killer's instincts. How your pulse raced every time your attention fixed on Wilmer. But you get to hide your instincts behind a sign on your office door, one that licenses you to pretend only to sleuthery. Detective? A line of business that guarantees you'll mix it up with killers."

Spade walked from the doorway to the sofa, pivoted, dropped his body onto it, and threw his arms behind his head, lacing his fingers together behind his neck. He pushed out his lower lip and nodded.

"Your generous signal for me to continue, I am to presume?" Brigid purred.

"Fourth. Truly impossible, is it, to let me go without getting yourself dragged to the gallows? You recited that line all night. But it doesn't wash. You can unravel the riddles to Lieutenant Dundy, cut through the knot of this whole thing. And you can make it stick that Wilmer rubbed out Thursby and your partner. You've said yourself that all the cops want is one fall guy. They'll get him. You don't have to send me over to save your neck. And you know it. How can you, who derides lies and liars, stand your own humbuggery?"

"I don't suppose you could shut your beautiful, goddamned lips," Spade said, yawning. "Maybe we could practice sitting silent in the gray, cold light of morning while we wait for San Francisco's finest?"

"No, Sam," she whispered, the throb back in her voice. She lifted herself from the chair, brushed the wrinkles from her dress, stepped across to the sofa, and eased herself onto its arm next to Spade. "Not yet. I'm not quite done. My beautiful, goddamned lips have more than savory kisses in them. After all, you're the truth seeker, aren't you? Well, it so happens I've found some truth too. About you. It's that you are running scared, are frightened, as your last three reasons prove.

"Five. If you let me off, I'd 'have something' on you, something I 'could use whenever' I wanted? What's your fear, Sam?" she asked, a pout in her voice as she traced his hairline with a finger. "I'll bet you've never told anyone your history, afraid it would be made light of. Why not join the human race? It doesn't take too much out of a man—any human—to tell what happened, way back when. Got used by somebody, got hurt, by some female probably? Mother betray you? Preferred father's company to yours? Gave birth to baby brother? Treacherously showed that her love for you wasn't exclusive? Or maybe it was a girlfriend? Gave you an apple? Said she'd bought it for you? But as you took that crunchy first bite, who came 'round the corner and caught you gnawing on his stolen apple but the greengrocer?"

Spade looked up at her, laughed, and pulled her finger away from his temple. "Chewing gum and Freudian guesses, is it, angel?" he said. He looked away and shook his head slowly.

"Glad to know you've heard of the Viennese doctor. And do lift again that lip over your dogtooth. You do it so well, the result of much practice before a glass, I'm sure. But whatever it was that happened way back when, you early vowed, didn't you, that you'd never let someone get something on you again? 'Once burned, twice shy?' You shatter that cliche: Once burned, always shy. That's Samuel Spade."

Spade unlaced his fingers from behind his head and brought a soft fist to his mouth, covering another yawn that spread open his face. "Any chance you could speed it up? I wouldn't want an interruption to deprive me of your goofy autopsy of my character." A pleasant smile illuminated his face.

"Six: you fear someday I'd 'shoot a hole' in you. That's called paranoia, Sam. Sure, I'm treacherous. But treachery is what humans have in common. We hurt one another, can't help but betray each other, sooner or later. Not just friends and enemies. But lovers and strangers, husbands and wives. And certainly brothers and sisters. But that's how we're made, Sam, full of conflicting drives and wishes. But this reason for sending me over—to keep me from shooting a hole in you—confesses your fear of being human, your fear of getting hurt, by me or anyone else. You're a crip—a cripple if you want the word whole. Maimed, part-human, you need more help than any doctor can give you."

"I'm beginning to imagine how Effie's relative must bore the college kids in his history courses across the bay," Spade said, grinning like a lewd satyr. "But we must have reached the end, my dislike of the notion that there'd be 'one chance in a hundred that you'd played me for a sucker.' With bated breath I await your explanation of what reason seven reveals."

Brigid rose from the arm of the sofa and walked to the doorway of the kitchen. She stepped into the kitchen and back out, slowly turned, and leaned against the doorway, rubbing her back against it. Her breasts gently bobbed, her belly undulated. Spade leaned forward on the sofa, head between hands, elbows on knees, and stared at the floor between his feet.

"Glad to oblige, Sam. A woman's duty—to please. Another deep-seated fear of yours, to be a sucker or sap, huh? With some reason, I'll grant, for suckers and saps never leave off believing they can trust other people. They persist in pretending, even when they know better, that people are basically good. But most people choose to be suckers and saps, gullible chumps who keep getting burned by their fellow humans. Why? Because in between burnings they have good relationships, times of shared things. Sure, that makes them pathetic. But not as pathetic as a crip. A crip, like you, is terrified of getting burned in a human relationship. Rather than run that risk, you'll show your heel to anyone who asks you to make yourself emotionally vulnerable."

Spade pulled from his pocket his lighter. Firing it, he held it horizontal, looking at its small flame as Brigid went on.

"You pride yourself on not being a sucker. And I'll hand it to you. You impressed me at first, made me believe that you were absolutely the wildest, most unpredictable person I'd ever known. I take that all back, Sam. You're so predictable that you rival a day-old corpse for stiffness. You're what's called a hard-boiled realist, aren't you? You never fool yourself into believing that what's true isn't, never wish that what has to happen can't. You've nothing in common with Iva, who knows you don't love her, care for her, even need her. But she'll be at your office door first thing in the morning—after news of my arrest hits the streets—hoping you're eager to bed her again. You've less in common with your secretary Effie, who's crossing her fingers for me, unwilling to believe I'm a murderess. Even Gutman, who knows that Wilmer will gun him down before he gets another chance at finding that falcon, is wishing right now for that chance. Suckers all."

"And you're a sucker, angel," Spade scoffed, sneering across at her, "for thinking there's any chance I'll find a way out for you." He blew out the flame and made a harsh derisive snort.

"Oh, I've accepted the inevitable, knowing now who I'm dealing with, never-a-sucker Sam. Why if the world could only find out about you there'd be a brigade of hard-boiled detectives, just like you, in a matter of months. You'd set a new style," she said as she sauntered to the edge of the window between the sofa and the armchair. "Lots of guys'd fall for it. Women, too. But it's not much of an accomplishment, to reject the emotions of trust, love, compassion, forgiveness, tenderness—the emotions of suckers. It's easy to walk the one-way street you're on," she said, peering out the window. "But it leads to isolation."

She reached over and patted him consolingly on the shoulder. "Yes, it leads to the cold comforts of a career, to the life of a private I, spelled like the letter, not 'e-y-e.'"

"My fear of emotional vulnerability again? Sounds like it to me, darling," said Spade, feigning concern as he turned up to her then looked away to study his closely clipped fingernails. "That's a luxury in this business, one that only gets a guy in trouble. Your disposal of Archer proves that, wouldn't you say?"

Suddenly Brigid reached down with her right hand and softly raked a kitchen knife against the side of his throat. He came alive. He leaned into her, grabbed her wrist, pulled her off balance, and rolled her body over his shoulder and onto the floor. She hit hard and grunted. Spade quickly straddled her, pinned her arms to the floor with his knees, and thumped her face with several backhanded slaps of his knuckles. Her eyes blazed up at him.

He got up, the knife in his hand. He lobbed it over onto the table. He brushed himself off and felt at the slight welt on his neck. She raised herself on an elbow, feeling her chin as he sat down in the armchair.

She chuckled between short breaths. "Maybe I'll get liver-colored bruises. They'd match the one on your temple, wouldn't they? But your neck, Sam," she said, slowly getting up and straightening her clothes and hair. "Can it be very bad? You knew it was too dull to cut. It wasn't so dull when I cut up sandwiches earlier, was it? So when did you dull it, Sam? Sometime after you'd dulled your straightedge, I suppose. Of course I checked it out in the bathroom when I was putting my clothes back on. Felt like you'd dulled the blade against the sink, Sam. Anticipated some showdown in your rooms, it seems?"

"Like I said, angel," Spade snarled, kneading his knuckles, "trust is a luxury no detective can afford. You palmed that knife from the sink-board and proved it. So now will you sit down and shut up?"

"That dulled knife on the sink board proved something more than that, Sam," she snapped back at him. "Christ, you planted it there, hoping that someone would pick it up and try to use it. I left it on the table in the nook, still sharp. You dulled it and placed it, handle to the doorway, so that someone would fall to its temptation."

"And you fell. So you've got no gripe coming to you."

"Had I fallen, Sam, you'd have a real welt on your neck. Sure. Feel again. Could it be that I gave you a soft stroke on the neck, just to see what you'd do?"

And then came a torrent, Brigid's face reddening with heat. "Christ but that planted knife and its dulled blade say a lot about why you're a detective, Sam. It gives you all the chances you want to find the weak spots in other people, to learn the smut, the dirt, the soiled truth about them. Lets you feel ever so superior, ever so contemptuous of their frailties and fears. Lets you muck around in murder and see what happens to guys and gals who make themselves vulnerable. Lets you witness the steady flow of treachery, deceit, and double-crossing that they deal out and get dealt. Lets you get close enough to see the decks they deal from. Lets you reaffirm your certainty that humans are hatefully untrustworthy. Lets you strip them to the skin, as you forced me to do, removing the shields that allow them any sense of privacy and decency."

She stopped and took a deep breath, wagging her head at Spade, who had picked up his volume of *Celebrated Criminal Cases of America* and was thumbing his way through it. "Being a detective makes you physically vulnerable—to cuffs from Dundy, kicks from Wilmer, druggings from Gutman, and now a knife raking from me. But you invite those, Sam. For you think they're the same as making yourself emotionally vulnerable. Maybe Gutman and Cairo and Wilmer are—what did you call them?—lollipops. But I'm not."

Spade wiped the stubbled, yellow, wet skin above his lip with a stiff finger. He pulled himself from the armchair, sloshed a glass half full of rum, and walked over to Brigid. He held it out to her.

She turned up her palm, expecting the glass, lifted her eyebrows, and smiled.

Spade put the glass to his own lips and drank down its liquid. "Since you know so much, angel, you must know how to pour your own drink," he snarled wolfishly, showing his jaw-teeth.

By the time he turned to seat himself on the sofa Brigid was at the table. She raised the bottle to her lips. Her Adam's apple bobbed once, paused, then bobbed twice more. She set the bottle down and shuddered briefly. Outside brakes barked and metal doors slammed.

"Fine timing, just as the curtain drops on your Punch-and-Judy show," said Spade. "Act five scene five: enter the San Francisco PD, the Polhaus-Dundy duo." Spade rolled back on the sofa, lazily stuffing a pillow behind his head. "The better to hear you with, my dear," he said. "For the abstract look on your lovely face warns me of an epilogue. Make it brief, please. The elevator will be on its way up."

"I'm thinking about your Flitcraft philosophy, Sam. You coddle that story, don't you? Earlier I thought it interesting but pointless. Wrong again. Charles Flitcraft nearly got bonked by a falling beam one fine day. So he—how did you put it, Sam? Surely you've memorized that story and can recite book, chapter, and verse."

"You bet, angel. After that brush with death, Flitcraft 'felt like somebody had taken the lid off life and let him look at the works.' And let me hurry you along, sweetheart, with more. A refresher. Flitcraft 'was a man who was most comfortable in step with his surroundings. He had been raised that way. The people he knew were like that. The life he knew was a clean orderly sane responsible' (no commas, mind you) 'affair. Now a falling beam had shown him that life was fundamentally none of these things. He, the good citizen-husband-father, could be wiped out between office and restaurant by the accident of a falling beam.' Now pay attention, darling. Here's the important line: 'He knew then that men died at haphazard like that, and lived only while blind chance spared them.' End of recitation. Performer awaits applause of audience before bowing."

Brigid fluffed her hair and set an eyebrow. "A great anecdote, Sam. A parable for living. But it's a parable for crips. How you suckle at that slogan. That men die haphazardly. That they live only while blind chance spares them. A lollipop creed!" she scoffed coldly. "It discards all appeals to order, honor, or nobility. It underwrites irrationality, ruthlessness, irresponsibility. In any order that suits you. A philosophy for crips, who need to believe that nothing matters, that meaning's an absurd notion, that life's a willy-nilly affair."

The elevator cage sounded its steel clashes from the end of the hall. A flurry of footsteps beat out varied rhythms in the hallway. When they reached the doorway, Brigid called out, "Come on in, gumshoes. The door's unlocked. And," her voice lowered again, now that Polhaus and Dundy were entering, "and the villain has been found out."

"What the hell, Spade," grumbled Lt. Dundy, as he came through the passageway, followed by Polhaus and two policemen.

Spade slowly got up from the sofa and poured himself another tumbler of rum. He rinsed his mouth with the drink, swallowed it, then fluttered his open hand aimlessly. "Here's Miles's murderess. I've got the proof. And I've got some exhibits—the boy's guns, one of Cairo's, a black statuette that all the hell was about, and a thousand-dollar bill that I was supposed to be bribed with. But Christ, get this one out of here. She's been babbling at me for half an hour and . . ."

"Hold it, Dundy," interrupted Brigid. "One last thing. You've got the proof, Sam? Wait a minute. Now I see it all. You've had the proof, had it all along. Of course. Once you figured out that Iva didn't kill your partner, you were certain I'd done it. But you didn't let on. Until a half an hour ago you'd led me to think you didn't know I'd shot him. But you've known all along, known that only someone with sexual drag, someone he'd already met, could lure him into an alley close enough to blow him away before he could get his own rod out."

Her strawberry-red hair flouncing against her shoulders, Brigid stepped up to Spade. Her lips held a rich smile of contempt. And her left eyebrow arched high, scrolling a graceful curve on her forehead. "At ease, Lieutenant," she said, without looking in his direction. "I'm quite without a weapon, quite harmless."

Then, in a slow cadence, she said, "Sam's the harmful one, aren't you, Sam? Oh, of course not physically. That's finally not your game. Your game is psychological. You've encouraged my treachery by keeping from me what you learned early on. You withheld that knowledge so that I'd do the things that would prove to you what you wanted confirmed about me: that I was a treacherous swine-maker."

"As good a label as any I can think of, angel," Spade said. "I gave you chances to prove you weren't one. But at every turn you manipulated, deceived, tried to victimize me."

"Oh, Spade. I'm the only victimizer?" she asked, her voice rippling with disgust.

"You'd better believe it. You played me false. That alone warrants my sending you over. Tom, can't you prod your partner into action, get this black widow out of here?"

Lt. Dundy held his hand up to Polhaus, his gesture commanding silence.

"So I'm the only villain in this melodrama, Sam?" asked Brigid. What about your toying with me? Haven't I been *your* victim? You gave me chances, all right, to prove my trust. But every one invited me to become snared in your secret webs, your sticky, nasty, insidious nets. The kitchen-knife ploy, Sam. You never once leveled with me. Yet you expected me to level with you. Sounds like the age-old prerogative of the male. But I doubt if that line will win me any sympathy in this clutch of hungry men."

"Did you do it, lady?" asked Lt. Dundy.

"Do it? Kill Spade's partner, you mean, Lieutenant? Yes, by all means. But it was only physical. Tepid stuff when stood next to the psychological homicide Spade practices. But that's a bit beyond your comprehension, I suppose."

Dundy broke into a wide grin. "Tell them, Polhaus," he ordered, his eyes flicking from Spade to Brigid and back again.

"Gutman's dead. The kid had just finished shooting him up when we got there. Gutman had breath enough only to tell us that the kid killed Thursby." He paused. "And Archer. We got the same from Cairo," Polhaus added, apologetically.

"So you were home free, lady. Until you confessed. And for that we must thank your friend here, I suppose," said Dundy. "Thanks, Spade, for working her up."

Spade turned and stepped to the window. He leaned and peered out into the fog.

Brigid chuckled. "The laugh's on us, Sam. It'll probably be San Quentin for me, if I'm lucky, Lieutenant? If you're lucky, Sam, you'll soon end up at the coroner's, alone on a cold slab. Not a big change from where you are now. If you're unlucky, you'll probably do time in an institution, too. But yours will be in Napa, the State Asylum."

Spade wheeled from the window. He stared at her mocking face, wagged his head, and shuffled to her, halting less than a foot from her. He sucked his cheeks. Suddenly but calmly he spit into her face.

Dundy jumped toward the pair.

"Don't fret, Lieutenant," Brigid said, as she slowly lifted her right hand. She wiped her face then looked at her hand, before she dried it on her hip. "Sam's gesture deserves no reaction from me. He gave the only thing he has to offer anyone: slime. But watch him, Detective-Sergeant Polhaus. He doesn't use chypre to scent his snot rag with. But he's as queer as Cairo. So don't be surprised when his needs get the better of him, when an officer nabs him in some public latrine and hauls him to the station on a 'morals' charge. And as long as we're setting the record straight, you might appreciate getting my real name: Judith. Judith Weisstein. Double ess, please. Not that any of you would be genuinely interested in the personal history of a woman. Interested only in the facts of my crime, right Lieutenant?"

Lt. Dundy nodded woodenly.

"Now, gentlemen," she said acidly, "would you kindly see me out of this rathole and into that birdcage elevator?"

Polhaus looked questioningly at Spade.

"You heard the lady," Spade said, a growling animal noise welling up out of his throat. "Get her out of here. Now, goddammit."

Once A Rabbit, Always?

A Feminist Interview with
Hemingway's María

INTERVIEWER: It was most kind of you to agree to this interview. At your advanced age I can well imagine the difficulty of answering questions about seventy-two hours from a life long ago.

MARÍA: Perhaps. But please to proceed.

INTERVIEWER: Like other personages upon whom Hemingway based his novel's characters, you, I trust, have read his novel as a version of your Civil War experiences?

MARÍA: Truly. It is a version. And thy interview? Its purpose, if I may ask?

INTERVIEWER: Naturally. I'm interviewing marginalized women who have figured in various cultural texts—from novels to historical documents. I'm asking for their views on the experiences that male authors have recorded them as having had—to see if there might be some discrepancy between the actual and the recorded accounts. And I wish to probe for explanation of why those women conducted themselves as they did. I'll compile the interviews in an anthology.

MARÍA: The title of thy anthology, please?

INTERVIEWER: Its working title is, well, is *Backward Gazes: A Gallery of Phallocentric Women.*

MARÍA: Thy reason for including an interview with me?

INTERVIEWER: In candor, because you're one of the backward women. You represent the classic stereotype who continues to impede the cause of women's liberation. You're the nubilized princess, the fantasized dream maiden whose infantilized dependency and submissive eroticism caters to all that feminists find most reprehensible in the male gaze.

MARÍA: Que va. I fear thou art another Fernando. Thou hast his capacity to make a bureaucracy with thy mouth. It is thy wish, then, to abuse me for the young woman I was during those seventy-two hours?

INTERVIEWER: Quite correct. Given Hemingway's to me unfathomable ability to endure—his unflagging popularity among readers worldwide—well, his chauvinistic novel about you and Robert Jordan continues to be read by benighted readers who find in you a role model, an image of a desirable type of woman.

MARÍA: That image is harmful, I am to believe?

INTERVIEWER: Quite harmful. After all, María, unless male and female readers correctly see the anathema you are to actualized womanhood, they'll be misled to think of you—if they're female—as an exemplar they should emulate or—if they're male—as an ideal they should search for: they'll believe that such women—as Hemingway characterized you—really do exist.

MARÍA: Thou dost make it difficult, at my age, not to feel flattered by thy accusations of my seductive power. But should not men and women value that sexual pleasure which often attaches to the image of thy nubilized maiden?

INTERVIEWER: Indeed, indeed. But being a woman is more than clinching in a sleeping bag with a man who mutters banalities about "now, always now, always now, going now, rising now, sailing now, leaving now, wheeling now, soaring now, away now, all the way now, all of all the way now."[1] A woman is more than an embrace-mate in the heather to a chorus of nowheres upon nowheres, "once again to nowhere, always and forever to nowhere, heavy on the elbows in the earth to nowhere, hung on all time always to unknowing nowhere" (159). Women are for more than submissively acquiescing to a man's orders to tend the horses or to dry his feet or fetch dry stockings; for more than playing adolescent servant submitting to her dying lover's commands; for more than kowtowing to his paradoxical psychoblather that instructs her, "Thou wilt go now, rabbit. But I go with thee. As long as there is one of us there is both of us." "If thou goest then I go, too." "Whichever one there is, is both." "We both go in thee now." "Thou art me too now" (463–64). There's more to being a woman than experiencing *la gloria*, more than dissolving in the convulsive shudder of earthmoving orgasms.

MARÍA: I see. I see. Truly it is embarrassing to hear thy recitations of Roberto's love talk. Yet it doth seem rare that thou hast memorized such talk. But dost thou truly believe I know not what a woman is? Dost thou think I see not the infant I was in Mr. Hemingway's book?

INTERVIEWER: Well, María, that's precisely why I sought you out for this interview: to determine whether in the intervening years you'd gained insight on your identity as a woman.

MARÍA: Truly I did. After I recovered.

INTERVIEWER: You were injured in the war, after you *left* the Guadarrama mountain pass?

MARÍA: Que va. After I recovered from the injury of Roberto's rejection.

INTERVIEWER: You mean that you suffered from some sort of breakdown after you *left* him at the pass?

MARÍA: Left, nothing. Was *taken* from him at the pass. Was *led off*, forcibly, from him. Was all but *handcuffed* by the Pilar and Pablo. Was *rejected* by Roberto. Thou dost remember my pleas to him, as my horse was being driven away: "Let me stay! Let me stay!" Thou dost remember too his shouting, "I am with thee. I am with thee now. We both are there. Go!" (465). Many women—had they suffered at the brutal hands of the fascist barbarians and had they gone crazy after that experience—many women might have gone crazy again after a lover's sudden rejection. That rejection: I had in no way expected or deserved it, thou canst be certain.

INTERVIEWER: I am most sorry to hear of your relapse, caused by this additional trauma. Please accept my sympathy. But, dear María, that has little to do, I'm afraid, with Hemingway's characterization of you during the seventy-two hours of the novel.

MARÍA: I beg to differ. It has everything. The Pilar was untruthful in telling Roberto, in his first hours among us, "I do not want her crazy here after you will go. I have had her crazy before and I have enough without that" (33). As if I were not still crazy during his time among us! Truly it embarrasses me to reread Mr.

Hemingway's novel and to discover what an infant I was. Dost thou believe I was such an innocent before the barbarities in our village? Dost thou believe that I, a mayor's daughter, was such an obedient, unassertive child among my family and friends before the war? Dost thou believe that a Spanish girl of my upbringing and pride would so demean herself to a stranger and to her people unless she were crazy? Surely thou canst comprehend: my traumas were responsible for those disgraceful hours with Roberto. I spit on my conduct. I behaved as an eight-year-old girl with a (how dost thou call it?) a crash?

INTERVIEWER: Crush?

MARÍA: Yes, with a crush on an older, handsome man.

INTERVIEWER: Well, María, this explains a good bit of your behavior, for it is certainly infantilized throughout the novel. But it makes your Roberto a more despicable chauvinist than I've previously regarded him.

MARÍA: What dost thou mean?

INTERVIEWER: Well, for all of his love talk to you, quite clearly you were little more than a convenient receptacle for his liquid manhood, a creature whom he spent little time finding anything about, certainly no time learning to know. He certainly left you with no means by which to contact his family in Montana, should you have needed their help after the war. And his attitude toward you—or any woman—is summed up in his nickname for you. *Guapa!* A slang word for female genitalia! In our country it's as if he called you "cunt" or "pussy." And then to translate the term as if it meant rabbit, when *conejo* is the only correct term for rabbit.[2] Affectionately though he may have meant the nickname, it reeks of conventional stereotyping by reducing a woman to an animated stuffed animal, a plaything known best for its reproductive fecundity.

MARÍA: Roberto angers thee.

INTERVIEWER: That's understatement. It enrages me to listen to him commanding you what to do at the end of the novel, ordering you about, as if you were but a child, with his fancy double-talk: "I go always with thee wherever thou goest." "Thou wilt go now. But I go with thee." "If thou goest then I go, too." "Now I put my hand there. Good. Thou art so good. Now do not think more. Now art thou doing what thou should. Now thou art obeying" (463–64). He exemplifies patriarchal ideology in its most insulting role as benevolent father. It is he, of course, who knows what's best for a woman, whose masculinity dominates speech. Like all who share your Roberto's phallogocentric hegemony, he permits woman either the choice to imagine and represent herself as men imagine and represent her (that is, to speak, but to do so only as a man would speak)—

MARÍA: And that woman is the Pilar?

INTERVIEWER: Yes. Of course. Or he permits her the choice to be but a "gap" in the world of masculine discourse, to choose silence, becoming, thereby, the "invisible and unheard sex."[3]

MARÍA: By which thou meanst me.

INTERVIEWER: Quite so. For just how much does your Roberto let you speak? I think of your narrative of the barbershop scene in which you were brutally shorn of your hair. It is your longest speech in the novel. But what is your Roberto's refrain? "Do not tell it." "Do not talk more." "Do not tell me any more." "Do not talk of it" (350–53). Your Roberto reveals his preference for your silence when, before your recitation, he tells you, in a sentence notable for its confusion of *thees* without *mes*, "I love thee thus lying beside thee and touching thee and knowing thou art truly there" (349). And when you are led away from his injured body at the end, he desires your obedience, not your language.

MARÍA: And thou hast more cause for thy anger against Roberto?

INTERVIEWER: Indeed. I loathe his privileging of patriarchal provincialism.

MARÍA: By which thou meanst . . .

INTERVIEWER: By which I meanst, uh, rather mean the ideological narrow-mindedness of his dilemma. Oh, to be caught, poor Roberto, in such a tug of war, such a mirroring civil war of imperatives. On one hand he must honor his political duty, his allegiance to his comrades and the communist cause, for whom his bridge-blowing mission is a pragmatic means to the greater end of freeing Spain from fascism. On the other hand, he must honor his ethical obligations, his responsibilities for the consequences of his political action on Pablo and Pilar's band. To bring suffering to innocent people, all in the name of right action, is as wrong as to refuse his appointed date with destiny at the bridge.

MARÍA: Doth not such a dilemma humanize him? Doth it not keep him from being an ideologue?

INTERVIEWER: But don't you see, María? That's an antiquated patriarchal dilemma. It sees issues only in terms of whether one should honor the father's call to patriotism or his call to paternalism. And what gets left out of the dilemma? It's the competing claim you represented—the woman's call to personal obligation, an obligation of intimacy that Robert Jordan betrays when he sends you off with the band. Typical of phallocentric patriarchalists, your Roberto illustrates that ideological causes always take precedence over human beings, especially when those humans are mere women.

MARÍA: And thou hast yet more cause for thy anger against Roberto?

INTERVIEWER: Yes. But wait a minute here. I'm the interviewer. Let me ask the question of moment: have you no anger toward your Roberto?

MARÍA: None.

INTERVIEWER: Do you mean to say that you still love him?

MARÍA: By no means. But he angers me not at all. For him I feel pity.

INTERVIEWER: Pity?

MARÍA: Truly. For I have come to realize that he was a deeply confused, nay, a pathetic man.

INTERVIEWER:

MARÍA: Thy silence, I take it, awaits some explanation?

INTERVIEWER: If you please.

MARÍA: He was no chauvinist, as thou dost call him. To tell truly, his sexuality was confused. Oh, thou hast not to worry that I will claim some overt homosexual act that only I had knowledge of. But surely thou canst understand his attraction to me with my cropped hair, canst thou not?

INTERVIEWER: Your resemblance, you mean, to a man?

MARÍA: My resemblance to a cropped-haired boy, if you will. Perhaps I resembled some playmate, brother or sister, some friend from his infancy or youth. I was someone whose uncertain sex contributed to his prompt love for me. Truly I had beautiful hair.

INTERVIEWER: Pretty plumage once?

MARÍA: Perhaps so. But for him it was tawny wheat, burned gold. Poetic compliments, perhaps. But I was no field to be harvested, no rare metal to be beaten.

INTERVIEWER: Ah! It must be your genderlessness to him, then, that explains that oddest of descriptions of your hair. It occurs on your last night together. He felt—I'm sure I can quote the sentence—"he felt the cropped head against his cheek, and it was as soft but as alive and silkily rolling as when a marten's fur rises under the caress of your hand"—now listen—"when you spread the trap jaws open and lift the marten clear and, holding it, stroke the fur smooth" (378).

MARÍA: Truly a rare comparison to make. Perhaps it shows some wish to regard me an animal, a dead one at that. *Aiee*, to be caught in the jaws of a lethal trap.

INTERVIEWER: Certainly it suggests his wish to detach your hair from your body, as though his lovemaking could occur with anyone with such hair, male or female. And it may explain his calling you rabbit, suggesting as that creature may, the downy fur of your mound of Venus—or of any youth's pubic area, male or female. But I'm afraid, María, willing though I am, I'm not convinced of your allegations of Jordan's confused sexuality.

MARÍA: Truly it is difficult to see, I confess. But recall thou our love scenes. Consider the language of them. Is the dark passage that he makes his incantations over, is that the entrance into my womb? Or could it be some nearby dark passage? I wish not to be vulgar or obscene. But pride in my womanhood suffers when I read those passages, whether we are lying in the heather or on his pine-bough bed, whether we are walking hand in hand or lying flank to flank. One and all, they blur my sex.

INTERVIEWER: You mean, I take it, that each of those scenes could as easily refer to the erotic pleasure of two men as of a man and a woman?

MARÍA: Truly.

INTERVIEWER: But you must remember the time in which Hemingway published his version of your story: censorship laws and public decency would have prohibited any frank references to your body parts. As I recall, there was sufficient controversy over the sleeping-bag scenes anyway.

MARÍA: Thou dost misunderstand me. Mr. Hemingway's descriptions of our love reflect well Roberto's state of mind. But the language of those passages is alien to heterosexual love.

INTERVIEWER: Well, now that I think back on some of those passages, there may be some merit in what you claim. The language is curiously lacking in phallogocentricity. Hmmm. I must confess that were I to read one of the earth-moving passages out of context, I might well conclude its author was a woman. Yes,

"They were having now and before and always and now and now and now. Oh, now, now, now, the only now, and above all now, and there is no other now but thou now and now is thy prophet. Now and forever now. Come now, now, for there is no now but now. Yes, now. Now, please now, only now, not anything else only this now, and where are you and where am I and where is the other one, and not why, not ever why, only this now; and on and always please then always now, always now, for now always one now . . . ." And then, "one and one is one, is one, is one, is one, is still one, is still one, is one descendingly, is one softly, is one longingly, is one kindly, is one happily, is one in goodness, is one to cherish, is one now on earth with elbows against the cut and slept-on branches of the pine tree with the smell of the pine boughs and the night; to earth conclusively now, and with the morning of the day to come. Then he said, for the other was only in his head and he had said nothing, 'Oh, María, I love thee and I thank thee for this.'" (379)

Well, now, just who is "the other" who was "only in his head?" But more, the whole passage reads like the semiotic style that Kristeva associates with women—repetitive, spasmodic, rhythmic, nonstructured.[4] And the geography of the pleasure, as Irigaray would say, describes *jouissance* in a diversified, complex way that borders on autoeroticism.[5] Indeed, the lack of phallic regionalization in these love scenes suggests an antiphallocentric text that Cixous might well find deserving of comment.[6]

MARÍA: I beg thy pardon. Thou dost seem distracted. I know not these names. Are they other women thou hast interviewed for thy *Gallery of Backward Women*?

INTERVIEWER: Scarcely. But why not just lay your cards on the table? What else leads you to suspect your Roberto of homoerotic tendencies?

MARÍA: Surely there is his preoccupation with his father and the Pablo, a pair of men whose disgraceful acts deeply injured him. Canst thou imagine my surprise when I read of the handshake between Roberto and the returned Pablo? In that handshake is more emotion than in our sleeping bag. Surely my Roberto took great pleasure in the hard gripping and frank pressing of hands. It led him to remark to himself that "Pablo had a good hand in the dark and feeling it gave Robert Jordan the strangest feeling he had felt that morning" (404). Such words gave me cause for much jealousy when first I read them. And Roberto continued to grip "the strange, firm, purposeful hand hard." That deserved the Pilar's sarcastic question, "What are you two doing? Becoming *maricones*?"

INTERVIEWER: By which she meant homosexuals, not just sissies?

MARÍA: Truly.

INTERVIEWER: Well, there's certainly a male conspiracy between the two after your Roberto's leg was crushed. Two men, willfully asserting their medical knowledge, pigheadedly vaunting their certainty of your Roberto's imminent death, letting him play the martyr on the mountaintop.

MARÍA: But I think you confuse the scene. You release more of your anger at Roberto. You should feel pity for his confused action. He thinks his martyrdom is for the noble cause of Republican Spain. He thinks it is payment to our band in exchange for having come among us and ruined our serenity. But his sacrifice shows his love for Pablo, a redeemed father. He must have hoped that the Pablo would value his sacrifice above all other acts of male camaraderie.

INTERVIEWER: And so I suppose it would have given homoerotic pleasure to your Roberto, had he known the identity of the officer leading the cavalry to him?

MARÍA: Truly it would have pleased him to die on the field of battle with the young Lieutenant Berrendo. It would repeat for him his pleasure in killing the young cavalryman who came upon us in the sleeping bag on the second morning.

INTERVIEWER: Well, María, I must admit that your Roberto seems unusually fixated on male figures, strangely braids with erotic aggression his male relationships, as with Kashkin, whom he kills in an act of mercy, or with Karkov, whose lovemaking with his wife and at least two mistresses seems to reveal the maricones' fascination with collective sexuality.

MARÍA: Dost thou think it can be that Roberto's eyes are upon Karkov as lover, not upon Karkov's women?

INTERVIEWER: Why not? If, as alleged, there is some homosexual component in group scenes of violence, then that explains his fascination with Pilar's narrative of the extermination of the fascists in Pablo's town, suggests that the erotic intensification of the collective sadism stirred Robert Jordan deeply.

MARÍA: Que va. Roberto listened in rapt attention to the Pilar's account.

INTERVIEWER: As he did to your account of the barbaric shearing of your hair in the barbershop. Yes, I see now: he desired your silence as you began telling him that event, wanting you to be the silent woman. But he desired more to hear what was done to you so that he could imagine the men whose cruel pleasure he luxuriated in, even though he would not admit to such luxury. What homoerotic delight he would have found in El Sordo's last hours I can well imagine.

MARÍA: Think you so? Can there be erotic pleasure in such a scene?

INTERVIEWER: Indeed. For is there not the pleasure of awaiting a dangerous lover's approach? Of taking with surprise the aggressive male, the Comrade Voyager, the Captain Mora of the red face and blond hair and British mustache and blue eyes? Of dropping the arrogant paternalist with the phallic spray of three shots from an automatic weapon? Yes, your Roberto would take pleasure in that violence and would enjoy his grief in the death of the young boy Joaquin.

MARÍA: Truly in Joaquin's death. For dost thou recall the episode of the Belgian boy?

INTERVIEWER: I don't believe I do.

MARÍA: Roberto remembers a boy from the Eleventh Brigade. His fellow villagers, five boys, had been killed early in the war. The boy was made an orderly. But he could do nothing without weeping or crying. All treated him very gently. Roberto resolved: "He would have to find out what became of him and

whether he ever cleared up and was fit for soldiering again"
(136). But why should Roberto compassionate that one young
man?

INTERVIEWER: Well, his empathetic attentiveness seems commendable, to be
sure. But it also smacks of sentimentality. Perhaps his humanistic, even feminized, sympathies sublimate his homoerotic interest in the orderly? Is that what you wish to imply?

MARÍA: I remark the episode because it shows a sensitivity in Roberto
that was strongly at odds with his masculinity, a sensitivity that
ran toward men, especially young or injured or emasculated men.

INTERVIEWER: It would seem to show that he had much in common with
America's good gray poet, Walt Whitman. But to think of literary correspondences brings to mind a tradition of orderlies
serving as the objects of homosexual officers, the best known
of them being one in a story by a British writer. But if I recall
correctly, Hemingway has a little-read story of a homosexual
proposition a major makes to an orderly. "A Simple Enquiry,"
it's called. And I've recently heard it reported that in an early
draft of "A Way You'll Never Be" two soldiers are brought before a captain and charged with homosexuality.[7] There are
other stories of homosexuality, I am quite sure. So it should
not surprise us that your Roberto was but one in a line of men
whose virile masculinity should be strongly questioned and
whose recurrent presence should tell something about their
author.

MARÍA: Nor should it surprise thee to learn the identity of Roberto's
personal hero, unnamed though he is in Mr. Hemingway's book.

INTERVIEWER: I know not to whom you refer.

MARÍA: Thou knowest not? Thou, a woman schooled in literary texts?
Who else, early in our waning century, boldly put himself into
the pantheon of military heroism with feats of derring-do
among an alien people? What silk-robed hero legendized himself by learning strange tongues and dialects, inspired natives,
and unified feuding desert tribes? Who became an explosives
expert, engaged in harassing attacks on Turkish outposts, troop
and supply trains, and fought guerilla-fashion, leading a camel
corps?

INTERVIEWER: You can only mean, of course, T. E. Lawrence—of Arabia. Now there's a topic for some scholar to make a name for himself with.[8]

MARÍA: Truly. Roberto idolized Colonel Lawrence for his heroics. But he also found alluring the homosexuality of his personal life, ignore that allure though he tried.

INTERVIEWER: Be that as it may, María, why has this—and all of the other signs of your Roberto's homosexuality—led you to pity him?

MARÍA: Que va. But was he not pathetically confused, unable to reconcile to himself his homosexual longing? Did that not contribute to his yearning for death, his deliberate desire to place himself in jeopardy, as if in expiation for his tabooed desires? Did it not explain, perhaps in part, his expatriation from the American West, where there could be little tolerance for a man of homosexual leanings? What could torture Roberto more than teaching in a small-town western university where constant contact with young men like Paco Berrendo, the Belgian boy, Joaquin, Andres, and other cropped-haired farm youths would unbearably strain his ability to instruct them only in Spanish? Far from being thy stereotyped chauvinist, was he not deeply divided? Truly he wished to act out the patriarchal masculinity you vilify him for. But he wished too to indulge in the nurturing maternalism that led him to grieve over injured young boys and to pride himself on packing his explosives as carefully "as he had packed his collection of wild bird eggs when he was a boy" (48). Ah, that he wished to become a writer, but told me no such thing. Would he return to teaching or continue with war games? Would we have any domestic life without him searching out new political causes? Ahh. Many, many are the signs of my Roberto's deep confusions. They would have made life with him unendurable, I am quite sure, had he survived that agony of my country.

INTERVIEWER: And what about your life, María, since you rode away from that Guadarrama mountain pass? Did you marry? Did you have children? Why do you still live here in Gredos?

MARÍA: Such questions, I believe, exceed the scope of thy interview, do they not? Enough of my private life has been revealed already, even though it was but some seventy hours. So of thee, my interviewer: to whom dost thou now turn for the next of thy interviews, thy next backward woman?

INTERVIEWER: It would not surprise you, would it, if I told you Pilar?

MARÍA: Not at all. But she has grown even more irascible than she was a half century ago. She confuses herself with other women, Mr. Hemingway's mother and that lesbian writer who held court in Paris.

INTERVIEWER: Gertrude Stein?

MARÍA: Yes. But thou knowest how to reach the Pilar, knowest the home to which she has been committed?

INTERVIEWER: Quite so. May I take along your regards to her?

MARÍA: Please to do so. And please be so kind, shouldst thou publish our interview in thy anthology, to accent properly the letter "i" in María. It would displease me to see it again anglicized, as it was by thy Mr. Hemingway, who foolishly vaunted himself on his linguistic ability, and whose errors went uncorrected by his shameless publishing house, Scrubbers.

INTERVIEWER: Scribner's, it is. Thank you, María, for so graciously and generously giving your time for this interview.

MARÍA: *Nada.* Good luck with the Pilar. Thou shalt need it. And be thou advised: do not be such a fool as to allow her to read the palm of thy hand.

Manolin on Hemingway's Santiago
A Fictive Interview

INTERVIEWER: I appreciate your willingness to be interviewed. Naturally your recent behavior drew the attention of fellow fishermen and townspeople. After so many years of a spartan and solitary life, of devotion to the art of fishing, and of remarked humility—well, it's a small wonder that news of your changed behavior spread. Indeed, spread to the mainland where I first got wind of it.

MANOLIN: Ha! With a wind in the east a smell comes across the harbor from the shark factory?

INTERVIEWER: Pardon? Ah, some line, I suppose, from the book? Tease me if you wish. But for the record: Are the reports accurate? Have you stopped fishing altogether? Do you spend your days, as they say, frequenting the library and either sitting on the beach, reading the little book, throwing pebbles into your waterlogged skiff and knotting your rotted lines, or meandering along the shore and about the countryside, muttering and laughing to yourself?

MANOLIN: Truly. I would not deny such reports. And so it must appear, ha, that I am crazed, a man harmed by too much sun, or by too little luck, or—how is it called?—by a crisis in the middle of the life. But it is of no import, señor.

INTERVIEWER: Well, it is of import. For your changed behavior, if it is not to be termed crazy, must have some explanation. It is for that explanation, if you don't mind, that I have traveled from Key West. After all, there are many who, knowing you to be the first disciple of Santiago, many who would find disturbing—

MANOLIN: Ha. Yes. The first disciple. It would disturb them that I had shed my discipleship, had become, yes, a turncoat?

INTERVIEWER: That explains your behavior? You have recanted your belief in Santiago, your devotion to the Exemplary Fisherman?

191

MANOLIN: And why not? For tardily have I come to see that truly he was *salao* [unlucky]—for me. And bad luck, too, for other simple-tons taken in by what I have commenced to call his pernicious manipulations.

INTERVIEWER: Pernicious manipulations, is it? Well now. Is there cause for your tardy recognition, some assignable event that prompted your about-face?

MANOLIN: Ah, a cause-monger? Maybe it was some cynical tourist's off-hand remark that Santiago was a hypocrite? Maybe it was report of Dick Sisler's mockery of the fiction that he had fished here? Maybe it was a rumor of a published sneer that the book "was as sickly a bucket of sentimental slop as was ever scrubbed off the bar-room floor"? Maybe I tired of imitating Santiago's ways? Or maybe it was Paco's tragedy?

INTERVIEWER: You refer, I assume, to the news story of last September? Of the boy whose mutilated body washed ashore here, a day after the arrival of his skiff, to which was lashed the skeleton of a marlin, scarce half the size of Santiago's? But such fatalities are common enough among fishermen. I should think Paco's death insuffi-cient to cause your recantation, your loss of faith.

MANOLIN: As you wish. But might not such a "common fatality," as you call it, make one wonder at Paco's foolishness? For truly, by lashing to his skiff the harpooned marlin, he mailed a dinner invitation to neighboring sharks. And stamped it with a trail of blood.

INTERVIEWER: Such a line of thinking, I suppose, made you regard as equally foolish Santiago's act of lashing his harpooned marlin to his skiff?

MANOLIN: Ha. More than foolish! Made me to ask, after so many years, why did he not cut away slabs of the dead marlin and haul them into the boat? And, after doing that, why did he not cut away the marlin's head or sword, boat it, and release the rest of the fish's body? The sword alone would have revealed the hugeness of the fish.

INTERVIEWER: But surely, to have filleted slabs would have mutilated—no, desecrated—the noble marlin, a creature whose beauty still in-spires awe in me when I think of the fish, "long, deep, wide, sil-ver and barred with purple and interminable in the water"; when I think of its "big scythe blade . . . very pale lavender above the dark blue . . . ."

MANOLIN: It was, do you think, señor, better to let sharks—makos and galanos—mutilate and desecrate it? I see little difference. *Jesus!* If the noble creature's beauty truly mattered to Santiago, then he would not have killed it. Much less would he have brought its desecrated beauty home for villagers to get frog-eyed over and for tourists to mistakenly identify, ha, as *tiburon*, as a shark.

INTERVIEWER: Unless, if I understand you correctly, unless Santiago was concerned less with dishonoring the fish than with losing the opportunity to gather glory to himself as a Great Fisherman?

MANOLIN: Truly that. And to guarantee my pledge of discipleship to him. Ha. Which I honored for over thirty years, exploited as I was by his pernicious manipulations.

INTERVIEWER: *Moment, por favore.* Let me return to the first motive you accuse Santiago of. Must his return with the fish be regarded an act swollen with the motive of self-glorification? Cannot exhaustion after his battle with the sharks explain why he arrived with the marlin still lashed to his skiff? Or if there are traces of self-glorification, cannot they reflect human frailty? Can they not be tolerated, overlooked, forgiven as—

MANOLIN: Ha. Do you take me for the witless schoolboy that Santiago's story portrayed me as? Can you not tolerate the idea that I put on intelligence with my manhood, late though it was in arriving? Let me assign him another motive: self-vindication. Did he return with the carcass because he was too exhausted to think of cutting it loose? Or because he was resolved to vindicate himself? To lay before those fellow fishermen who slighted his ability an accomplishment of such magnitude that *they*, ha, would have to rub their own faces in their grievous misjudgment of his skill? And a third motive for returning with the fish, señor: vindictiveness?

INTERVIEWER: Well, I suppose a cynic might say that Santiago's return with the fish revealed a motive to avenge himself upon your father. For it was he, after all, who had so little faith in Santiago's superiority as a fisherman that he ordered you—whom Santiago had taught since you were but five—to fish with another man after forty fishless days.

MANOLIN: And no vindictiveness beyond that?

INTERVIEWER: Well, there was no one else for whom he harbored hostility, on whom he sought revenge.

MANOLIN: No one, señor? Not even me?

INTERVIEWER: You?

MANOLIN: "You," he asks in disbelief? You wish me to spit, sir, in the sand of thy stupidity?

INTERVIEWER: Clearly I do not follow you.

MANOLIN: Maybe the reports of my lunacy are true? Ha. You poorly remember the ending of the book? Do you forget, when I brought him coffee the morning after his return, his telling me, "I missed you"?

INTERVIEWER: Well? Still I do not follow. My wife will say the same when I return home.

MANOLIN: With no difference? Listen, then. Countless times after his death I asked myself questions. When Santiago died, did he do so merely because of his age, because his time had come? Or did he die because he had been so worn and battered by his lonely ordeal with the marlin? And should I not punish myself for having been absent, for not having shared or shouldered some of his ordeal? True. He missed me. But equally true is this: he made certain to let me know he missed me. By saying, "I missed you," he scarred my conscience for over thirty years with guilt because I had failed to pledge my discipleship *before* his ordeal with the marlin.

INTERVIEWER: Small evidence, if you'll permit my saying so, on which to accuse him of vindictiveness.

MANOLIN: Ha. So you taunt me to fry my other fish? So be it. You recall his refusal to reply to my declaration of discipleship, do you not? After I asked about the marlin's spear? He said, "You keep it if you want it . . . ."

INTERVIEWER: There's some ironic understatement in that "if you want it," I'll admit.

MANOLIN: Please. Not to interrupt. When he said, "You keep it if you want it," not only did I declare, "I want it." Also I pledged, "Now *we* must make *our* plans about other things." But did he acknowledge my pledge? Did he appreciate the import of my first-person plural pronouns? Did he accept my commitment? No, señor. He disdained an answer. He brushed aside my statement. Instead he lanced my sincerity with a poisoned barb. He asked, "Did they search for me?" By questioning so pointedly what *they* did for him in his absence, he all but accused me of failing to have done any significant thing for him before he left. And he slighted my offer to make amends, to do things for him in the future.

INTERVIEWER: Well, perhaps he did harbor some resentment against you. And now that I think about it, I can see how you might also view his wishes that you were with him in the boat: "I wish I had the boy." To someone overly sensitive or guilt-inclined, such a repeated wish might be felt a curse for being absent, might amount to a guilt trip for not having been a Brother's—or Spiritual Father's—Keeper. But, Manolin, you have taken the whip to yourself.

MANOLIN: Ha. Truly. But he handed me the whip. For do you ignore the treachery of his words? Just after he declared he missed me, he asked, "What did you catch?"

INTERVIEWER: No treachery that I can hear in that question.

MANOLIN: Unless you listen to its submerged question: of whether I caught *anything* to compare with his catch.

INTERVIEWER: There are, I'm told, offenses given and offenses taken.

MANOLIN: And did he not give them? Yes, he approved of the four fish I caught during his ordeal. But his "Very good" had such a distant and cold formality that I was hurt by it. To think that he could question my catch as though we were strangers wounded me. I interrupted, you remember, restating my pledge to him: "Now we will fish together." And how did he answer? With false modesty: "No. I am not lucky. I am not lucky anymore."

INTERVIEWER: To which you responded by sending luck to hell.

MANOLIN: Truly, señor. For it was to such a point of anger that he had manipulated me. So shrewd was he, leading me by the nose to the real *point* of his treacherous conversation: "What will your family say?" Oh, so confident was he that I, full of pity and guilt, would renounce my family for him.

INTERVIEWER: As you did.

MANOLIN: Truly, took a new father, for over thirty years.

INTERVIEWER: Yes: traveled the familiar road of the Family romance, arrived early at the end of every boy's Quest for the Royal Father.

MANOLIN: I care little for your riddling formulas, and less for your sneers. Perhaps our interview is finished?

INTERVIEWER: No. Please sit down again. Please sit. Your view of Santiago's be-
               havior unsettles me. Indeed, I think your harsh reconstruction of
               his vindictiveness toward you in the closing pages of the book
               needs to be seen in the context of his ordeal and his exhaustion
               during the interval of that conversation. That is to say, he was
               not quite himself. And so his behavior to you must be excused,
               so out of keeping is it with his sincere regard for you during the
               rest of the book.

MANOLIN: So, too, did I think him for too many years: sincere. But do you
               not now see what explains my reported change of behavior, my
               muttering and laughing? It gushes forth when I think about the
               fraud I so long revered.

INTERVIEWER: Again I'm at your mercy for instruction.

MANOLIN: So be it. His humility, his fraternal ethic, his serene benevolence
               toward all his brothers? All duplicity, señor. Yes, duplicity that
               he patiently cultivated, pretense that he employed to slowly
               stake his claim upon me, a claim I honored by, how do you say,
               yes, by *aping* his conduct and ethic. Yes, his methods of manip-
               ulation treated me as an object to use and an agent to turn. Such
               treatment, señor, is impiety, for it did injury to my soul.

INTERVIEWER: Perhaps some evidence of these allegations of his fraud?

MANOLIN: Is it not abundant? Tally up his innumerable fictions. Long I
               thought them harmless games. But now I wonder at what I
               should laugh more: my gullibility or his duplicity. Truly? You
               need a list? Well, are there not the so-called fictions of the cast
               net and the pot of yellow rice with fish? And the fictions: that
               eighty-five was a lucky number. That either of us could borrow
               two-and-a-half dollars for the lottery. That Perico at the bodega
               daily gave him the day-old paper to read the baseball scores.
               That he knew the Yankees had won on the previous day. That
               he had waited to eat dinner and drink the beer I brought from
               Martin until he had washed—

INTERVIEWER: Such fictions are but shared intimacies between trusted friends.

MANOLIN: And like the tips of icebergs may they not also reveal a broad and
               deep and dark streak of duplicity? As when one shares an inti-
               mate declaration with a noble fish, fraternally calling it one's
               brother, only to nudge—hypocritically and lethally—an intimate
               harpoon, ha! into its trusting heart?

INTERVIEWER: But the killing of the marlin was to be done. I expect nothing less from a man who was born to fish.

MANOLIN: Ah. And so do I. But a fisherman who claims to be *strange* and asks me to regard him as extraordinary, he should do nothing normal—like kill a fish of legendary size and tow its mutilated carcass to shore. A strange fisherman, truly, would have brought the fish to the boat. But by rolling it belly up and making it vulnerable to the harpoon, *that* would have shown his conquest of the fish. And then he should have released it.

INTERVIEWER: But such an exhausted, deeply hooked fish would surely have died, would have become a pathetic meal for predators.

MANOLIN: Truly. But a strange fisherman would not have needed to witness its death. Nor would he have to go through the vainglorious stupidity of trying to protect it from sharks. Nor the silliness of lamenting its predictable mutilation.

INTERVIEWER: Next I suppose you'll find fault with his self-reproaches for having gone out too far.

MANOLIN: Ha. His refrain, señor, with all its high-sounding, gilded guilt? Just another of his fictions, do you not see? By expressing guilt, he cleverly defends himself against charges of swollen pride in his accomplishment. As did I for many years, so, too, do you listen to his statements from the wrong end: you hear what he wants heard—humility and guilt—not what he wants hidden— his obsession with heroic achievement.

INTERVIEWER: Well, I'll admit that by bringing back the skeleton Santiago could be said to be showing off to others what he alone did. But I find little obsession with heroic achievement in that.

MANOLIN: Unless it's at one with his constant need to link himself to other heroes, to royal giants, the glory of whose light he would shine upon himself? Do not forget his fondness for speaking of Joe DiMaggio as though he were an old friend. As well remember his pride in having "beaten" (mind you, señor, "beaten," not endured or outlasted) at arm wrestling the negro of Cienfuegos. For that he became known as *el campéon*, a (how do you call it?) "Nickname" he suffered easily. Remember, too, those other creatures of power to whom he insists we link him? He will dream of lions regally romping on African beaches. But never will he dream of jellyfish or songbirds or rabbits or kittens.

INTERVIEWER: So he had grandiose fantasies? His "pernicious manipulations," as you call them, got him only you. A single disciple shows little proof of power politics.

MANOLIN: Only in large, public arenas, señor, does power politics show its ugly face? It is absent, is it, in domestic scenes, at family hearths, and even in small offices where, I imagine, you work? And you are the educated interviewer, are you not? I think you waste my time.

INTERVIEWER: Okay. So I'm taunting you, trying to draw you out. But surely you'll admit that even if Santiago manipulated you, deliberately sought to make you his disciple, you've little cause to complain. You've had a good life, been an example in turn to other young fishermen, even had your own flock of distant disciples, until your behavior recently changed.

MANOLIN: Ha. Can it be that you understand so little about heroes and the subtle, stern and, *Ay*, cruel demands they lay on those who would follow in their footsteps? Can you not truly imagine, after Santiago died, just how restricted was the conduct of my living? For over thirty years I lived that "spartan and solitary life" you spoke of when we began. I devoted my life to the art of fishing, was noted among my people for my humility. And there was no pretense in my conduct, neither insincerity nor intimate fictions with others. But I was, simply, a misfit. By pledging my discipleship to Santiago, I imitated, as best I could, his ways. And I measured every act against his actions, which I enshrined in memory. Those actions I could not help but fall far short of, year after year, señor.

INTERVIEWER: You'll permit me to ask if there's some self-pity in your account?

MANOLIN: Judge for yourself. But who became estranged from his living fellow men? Who abstained from sexual relationships? Who withdrew from family circles? Who circumscribed himself within a narrow compass of activity? And who perpetually interrogated himself to determine whether The Master would have behaved similarly? Who strove, year after year, to honor Santiago's name by attempting to fill his shoes and by suffering the laughter of family and friends? Who felt compelled to hold himself above his fellows, practiced humility and did not understand those who labeled it a mask behind which lay a "holier-than-thou" visage? And who was frustrated, year upon year, at never catching a marlin that was even as big as the one Paco caught? Need I tell you who became known as a strange man? Or who frequently asked himself whether he had gone out too far?

INTERVIEWER: No, certainly not. But then like Santiago, you went out too far?

MANOLIN: Truly. But I did not go of my own will. No. Santiago drove me out that far, subtly inculcated me in his ways—from the time I was five, you remember. Yes, he fostered my worship of his heroic achievements, all the while keeping me blind to the power games his duplicity practiced on me. Ha. He suckled me on small but toxic doses of his poisonous virtue.

INTERVIEWER: Whew! Now you make him sound like some cult leader who, under the mantle of spiritual vision, brainwashes his devotees. But little in his conversation with you shows such brainwashing. After all, he displays respect and generosity toward others. He's tolerant of your father's lack of faith in him, and he has compassion for your other fisherman's near-blindness.

MANOLIN: I think I grow weary of your stupidity or of the cheap irony of your statements. For you ignore, of course, the tiny harpoons of Santiago's malice. He sticks one into my other fisherman, who had never gone turtle-ing, as Santiago had for years off the Mosquito Coast. And so, unlike Santiago, he had no excuse for growing almost blind—except his lesser capacities as a human being. And Santiago sticks another barb into my father, who judged McGraw as baseball's greatest manager. That, you recall, drew Santiago's disdain. He declared that my father would have given such stature to any manager who, cash in hand, came here every year—even the Leo, Durocher. Can you truly not see in such belittlement Santiago's insidious schooling? Perniciously and patiently he wooed me from my family.

INTERVIEWER: But even if such schooling is a form of brainwashing, Santiago inculcated such views with no authoritarian decalogue of thou shalts and shalt nots.

MANOLIN: Truly, he catechized me in no commandments. But such commandments are methods for lesser men. Santiago's methods were psychological: he knew how to wound with, as well as without, a harpoon. As when, the night before he embarked on his ordeal, I brought our dinner and he declared that he was ready to eat, having "only needed time to wash." You remember my guilt for having been so thoughtless? I neglected to bring him wash water and soap and a towel. I was stung to the quick to realize that I needed to see to a shirt and jacket and shoes and a blanket for him against the coming of winter.

INTERVIEWER: But you confuse guilt with love. Your self-scolding for thoughtlessness little more than reflects your affection for him, your wish to care for a man you esteemed.

MANOLIN: Truly, a measure of that. But you pretend blindness to his pedagogy, his resolution to guarantee my guilty discipleship. Ha. He would not stoop to scold me for my neglect. Nor would he stoop to ask me for anything—baits, beer, meals, water. For well did he know that his silence spoke loudly of my self-centeredness. The voice of his disappointment came from me, so able was he to make me put him inside myself. How often I laugh now, to recall his saying, "I know many tricks and I have resolution," and to realize that he spoke of more than fishing.

INTERVIEWER: But even if his instruction was a form of brainwashing, he held no threat over you, did not force you to follow in his footsteps.

MANOLIN: So naive, are you, to the ways of intimidation, señor? Why, from the very earliest days he made his power known to me. Do you forget the early episode when I was his new pupil and he boated a fish too green?

INTERVIEWER: Yes, brought it into the boat before it was played out, exhausted. So it thrashed about the boat, causing havoc, I think I remember.

MANOLIN: The fish "nearly tore the boat to pieces." But was that boating of a green fish accident or design, do you think? Was Santiago an unskilled fisherman when I was five? Was he so unnerved by my presence that he rushed the boating? Or was he deliberately trying to intimidate me?

INTERVIEWER: All right. Please recite the passage. For it's clear you've memorized it.

MANOLIN: Truly I have: "I can remember the tail slapping and banging and the thwart breaking and the noise of the clubbing. I can remember you throwing me into the bow where the wet coiled lines were and feeling the whole boat shiver and the noise of you clubbing him like chopping a tree down and the sweet blood smell all over me."

INTERVIEWER: You remember the event with great clarity. I applaud your fine memory.

MANOLIN: Or should you note that my recall has the vividness of what I have learned is called a traumatic childhood event? For truly those moments in the small boat terrified me, most because of Santiago's capacity for such violence, his clubbing brutality. You scarce need me to tell you of the scenes of terror I imagined and had nightmares about. Nor to tell you who that green fish became. Nor whose sweet blood smell I smelled.

INTERVIEWER: Yes, I suppose that to a young boy such an experience would be intimidating, could make you feel that disobedience to his wishes or instructions might well cause him to erupt in similar violence. So, part of your discipleship had a root in that possibility, in your fear of him?

MANOLIN: Do not all disciples have such fear? Is it not that which contributes to their awe of their leader? Truly, heroes who resemble Santiago, who perform heroic deeds beneath the cloak of fraternity, must all strike awe in their followers, regardless of the pacifism they preach and pretend to exhibit.

INTERVIEWER: Well, I think now you do go out too far, exceed the limits of our interview. So let me bring us to an end with two final questions. First, is not your changed behavior an overreaction, a response so excessive that you've become another kind of misfit, a thoroughgoing cynic?

MANOLIN: Ha. I think not, sir. But it is easy to regard me that way, I realize. But if my change is overreaction, then it overreacts to a man of exaggerated traits. Santiago may be acclaimed for his boundless, his infinite fraternalism as well as for his enviable serenity. But the exaggeration of those traits seems to me to silhouette some dark shadow or disturbing knot in Santiago's mind. They reveal a messianic lust to be savior to at least one person, to ensnare the worship of one disciple. They give air to a rancid ego, which sought promise of my lifelong genuflection. In a word, señor, Santiago was no Hero. Rather he was a Trickster, a figure short on humor and comedy, long on twisted manipulations. But ha! Your cocked eyebrow would prick my peroration, would it not? So be it. To your last question?

INTERVIEWER: Your future? What will you do, once you weary of this stage in your development?

MANOLIN: Perhaps the answer approaches, over there?

INTERVIEWER: That rabble? Those union roughnecks who would organize you, would bargain, presumably on behalf of your collective interests, against the cannery owners?

MANOLIN: Or those others, behind them, who also ask for brotherhood?

INTERVIEWER: What, the small band of, what are they, environmentalists, opposed to the exploitation of the sea, opposed to the domination of nature by man's arrogant . . . ? Manolin? One more minute? Manolin? THANK . . . you. For the interview.

Psychoanalytic Training Report #3
The Patient Meursault

Part I: Formally Enumerate the Methodological Constraints an Analytic Interpretation of Patient Meursault Poses to an Analyst

A. Working from a Transcribed Audiotape of Patient Meursault's Monologue

By not being present during Patient Meursault's recumbent recitation, the analyst is denied the advantage of hearing *how* he says what he says, of carefully listening to his emphases or inflections, his vocal rendering and coloring of his account. The analyst is further deprived of the opportunity, especially significant in this case, of hearing whether the affectless manner or style indicated by the transcription of his monologue's mere words was offset or nuanced either by any emotionality in his actual telling or by any verbal markers that convey the nature of his relationship with his therapist (see section C below). Indeed, it would have been helpful to the analyst to know the pace of his monologue and whether and where—besides at the eleven chapterlike numberings—he paused or hesitated in talking out his story. In addition, did Patient Meursault mark with any vocal indicators the conspicuous discontinuities and inconsistencies in his narration of events, which mixes and confuses the present with the past? Moreover, the analyst could profit from knowing whether the two primary parts of the monologue constituted two very lengthy, unconventional sessions, whether each of the sessions had one or more interruptions, whether they occurred at points other than the eleven formally designated interruptions, and whether those eleven "installments" were conventional fifty-minute sessions.

B. Working from a Text Whose Patient's Fate Is Unclear

If Patient Meursault has been beheaded in a public execution, the assigned case is either cruel or academic, inflicting upon the analyst a patient whom she cannot help, thereby defeating the purpose of our therapeutic practice. If

Patient Meursault faces the sentence of a public execution, the analyst is being asked to be complicit in diagnosing and treating a patient whose cure will make him fit for that execution, an unethical application of our profession. If Patient Meursault is alive, if his sentence of public execution is imaginary, and if his "free-association" monologue transcribes a recent set of sessions, then that transcription provides the analyst with a disjunctive bricolage of diary, journal, memoir, and reconstructed events; and a bizarre tapestry of memory, wish, fantasy, dream, and defense. From such a monologue of a living person, the analyst can usefully work, despite the constraints below. Her interpretations, that is, are capable of changing the way Patient Meursault views his symptoms and, thereby, of freeing him to see them—and himself—in a new way, from a perspective different than his customary one.

C. *Working without the Collaboration of Patient Meursault*

The interpretations arrived at in the formal analysis below are disadvantaged by the analyst's not having access to the patient and, thereby, not being able to discuss his monologue with him. This unilateral relationship violates the vital convention that an analyst share her tentative conclusions and interpretations with a patient so as to get his concurrence, correction, or reconstruction before proceeding to treatment. Consequently, the analyst's conclusions will be of limited, if any, therapeutic value to Patient Meursault unless she can establish a live relationship with him and can pinpoint the symptoms that signify behaviors that will resonate with Mr. Meursault in such a way as to illumine or reveal his repressed desires and unconscious motives and, thereby, enable him to better or more fully understand himself.

D. *Working without Knowledge of the Identity of Patient Meursault's Auditor*

It should go without saying that no patient's talking occurs in a void, is never a mere transfer of information onto a blank page—much less into an unresponsive recording machine for transcription and for distanced and cold analysis. Rather, it is always part of a relationship between two people. Consequently, it is imperative that an analyst in training not be left in the dark as regards the identity, or at least a characterization, of the actual analyst who listened to and responded to the monologue spoken by Patient Meursault. For to a greater or lesser degree, his monologue was surely affected by the relationship he sought, felt compelled to establish, or unwittingly fell into with his analyst, especially were the analyst male, not female. The quality and kind of teller–listener relationship in transference and countertransference bears strongly on the meanings and significance inferred from, as well as the effectiveness of, an analyst's work. Consequently, contradictions, oversimplifications, or errors in the report below may well result from this analyst's inference that Patient Meursault's transcription was from an account told a male analyst.

E. Working with a Foreign-Born Patient

A number of details and references indicate that Patient Meursault is a foreigner, indeed is a Frenchman living in Algiers, is what is called a "*pied-noir*," a European born in Algiers. This further complicates an analysis if the analyst has no depth of understanding or knowledge of that culture, its history, or the place of colonial Europeans in a North African state at the time of the monologue. (If the transcription is also a translation, the analysis is further complicated, it should go without saying.) Notwithstanding these impediments, the analyst is still in a position to hear Patient Meursault's account as if it were that of a human being in any culture burdened with minority discrimination, class conflict, political tension, religious difference, and, especially in this case, quite marked gender roles. Although this analyst brings a limited knowledge of Islamic traditions to her interpretations of Patient Meursault's attitudes toward three significant, but unnamed, Arabs in his story, she concurrently avails herself—perhaps too boldly—of the opportunity to analyze a man whose monologue frees her from succumbing to the temptations of, or being unduly constrained by, the referential fallacy. I refer, of course, to that error of being compelled to ground all understandings and interpretations of a human being's behavior patterns and symptoms in the stultifying and inhibiting knowledge of the historical, cultural, and linguistic context inscribed in the patient. Such knowledge all too often unduly distorts with static the "free listening" that a patient's "free association" requires.

F. Working with Eclectic Psychoanalytic Methodologies

While this analyst prefers to apply methodologies developed by post-Freudian schools (e.g., Klein, Lacan, Kohut, object relations, relational analysis, feminist theory, and the Stone Center model), she tries also to demonstrate that unlike many modern analysts she is adequately schooled in classical Freudian analysis and can apply its methodology and terms, despite its scientific unverifiability and the problematics of its reductive power. Regardless of methodologies, the report that follows aspires to demonstrate the analyst's neutrality and ability to bestow upon the whole text what the father of psychoanalysis calls an "evenly hovering attention" over all of its details, significant and reputedly insignificant.

Part II: Formulate Your Case (a Coherent Interpretation)
of Patient Meursault *But Not* Your Therapeutic Treatment

A. Abstract

An examination of the conflicting functions and multiple interpretations of a minor episode links its dominant misogyny to a complex pattern of similar events and relationships that assist an understanding, first, of Mr. Meursault's killing of the Arab—exposing the disguises, displacements, condensations, defenses, and repressed motives necessary to unraveling the strands surprisingly interwoven in that singular action of matricide—and, second, of the etiology of Mr. Meursault's essentially narcissistic act. At all stages of interpretation, the question guiding this analyst's answers is Why is the patient now doing what to whom?

B. *The Story of the Czech Traveler: A Resonant Incidental*

The episode most curious in Mr. Meursault's monologue is his inclusion of the news story he found between his mattress and the bed planks, a "story about the Czechoslovakian." He refers to it, proprietorially, as "my crime story." Although it was yellowed with age, its top part was missing, and it had been half-stuck to the mattress's canvas, he nevertheless insists that he "must have read" this "old scrap of newspaper" a thousand times. The story is of a son who returns to the village of his birth twenty-five years after he'd gone to seek his fortune. Wealthy, married, and father of a child, he leaves his wife and child at one village hotel so as to try to surprise his aged mother and sister by taking lodgings under a false name at the hotel they run in the same village. They don't recognize him. But they do recognize the wealth he conspicuously shows off before them. In the night they enter his room, beat him to death with a hammer, rob him, and throw his body into the river. His wife comes to their hotel the next morning and reveals the traveler's identity, which prompts the mother to hang herself and the sister to drown herself in a well.

In addition to Mr. Meursault's *claim* that he read the story "a thousand times," three other details warrant rumination. First, he *questions* the story's credibility, saying that "it wasn't very likely," but then decides "it was perfectly natural." Second, he *judges* the Czech traveler, ruling that "he pretty much deserved what he got." Third, he *moralizes*, concluding that "you should never play games."

The "fact" that Mr. Meursault *claims* to have hoarded this fugitive scrap of newspaper and obsessed over its story, presumably reading it over and over again, unquestionably establishes its significance to him and to an understanding of his character and his relationships. If understood literally, the manifest content of the virtually memorized story invites his auditor/reader/judge/analyst[1] to view Mr. Meursault to be both a casual anecdotalist who reports on an event merely to entertain a listener with an odd story of human relationships that end disastrously, and to be a tendentious raconteur who seizes on an arresting narrative about a family calamity to serve his own interests. Although a casual listener, careless reader, or empathic stranger might regard the story as the first, a more discerning listener or reader would surely find Mr. Meursault, on trial for or appealing for his very life, cleverly looking out for his neck. Consequently, a *moral* of his tendentious, cautionary tale is certainly to warn against playing pranks, especially ones that threaten to humiliate or mortify one's family by appearing to them in what could be construed as a disguise and by foolishly leading them to commit the horrifying acts of infanticide and fratricide. Mr. Meursault's ability to come to such a moralizing inference indicates that under most circumstances he can differentiate right from wrong behavior and freely exercises that ability—even though he makes no explicit or conscious connection between the morality of what he curiously appropriates as "my crime story" and his own actual crime, his murder of an Arab. Moreover, Mr. Meursault, mirroring the trial in which he's recently been the defendant, wastes no time *judging* the behavior of the Czech traveler. He pronounces that the mother and sister were justified in their homicide of the traveler and that the punishment they meted out was appropriate to the cruel game he had subjected them to: death by hammer blows was what he "deserved." In a word, he insinuates his ability to sit in a jury box and judge the behavior of three people, ruling against a man's joke and in favor of two women, even though their acts are murderous. By siding with the justness of the women's actions in killing the traveler, Mr. Meursault again exposes the tendentiousness of his story: If their murder can be exonerated, so too can his. Finally, Mr. Meursault's capacity for regarding the news story's *plausibility*, as being "perfectly natural," contributes to the impression of his open-mindedness, his willingness to allow that events which seem premeditated or calculated may be without a plan or agenda. "Things just happen," he strongly implies, "irrespective of conscious volition or unconscious desire." He would of course have every reason to hope that his auditor/reader/judge/analyst would believe the same to be true about his own case.

To take Mr. Meursault "at his word," as an honest and sincere reporter of events and especially of this memory, is to find him altogether normal, stable, even pedestrian. "One of us," he reads a story and interprets its characters, events, and point with empathy, even though his vindication of the murdering mother and sister may be more liberal than a real jury's would be.

It is precisely that liberality of mind, his favoring of the women over the foolish traveler that opens a seam in what can no longer be regarded as simply his *memory* of that yellowed, torn, incomplete "story." His story is also a gratifying *fantasy* and a recurrent and regressive *dream*, which may explain why, significantly, he makes a point of reporting that he found the "news story" in that altogether appropriate place of daydream, sleep, and dream, between the canvas mattress and the bed planks. But whether memory, fantasy or dream, the important matter is how each mode of presentation functions in a fuller understanding of Mr. Meursault as a patient whose entire monologue—or any symptomatic segment of it—can establish different perspectives that will elucidate his rhetorical strategies vis-à-vis his auditor/reader/judge/analyst, strategies that may clarify his self-perception and are capable of revealing himself to himself.

When regarded as a *fantasy*, Mr. Meursault's story distills into a commonplace of an infant's wish-world: although the sex of the child who accompanies the traveler and wife back to the traveler's birthplace is unidentified, it can only be masculine, for the events gratify that recurrent Oedipal wish of a male narrator to slay father in order to bed mother. This primary fantasy, of course, is defended against in Mr. Meursault's account of it. Not only does he deliberately obscure or conveniently forget the child's sex, but he also projects his patricidal wish onto displaced aggressive surrogates, grandmother and aunt, who unimaginatively bash the traveler's head in with a hammer. The mother's complicity in the boy-child's Oedipal fantasy is gratified by her revelation, "without knowing it," of her husband's identity to her mother- and sister-in-law, which effectively leads to their suicides, leaving the Oedipal dyad of mother and son, which the fantasist desires. Given Mr. Meursault's information about the death of his own father, whom "I never knew"; given the duration of Mr. Meursault's shared life with only his mother; and given his demeaning portrait of his mother's late-life relationship with Thomas Pérez, who, he claims, faints during the burial of Mr. Meursault's mother at the cemetery "(he crumpled like a rag doll)"—given these factors, it's clear why Mr. Meursault treated himself "a thousand times" to the Oedipally gratifying fantasy of the Czech traveler: It recapitulates and perpetuates his biographical experiences (however minimally reported), thereby confirming the relationship by which he seeks to define himself as a loving son. Surely his bachelorhood reflects positively on his deep love for his mother, whose death may be said to have constituted a traumatic event that may explain or mitigate his "automatic," indifferent, affectless, or unreflective behavior after her death.

This fantasy version of Mr. Meursault's "news story" radically readjusts an auditor's/reader's/judge's/analyst's vision by challenging not only the values assigned to the story's characters but also their identities. But to sustain this fantasy of a boy's Oedipal love requires freezing the values and identities and then aligning them with other patterns in Mr. Meursault's larger monologue, patterns that must corroborate only those values and identities. To that corroboration I could proceed, were the fantasy version the controlling fantasy of the entire monologue. However, it is not the controlling fantasy. A more complex dream version unravels it or, better, shows that a later stage of development in Mr. Meursault generates a permutation that reorganizes the story's meaning and significance and, thus, an analysis of Mr. Meursault's character.

By regarding his "crime story" as a *dream*—by casting a skeptical eye on both the manifest tendentious memory and the latent Oedipal fantasy in Mr. Meursault's story—both it and his judgments turn upside down to reveal his predominant need and controlling desire to be a deep hostility to women and his disguised outrage at their brutality. In other words, the Oedipal fantasy, which, like all fantasies, fulfills a wish, obscures or distorts the regressive function of Mr. Meursault's dream, which meets Freud's famous formula: "Every dream is the (disguised) fulfillment of a (repressed) wish."

True, the traveler tries to dupe his sister and mother. But it's all in the name of heightening their private surprise and joy when he will discover to them his identity, his gift; they'll not be subjected to public embarrassment or mortification, unless they're gossips who tattle on themselves. Under cover of darkness, however, they shed their disguises as welcoming hostesses and stand forth as greedy, ruthless monsters. The sight of his wealth brews resentment that no blood relation, much less that son/brother who abandoned them to seek his own fortune, has ever shared such wealth with them or sought to ease the burdensomeness of their lives as innkeepers. Seizing the opportunity that his sleep affords, they bludgeon him to death and dump his body in the river, manifesting, in Mr. Meursault's mind, their own and thus their sex's fundamental viciousness. Although Mr. Meursault's dream has the mother and daughter inflict mortal punishment upon themselves, their self-destruction is a distortion and displacement of his wish that they and the sisterhood to which they belong, "bad objects" all, be hanged and drowned as creatures who deserve "what they get." Moreover, their brutality is, "on the one hand . . . perfectly natural," his dream suggests, for homicidal aggressions are as native to their breasts as is the milk that sometimes flows from them; and "on the other" hand, their behavior is all too "likely," part of a predictable pattern of behavior that metes out cruelty the traveler did not "deserve." Mr. Meursault's dream cautions himself as a traveler who returns to the place of his birth that like all men, he must beware women. Rather than buy into the moral that "you should never play games," Mr. Meursault's dream cautions that because a man is condemned to "play games" with women, he had best be on guard to always play shrewdly and in dead earnest to keep them from attaining knowledge, advantage and, thereby, power over a man.

In this construction of Mr. Meursault's dark dream of evil women, even the traveler's wife is complicit and vilified, no longer the object of Oedipal desire. According to Mr. Meursault, on the morning after the Czech, his wife, and child arrived in the village, the wife came to her mother- and sister-in-law's hotel and, "without knowing it, gave away the traveler's identity." The expression of "giving away his identity" suggests that she freely betrays him rather than merely discloses or reveals who their overnight guest was. And why does Mr. Meursault include the phrase "without knowing it"? Is this to suggest that her disclosure was unintentional but that she was a bungler who was actually trying to carry on his prank, that she didn't realize what she was stupidly revealing? Is it to suggest that her "Freudian slip," her *vergreifen* or "bungled action," reveals what she unconsciously wants revealed, so as to do him and them harm? Is it also to indicate that, contrary to what is said, she knew what she was disclosing and actually delighted in revealing to the two women what they had accomplished, gratifying her wish as well as theirs?

By expanding the web of associations and meanings inhering in Mr. Meursault's story, I'm taking liberties with it and its small place in his overall monologue, the whole transcription. But my "systematic impiety," colliding interpretations, and alternative meanings aim at engaging in the psychoanalytic process of shifting perspectives so as to condense particular details into a single, though temporary, focusing insight, not to insist on an authoritative interpretation or diagnosis, much less to set up some question-begging dichotomies that set a historical news story against a memory, fantasy, and dream as rival modes of presentation. That is, while it may be excessive or erroneous to attach so much importance to a simple news story that Mr. Meursault, by pure happenstance, found in his jail cell, an auditor/reader/judge/analyst must not forget that it is Mr. Meursault who attaches the importance. After all, he could have mentioned that he found a yellowed old news story about a crime that took place in another country, but that he threw it out with other refuse because it seemed implausible or was upsetting. Indeed, inasmuch as no one else who visits him in jail mentions knowing about the Czech's "crime story," it's possible that the story is a complete fabrication, a narrative imagined—or dreamed—by Mr. Meursault. In any case, while Mr. Meursault's memory may be at work in capturing this event and including it in his monologue, his memory, like anyone's, recovers events because they contain meaning, value, significance, and gratification.

By way of recapitulation and clarification, let me return to the axiomatic question crucial to a modern analyst's work: Why is the patient now doing what to whom? Mr. Meursault's motives for telling about "[his] crime story" of the Czech traveler—and to whom—invites at least five alternatives, each peeling away a deeper or darker layer of motivation and each influenced by his relationship with his analyst. First, what he is "doing" is reporting on a *news story* that often diverted or entertained him during his incarceration, trying to impress upon his auditor/reader/judge/analyst that he is an unguarded autobiographer with no aces up his sleeve or hidden agendas behind his roughly chronological and itemized recitation of a framed interval of his life. Second, what he is "doing" is exploiting a story or *memory* to present himself to his auditor/reader/judge/analyst as sensitive moralist, someone who appreciates the punishment both meted out against duplicitous, and self-inflicted by guilty, people, which appreciation aims to make him, thereby, someone deserving of consideration for a remitted or mitigated sentence—if not exculpation, pardon, or forgiveness—for his own crime against an Arab. Third, what he is "doing" is telling a *fantasy* that gratifies his Oedipal wishes and, whether his auditor/reader/judge/analyst is male or female, will unconsciously gratify him or her, too, even if interpreting the fantasy as a homosexual (negative-Oedipal) wish, which requires simply turning the traveler's child into a girl. Fourth, what he is "doing" is providing a secondary revision of a *dream* in whose manifest content he finds cause to blame the traveler for precipitating women's cruel acts and, by commiserating with their self-inflicted punishments, tries to enlist empathy from his auditor/reader judge/analyst and, thereby, win approval as a man whose forthcoming sentence deserves extenuation because of his ability to recognize the precipitating agent in others' crimes. Fifth, what he is "doing" is decoding a *dream*'s latent content, which allows him to unconsciously vent his hostility toward women for their natural barbarity, to unconsciously appeal to those misogynists among his auditors/readers/judges/analysts who share his displaced libidinal and narcissistic pleasure in the exposure and extermination of women as murderous agents, and to unconsciously express his guilt over the gratification of the patricidal component of his Oedipal wish.

C. The Disguised Patterns of Misogyny in Mr. Meursault's Monologue

Having exhumed what I interpret to be the latent misogyny in Mr. Meursault's deepest-seated, disguised, predominant, and narcissistic desire to malign women, I now proceed to assemble the corroborating episodes and evidence which integrate—be they echoes, mirrors, shadows, parallels, or analogies— with his eroticized hostility against women. And in the repetitious pattern of those episodes and evidence—primarily his relationships with Raymond, Salamano, and Marie—I will establish the presence of his relentless hostility, whose matricidal objective serves his narcissism.

Before I turn to the events and relationships concurrent with or just prior to his killing of the Arab, however, one episode during Mr. Meursault's imprisonment begs for analysis. While it seems superficially so inconsequential, it contributes to my interpretation of his narcissistic need to devalue others, but especially women. I refer to the day Marie, his lover, comes to visit him in prison. Rivaling the importance to him of Marie's presence and their brief conversation are the two women, one Moorish and one French, who immediately flank her and to whose presence during the episode he keeps returning: "a little, thin-lipped old woman dressed in black and a fat, bareheaded woman who was talking at the top of her voice and making lots of gestures." Although the thin-lipped Arab woman in black is visiting her small, delicate-handed son, she utters not a single word to him. She only stares at him. Only after he is called to return to his cell and he bids her good-bye does she reach between the bars on her side of the room, eight to ten meters from him, and "give him a long, slow little wave."

To answer the question Why is the patient now doing what to whom? requires some circuitous explanation. Curiously, Mr. Meursault registers no details about any facial expressions the thin-lipped woman communicates. He allows an auditor/reader/judge/analyst to interpret her on the one hand with empathy: she is a morose mourner who is so disconsolate over her son's shame that she cannot bring herself to falsely pretend otherwise and earnestly but silently communicates with him by way of her concentrated gaze. But Mr. Meursault allows, on the other hand, an interpretation whose attitude is disgust: she is a resentful scold who is so ashamed of the disgrace her son has brought upon the family name that she punishes him with the withering and sustained disapproval of bitter silence. Whether she consoles him or exacerbates his shame is unclear. True, Mr. Meursault regards the silence between the mother and son to be an "oasis of silence" in the din of murmuring and shouting that goes on in the visiting room. But his oasis image addresses only what her silence does for *him*, not for or to her son. Her significance lies in her silence, which links her to Mr. Meursault's mother, whose silences are her most memorable trait. It also links her to the little robot woman who attends his trial and to whom he had paid such close attention on the evening she'd taken a seat at his table in Céleste's restaurant. In return for his attention on that evening she had altogether ignored him and proceeded to methodically check off the radio programs on the magazine that occupied her exclusive attention throughout her dinner. Remarkable as a solitaire, her presence at that dinner and later at his trial makes her a surrogate for his mother, and her silence, in his mind, communicates both her judgmental contempt for, and her humiliated shame of, him: her total disregard, which suggests to him that he amounts to nothing more than a badly made or functionless piece of furniture, injures his ever-vulnerable narcissistic self-esteem. Indeed, her silence also allies her with the silent brutality of the Czech traveler's mother and sister. Their stretched neck and suffocating mouth, respectively, are lethal oral injuries that become specifically and uncannily congruent with the muteness of the tight-lipped, prisoner-visiting mother in black and Mr. Meursault's effectively mute mother.

This repetitious presence of silent women whom Mr. Meursault clusters as malignant agents deserving oblique and disguised vilification is reinforced by that other visiting woman flanking Marie in the prison, the fat, bareheaded, loud-mouthed woman. Her shouts, her report on a woman's refusal to do something that would help Mr. Meursault's fellow inmate out ("'Jeanne wouldn't take him'"), and her listing of the items she had put in a basket she brought and left at the prison clerk's office for him—these construct one more image of a male–female relationship in which the man appears to be paying the price for some misdeed, as if to suggest that men are victims, sacrificed by women on their altar.

These parallels—unless or until riveted to more substantial girders—are much too tenuous to build Mr. Meursault's misogyny on. But the girders, once made visible, more than adequately support my analysis.

The central girder is Mr. Meursault's friendship with the sharp-dressing pimp Raymond Sintès, about whom he significantly says, "I find what he has to say interesting. Besides, I don't have any reason not to talk to him."

Inasmuch as a pimp or procurer regards the women whose flesh he traffics in as objects to be exploited, his livelihood rests on a contempt for or methodical degradation of women. For Mr. Meursault to be friends with a pimp—to have no reason to repulse his friendship—proves he shares that contempt, even though he never overtly celebrates Raymond's attitude or much else, for that matter. As if that were not enough, Mr. Meursault readily accepts without question Raymond's self-serving versions of five stories: of the fight he'd gotten into, of how his mistress/prostitute had betrayed or two-timed him, of why he had "smacked her around," of why he needs Mr. Meursault's help in writing a letter to her, and of why his plan of entrapment and retaliation against her is appropriate or just. Most telling is Mr. Meursault's unhesitating complicity in writing the letter that induces her to return to Raymond. That act might well reflect the higher value he places on brotherliness or camaraderie, were it not for the female target of Raymond's abusiveness. As if her status as a prostitute weren't degrading enough, she's further demeaned by her identity as a Moor, a racial and ethnic populace whom a colonial culture feels justified, if not obligated, to mistreat as inferiors. (Even more, although the transcript's ambiguous strikeovers seem intended to cross out several phrases in this episode, Raymond further denigrates his mistress by telling Mr. Meursault that "she amuses herself with her thing." By insinuating that she masturbates, he invites Mr. Meursault to view her "perverse" or "unnatural" self-amusement as deserving the punishment he has planned.) And when Raymond's plan succeeds and he beats up on his allegedly cheating mistress, Mr. Meursault refuses to honor his own lover's, Marie's, request to fetch a policeman. He explains that he "didn't like cops," which rationalization conceals the gratification he derives from Raymond's prolonged beating of the woman. Even Mr. Meursault's perjurious statement at the police station, swearing that the woman had cheated on Raymond, attempts to hide his deep hostility for women behind his superficial male comradeship and the sexist justification that a cheating woman "deserves" physical abuse. As when he had written the letter for Raymond, he claims that in making his statement to the police he has again "tried my best to please Raymond because I didn't have any reason not to please him." Mr. Meursault's repetitious but bald emphasis on pleasing Raymond thinly disguises the fulfillment he derives from projecting onto Raymond—a "narcissistic extension" or "selfobject"—his own wish to devalue women through injury.

Why is the patient now doing what to whom? I should hope my answers are in the above, the crux of which is that Mr. Meursault willingly becomes a pimp's scribe or amanuensis and writes a duplicitous letter whose pretext, a sincere request for sexual rapprochement, successfully hides its real text, which is a spiteful ruse by which to act out sadistic aggressions. Indeed, the letter Raymond asks Mr. Meursault to write provides a pretext for a treacherous letter that Mr. Meursault himself desires an opportunity to write. He registers not the least bit of difficulty in writing it and earns Raymond's "pleased" gratitude: "'I could tell you knew about these things.'" Raymond grants him status as a "pal," the equivalent of informal initiation into the brotherhood of women-haters.

A second girder supporting the misogyny of Mr. Meursault takes form in the attention and space he devotes to "the couple" who reside across the landing, Salamano and his dog. A widower who acquired a spaniel puppy shortly after his wife died, the now skin-diseased, decrepit Salamano treats his now-mangy, aged, but never-named dog to an unvarying regimen of twice-a-day walks, predictable beatings, and repetitive verbal abuse. One day while Salamano is distracted in a crowd, the dog slips its collar and disappears. Salamano is beside himself with his loss, turns to Mr. Meursault for advice, and on his suggestions contacts the animal pound and the police, but to no avail.

Although Mr. Meursault empathizes with old Salamano's literal situation, his interest and the detail of his recollection of the "couple's" relationship screen the gratification he derives from the relationship's underlying misogyny and his brotherhood with Salamano. In the first place the spaniel, reluctantly or tardily identified as a "he," is a surrogate for Salamano's dead wife, whom, Mr. Meursault pointedly tells, Salamano admits he had never been happy with. The beatings and abuse he publicly administers on the dog act out his hostilities against that displaced wife, despite his dependency on "her" companionship, his genuine grief over his loss of "her," and his anger at being deprived of a submissive object upon which to inflict his nasty will. In this regard, Salamano's wish for the return of his dog concurrently parallels Raymond's desire for the return of his Moorish mistress so that he, too, can bloody her again with his persecutory beatings. Salamano's mention that Mr. Meursault's mother "was very fond of his dog" further buttresses an interpretation that Mr. Meursault finds gratification in the episode of another man's loss, especially when that loss is prefaced by a long history of mistreatment of an unnamed creature who also mirrors Mr. Meursault's mother, a woman without name.

The third girder on which Mr. Meursault's misogyny rests is his relationship with Marie Cardona, the former office typist whom he'd "had a thing for at the time" of her employment but hadn't pursued. Meeting her by chance at the public beach the day after his return from his mother's burial, he wastes no time making amorous advances that she laughingly encourages, whether he's brushing against her breasts, resting his head on her stomach as they dry out in the sun on the float, or swimming back to the dock together, his arm around her waist. Between then and the next morning when she departs from him to meet an obligation to her aunt, she has permitted him to freely fondle her breasts and kiss her during the comic film they had gone to; and she has accompanied him "home," where his bed straightaway becomes the site for their first sexual relations. In common parlance, Mr. Meursault presents her to be an "easy lay," an impulsive hedonist with few moral scruples, perhaps even a capricious slut who enjoys the pleasures of casual sex. Not once after he wakes that Sunday does he include in his extensively itemized chronology of the day a single thought or mention of her, suggesting that mentally he smears her as just "a piece," a convenient and pleasing orgasmic container.

Inasmuch as a full week goes by before Mr. Meursault and Marie, "as we'd planned," get together, bus off for a beach outing, then eagerly return to "throw ourselves onto my bed," it is clear that she has no fast hold on his affection or regard. He confirms that when, the following morning, she asks if he loves her; he tells her that "it didn't mean anything but that I didn't think so." And when she visits him the following evening and, point-blank, asks if he wants to marry her, he tells her that "it didn't make any difference to me and that we could if she wanted to." As if this repetition of indifference weren't insulting enough to silence her, she plunges heedlessly on and asks whether he would have accepted her "proposal from another woman with whom [he] was involved in the same way," to which he tells her simply, "'Sure.'" Her failure to react to his cavalier dismissal and to spurn any further relationship with him proves her utter lack of pride, justifies his fundamental contempt for her, and gratifies his narcissistic need to exploit relationships with inferiors whose inadequacies attest to his superior worth.

Other details could be adduced at this point, but even though Mr. Meursault never expresses himself with overt sarcasm or malice, the pattern of his disdain for Marie as just "another woman" is incontestable, despite the erotic gratification she provides him. Indeed, during the eleven months of confinement before the investigation of his case is completed and he is brought before the court, he declares that while his erotic desire for a woman tormented him, he "never thought specifically of Marie." Instead he claims that he was a veritable Lothario: "I thought so much about a woman, about women, about all the ones I had known, about the circumstances in which I had enjoyed them, that my cell would be filled with their faces and crowded with my desires." If he was in fact a womanizer, whose chief interest is in seducing women—"I had enjoyed them," he selfishly admits—then Mr. Meursault, this pied-noir Don Juan, fits the pattern of a man whose erotic attentions also mask his aggressive hostility for the very objects of his attention. Marie's lack of self-respect and diminished sense of self-worth make her, consequently, an appropriate target of his contempt.

To collect and move my points forward, my analysis finds that Mr. Meursault's hostility towards Marie, Raymond's Arab mistress, and Salamano's spaniel constitutes forms of displaced hostility toward his mother, which indirectly explains his unconscious motive for violating the conventions of filial grief after his mother died. He, of course, describes each of his behaviors as best he can and tries to mock the judgment against him that he's to be executed for failing to weep at his mother's funeral. But despite the bizarre case the prosecuting attorney puts together, Mr. Meursault's monologue has it right: his murder of the Arab has everything to do with his unconventional response to his mother's death and funeral; his murder of the Arab is a displacement of the erotics of his matricidal desire.

But to address that murder of the Arab—rather what Mr. Meursault's killing of the Arab means—requires explaining two additional manifestations of Mr. Meursault's hostile relationships with women. I refer to his relationships with the examining magistrate and the prison chaplain, both of whom display forms of inferiority hateful to Mr. Meursault.

With the former, Mr. Meursault seems to enjoy his own flat but detailed narration and "accurate" quotation or report of the magistrate's words and behavior during their second meeting. His account, despite its deadpan manner, satirizes the outrageously hysterical outburst of the examining magistrate whose fierce affiliation with and subordination to Christianity and its icon of the silver crucifix has nothing to do with the facts of the killing. Nevertheless, the magistrate's *function*, rather than his *sex*, compels interpreting him with derision to be a manic devotee, a person enslaved in a "feminized" form of ideological infatuation or what Freud calls "infantile helplessness." The magistrate's frantic dependency on his crucified Jesus is akin to the other forms of "female" dependency in Mr. Meursault's world: be it the spaniel to Salamano, the Arab mistress to Raymond and her brother, Marie to Mr. Meursault, or the monologue's other loud person, the bareheaded woman next to Marie in the prison's visiting room who converses with her husband only in shouts. By the end of the magistrate's eleven-month investigation, Mr. Meursault's "ridiculous impression of being 'one of the family'" speaks directly to the magistrate's function as a surrogate mother; after all, Mr. Meursault's family, for all intents and purposes, consisted exclusively of him and his mother, his father apparently having died or abandoned his wife and child during Mr. Meursault's infancy.

Mr. Meursault's relationship with the prison chaplain also translates into a mother–son exchange. When stripped of its particulars, the chaplain's attempts at interceding for his "son" replicate a mother's efforts at communicating with and instructing a son whose characteristically aggressive misbehavior has required solitary punishment. The chaplain's patient but sustained efforts, however well-intentioned, constitute a form of maternal meddlesomeness against which full-blooded young sons and daughters would strongly, if not violently and justifiably, rebel. More, the chaplain's interference sufficiently provokes Mr. Meursault so that his exploding emotion, verbal upbraiding, and physical aggressions—which require prison guards to extricate the chaplain from his grip—act out the long-repressed and deeply disguised or shrewdly displaced matricidal hostility he has long harbored against the women represented in the chaplain, wearing a cassock with its dresslike skirts and bonnetlike hood.

D. Mr. Meursault's Murder of the Nameless Arab: Motive, Meaning, and Origin

Can an argument now be constructed to show that the Arab whom Mr. Meursault kills with five bullets is *also* a woman? Such a transformation is unnecessary here, for explaining the motive behind the killing of that Arab is considerably simpler, if the analysis already presented has effectively done its preparatory and recuperative work of translation and interpretation.

Quite simply, the Arab brother of Raymond's mistress is a man who *values* a woman. And in the Arab's sister is condensed his mother, women in general, and—given the political, religious, and cultural situation of the colonialized state he lives in—his country, and, indeed, his "motherland." It may well be that his sister has violated Arabic, Moorish, Islamic, and Algerian cultural norms by having become a prostitute. It may well be that she has further breached those norms by performing her scandalous and blasphemous duties under the control and domination of a colonial Frenchman, Raymond Sintès. But nothing she does entitles that Frenchman—be he her lover, "employer," imperialistic colonizer, or all three—to be the agent entitled to physically abuse her, to so beat her up that she returns home bloodied. The outcome of the Arab's first fight with Raymond, in which Raymond gives *him* a drubbing, neither intimidates him, diminishes his fraternal obligation to honor and protect his sister, or thwarts his religious duty to intervene in the wayward behavior of a Muslim woman who, regardless of her actions, still represents a cultural icon. So when Mr. Meursault's letter, composed and written without any dictated instructions from Raymond, lures her into a trap that results in her victimization at Raymond's hands again, the Arab stalks Raymond for an opportunity to try again to avenge the wrong done his sister, his family's honor, his culture, and his religion. By following him a week later to the beach where he slashes Raymond's arm and mouth, he succeeds by "marking" Raymond visibly as an offender. His success, however, sufficiently aggravates Mr. Meursault to track him down on the beach and shoot him, five times, but not simply out of fraternal friendship for Raymond or adherence to some primitive code of retributive justice, much less because of a cruel sun glinting off a knife's blade. Rather, Mr. Meursault chose to enter into a relationship with Raymond because of Raymond's dynamic—not formulaic—role as Mr. Meursault's pawn and double, his "selfobject." Raymond gratifies the psychic economy of Mr. Meursault's misogynistic desire at every interval in the relationship: Mr. Meursault listens to the "history" of the cheating Arab mistress, writes the disingenuous letter to her, witnesses the beating of her, lies to police about her, and, now, slays her defender, who is, in a word, his antithesis. That Mr. Meursault's murder of the Arab requires the punishments of incarceration, a trial, and execution does nothing to minimize, deflect, undo, or qualify his accomplishment. Indeed, they can be said to be obligatory mitigations necessary to disguising the fulfillment of his desire, thereby validating again Freud's formula: "Every dream is the (disguised) fulfillment of a (repressed) wish." In other words, the space and detail that Mr. Meursault lavishes on his incarceration and the sustained legal processes in part 2 of his monologue richly disguise the narcissistic fulfillment of his matricidal wish by making himself appear to be the victim of an irrational culture and persecutory fanatics.

Why Mr. Meursault fires four additional bullets into the already dying Arab's body of course makes "no sense." But that very senselessness has its explanation in the strength of Mr. Meursault's misogyny and the depth of his matricidal desire. It would be silly or pointless to try to apportion each of the five bullets to an appointed women, even though the first of Mr. Meursault's two-part monologue singles out five irritating women: Maman, Raymond's Arab mistress, the robot woman, Marie, and the aged woman who cries incessantly during the vigil in the little mortuary on the eve of the funeral in Marengo. The five shots instead tell, one by one, of Mr. Meursault's long-repressed but now-gratified hostility toward women, however configured, disguised, or displaced they are in an Arab whose very lack of a name makes him a signifier whose referents, while ambiguous, congeal around women. The five shots also signify Mr. Meursault's repetition compulsion, their target a recumbent, partly naked human body he equates with women.

That the case the courtroom will hear following Mr. Meursault's is a case of parricide—information emphasized by his lawyer, reporters, and the prosecutor—further connects to Mr. Meursault's misogyny. It's common to assume that parricide means murder of a father, which is how Mr. Meursault's prosecutor alludes to the case to follow. But since that precise term is generic for murder of a parent of either sex (in contrast to "patricide," which signifies exclusively "murder of a father"), the prosecutor is uncannily correct when, in his rhetorically irrational peroration at the end of his final argument, he considers Mr. Meursault's deeds the moral equivalent of "killing his mother." "I am convinced, gentlemen," he declares, ". . . that you will not think it too bold of me if I suggest to you that the man who is seated in the dock is also guilty of the murder to be tried in this court tomorrow." In a word, Mr. Meursault is guilty of two murders that are condensed in the single murder of the Arab.

The remaining matter is to explain *why* Mr. Meursault harbors such an intense misogyny and to trace it and its corollary, his matricidal hostility, to its origins, to discover its etiology. The answer is not easy to come by, however overdetermined it might be, for he provides almost no information about his infancy, development, or relationship with his mother, familial relations, or other women. So about this part of my analysis I must be less confident.

The only memory Mr. Meursault has about his father, as I mentioned earlier, is his mother's *story* of his father's reaction to watching a murderer be executed. But while Mr. Meursault tells that he felt "a little disgusted by him" for returning home and throwing up "half the morning," his father's reaction doesn't appear to come close to anything resembling a traumatic event in Mr. Meursault's development. Moreover, he makes no effort to question his mother's motive for choosing to tell him only that story about his father, rather than some other story or, for that matter, a raft of other stories. Nonetheless, it is that father's absence, from his life and memory, that hovers, an ominous dark cloud, over Mr. Meursault's character; this deficit in Mr. Meursault's background and inner life explains his narcissism, for the deficit causes him to feel shame that his insufficiency, weakness, and inferiority are responsible for his father's absence. Only compensatory behavior will repudiate his responsibility.

What accounts for my father's absence? Did he die, and if so, how? If he abandoned us, why did he do so? Those are the questions that have to have long plagued Mr. Meursault. And they are the very questions the child of the Czech traveler will doubtless ask his mother, which correspondence of plots establishes the centrality of the "news story" I began with. Mr. Meursault's mother's unwillingness or inability to make known to him either how his father died or why he abandoned them or what some other reminiscences about him were, this lack of information makes *her* culpable for his disappearance and suggests that guilt dictates her silence. In effect, to Mr. Meursault, his mother did something to deprive him of his father; if that Czech traveler "deserved" to have his head hammered in for trying to surprise his mother with a game of disguised identity, then certainly Mr. Meursault's mother's eradication of his father "deserves" the punishment of any hostile act he himself can come up with. Indeed, inasmuch as he blames his shooting of the Arab on the dazzling spears of sunlight glinting off the Arab's knife blade and stabbing at his "stinging eyes"; and inasmuch as a man's eyes are a classic displacement of his testicles (vide Oedipus's self-mutilation); and inasmuch as the Arab is a condensation for Mr. Meursault of women turned aggressive, then it would seem fair to conclude, in classical fashion, that Mr. Meursault's shooting of the Arab is a retaliatory act against his mother's castration of his father and, thus, her threat to himself as well.

Early in his monologue Mr. Meursault mentions, "When she was at home with me, Maman used to spend her time following me with her eyes, not saying a thing." Her actions appear innocuous enough—as if she were a fond mother enjoying the pleasure of watching the child of her womb engaged in his routines. But her actions are also threatening, as if she's both waiting for the right moment to pounce aggressively upon him and recording carefully each of his inadequacies—his ugliness, impotence, and helplessness—so as to shame him for each of them. Her silence, all by itself, is as menacing and belittling as the stares of the robot woman, the Arab mother during the prison visitation, and Arab men who silently take the measure of the beach-bound trio of Raymond, Marie, and Mr. Meursault on that fateful Sunday morning. Her silence suggests that she's little interested in any communication with someone so inferior as he, that his presence, like his father's, is unwelcome. In a word, his removal of his mother to the convalescent home three years before her death constitutes a retaliatory act against her. But its matricidal aggression is so attenuated, if not sublimated, that it afforded Mr. Meursault little fulfillment of his hostile wish. Raymond's entanglement, however, gives Mr. Meursault a set of opportunities that, as they unfold, fully gratify his hostile and narcissistic wishes.

And Mr. Meursault's professed pleasure in the prospect of being beheaded before a large crowd of people whom he wishes will greet him "with cries of hate"? How does that fit into this analysis? Foremost, it restores to Mr. Meursault the presence of his absent father by placing himself in the only place he can connect his father with, despite his father's revulsion at the execution he witnessed. It also confirms that the beheading he faces will replicate the castration he imagines his father suffered as Maman's victim and that he himself will now fully suffer in a disguised form. The crowd's "cries of hate" gratify his narcissism by demonstrating not only *their* inferiority (they have not the least glimmer of what his murder signified) and *their* envy (their hatred will constitute nothing more than reaction formation, excessively decrying his action because it acts out the deeply repressed wish they share with him), but also his fervent desire to connect with others, regardless of the manner or means. His execution will also unconsciously reward him with the punishment he desires for harboring parricidal wishes and for, like the Czech traveler, playing games whose secrets and intentions he disguises and hides.

Finally, as Mr. Meursault's monologue reveals throughout, having individuals, clusters, or throngs of people look at him—across the little mortuary, in the courtroom, in his jail cell, at his execution—gratifies his narcissism. His monologue is further proof of that narcissism: he loves to hear himself talk. And he loves an audience, be it in his analyst's sanctuary or before an imagined crowd, for he is confident that it will react to him, the crowd with "cries of hatred," his analyst, of course, with a cogent interpretation, herewith concluded, upon which a beneficial treatment program can be built.

Part III: Freely Express Residual Questions or Problems

Dear Dr. Schoenbergen,

Having concluded this advanced training assignment, I hope I've accomplished one objective you continue to impress on me, the need to keep jargon out of an analysis or to a minimum and, thereby, to make it comprehensible without sacrificing complexity. Nevertheless, I end with three questions and hope you'll take time to respond to each of them.

First, I must ask whether, given my background, which by this stage in my training you know all too well, whether you handpicked this patient and case for me? Was it your intent to test me on whether the various and profuse manifestations of Mr. Meursault's misogyny and matricidal hostility, which led to my description and diagnosis, would so irritate me as to cause me to rupture the analytic "objectivity" of my report with subjective outbursts, as happened on an earlier assignment? Moreover, because Mr. Meursault would be a difficult patient to treat and would surely obstruct the collaborative therapeutic relationship a therapist would strive to develop with him, did you assign me this case to magnify the countertransference problems it seems laden with? After all, the transcribed monologue suggests that Mr. Meursault—as can be expected in a narcissistic patient—seems to have obliterated his therapist, utterly devalued his auditor as a projected "narcissistic extension" or, perhaps, "selfobject."

Second, if Mr. Meursault's rudimentary desire—the target of his double-helixed erotic and aggressive drives—is to do away with his mother, the fulfillment of that desire would, under normal circumstances, activate the negative-Oedipal formula, which requires interpreting events and relationships as displacements of and defenses against his homosexual desire for his father. But inasmuch as Mr. Meursault had no relationship with his father, and inasmuch as I am unable—without ingenious mental gymnastics and substitutions—to construct a coherent or intelligible case that Mr. Meursault's relationships with Raymond, Salamano, Tomas Pérez, Masson, Céleste, or the Arab constellate into a "queer reading" or a disguised pattern of repressed homosexual gratification, would it be correct to locate the monologue at a pre-Oedipal stage of Mr. Meursault's development? And if so, then would the eradication of Maman and the hostilities against women express Mr. Meursault's exclusive desire for pre-Oedipal, narcissistic gratification, even if it paradoxically requires decapitation and the loss of the oral organ by which that primary stage is gratified? Or should I read that decapitation and loss of oral organ also as a displacement of castration, both losses, of voice and phallic member, compounding the deficit model upon which narcissistic personalities come to rest?

Third, in listening to my summary and discussion of Mr Meursault's monologue, my partner suggested that it seemed as if the case could easily be passed off as a literary text, that the problematic issues in the monologue resembled any number of first-person narratives or dramatic monologues studied in college literature courses; my partner even went so far as to wonder if you'd given me an actual work of literature. I instantly scorned the idea, as you can imagine. But my partner is asking around. If it is an actual work of literature, why would the assignment have withheld that information? What kind of a test have I been given? Surely my instructors don't want trainees to think that analysis and the helping profession to which I aspire is merely a form of literary criticism, which I've long been conditioned to consider to be nothing more than academic onanism, do they?

Well, yes, it is well past time that I end this assignment. Dare I say, however, that while I enjoyed this latest task in my progress toward "certification," two matters nagged. First, I chafed throughout at the restriction forbidding me from taking the case to the vital next step of recommending a therapeutic treatment plan. Second, I wondered at several points about the professional constraints and ethical dilemmas that working in a correctional setting would pose. These aside, I look forward to your responses. Where I have overlooked, oversimplified, or overcomplicated matters, you will, I trust, point out my errors, stupidities, excesses, and myopia, as you have so conscientiously done in the earlier stages of my training. Where I need more training, you will, I trust, direct me. And where I show discernment and insight, you will, I trust, commend me.

Respectfully submitted,
(Signed) Dora V.

Notes

Notes to Introduction

1. See, respectively, Stanley Eugene Fish, *Self-Consuming Artifacts: The Experience of Seventeenth-Century Literature* (Berkeley: U of California P, 1972) and *Is There a Text in This Class? The Authority of Interpretive Communities* (Cambridge: Harvard UP, 1980); Norman N. Holland, *5 Readers Reading* (New Haven: Yale UP, 1975); David Bleich, *Subjective Criticism* (Baltimore: Johns Hopkins UP, 1978); Steven Mailloux, *Interpretive Conventions: The Reader in the Study of American Fiction* (Ithaca: Cornell UP, 1982) and *Rhetorical Power* (Ithaca: Cornell UP, 1989); Judith Fetterley, *The Resisting Reader: A Feminist Approach to American Fiction* (Bloomington: Indiana UP, 1979); Wolfgang Iser, *The Implied Reader: Patterns of Communication in Prose Fiction from Bunyan to Beckett* (Baltimore: Johns Hopkins UP, 1974), *The Act of Reading: A Theory of Aesthetic Response* (Baltimore: Johns Hopkins UP, 1978), and *The Range of Interpretation* (New York: Columbia UP, 2000). For an incisive, brilliant analysis of the wide range of reader-response criticism, see Elizabeth Freund, *The Return of the Reader: Reader-Response Criticism* (London: Methuen, 1987).

2. I am indebted to the work of British philosopher J. L. Austin and speech–act theorists who follow his lead, among them John Searle, Richard Ohmann, Wolfgang Iser, Mary Louise Pratt, and Shoshana Felman. Granted his ideas have all met with important challenges: his distinction between constative and performative utterances; his divisions among locutionary acts (conveying meaning), illocutionary acts (conveying the force of tone, attitude, feeling, motive, or intention), and perlocutionary acts (conveying consequences upon speaker, audience, or others); and his insistence that literary language be excluded from his categories. But his work has nonetheless promoted explorations of the function of utterances as articulations that make things happen (rather than merely have meaning) and facilitated the study of all texts as performative.

3. *The Gazer's Spirit: Poems Speaking to Silent Works of Art* (Chicago: U of Chicago P, 1995). *Intertextuality* defines the common if not universal practice of authors and artists who, when composing their own works, build on, react to, or reenvision previous texts or a set of texts whose presence may be boldly or delicately woven into their own. Hollander's term, *interfigurality*, similarly defines the practice of authors whose work appropriates other artists' characters

and narrative situations—their "figures"—to construct a narrative of the same situation. Hence, his book is interested in poets examining and writing about works of art, creating narrators who give voice to a voiceless, visual experience.

4. "On the Nature and Status of Covert Texts: A Reply to Gerry Brenner's 'Letter to "De Ole True Huck,"'" *The Journal of Narrative Technique* 20 (Spring 1990): 235–47. Rpt. in *Mark Twain: Adventures of Huckleberry Finn: A Case Study in Critical Controversy*, ed. Gerald Graff and James Phelan (Boston: Bedford/St. Martin's, 1995) 468–79; citations to Phelan's essay are from this edition.

5. I refer to Peter J. Rabinowitz, *Before Reading: Narrative Conventions and the Politics of Interpretation* (Ithaca: Cornell UP, 1987), who identifies four rules of reading. Rules of "notice" alert readers to important parts of a narrative; rules of "signification" to details with reliable, secondary or special meaning; rules of "configuration" to details that fit into familiar patterns; and rules of "coherence" to the way a narrative fits together into a whole.

6. "Misreading as a Historical Act: Cultural Rhetoric, Bible Politics, and Fuller's 1845 Review of Douglass's *Narrative*," *Readers in History: Nineteenth-Century American Literature and the Contexts of Response*, ed. James L. Machor (Baltimore: Johns Hopkins UP, 1993) 5.

7. Jonathan Culler, *The Pursuit of Signs: Semiotics, Literature, Deconstruction* (Ithaca: Cornell UP, 1981).

8. See Frederick M. Keener, *English Dialogues of the Dead* (New York: Columbia UP, 1973).

9. *Recalcitrance, Faulkner, and the Professors: A Critical Fiction* (Iowa City: U of Iowa P, 1990).

10. *After Dickens: Reading, Adaptation and Performance* (Cambridge: Cambridge UP, 1999).

11. See her *Unmarked: The Politics of Performance* (New York: Routledge, 1993); and *Mourning Sex: Performing Public Memories* (London: Routledge, 1997).

12. See, for example, Mary Poovey, "Creative Criticism: Adaptation, Performative Writing, and the Problem of Objectivity," *Narrative* 8 (May 2000): 109–33.

13. *Harper's*, 300 (June 2000): 110–14.

Notes to An Interview with Biblical Ruth

1. These are the first distinguishable words in the damaged beginning of the audiotape from which this transcription has been made. It seems reasonable to assume that Ruth has asked the interviewer to forgo the usual preliminaries, for his inflection of the words within quotation marks sounds like an echo of her request.

2. The interviewer must here be alluding to two authors whose articles have met with some scorn from scholars: H. G. May, "Ruth's Visit to the High Place at Bethlehem," *Journal of the Royal Asiatic Society of Great Britain and Ireland* (1939): 75–78, who finds evidence that Boaz's gift to Ruth of six measures of barley when she departs from the threshing-floor is the price customarily paid sacred prostitutes(!); and Calum M. Carmichael, "A Ceremonial Crux: Removing a Man's Sandal as a Female Gesture of Contempt," *Journal of Biblical Literature* 96 (1977): 321–36, who finds such clear sexual symbolism in Ruth's visit to Boaz at the threshing-floor that mere mention of "feet" and "skirt" makes it manifestly transparent both that "[t]he original recipients of the story of Ruth would have fully understood the meaning of the language and gestures at the threshing-floor," and that they would have unhesitatingly recognized the "hidden significance of the event" (333). For a corrective to the outlandishness of each, see, respectively, H. H. Rowley, "The Marriage of Ruth," *The Servant of the Lord and Other Essays on the Old Testament* 2nd ed. (Oxford: Basil Blackwell & Mott, 1965) 189n; and Jack M. Sasson, *Ruth: A New Translation with a Philological Commentary and a Formalist–Folklorist Interpretation* (Baltimore: Johns Hopkins UP, 1979) 71. But then see as well, Mieke Bal, *Lethal Love: Feminist Literary Readings of Biblical Love Stories* (Bloomington: Indiana UP, 1987), who remarks the ambiguity of the Hebrew word *skirt*, which Ruth lifts when she goes to lie beside Boaz on the threshing floor, a word that also means "testicles," 70.

3. The interviewer here seems to seek answer to whether Boaz was Naomi's contemporary or younger, the former answer put forth by Rowley 192; and argued by Edward F. Campbell, Jr., *Ruth: A New Translation with Introduction, Notes, and Commentary* (Garden City, NY: Doubleday, 1975) 110; an answer rejected by Sasson 85–86.

4. The interviewer's emphasis on "sell" appears to acknowledge the considerable discussion of Naomi's property rights and of precisely what Boaz's terms meant; for which see D. R. Ap-Thomas, "The Book of Ruth," *The Expository Times* 79 (1967–68): 372; Robert Gordis, "Love, Marriage, and Business in the Book of Ruth: A Chapter in Hebrew Customary Law," *A Light unto My Path: Old Testament Studies in Honor of Jacob M. Myers*, ed. Howard N. Bream, Ralph D. Heim, and Carey A. Moore (Philadelphia: Temple UP, 1974) 252–59; and Sasson 108–15.

5. Ruth's question has fueled no few commentators. Customarily they endorse a "hidden-God theology"; for example, Oswald Loretz, "The Theme of the Ruth Story," *Catholic Biblical Quarterly* 22 (1960): 391–99; Ronald M. Hals, *The Theology of the Book of Ruth* (Philadelphia: Fortress, 1969); and Campbell 28–29. Sasson's translation, however, renders *Ruth* a "secular" text; and he argues against theologizing the book, both in his commentary and in his odd review of Campbell's translation, "Divine Providence or Human Plan," *Interpretation* 30 (1976): 417–18. Most recently Jan Wojcik, "Improvising Rules in the Book of

Ruth," *PMLA* 100 (1985): 145–53, agrees with Sasson's "secular" reading, but unwittingly misreads Sasson (153n), for he assumes that Sasson's quotation (44) *from* Hals (11–12) is Sasson's *own* position.

6. Ruth appears to be twitting her interviewer here, for some of her questions, like those of the interviewer, may well have their origin in questions assembled in Campbell's "The Hebrew Short Story: A Study of Ruth," *A Light unto My Path* 84.

7. For discussion of the problems surrounding his name, see Ap-Roberts 370–71.

8. The interviewer seems to have ignored Campbell's judicious commentary, which declares "there can be no dangerous implication" in Boaz's instruction that Ruth spend the remainder of the night with him (137). For, as he properly notes, Boaz's instruction is free from all ambiguity, having avoided the verb *to lie down* and having chosen instead the Hebrew verb *lwn/lyn* ("to lodge"), which is "never used in the Hebrew Bible with any sexual undertone"; moreover, Campbell explains that Ruth and Boaz are humans who "will do things in righteous fashion," and he concludes by pronouncing, "It is not prudery which compels the conclusion that there was no sexual intercourse at the threshing floor; it is the *utter irrelevance of such a speculation*" (138; emphasis added).

9. Here the interviewer seems to allude to a mildly feminist analysis. See Phyllis Trible's "Two Women in a Man's World: A Reading of The Book of Ruth," *Soundings* 59 (1976): 251–79, in which "Ruth and the females of Bethlehem work as paradigms for radicality. All together they are women in culture, women against culture, and women transforming culture"(279). For a slightly expanded version of this essay, see "A Human Comedy" in Trible's *God and the Rhetoric of Sexuality* (Philadelphia: Fortress, 1978) 166–99. But Ruth may also be alluding here to Bal's discussion of the unconventionally male bond that Ruth has had with Naomi, to whom she "clave," as wives were to cleave to husbands (72, 83, 85).

10. See Sasson's illuminating remarks on this point (62).

11. Here our interviewer expresses an idea for which courtesy demands proper acknowledgment; namely, Trible 257–58.

12. Ruth appears to question, perhaps unintentionally, Campbell's claim— for which it must be admitted there is no textual evidence—that "we get a glimpse of Naomi in wide-eyed astonishment as her daughter-in-law returns with an abundant supply of barley" (105).

13. Sasson notes this very difference (47–48, 49, 56).

14. The allusion, of course, is to Proverbs 11:22: "Like a gold ring in a pig's snout / Is a beautiful woman without discretion."

15. Although I have been unable to identify the "persuader" of the interviewer's latter notion, Campbell attributes a strikingly similar notion to C. F.

Keil, referring, he leaves me to guess, to C. F. Keil and F. Delitzsch, *Joshua, Judges and Ruth* (Edinburgh: n.p., 1876).

16. Ruth here alludes to Campbell 64.

17. Ruth here must be deriding Sasson's description of Naomi (24).

18. The interviewer here seems to allude to an article which advances this argument: Edward Robertson, "The Plot of the Book of Ruth," *Bulletin of the John Rylands Library, Manchester* 32 (1949–50): 207–28.

19. Here Ruth appears to take issue with Wojcik's discussion of her oath, for the simile occurs in his article (148).

20. Unquestionably the interviewer alludes to the lightly regarded comment of Thomas J. Meek, "Translating the Hebrew Bible," *Journal of Biblical Literature* 79 (1960): 333, a comment, however, which may need reassessment in the light of what lies ahead in this interview, for Meek continues by claiming, "It is one of the delicate touches in the book that Ruth should be represented as slightly exaggerating the status of Boaz in order to further his interest in her."

21. Unnecessary though it should be to do so, I identify the source for unschooled readers, should there be any: Proverbs 12:1.

22. The interviewer refers to Sasson's translation and commentary (38–48) on which salient portions of his subsequent discussion draws.

23. Campbell corroborates that Ruth's Hebrew statement "uses the so-called cohortative first person, which can express a request for permission *or a firm determination*"; given this ambiguity, he credits Ruth with "having taken stock of the general situation" and with stating "her determination to set about meeting it" (91–92; emphasis added), thus explaining *his* translation of 2:2, "'I am going out to the field and glean barley spears after someone in whose eyes I find favor'" (85). In a recent conversation my esteemed colleague N. D. Friedmann directed me to T. O. Lambdin's discussion of the cohortative; indeed his *Introduction to Biblical Hebrew* (New York: Scribner's, 1971) buttresses Campbell's translation, explaining that the cohortative first person establishes "a logical consequence, either of an immediately preceding statement or of the general situation in which it is uttered" (170).

24. Here Ruth can only be referring to Bal's "analysis of narratological subject positions," which finds that "Ruth's subject position, however autonomous it sometimes seems to be, is formally derived from the two elders" (78).

25. I quash Sasson's rejection of the accepted view of God's role in Ruth's arrival at Boaz's field—from which the interviewer here quotes (45)—in my article "*Qārāh*: What 'Happens' in *Ruth*: Dismantling a Secular Commentary," forthcoming in *Journal of Biblical Literature*.

26. Trible answers Ruth's question affirmatively, if not dogmatically (260).

27. Ruth and the interviewer joust with Campell's and Sasson's translations (86–87 and 49, respectively); for Sasson's refusal to allow the optative, see 52–53.

28. Campbell notes this as a possible meaning but rightly dismisses it (100–01); Sasson, too, discounts the possibility of reading *wekî dibbartā àl-lēb šiphātekā* as belonging to the language of courtship: "It would simply be too presumptuous of Ruth to employ such a vocabulary so prematurely" (53). But surely we must now begin to wonder.

29. Ruth seems to refer to the difference between her use here of *šiphāh* (maid-servant) and her use in 3:9 of *'āmāh* (handmaiden), for commentary on which see Campbell 101, or Sasson, 53–54.

30. Ruth refers here (quite superciliously, I must be allowed to interject) to Campbell 101.

31. This translation, of course, is that of the New English Bible.

32. The source for Ruth's quotation has wasted no little of my research time. And I must confess that I have drawn an empty net for my efforts. However, an English professor who insists upon her anonymity, learning of my inquiries, believed the source to be Charles Dickens's *The Pickwick Papers*; but such a source seemed too unlikely to deserve the time it would take to sift that book's 900-plus pages.

33. Sasson's reading of Boaz as trickster is on 230–32, but much of his philological and folklorist analysis also points to such a reading; see especially his commentary on what he designates "Legal Discussions" (4:1–12), to which he relegates fully one-third of his entire commentary (102-57).

34. Ruth's glib comments here allude to Sasson 216 ff.

35. Ruth alludes to Stephen Bertman's "Symmetrical Design in The Book of Ruth," *Journal of Biblical Literature* 84 (1965): 165–68, which includes in its conclusion this explanation for the style of the book's architecture: "Possibly it is the result of a psychological disposition, a way of conceiving of things which affects the shape of the created work, a disposition by virtue of which things are thought of not separately but together, not singly but in balanced relation . . . ."

36. The former reference is certainly to Vladimir Propp, upon whose work Sasson's interpretation of *Ruth* is admittedly indebted; I am advised that the latter reference may be to Bruno Bettelheim, *The Uses of Enchantment: The Meaning and Importance of Fairy Tales* (New York: Knopf, 1976). Fairy tales, indeed!

37. Campbell is the interviewer's source for this idea (101).

38. The former idea is developed by Sasson 74–78. But the curious implication in the latter is contained in Ruth's "more of his seed," for this suggests that possibly Boaz's well-remarked "shudder" was not one of fright but one of nocturnal emission. Odd that the otherwise alert interviewer allows this to slip past him, as the rest of the interview will disclose. Indeed, if Boaz's shudder does signify an ejaculation, Ruth may have provided grounds for arguing that the remainder of her nighttime stay with Boaz was erotically uneventful. If my reader will permit what may appear to be an uncircumspect thought, which I

offer in all scholarly sobriety, we may even have uncovered a reason for Ruth's reference to herself as Boaz's "*hand*-maiden."

39. Sasson carefully analyzes the fact that Ruth's statement contains both of these issues (80–83).

40. The interviewer appears to insinuate Ruth's kinship with Tamar as a scheming woman—even though her schemes might have been justified; Tamar, of course, disguised herself as a harlot and bore her father-in-law, Judah, a son because of his refusal to honor his levirate obligation. For additional (but, I dare say, opaquely Lacanian) commentary on Ruth's "kinship" to Tamar, Rachel, and Leah, see Bal, 76, 83–87.

41. Cf. note 33.

42. Given the rich ambiguities of the tale's artistic wordplay, I can no longer refrain from remarking on the excessive frequency of one word in each of the tale's four chapters, respectively "return" (*šûb*), "glean" (*lāqat*), "threshing-floor" (*gōren*), and "redeem" (*gā'al*). Although necessary to the tale's events, the words form an ostinato which may well hint at a subtext planted by the tale's story-teller: "return" to the text, "glean" it for dropped or neglected grains, and carefully winnow it on the "threshing-floor" so as to "redeem" its overlooked splendors.

43. The audiotape abruptly breaks off with this unfinished sentence. As a matter of fact, it ends, I must remark, with a loud but unidentifiable sound, sig-nifying only God knows what. Thus one cannot ascertain how to construe the interview's closing exchange: whether Ruth's amazement is to be taken as ac-knowledgment of her surprise at the interviewer's sudden perspicacity, his rev-elation of her deepest motive—that her actions were prompted, one and all, out of love of Mahlon—or as incredulous disgust at the interviewer's outlandish idea. I can only report that the intonations of Ruth's response make it highly ambiguous. Needless to say, I have my own thoughts on the matter, but my commission to transcribe and annotate the interview forbade me to indulge in such speculation. Finally, I must apologize to my readers for not having informed them earlier of two matters: that they were reading an incomplete interview, and that I was handcuffed from divulging the identity of the inter-viewer. But such stipulations were written into the grant which funded this en-terprise, a grant whose benefactors I have no way of identifying because of the secrecy in which the entire transaction was conducted. I was informed only of the benefactors' belief in the worth of the interview to scholarly notice. (But whether scholars will find worth in the interview I must leave to them.)

Notes to A Rejection Letter—and More—for Melville's "The Bell-Tower"

1. Curtis's role at Harper's—as well as the authenticity of the statements Curtis attributes to the Harper brothers in Item 135—is vouched for in detail

by J. Henry Harper's *The House of Harper: A Century of Publishing in Franklin Square* (New York: Harper's, 1912). Curtis's biographers are Edward Cary, *George William Curtis* (Boston: Houghton, 1894) and Gordon Milne, *George William Curtis & the Genteel Tradition* (Bloomington: Indiana UP, 1956).

2. The judgment of "most inept" is from the editorial note to the story in Werner Berthoff, ed., *Great Short Works of Herman Melville*, (New York: Harper, 1970) 233. Critical commentary on the story includes: Charles A. Fenton, "'The Bell-Tower': Melville and Technology," *American Literature* 23 (1951): 219–32; Richard H. Fogle, "The Bell-Tower," *Melville's Shorter Tales* (Norman: U of Oklahoma P, 1960) 63–72; Valeria Verucci, "*The Bell Tower di Herman Melville*," *Studi Americani* 8 (1963): 91–119; Marvin Fisher, "Melville's 'Bell-Tower': A Double Thrust," *American Quarterly* 18 (1966): 200–207. Rpt. in his *Going Under: Melville's Short Fiction and the American 1850s* (Baton Rouge: Louisiana State UP, 1977) 95–104; John Vernon, "Melville's 'The Bell-Tower,'" *Studies in Short Fiction* 7 (1970): 264–76; Robert E. Morsberger, "Melville's 'The Bell-Tower' and Benvenuto Cellini," *American Literature* 44 (1972): 456–62; Jacqueline D. Costello and Robert J. Kloss, "The Psychological Depths of Melville's 'The Bell-Tower,'" *Emerson Society Quarterly* 19 (1973): 254–60; R. Bruce Bickley, Jr., "The Bell-Tower," *The Method of Melville's Short Fiction* (Durham: Duke UP, 1975) 96–100; Wayne R. Kime, "'The Bell-Tower': Melville's Reply to a Review," *Emerson Society Quarterly* 22 (1976): 28–38; William B. Dillingham, "Cynic Solitaire: 'The Bell-Tower,'" *Melville's Short Fiction, 1853–1856* (Athens: U Georgia P, 1977) 208–26; Hennig Cohen, "Bannadonna's Bell Ritual," *Melville Society Extracts* 36 (1978): 7–8; and Klaus Benesch, "Figuring Modern Authorship: Melville's Narratives of Technological Encroachment," *Romantic Cyborgs: Authorship and Technology in the American Renaissance* (Amherst: U of Massachusetts P, 2002) 129–56.

3. For the publication history of Melville's stories, see Morton M. Sealts, Jr., "The Chronology of Melville's Short Fiction, 1853–1856," *Harvard Library Bulletin* 28 (1980): 391–403. Rpt. in his *Pursuing Melville: 1940–1980* (Madison: U Wisconsin P, 1982) 221–31.

4. Jay Leyda, *The Melville Log: A Documentary Life of Herman Melville, 1819–1891*, 2 vols. (New York: Harcourt, 1951); and Merrell R. Davis and William H. Gilman, eds., *The Letters of Herman Melville* (New Haven: Yale UP, 1960).

5. In their notes Davis and Gilman remark on one other instance of a letter to Harper Brothers in 1854, one that was not on the customary "faded blue paper, with blue lines" (354). I am indebted to Sealts's "Chronology" for calling this to my attention; see his *Pursuing Melville* 373n.

6. Curtis's friendship with Hawthorne dates from his eighteen-month residence, with his older brother Burrill, at Brook Farm in 1842 and 1843. The

following two years found Curtis and Burrill residing in Concord, Massachusetts, where the friendship—and Curtis's further acquaintance with the day's literary lights—grew. See Milne, *Curtis* 10–32.

7. "Our Young Authors—Melville," *Putnam's Monthly Magazine* 1 (February 1853): 163.

8. See Milne, *Curtis* 67.

9. Although most of Melville's stories were published anonymously, *The Encantadas* was printed under the pseudonym to which Curtis's letter alludes.

10. The "Editor's Easy Chair" column of May 1854 had discoursed on both these subjects (841 and 844–45, respectively).

11. These fictitious names allude to "Editor's Easy Chair" columns of January 1854, 272; February 1854, 415–16; and December 1853, 132; respectively.

12. "Editor's Easy Chair," April 1854, 696–97.

13. Curtis seems to refer to Babbalanja's "nursery tale" about the nine blind men's "discoveries" of the trunk of the banyan tree in chapter 115 of *Mardi* (New York: New American Library, 1964).

14. Curtis was married to Anna Shaw on Thanksgiving Day, November 26, 1856. But no family lines connected Melville's and Curtis's wives.

Notes to Hemingway's "María"

1. Ernest Hemingway, *For Whom the Bell Tolls* (New York: Scribner's, 1940) 379. Further references will be cited in parenthesis in the text.

2. See Allen Josephs, "Hemingway's Poor Spanish: Chauvinism and Loss of Credibility in *For Whom the Bell Tolls*," *Hemingway: A Revaluation*, ed. Donald R. Noble (Troy, NY: Whitston, 1983) 211–12.

3. See Ann Rosalind Jones, "Inscribing Femininity: French Theories of the Feminine," *Making a Difference: Feminist Literary Criticism*, ed. Gayle Green and Coppelia Kahn (London: Methuen, 1985) 83.

4. See Ann Rosalind Jones, "Writing the Body: Toward an Understanding of *l'Écriture feminine*," *The New Feminist Criticism: Essays on Women, Literature, and Theory*, ed. Elaine Showalter (New York: Pantheon, 1985) 363.

5. See Luce Irigaray, *This Sex Which Is Not One*, trans. Catherine Porter (Ithaca: Cornell UP, 1985) 101–03.

6. Jones, "Writing the Body" 365.

7. See Paul Smith, "'Daffodils and Stories': The Re-writing of 'A Way You'll Never Be'," unpublished essay, presented at the Mid-Hudson-MLA, Poughkeepsie, NY, December 1987.

8. Michael Reynolds, "*For Whom the Bell Tolls*: Colonel Lawrence Rings the Changes," unpublished essay, presented at the Mid-Hudson-MLA, Poughkeepsie, NY, December 1987.

Note to Psychoanalytic Training Report #3

1. I resort to this set of four roles to suggest that while I attend to Mr. Meursault's monologue professionally, I cannot shut off the fact that it affects me—and perhaps any engaged reader of the transcription—in different ways, depending on which perspective I choose to adopt: listening to an imagined, dramatic voice; cognitively interacting with an exotic, printed tale; bearing witness to a legal deposition; or analyzing an account to describe and diagnose its dynamic, economic, genetic, and adaptive functions.

Index

233